THE INTRUDERS

Jason could simply flee, disappear into the night. But where? Anyone who had tracked him this far was not going to be discouraged by not finding him at home and the islands presented few hiding places. No, he was going to have to terminate this venture here and now.

Jason sighed. His fight had been from the first very, very personal. He had taken satisfaction from the expression on the faces of men who knew they would be dead within the next second. Satisfaction and a small degree of revenge, a minute reprisal for his loss. Tonight there would only be impersonal killing from which he would derive little vindication.

Well, with one exception.

Jason crept forward on his knees and elbows, the plastic device between his teeth and the shotgun held in both hands. When he was close enough to see the sentry against the sky, he stood.

"Welcome to North Caicos," Jason said softly....

GATES OF
HADES

GREGG LOOMIS

LEISURE BOOKS NEW YORK CITY

This book is for Suzanne.
Thank you.

A LEISURE BOOK®

June 2007

Published by

Dorchester Publishing Co., Inc.
200 Madison Avenue
New York, NY 10016

ISBN-10: 0-8439-5894-4
ISBN-13: 978-0-8439-5894-2

The name "Leisure Books" and the stylized "L" with design are trademarks of Dorchester Publishing Co., Inc.

Printed in the United States of America.

Visit us on the web at www.dorchesterpub.com.

ACKNOWLEDGMENTS

The common misconception is that writing is a lonely craft. This might have been true when Dickens dipped his quill into an inkwell or even when Mark Twain was the first to use a typewriter to create a novel. Today, with e-mail, phone and fax connections, I'm not only not alone, I have immediate assistance and advice from my ever-patient agent, Mary Jack Wald, and my editor, Don D'Auria, who is both quick and tactful in separating the good ideas from the not-so-good. Without either of these professionals, this book would not have happened.

Thanks also to Suzanne my wife, who loves to poke into the dimmer corners of history.

The scenes and much of the history of the ancient underworld come from my interpretation of Robert Temple's *Netherworld*, a photographically illustrated account of an actual descent into and exploration of the Oracle of the Dead, or Hades, at Baia in 2001. As stated in the book, the site was sealed again after Temple's exploration.

The cave of the Sybil of Cumae, though perhaps requiring a seeress to find, is open to the public.

DISCOVERY OF HADES AT BAIA

In the 1960s, Robert Padget, an amateur archeologist, had retired from his job in England and was living in the Naples area. For unclear reasons, he suspected there was a historical basis for parts of the epics of Homer and Virgil, particularly those dealing with the Sibyl of Cumae and, nearby, Hades.

When a cave that fit the classical description of the Sibyl's was discovered, Padget was certain that Hades must also exist.

In 1962, he found a series of man-made caverns at the ancient resort town of Baia that included sacrificial altars and tunnels that would have allowed the seemingly mystical appearance and disappearance of priests (as described in the classics). And there was a shallow underground river, the Styx. The series of caves had been methodically filled with dirt, rocks and rubble, the latter dated to the last years of Augustus Caesar (27 B.C. – 14 A.D.). There were traces of sulfur gases but none of the potentially poisonous vapors associated with volcanic regions.

Padget scheduled a press conference in London to announce his discovery, but the timing could not have been worse: November 22, 1963 at 6:00 p.m., or early afternoon in Dallas, Texas. Apparently, the conference was never rescheduled and the caves were decreed a hazard by the Italian government and ordered to be sealed.

In 1992, Robert Temple convinced the Italian authorities to let him follow Padget's path. He and his crew took photographs this time, which were reproduced in his book, *Netherworld*.

Again, the Italians sealed the cave, citing the possibilities of poison gases, unstable earth, etc.

PROLOGUE

55 o, 47', 21 " ' N
173 o, 40', 14" W
North of Atka, Andrean of Islands, Bering Sea
June 12, 0618 Hours

The Russian fishing trawler had to have been the source of the SOS. As big as a WWII aircraft carrier, it was designed to catch, process, and freeze tons of North Pacific cod without leaving the fishing grounds. That was why a number of countries had banned these superships: two or three of them could wipe out a breeding ground in days.

But fishing wasn't what it was doing now.

Captain Edward "Easy" Rumpmiller stood on the small bridge of the U.S. Coast Guard cutter *Reynolds* and studied the massive craft through binoculars. Even in the glare of the subarctic spring sun, he could see there were no nets out. The open hatches to the huge holds were covered in a white cloud of gulls feasting on a catch left available to them. The craft was wallowing in the swell, not under power.

That was the reason for the distress signal, of course.

He grimaced. *Damn Russians.* Fishing illegally within

the two-hundred-mile area claimed by the United States, they had the balls to call the U.S. Coast Guard when something happened to their engines. If the world were a sane place, he'd have authority to at least confiscate their catch to cover the taxpayers' expense in rescuing the bastards.

But it wasn't and he didn't.

So, what good was a territorial limit when it only meant you had to help somebody trespassing in it?

"No response, Cap'n."

Rumpmiller's thoughts on political complexities scattered like a covey of frightened birds as he put down the glasses and nodded to his radioman, Third Class O. D. Peschky. He'd never asked what the initials stood for.

"Try again, all international frequencies."

He wasn't surprised when that didn't work, either.

He sighed deeply, a man put to useless effort. "Blast the siren a couple of times. That should wake 'em up."

Just like the Russians: lose both engines, call for help, and get tanked up on vodka while they waited.

He made a minute adjustment to the binoculars as the shrill clarion echoed across the gray water. Nobody stirring. Bastards must have all passed out. Nothing to do but board, a problematic task since the trawler's deck towered a good thirty feet above his head.

Then he saw it: a rope boarding ladder dangled from just behind the trawler's bow, like the Russkies had anticipated the problem and left it before drinking themselves into a stupor.

"All ahead, prepare boarding party."

Rumpmiller buckled on the webbed gun belt required for boarding operations. He didn't like this one bit. Climbing up a ladder onto a ship in distress should be all in a day's work, but there was something sinister about the trawler, something he could not have explained.

For the first time in years, he slid back the action of his navy-issue Beretta, making sure he had a full load.

On board, the Russian craft appeared as deserted as it

had from the bridge of the *Reynolds*. Huge hatches yawned open, and the smell of fish about to go bad filled the air, along with the raucous protests of birds frightened away from what was probably the only free meal the Northern Pacific would ever yield them. There was no one on deck, nor could he see anyone through the glass of the bridge above his head.

Rumpmiller could not have explained why he used hand motions rather than verbal orders to direct his armed five-man party to split up and search the ship.

Minutes later, Chief Petty Officer Wilson was back, his face white. "Sir, you'd better see this."

"What . . ."

But Wilson had already turned his back to lead the way, and the light breeze snatched the words into the emptiness of the Pacific.

At first, Rumpmiller thought his original hypothesis about vodka had been correct; in dealing with Russian seamen, it usually was. The men lying in a lake of drying blood, all eight of them, seemed to have two mouths, the lower one set in a grin.

Acid bile rose in his throat as he realized each man had had his throat cut.

For an instant, Rumpmiller thought he was going to be sick. Somehow he managed to swallow, hoping he was keeping his composure in front of the petty officer. "Chief, gather the boarding party and search every inch of the ship. Shoot anyone who even looks unfriendly."

The petty officer started to turn, stopped, and asked, "Even the holds, sir?"

Rumpmiller wasn't about to have his men smelling like overripe fish if he could avoid it. "No, secure the holds. Nothing gets in or out. They can be searched when the ship is towed to port."

Rumpmiller could hear feet running across the steel deck as Wilson's foghorn voice bellowed orders. He swallowed again and felt a little better as he looked around the room. A mess area, he surmised, since a small galley was adjacent. The plastic tabletop was pocked with cigarette burns from overflowing ashtrays. A number of glasses rolled across the floor as the ship rocked back and forth. He had no idea what the ship's full complement would be, but he knew these trawlers were built for a maximum of mechanization and a minimum of manpower. It was possible the whole crew was right here, lying in sticky puddles of their own life fluids.

He shook his head.

Impossible.

If all the crew were here, then who had manned the ship while its crew was being slaughtered like so much beef? Who had sent the SOS; who had put down the boarding ladder?

He stepped over the coaming into the galley. Eight plates were stacked in the stainless-steel sink. A nearly empty bottle stood nearby. He didn't need to read the Cyrillic label to tell him at least part of his original premise was true.

For the first time, he noted the smell of something burned, an odor over the metallic smell of drying blood. Not marijuana. He'd smelled enough of that during his stint on the East Coast, where years ago it had not been uncommon to encounter armadas of bales of cannabis either jettisoned by a pursued dope runner or waiting to be picked up by one. The coast guard had burned enough of the contraband that he would never forget the scent.

Which this wasn't.

More like sulfur, maybe struck matches. Although it was unlikely, the smell was strongest near what looked like a small rock garden in one corner, round white stones surrounded by a pair of very ugly plants. Why would a fishing trawler carry rocks and spindly plants? Maybe the captain wanted it there. Whatever, the stones and plants were not the problem at hand.

Nothing else caught his attention, nothing that might indicate how or why these men were dead and the ship left abandoned.

The question brought on a queasiness worse than he had felt when he saw the bodies. It was as if the killer or killers had wanted the ship and its macabre cargo to be found, wanted to make sure the world noted his or their handiwork.

A message of some sort?

If so, sending the distress signal and leaving the boarding ladder made a certain sick sense.

Very sick.

Even so, that didn't answer other questions, like how had eight seamen been overcome with not even a struggle? He saw no defensive wounds.

Any way he looked at it, the problem would not be Rumpmiller's for long—no longer than it took to radio Dutch Harbor.

Atlanta Journal Constitution,
August 16

MEN STABBED IN NATIONAL FOR-
EST

Chattahoochee National Park, Tallu-lah Falls, GA:

The bodies of six employees of the Georgia Timber Company were found stabbed to death at a logging site near this mountain resort area yesterday. Police have not released names pending notification of family.

The exact cause of death has not yet been formally determined by the Raburn County Medical Examiner, Dr. Charles Walker, but he speculates some sort of chemical inhalation played a part, although the actual cause of death appeared to be stab wounds.

"There was no sign of a struggle," Dr. Walker was quoted as saying, "and I can't imagine six healthy lumberjacks standing by while being attacked. Something disabled them."

Georgia Timber has come under criticism from a number of environmental groups in the last year for its cutting of trees in national forests. Company spokespersons declined comment but referred to a previous statement: "Georgia Timber won the bidding competition with the federal government for limited cutting in the Chattahoochee National Forest, and the taxpayers will benefit from careful and responsible removal of replaceable hardwoods."

PART I

CHAPTER ONE

Princess Juliana International Airport
Philipsburg, St. Maarten, Netherlands Antilles
December 20

Williford Watkins liked Americans. Were it not for Americans, he would have to live solely on what he got for working in the tower at the island's airport, a salary that never would have paid for the used twenty-eight-foot sport fisherman in which he took American tourists diving, snorkeling, and fishing for as much as a thousand dollars a day. His job, the one in the tower, consisted of eight tedious hours five days a week, doing little more than making sure the runway was clear of aircraft and telling the Air France or Lufthansa pilots, "Cleared to land."

The boring nature of his job was why he let his curiosity take hold when that particular Gulfstream IV landed. According to the routing slip Williford picked up from the rack, the plane was Swiss, but the numbers painted on the tail were unlike any Swiss registration he had ever seen.

Since his shift was over, or near enough by island standards, he walked downstairs and over to the customs and immigration section of the terminal. He had a charter at the dock at Marigot, over on the French side of the island, but the fish weren't going anywhere and the anglers could wait. This was, after all, the Caribbean, where time was approximate at best.

The two pilots from the Gulfstream were filing their general declarations, the papers every country of entry required that listed passengers, cargo, and point of departure. His curiosity stirred once again when he noted there was only one passenger, a swarthy man with angry eyes. The dark man glared at Williford's dreadlocks and Bob Marley T-shirt. Williford smiled at him, just the way the tourism bureau said to do to all white folks. The dark man turned away.

That was unusual, too. *Most mon come to St. Maarten, they be happy, not angry.* The charter could wait a little longer.

Williford went outside into the brilliant sunshine of another day in paradise. His sunglasses, cooled by the aggressive air-conditioning inside, fogged over in the humid heat. The parking lot where he had left the Samurai he had bought with the money from his American charter customers was to his right. He turned left toward the flight operations building.

After exchanging some good-natured insults with the men in the single room, he found a copy of *World Aircraft Registrations*, thumbed through the country-by-country directory, and turned to Switzerland. He had been right: the Gulfstream's registration was not listed. Putting the heavy volume on a table, he tried the directory by registration letters. Fortunately, the United States was the only nation that had so many aircraft it used numbers instead of letters.

It took him only a few minutes to find out that the Gulfstream, or at least its numbers, were Syrian.

Williford checked his watch. His charter customers weren't going to be happy, but he couldn't quit now. Crossing the room, he picked up a telephone connected to the small air-traffic control center located in the base of the tower he had just left.

"Freddy," he said when a familiar voice came on the line, "th' Gulfstream you mons worked a few minutes ago; where it come from?"

What he heard made his curiosity sit up and take notice. The plane had been handed off from San Juan Center, the air-traffic control facility for high-altitude traffic in this part of the Caribbean, but it had *not* been handed off in sequence from London to Greenland to New York to Miami centers, the normal sequence for flights from Europe. Instead, it had commenced the transatlantic part of its journey with Tenerife Center in the Canary Islands. Williford wasn't sure what part of the Caribbean those islands occupied, but he did know something was crazy as a marlin with its bill stuck in a boat hull.

There was something he had read in the men's room while he was taking a break a few weeks ago, something about the Americans wanting to know about suspicious flights. He supposed they wanted to further their endless (and, in Williford's opinion, hopeless) effort against the drugs that journeyed northbound in volumes unequaled by tropical fruit. Maybe if he called the Americans, they could somehow send him charter business six months from now, in the summer, when things got slack.

He dialed the number of Miami Center.

The next morning, Williford figured the Americans had sent at least one charter, lack of summer notwithstanding. Except the four men who knocked on his door at sunup were already sweating in suits and ties.

"Can't go now, mon," Williford said. "Can't go till afta work."

One of the men gave him a smile with no humor in it. "We'll only be a minute, Mr. Watkins. You'll be on your way in no time. We need your help."

From the looks of them, four large men whose wilting suits did little to conceal muscle, they didn't need help from anyone. They also didn't look like the kind who would go away just to make sure a man got to work on time.

Williford really hadn't intended for them to come into his two-room cottage, not till his wife, Caroline, could get the place cleaned up a little, but they pushed right past him into the half of the house that served as a living room.

One of the men was carrying a book of photos. He sat in Williford's easy chair, the only upholstered one in the house, and opened the book. "We'd like you to take a look. . . ."

Caroline emerged from behind the sheet that divided off the bedroom and gave Williford a look that could have burned a hole in the linen before she left without a word on her way to her job at Mullet Bay, one of the resorts along the beach. She didn't like to have company in the house before she was dressed.

The four men in suits seemed not to notice as the one with the book continued. "See if any of these men are the passenger on that Gulfstream."

And he was. An unmistakable likeness was on the second page. Williford pointed, and all four of his visitors nodded as though sharing a secret.

"Who he be?" Williford naturally wanted to know.

"A man we got business with," the man with the book said, and gave another smile, one that reminded Williford of a shark approaching a wounded fish.

CHAPTER TWO

Washington, D.C.
The White House, Oval Office at the same time

In the opinion of Sam Hoffman, senior senator from Georgia, the president's plan was irrational, ill-considered, and utter rubbish. Worse, it would be seen for what it was: an effort to appease the opposition. Still worse, it could cost the party support from its most generous constituency.

It wasn't all the president's fault his poll numbers were now pushing Nixon's. The people screaming the loudest about gasoline prices were largely the same ones who had stridently opposed the building of new refineries, expanded drilling in Alaska, or nuclear power. Those demanding "affordable housing" howled when he permitted limited cutting in national forests to increase the supply of wood, the backbone of the home-building industry.

The list was nearly endless.

Actually, the president was well intentioned. A Vietnam veteran who had never even been mentioned in the same breath as any scandal, he had served his state and his country for over thirty years in every capacity, from state school superintendent to governor, from Congress to the

White House. Married for over forty years, church elder. The all-American Mr. Clean who was just now learning that, even as president, he really couldn't please everybody, a fact that disappointed him no end.

But the president's plan was far too transparent to jack a feather off the floor, let alone the president's abysmal polls.

Senator Sam, as he liked to be called by his constituents, was always awed by the White House. Scant places in America contained more history—history that few in Washington understood, much less read. In this town, history was what had been said last night by the talking heads on CNN. The president was a prime example. Seated behind the desk on which Lincoln had supposedly signed the Emancipation Proclamation, the man could give you the current poll numbers to two decimal points, but his knowledge of the past was a blank slate. Appeasing opposite interests didn't work.

Never had, never would.

Like all politicians, he was much more interested in the future.

Specifically, his future.

"I need your help on this, Sam," the president said. "As chairman of the Environmental Study Committee, your endorsement of the plan is essential if we're going to get bipartisan support."

Sam chose to ignore the *we*, which was either the royal plural or included him in a plan he viewed as both deceptive and useless. Neither was a pleasant possibility.

"What you propose doesn't need congressional approval, Mr. President," Sam said noncommittally.

The president smiled that million-vote grin. "I know, Sam, but your approval would generate support. After all, you're a very influential man."

Sam ignored the flattery. God, but would this, his last term, ever end? Another year and he could retire to his farm in the Appalachian foothills, where a man was as good as his last promise and bullshit was fertilizer, not an art form.

The president took his silence as acquiescence and plowed ahead. "Having various environmental groups here in Washington next year to discuss a single plan to mitigate global warming, create pure air and water, conserve of the earth's resources and all that should please the Sierra Clubbers and all the bunny huggers. Ten and a half million votes, I understand. Sam, we'll even offer to grant amnesty to those radicals who've committed crimes in the name of the environment, agree to a halt to drilling in the ANWR in exchange for no more bombing of oil platforms in the Gulf, no more destruction of property. We'll steal the opposition's whole Green vote."

Appease the advocates of the Key Largo cotton mouse and southern snail darter? Stop development and a slow but steady increase in the job market on behalf of the Virginia wild plum vine? Make peace with fruitcakes who had blown up mining equipment, sabotaged power grids, even killed people in the process?

"You sure you want to pardon criminals, Mr. President? Most conservationists may be liberals, but they're law-abiding citizens. I'm not sure the radicals compose that big a bloc of votes."

And certainly an even smaller group of contributors.

The president's face became serious, that almost-frown he used to stare into the TV cameras when urging his fellow Americans to accept something. "That's why I need you aboard, Sam. If you endorse the plan, the more conservative members of your committee will go for it. Tell you what." He looked around the room as though to make sure the two were alone before lowering his voice to a conspiratorial level. "You come out for my conference, you help me, and I think I can get the Defense Department to double that sub base on the Georgia coast. Over a thousand new jobs, Sam; think about it."

Sam did think about it, and it made his head hurt. The president wanted the same thing every first-term president wanted: a second term.

The trouble with appeasement of radicals was that it was like pissing down your leg to keep it warm: it worked only as long as you kept it up.

Sam glanced around the room, half expecting to see a picture of Neville Chamberlain beside those of Eisenhower and Reagan. Nixon was conspicuously absent. But then, this president had probably never heard of "peace in our time."

On the other hand, even if the conference generated only empty promises, the international publicity of hosting those who believed in global warming—that something could be done about it and the world could agree what that was—would generate hours of airtime, which translated into votes in next year's election, votes from people who, like the president, had no concept of history.

By the time the conference was fading newsprint and the election safely in the win column, the rich would return to seek wealth wherever it could be found, and the poor would continue to complain about it rather than helping themselves. That was what maintained class status quo.

Ah, well, Sam would be plain Citizen Sam by then, far from the poisonous political vapors of the Potomac.

"I'll give it some thought, Mr. President."

The president vaulted to his feet. Sam almost expected him to jump over the desk to shake hands, like the champion tennis player he had been in college. "I knew I could count on you, Sam."

Sam left the room with the pleasant thought that his imminent retirement enabled him to be a statesman thinking of the next generation instead of a politician thinking of the next election.

And being a statesman didn't include showcase conferences and amnesty solely for the purpose of vote pandering, not with misguided if intellectually honest conservationists, nor with their criminal fellow travelers.

CHAPTER THREE

Saint Barthélemy, French Antilles
Two days later

Jason Peters navigated the *Zodiac* across Gustavia Harbor to the public dock at the south end. Tying the small inflatable up to a cleat already crowded with several other hawsers, he climbed up and merged with the winter crowd of visitors shopping along the Rue du Bore de Mere. His white T-shirt and shorts might have led an observer to conclude he was just one more hired crew buying supplies for one of the dozen or so yachts that annually brought the rich, beautiful, and famous to the island's eight square miles of beaches, Parisian shops, and French cuisine. Ninety-nine meter ships, the largest the tiny inner harbor could accommodate, contained more living space than most people's homes. And more expensive art and furnishings.

Like an elite private club, St. Bart's was desirable more for who was excluded than included. With no chain hotels, high-rises, or mass-market resorts, the island was the playground of the wealthy. With hotel rooms or private villas at well over a thousand dollars a night during season, the average family was likely to look elsewhere for a vacation site. Even the airport catered to the select few. The narrow fifteen-hundred-foot strip required a special logbook endorsement from the French government after demonstration of specific skills. The laws of gravity required only small aircraft with STOL (short takeoff and landing) capabilities. Anything larger would either wind up very wet or part of the permanent scenery among the island's hills.

Instead of entering the chandler's shop or the grocery store, Jason paused in front of the Hermès window display of handbags bearing the price tags of small automobiles. He shifted position once, twice, until the reflections in the glass satisfied him he was not being followed.

A block farther he stopped again, this time to admire a young woman, one of those who came from France for a year or two's work to support their time on beaches where swimwear was optional and tans uniform. On St. Bart's, as the island was known, clothes were a fashion statement, not a requirement of modesty. Undergarments were virtually unknown.

His interest was more than returned. A number of these nymphlike creatures turned for a second look at Jason. He was obviously someone who had spent more than ten days or two weeks out-of-doors. His skin was an even copper color, not the red that resulted from an effort to get a tan in a limited time. His hair was sun-streaked and brushed back over the tops of his ears. Muscles stretched the sleeves of his shirt, and his stomach was flat, unlike those swollen by the rich fare for which the island's restaurants were famous. He was not only a handsome American, but, more important, he might be a rich one.

At the end of the street, he paused for a moment, watching the crowd in the open yard of La Select, a restaurant noted more as a meeting place for the young than for haute cuisine. The establishment basked in the story that its version of American junk food had inspired Jimmy Buffett's "Cheeseburger in Paradise." In fact, the musician's voice and the twang of the Coral Reefer Band could be heard on the sound system, but just barely over the jagged shouts of conversation of those occupying the plastic tables and those waiting for room to do so.

He doglegged left, then right onto Rue da la Républic. There was hardly room for him to squeeze between the slow parade of cars jammed into every available parking space along the street. He stopped in front of Le Comptoir du Cigare, a store that not only sold cigars but liquor, smoking accessories, and Panama hats almost as expensive as the Hermès bags.

Inside, a woman in her early twenties was seated outside the humidor, listlessly turning the pages of a magazine while her companion, an overweight man in his late forties or early fifties, inspected a Dunhill lighter and haggled with the proprietor in Parisian-accented French.

Jason made eye contact with a leggy girl whose physical attributes were hardly concealed by her ankle-length cotton dress. Her height was emphasized by the remarkably ugly four-inch rubber platform sandals that had inexplicably become fashionable that season. She followed him into the humidor, a twelve-by-twelve-foot room enclosed in glass. Besides keeping a large stock of Cuban tobacco moist, the glass was soundproof.

Reaching into one of the open boxes on a shelf, Jason ran a thick Hoyo de Monterrey under his nose and sniffed his satisfaction.

"May I help you?" she asked in heavily accented English.

Jason replaced the cigar and grinned as he nodded toward the couple outside. "Touching that a man would bring his daughter to St. Bart's."

She lengthened her face and gave him the shrug that was the unmistakable Gallic display of urbanity. *"Cinq à sept."*

Five to seven, the hours between work and home, the time a Parisian had for his mistress. Disdainful French idiom for such a relationship.

"You joke," she continued. "And I think you did not come to chose a cigar."

"You're right. I still have most of the box of Epicure Number Two's I bought from you yesterday. Besides, that Double Corona is too large to look good in my delicate hands, don't you think?"

"Always the joke, Jason. Soon someone else will want to look at the cigars and we cannot talk."

His smile vanished. "You're right. What did you find out?"

"He is on the *Fortune*. It has the Cayman flag."

Most of the superyachts in the harbor flew Cayman colors. Such conspicuous wealth would draw the unwanted attention of the tax man in other countries. The Caymans allowed anonymity by registering vessels to untraceable corporations.

"Unimaginative name." He turned and pretended to read the brightly colored brand names on a stack of cigar boxes. "The ship is the size of your average Holiday Inn. Where is the master stateroom?"

She glanced over her shoulder. "The sternmost stateroom on the second level. Almost directly under the salon. Go . . ." She picked up a cigar as the man with the girlfriend came into the humidor. "I believe you will find this one has the taste you describe."

The Frenchman surveyed the stock carefully before selecting a box of Partagas. He left to inquire as to price and argue with the store's proprietor again. Jason assumed the owner had properly inflated the cost. It was anathema to the French to pay the first price asked.

"Could you draw me a diagram?" Jason asked.

Turning to the wall so those outside could not see, the girl reached into the front of her dress, stepped back, and brushed against Jason. He felt a thick wad of paper slipped into his hand.

"It is the best I could do."

Jason stuffed the paper into a pocket of his shorts and

grinned salaciously. "The best you could do when you were doing something else?"

She looked as though she might have eaten a bad snail. "Do not overwork your, er, imagination. I delivered a box of cigars the ship's captain ordered for the crew the day before. Nothing more. Now go."

A few doors down the street, an art gallery was late removing the sunscreens in its windows after the afternoon quietus observed by most of the island's shops. Jason stopped so abruptly the couple behind him had to dodge into the street to avoid a collision on the narrow sidewalk. Jason stood in front of the store, all but oblivious to his surroundings. His attention was on an acrylic painting, a photorealistic depiction of a hummingbird feeding from a hibiscus blossom. The colors were vibrant, almost as though lit from within. Without being conscious of it, he grasped a small gold ring that hung on a chain around his neck.

What was the painting doing here? It had been sold to a wealthy developer in the Bahamas over five years ago. What were the odds of it being for sale again here in St. Bart's?

According to the date above the signature, it had been completed weeks before the artist's life had turned upside down.

Jason knew.

His name was on the canvas.

He shook his head as though to dispel the thoughts, the recollections. He would never be free of the memories; nor would he want to be. He reminded himself that he was here to get a job done, not reflect on the cruelties and uncertainties of life. He turned and walked back the way he had come. He forced himself to think of what had to be done, to exclude what had been.

On his way back to the *Zodiac*, Jason joined five or six people gathered around the stern of one of the yachts. Through the thick glass doors of the salon an American movie star whose name Jason could not recall could be seen having tea. Jason melted into the group, but his attention was directed toward the vessel moored to port, the *Fortune*.

Two large men stood at the head of the extended gangplank. Had their arms not been crossed, they might have been at attention. Their faces were impassive behind the shield of reflective sunglasses. In spite of the eighty-plus temperature, each wore a loose-fitting nylon jacket bearing the logo of a National League baseball team. Neither seemed bothered by the heat, not a drop of sweat between them.

The fame or notoriety of many of the occupants of the yachts necessitated posting a crew member or two to keep uninvited guests off the ship. Jason wondered if any other than those on the *Fortune* were armed.

Back in the *Zodiac*, Jason followed the contours of the harbor, gaping appropriately at the ships docked there. He was careful to spend no more time observing the *Fortune* than looking at vessels of similar size. The tinted glass of the bridge concealed the men Jason was certain were keeping watch on the forward part of the ship. He could see lights mounted halfway up the superstructure. No doubt they would illuminate the foredeck as bright as day should hidden electric beams be broken. Or perhaps they were wired to weight sensors. In any event, entry to the *Fortune* wasn't likely to be gained by climbing over the bow. Besides, the deck was, what, ten or fifteen feet above his head? One small noise, one bump against the ship's hull from the wake of a passing craft . . . Jason discarded the idea.

As the *Zodiac* continued its slow circuit, Jason noticed the twin anchors hanging from hatches that opened just above the waterline. The hatches were designed to close once the anchors were retrieved so that a streamlined surface would be presented to the sea when the vessel was under way. One end of the anchor chains disappeared into the water, the other into a port in the hull. Would it be possible . . . ?

Jason lazily turned to retrace his course and pass the line of yachts again. This time he stopped under the bow of the *Fortune*, the one place he could not be observed by anyone on board. He surveyed the anchor hatch carefully, mentally measuring the openings through which the anchor lines passed into the ship. He shook his head. Tight but unguarded.

He turned the *Zodiac*'s bow toward the harbor's mouth and sped toward the roads.

Minutes later he pulled abeam of a small sloop that bobbed gently at its anchor buoy. A United States flag hung limply from the rigging of the single mast, along with shirts, swimsuits, and other drying laundry. Canvas was draped over the mainsail's boom to shelter the cockpit from the afternoon sun. Salsa music, probably radio from Puerto Rico, filled the air. Its appearance was similar to the number of small craft gently rolling in the swells nearby, one more indistinguishable small American boat making a stop at St. Bart's in view of the town surrounded by verdant hills.

Carefully balancing against the motion of the *Zodiac*, he stood and rapped loudly on the fiberglass hull. "Paco, Paco, wake up!"

The reaction was immediate.

Joyous barking was followed by the scratch of paws on the deck. A shaggy canine head was followed by a thick brown body that vibrated with a furiously wagging tail. Deep brown eyes regarded Jason with what in a woman could have been described as lust.

The dog's appearance finally pushed the melancholy of the painting from Jason's mind like a breeze clearing away clouds. He couldn't have suppressed a smile had he wanted to. "Miss me, did you, Pangloss? Go get Paco."

The dog turned in a complete circle.

"Paco, wake Paco. There's a hamburger in it for you," Jason coaxed.

The dog disappeared. Seconds later there was an explosion of Spanish invective as the boat rocked from shifting weight. A man came into view, bare to the waist. Jason could see the network of pink scars across his chest, souvenirs of torture during captivity by Colombia's ruthless and brutal rebels, FARC. Rumor said every man who had so much as nicked Paco took days to die once he got free and turned on his captors. Large, with hair tousled from sleep, he was wiping a hand the size of a bear's paw across his dark face.

"Fookin' dog! He lick my face, mon. I *hate* bein' licked in th' face!"

"Lucky he didn't piss on you to get you awake." Jason tossed the *Zodiac*'s painter aboard the sloop. "How 'bout tying me off?"

Still grumbling, Paco made his way to the stern to secure the rubber craft, and Jason scrambled aboard.

"Don' know why you hadda bring th' fookin' dog." Paco was still griping as he made his way forward.

"Consider Pangloss cover." Jason was scratching between the animal's pointed ears. "Who would think a boat with a dog on board was on anything but a pleasure cruise?"

Pangloss combined the ears of a German shepherd with the long hair of a collie and the size of both. Jason was fairly certain there were other breeds in the animal's uncertain ancestry. Jason began to scratch underneath the pointed jaw. Pangloss was in ecstacy.

"Coulda brought a fookin' cat instead." Paco was headed below. "Cats don' lick your face."

Jason followed, Pangloss on his heels. "Whoever heard of a loyal cat? You think a cat would guard the ship while we're gone?"

"Cat wouldn't shit on the deck. Fookin' cats are clean, man."

Paco opened the small refrigerator in the tiny galley, popped open a bottle of Caribe beer, and offered it to Jason. "You want cover, we shoulda brought a couple of fookin' womens. They could guard the ship *and* not shit on the deck. An' we could get laid."

Jason sipped on the beer as Paco opened another and folded down the hinged galley table. "We finish here, you'll have all the time you need for women. And money."

Paco became serious. "You get what we need?"

Jason turned off the radio and slipped a CD into the stereo. Brisk but melodic strands of Vivaldi's violins replaced the Latin beat.

Paco shook his massive head. "Man, that moosic sound like a somebody put two cats in th' same sack."

Ignoring the complaint, Jason squeezed past the larger man to reach into the refrigerator and pull out a bit of ground beef. He had Pangloss's undivided attention. The dog sat, salivating.

Jason held out the treat. "Okay!"

The meat disappeared to the accompaniment of a satisfied gulp.

Jason took the paper from his pocket. "I think we have it. She drew a diagram showing the location of the master stateroom. As you know, we're doing a 'rendition,' capturing the guy here and then rendezvousing with the ship at sea to turn him over."

"Then what?"

"Not our business. Once the U.S. Navy has him safely out of somebody's territorial waters, I'd guess there'll be some fairly serious interrogation, something the Geneva Convention doesn't exactly cover."

Rendition was a CIA term for kidnapping someone from a sovereign nation and spiriting them away to where there were no bounds on interrogation methods. Having the actual capture performed by someone unconnected to the government gave at least technical truth to the constant denial of the practice.

Paco turned on a swivel-necked lamp, and both men stared at the paper before Paco said, "You fookin' better

hope she know what she doin', man. Won't be but one
chance."

Jason nodded. "One chance, if that."

"Who is this guy, anyway?" Paco wanted to know.

"Aziz Saud Alazar," Jason said. " 'Nother of those Saudi
princes who speaks Islam and acts Western. Bad dude, a
graduate of Christ College, Oxford, as well as a number of
schools for terrorists the Russkies operated in the seven-
ties. Got into the arms-smuggling business just before the
Evil Empire fell. Word on the street is he can broker the
sale of anything from a slightly used F-14 fighter to a small
Pakistani nuclear device. Sells to al-Qaeda, Hamas, Russian separatists, African dictators, anybody in the market
for death and destruction. I'd guess someone wants his
customer list."

Paco drained his beer and reached for the fridge to replace it. "So, what's one o' them camel fookers doin'
here? No mosque widdin a hunnert miles or more."

"Get me one too, will you? Alazar's not like your basic
fanatical fundamentalist, more like another Royal House
of Saud playboy. His religion apparently doesn't stand in
the way of his receiving a nice hunk of change for his efforts. He spends lavishly on the Riviera, the casino in
Monte Carlo, or on the slopes at St. Moritz. He was there
only until recognized. Then he disappeared minutes ahead
of the French security people. Probably returned to safe
haven in Syria."

Paco popped the tops and handed one of the frosty bottles to Jason. "Shudda known it'd be somebody causin'
shit. You don' do much other 'n spoil somebody else's
party, go after the guys dealin' in killin' folks. Almost like
you got somethin' personal against ordinary international
crooks."

The statement was more astute than Jason would have
expected from Paco. He took the beer and put it to his lips
before answering. "I just do my job and collect my pay."

It was obvious Paco didn't accept this observation, but

he didn't choose to challenge it, either. "Ho-kay. I unner-stan' we bring this one back alive to question."

Jason was on more certain ground. "Like I said, I'd guess our soon-to-be pal Alazar sold some really bad shit to the wrong people. Our customer would like to know what and who. We bring him back alive, turn him over to the spooks. They turn him over to someone who thinks the Geneva Convention is a meeting of watchmakers and chocolate manufacturers. They can make him talk. Some set of bad guys find out their secret isn't so secret anymore."

Paco had already emptied his bottle. He tossed it into the garbage with a wistful look at the refrigerator. "I get it: no more stink like the 'merican press made a few years back about puttin' panties on some fookers' heads, havin' dogs bark at 'em, in that prison in Iraq, Abu Ghraib."

Jason shrugged, a signal of indifference. "Suit me fine to punch his ticket right here, but orders are orders. Besides, taking him prisoner we got a real talking point, things don't go so well aboard that boat."

Paco was digging around in the little refrigerator for something to eat. Over his shoulder he asked, "How'd we know th' fooker was here, anyway?"

Jason shook his head. "Don't ask me; I just work here, same as you. I do know the boat flies the Cayman flag."

Under the table, where Paco thought it wouldn't be seen, his hand was rubbing Pangloss's long snout. Paco's dislike of the dog was a charade that gave the burly His-panic something to grouse about. "So does ever' big yacht in the Caribbean. No tellin' where it really came from."

"This one came from over there." He pointed to where the hills of St. Martin were clearly visible less than twenty miles away. "At least, that's where Alazar boarded her."

"Island's half French, half Dutch," Paco said, as though that explained its role as a point of origin.

"Yep," Jason agreed as he slid out a computer keyboard concealed underneath the table. He typed in a brief message. When he hit enter, the electronics would automatically encode and compress the words into an unintelligible beep of less than a second's time. A satellite overhead would relay what sounded like mere static to equipment that would decode and print the words. The signal would be untraceable and indecipherable.

He finished and pushed the keyboard back in, then lifted the tabletop. He stretched and yawned. "May as well nap. We aren't going to get a lot of sleep tonight."

Though neither would admit it to the other, both men knew there was no chance the adrenaline pumping through their systems would permit sleep.

By midnight the dark water of the harbor reflected lights from the adjacent bars and restaurants like jewels on black velvet. Music from Escalier, a gathering place for the younger visitors to the island, reverberated across the harbor with enough volume to cover the sounds of the small craft that scooted between entertainment establishments like water spiders. It was because of the activity of the island's nightlife that Jason and Paco had decided to move now, rather than wait for the silence of early morning, when the sound of an outboard might draw attention.

Jason maneuvered the *Zodiac* into the space between the *Fortune* and the ship to her port, where both hulls created a shadow on the water as black and viscous as used motor oil. For a full five minutes they listened to the tide sucking at the ship, the anchor chain's metallic groan, the sound of revelry across the harbor. Hair on the back of Jason's neck prickled like tiny antennae anticipating danger signals. It was a familiar experience.

The *Zodiac*'s arrival had not been noted. Jason tied the painter to the anchor chain.

There was a metallic click as Jason checked the nine-millimeter SIG Sauer P228 automatic. Thirteen rounds in the magazine, another in the chamber. Two spare clips in quick-release holders on his belt. A good compromise between weight and firepower, the Swiss pistol still was hardly a match for the weaponry Alazar was likely to have on board. Jason's plan required a quick in and out, something the weight of heavier equipment would only impede. If Jason and Paco needed superior armament, they would already be in serious trouble. Replacing the pistol in the holster slung over his Kevlar vest, Jason inspected the rest of his gear as best he could in the poor light.

"Ready?"

Paco's silhouette glanced up the anchor chain and shook its head slowly. "A fookin' rat couldn' get though there, man," he whispered.

"A fat rat, you mean." Jason tugged on a pair of work gloves, pulled himself out of the *Zodiac* by the anchor chain, and began to climb. "You'll have to suck in your gut."

When Jason was halfway up the chain, Paco began his climb. Both men moved slowly, aware that a slip, a mistake, could set the chain into motion, clanging against the steel skin of the ship like an alarm bell.

At the top of the chain Jason stood on the lip of the anchor hatch, holding on to the chain for balance. Darkness prevented him from seeing Paco, but the larger man's grunts marked his progress. When Paco stood panting alongside Jason, Jason took a small flashlight from his pocket and played its narrow beam on the opening where the chain disappeared into the hull.

"No fookin' way, man," Paco whispered. "No way I can squeeze through there."

He was right.

"You'll have to take off your vest," Jason said. "And lay off the beer and chips before the next time."

Headfirst, Jason crawled through the hole into stygian darkness. The flashlight revealed a triangular room of no more than fifty square feet containing coils of rope, a toolbox bolted to the wall, and a motor for the electric winches overhead. The apex of the triangle was the ship's bow; the bulkhead that was its base contained a small door.

Jason tried the door. It refused to yield.

"Fook! I'm stuck!" Paco's head and shoulders filled the opening.

Jason suppressed a grin before he realized his face was in darkness. "Wriggle a little more. You look like somebody's hunting trophy mounted on a wall."

"Real funny, man."

Jason switched off the light and returned his attention to the door, squatting to peer along the edges. There was no watertight seal above the coaming, as there would have been on a military vessel. Through the space between the door and its frame he could make out dim light. He removed a diver's knife from its sheath on his ankle.

A thud beside him announced that Paco had worked his way loose.

Jason ran the knife blade upward along the side of the door until he felt resistance. He increased pressure until there was a click, the sound of a simple bolt sliding from its catch. As he had guessed, there had been no complex locking mechanism. There was no reason to worry about the contents of the anchor locker. He pushed and the door swung an inch or so.

He turned to Paco. "You got that syringe ready?"

Paco held up a SIG Sauer like Jason's. "Yeah, but I'm cocked an' locked."

The two men crept up a dimly lit companionway to the middle level of the vessel. At the top of the stairs a door led to a passageway that resembled the hall of a plush apartment building more than anything nautical. Thick carpet covered floors bounded by highly polished teak walls.

"Last door on the left," Jason whispered.

Paco, weapon ready, watched Jason make his way to the end. Jason stood outside the door covering Paco until he, too, stood outside it. Jason held up one finger, then a second. On the third, he opened the door and entered while Paco stood ready to supply covering fire if needed.

The only light in the stateroom seeped through half-curtained portholes from the late-night bars along the dock. Paco slipped inside and softly closed the door. A muffled click announced that he had locked it. Both men flattened themselves against the bulkhead while their eyes became accustomed to what illumination there was. The sound of light snoring came from a bed that was a dark blob to their right. Jason was beside it in two steps, his gun ready when Paco flipped the light switch.

Both occupants of the bed came immediately awake.

Jason jammed the stubby barrel of his gun into the man's gaping mouth. "One sound and your brains'll be all over those silk sheets," he whispered.

Jason saw that the other body was that of a woman, no doubt an advance on Alazar's ration of heavenly virgins. She emitted a squeak of terror as Paco placed his weapon next to her head and made a quiet shushing sound. Her eyes darted from the gun to the syringe he held in his other hand and back again.

Jason gave a quick nod, and Paco pulled the woman from the protection of the bedclothes. She was nude. He roughly shoved her toward the adjacent bath.

"You shut up," Paco cautioned. "I hear anythin' from you, and you dead."

From the expression on her face before Paco closed the door, she believed him.

Jason was counting on the fact that, unlike many of his cllients, Alazar had no desire to meet Allah up close and personal just yet.

Alazar lay perfectly still, only a twitch of his eyes betraying his fear. Jason followed the direction in which the arms dealer had glanced. Without removing the gun from the man's mouth, Jason reached under a pillow and held up a .38 Beretta. He jammed it into the waist of his pants.

"Don't even think about it," he said as he held out a hand toward Paco.

Paco slapped the syringe into his palm.

Alazar began to squirm, a series of unintelligible protests leaking around the gun's muzzle.

Jason held the needle up, squeezing a few drops from the end to make sure there were no air bubbles.

"Hold still," he hissed. "If I were going to kill you, you'd be dead. You're going for a ride, and we want to make sure you don't become a party pooper on us."

He stuck the syringe into an arm.

Jason had not emptied the needle before Alazar's back arched. Teeth ground against the gun's barrel as the man's face contorted and spasmed. His arms flailed widely; then he moaned and was still. Dropping the syringe, Jason felt the neck for a pulse at the carotid artery. There was none. Blank eyes stared into eternity. As if he needed confirmation of the obvious, there was the smell of the result a recently relaxed sphincter muscle.

"Shit!" Jason spit. "There goes our security blanket. Some asshole overcooked the tranquilizer." He flung the syringe across the room. "Stupid bastards!"

Paco was puzzled. "Now what?"

Jason glanced around the stateroom. "Go through the bureau there; see if you can find papers, anything of interest."

As he spoke, Jason snatched a laptop computer from the table beside the bed. "With any luck at all, the recently departed used this for something other than games and porn."

Paco quickly completed his search of the bureau's drawers. "Nothin', man, nothin' other 'n some 'spensive silk shirts." He held up what looked like the bottom to a woman's bright red bikini. "An' these."

Jason put the computer under his left arm. "We can discuss Alazar's taste in underwear later. Right now, we're history. Make sure the woman isn't getting out in the next few minutes. You can tie the door. . . ."

There was a soft knock at the door to the passageway and muffled words Jason didn't understand.

A quick look around affirmed what he already knew: that door was the only exit from the stateroom. He pointed toward the bath, then the door. Paco understood. As Jason pressed himself against the bulkhead, Paco pulled the woman from the bathroom. Keeping her body and himself concealed behind the door, he opened it, pushing her head around the edge. His weapon rested along the back of her neck.

There was a murmured conversation.

Through the crack between the door and its frame, Jason could see a young man in a white jacket carrying what appeared to be a bottle of champagne like the two on the floor beside the bed. Alazar, it seemed, did not include bubbly in the prophet's injunction against alcohol.

In a single fluid movement, Jason stepped from behind the door, shoved the woman aside, and grabbed the astonished wine server's jacket with one hand while jamming the SIG Sauer between his eyes. The man offered no resistance as Jason snatched him into the room and gently closed the door. The only casualty of the maneuver was the champagne, which toppled from its tray. It had not been opened. Paco stooped.

"Leave it," Jason said. "Off vintage, anyway, I'll bet. The sort of crap the French would sell Arabs."

Paco picked the bottle up and stuffed it neck-first into his pants. "Mebbe off vintage, but th' fookin' price's hokay. Whatcha gonna do with 'em?"

The woman's fear-widened eyes were trying to avoid the body sprawled across the bed. The man could not tear his stare away.

"Rip the sheets into strips and tie and gag both of them. Let's hope nobody is scheduled to bring the caviar."

While both captives cowered under Jason's automatic, Paco tore strips from the bedsheets. Minutes later the man and woman were trussed like bucks slung over the hood of a pickup truck. Jason rummaged around the top of a bedside table until he found a set of keys, one of which he used to lock the stateroom once he and Paco were outside in the passageway.

They listened.

Silence is an absence of sound. But to someone whose adrenaline is pumping, someone whose life depends on his hearing at the moment, silence becomes a sound of its own, the sound of the heart thumping, of breaths taken deeply, and, loudest of all, the sound of emptiness and space that create a pressure upon the ears.

Jason's employer was going to be less than happy with a dead rather than captive arms salesman, but Jason and Paco hadn't formulated the contents of the deadly syringe. Maybe someone had planned for Alazar to die, lying to Jason for fear he would refuse to administer a fatal dose. If so, no one should have been concerned. Ridding the world of its Alazars was what Jason had sworn to do—kill all of them.

He would never be even for what they had done.

Alert to the possibility of being discovered, they began to move, to return the way they had come.

They had almost reached the anchor locker when they heard shouts and the sound of heavy and hurried feet. Jason and Paco traded stealth for haste.

Splinters, as deadly as bullets, flew from the ceiling over his head. He ducked reflexively as he and Paco stepped over the coaming and slammed the door.

In the cramped darkness of the tiny room they could see the harbor's water through the anchor port.

Jason motioned with his pistol. "You first. I'll cover."

"No, man. Take me too long to get through th' fookin' hole. You go."

The door trembled in its frame as jagged holes admitted light from the passageway outside. Wood fragments buzzed through the air like angry bees. No sound of gunshots. Silencers, Jason thought. They weren't using the arsenal of automatic weapons Alazar usually carried because rapid fire quickly burned out sound suppressors.

Jason fired two rounds through the shattered door. The SIG Sauer might as well have been a cannon in the confines of the small room. He didn't expect to hit anything, but the noise should back Alazar's men off for a moment or two, since their reluctance to use automatic weapons indicated that they wanted to avoid attracting the attention of anyone on shore, particularly the local cops.

His ears ringing, Jason stuck the gun into its holster, made sure the computer was securely inside the back of his belt, and grabbed the anchor chain with both hands as he swung his feet through the hawsehole. He squeezed through the aperture until only his head was still inside.

"C'mon, Paco!"

In the dim light reflected through the opening, he saw Paco grab the chain.

Jason was halfway down the anchor chain when Paco grunted. "I'm stuck! I can't get through! The fookin' bottle . . ."

Jason's feet were feeling for the *Zodiac*. "Dump the goddamn champagne bottle!"

Above his head Jason saw Paco's legs wrapped around the chain hawser. They struggled and went limp. Arms dragged Paco back inside.

A face appeared at the opening.

It was not Paco's.

Jason grabbed the pistol and squeezed off a shot, the report merging with the clang of the bullet ricocheting from the steel hull.

The face disappeared.

His weapon pointed at the anchor port, Jason used his other hand to snatch the inflatable's line from the anchor chain and shoved the craft clear. He was tugging at the outboard's lanyard when a spitting sound was followed by the hiss of escaping air.

Shit, somebody had hit the *Zodiac*.

The motor caught on the third pull. Lying flat against the coolness of the thin rubber, Jason opened the throttle and streaked for the middle of the harbor. Something whined overhead and hit the water with a crack.

When he was certain he was out of range, Jason cut the motor and considered his options. He wasn't concerned about the *Zodiac*. Its inflatable hull was compartmentalized; one puncture wouldn't sink it.

Paco.

Dead or wounded. A prisoner.

Jason tried not to imagine what would happen to his comrade if he were alive.

Orders were clear: If something went wrong, the mission was nothing more than an effort by individuals to revenge one of the many vistims of Alazar's business. Neither Jason nor Paco were employed by any government. The United States disavowed any connection with such a violation of France's sovereignty by mercenaries, even if one was a U.S. national. Any survivor was to vacate the area as quickly and quietly as possible, leaving his comrade to whatever fate he might suffer.

Rules of the game.

Fuck orders.

Had the syringe contained the nonlethal dose as advertised, a sedated Alazar could have been dragged with them, used as a shield or hostage. Because of someone's incompetence or dishonesty, a good man would likely die a very unpleasant death. Jason was not going to leave a comrade to the tender mercies of people whose stock in trade was death.

Water slopped over the deflated compartment of the Zodiac as Jason made for the harbor's mouth. Once he rounded the quay, he was out of sight from the *Fortune*. He beached the *Zodiac* on a rocky shore just beyond the lights of Chez Maya, a restaurant where waiters were stacking chairs on tables for the night. The place had a view of the roads as well as a small cemetery. Entirely appropriate in view of the evening's activities, Jason thought grimly.

Only when he beached the *Zodiac* did he remember Paco had the small cork attached to the keys to the sailboat, keys that not only allowed the single hatch and door to the cabin to be locked, but the ignition key to the small engine. At the moment, keys were the least of his worries.

It took nearly twenty minutes to make his way back to the harbor on foot along the narrow street. Keeping in the shadows was not difficult with the distance between the few streetlights and the occasional vehicular traffic. He was trying to formulate a plan when he rounded a curve and faced the straight stretch of pavement that bordered the harbor.

Half a mile ahead, the water, ships, and buildings were painted with flashing blue and red lights. The bleating of sirens bounced from the surrounding hills. Jason stopped. Dread grew in his chest like an undigested meal in his stomach—a dread that reached icy tentacles down his arms and legs.

Forcing himself to walk at a normal pace, he approached a small crowd of police, medics, and the curious at the edge of the dock. All he could see at first was a puddle of water with a pinkish tint he assumed was a reflection from a nearby ambulance. Closer inspection revealed something at the center of the group, something large, wet, and oozing red. A fish that some nocturnal fisherman had dragged ashore?

He knew better.

"What is it?" an anonymous dark form with an American accent asked another.

"A body," an earlier arrival answered. "Boat was headed out of the harbor and saw it. Thought somebody had fallen overboard."

Fighting back the acid bile that was rising in his throat, Jason slipped between several gawking spectators. A nude body of a man lay on the concrete, a stream of seawater and blood dripping from the jagged stump of a neck from which the head was missing. In the pulsating lights of emergency vehicles the network of scars across the chest was quite visible.

"Boy, I bet this causes an uproar," the first spectator observed as casually as though commenting on the nightly news. "A murder isn't going to do the island any good. Particularly one this grisly." He sounded as if he were enjoying the show.

"Murder?" the second man asked sarcastically. "What murder? It was a boating accident."

Jason turned his back on the following snicker. Where had these people become so emotionally calloused that they could view a decapitation with such equanimity? Violence had been part of his life for a long time, and he would never become accustomed to sights like that on the dock. Did American television and movies put *that* much bloodshed in the lives of normal people?

He looked for a place to throw up unobserved.

Almost unobserved.

One man in the crowd watched closely. Jason was too busy losing the afternoon's beers to note the small digital camera with its enhanced light lens.

CHAPTER FOUR

Costa Rica
December 26

It was unlikely anyone would have come upon the building. It was so well concealed in the rain forest that at first sight it seemed like a jungle cat pouncing from the green curtain of growth.

Otherwise, it was remarkable only in that it had a veneer of concrete rather than the cement block from which most native homes were built. What could not be observed in the remote chance of a passerby was that the structure was not a house at all. It concealed the entrance to an underground network. The massive ficus tree whose branches seemed to embrace the modest edifice concealed a dozen or so high-tech antennae. The strangler fig vines, thick as a man's wrist, that draped from the tree like ropes anchoring a balloon were actually electrical wires that ran to a generator far enough away that its gentle hum could not be heard here.

Not that sound mattered. The nearest settlement, a native village, was miles away, and the increasing number of tourists visiting the Costa Rican rain forest were content to remain in their vehicles on what served as a road on the opposite side of the mountain.

The government, always in pursuit of U.S. dollars, had happily allowed the construction of a nature laboratory to study and preserve the local flora and fauna. No one in San José had questioned the necessity of using nonlocal labor to build the facility, workers who melted away like mountain mist in the morning sun as soon as the job was complete. As long as certain officials received their monthly "consulting fee," no one questioned what was going on in the rain forest.

Only ten feet below the surface of volcanic rock, a room of roughly a thousand square feet was as brightly lit as an operating room. Two men sat in front of a computer screen.

Both were dressed in guayabera, the loose-fitting, four-pocket shirt the Latin America peasant wore outside rough white canvas pants rolled almost to the knees, with thong flip-flops. Notwithstanding the native attire, neither man would have been mistaken for a Costa Rican. Both were bulky, with the bodies of athletes from some sport where hurting someone was part of the game. The light from the computer reflected a bluish glow from two shaved scalps.

"You're sure that's him?" one asked the other.

"You can see the harbor of St. Bart's in the background," the other responded.

The first man shifted his position for a better view. "What do we know about him?"

The other touched a key on the board in front of him and read from the screen. "Very little so far. He was at one time employed by the army—we hacked into the military's files—but not much since he left in 2001."

"Echelon?"

The man referred to the supereavesdropping program that, from its place in England, monitored every e-mail and most telephone calls worldwide. The information gleaned was shared only by England, the United States, Canada, Australia, and New Zealand. The satellites and the system they made work had been in operation long before the American public learned that their communications could be intercepted. The sheer volume of transmissions made it highly unlikely that anyone would be listened to without already being of interest to one of the governments involved.

"Our person there has secretly tagged Peters's name, although that's more difficult than watching for a specific phone number or e-mail address. He may use an encryption device. In any case, we're tracing what we took from his companion. Is he a threat?"

"He or his employer has Alazar's computer."

The other man, perhaps a year or so younger than the first, reached into a bowl containing the small, sweet bananas grown nearby. He began to peel. "Surely he wasn't so careless as to . . ."

The older man snorted. "Alazar was not part of our cause. He was only in it for the money."

The other finished the banana in two bites. "We've found the location of his secret; we no longer need him. Perhaps his death was providential."

"Perhaps. But keep our people looking for Peters. We can't risk what might be on that computer. The secret he sold us is our greatest weapon against the despoilers of the earth."

JOURNAL OF SEVERENUS TACTUS EXCERPTED FROM ENO CALLIGINI, PH.D., *ORACLES, AUGURY, AND DIVINATION IN THE ANCIENT WORLD*. (TURIN: UNIVERSITY OF TURIN PRESS, 2003). TRANSLATION BY FREDERICK SOMMES, PH.D. CHAPEL HILL, N.C.: UNIVERSITY OF NORTH CAROLINA PRESS.

Cave of the Sibyl
Cumae, Gulf of Naples
Campania, Italy
Nones Iunius (June 1), Thirty-Seventh Year of the Reign
of Augustus Caesar (A.D. 10)

I, Severenus, son of Tactus, have decided to make this account of my descent into Hades[1] and, the gods willing, my return, so it may form a record of a remarkable journey. It is not a trip I undertake lightly, but one of necessity.

I am well aware many have crossed the River Styx never to return and that the trip is costly. In nearby Baia[2] already I have purchased from the priests three suitable bullocks and three lambs for sacrifice, as well as innumerable ducks and chickens so that these priest might augur the most favorable of times to enter the underworld.[3]

By inquiry, I ascertained that no one entered the underworld before visiting the Sibyl at Cumae a few miles north of my inn in Baia to ascertain if they would survive such a journey.[4] As Apollo's chariot reached its zenith for the day, I stood at the mouth of the cave, waiting for one of the Sibyl's priests to lead me inside. I stared into the alternating streaks of light and dark that marked the entrance, wondering again how wise were the actions I was preparing to take. I was half convinced consulting the seeress was the only sage part.

At least she could advise me of what will happen when I go down into Hades.

I only wished she could answer my question and obviate the necessity of confronting the shade of my dead father. Tactus was a difficult man and one who shared his secrets with no one. He had provided me and my siblings with a Greek slave to educate us, clothing, food and shelter, and little else, although he was one of the wealthiest merchants in Rome. When he died last year, my mother and siblings and I found his treasury nearly empty, both of goods and money. A diligent search and inquiry of his workers, both slave and freemen, revealed nothing. The only way to locate the fortune Tactus had secreted was to descend to the world of the dead and ask him.[5]

I was of the thought that it wasn't only Baia's mild climate, a refuge from the heat of Rome's summers, warm sulfur springs, and fat, purple oysters that had made the town the empire's premier resort location. More brothels than temples, more gambling halls than public buildings, exquisite baths. Seneca the Younger had described the place as a "vortex of luxury" and a "harbor of vice" two hundred years ago.

No, it wasn't the cooling breezes or the attractiveness of the prostitutes that had established the town.

It was the entrance to Hades.

My thoughts returned to the Sibyl. They said she dated to before man; and, at her request, the gods had granted her eternal life. She had not asked for eternal youth, an oversight that explained why she . . .

There was movement in the cave.

An androgynous figure, its face completely shadowed by a cloak, was coming toward me. Or was it? It alternately approached and disappeared like a ghost, getting closer with each reappearance.[6]

Wordlessly, a hand motioned me forward.

NOTES

1. Other than Virgil, Homer, and other Greco-Roman poets, this is the first account of such a journey, certainly the first by a nonheroic personality or in the first person, although there is little doubt that real persons in addition to legendary ones (Aeneas, Odysseus, etc.) risked such a venture. Then, of course, there was Persephone, who, kidnapped by Pluto, lord of the underworld, was allowed to return to the earth each spring for a visit.

2. The modern name for the town, used for convienince's sake. The Roman name was Bauli.

3. The selling of sacrificial livestock was a mainstay of the priests and attendants at oracles and sibyls throughout the ancient world. Not all the animals purchased for this purpose were slaughtered, allowing any number of resales.

4. Cumae is the oldest Greek settlement yet found in Italy. The Cumae Sibyl was regarded as one of the two or three most important sources of divination in the ancient world and was held in equal or higher esteem than the oracle at Delphi in Greece.

5. The easy solution would seem to be simply asking the Sibyl, but oracles dealt only with se-

crets of the future, not the past. Possibly this division of labor kept more priests profitably occupied, not unlike the strict division of tasks favored by today's labor unions.

6. The cave of the Sibyl at Cumae may be visited today. The approach is a number of equally wide pillars of stone and open space. In the afternoon sun, a person walking along this corridor would enter darkness and light at identical intervals, giving the illusion to the observer outside of alternately appearing and disappearing. We will further examine other tricks of showmanship designed to dazzle, or better yet, frighten, those who dealt with the cult of priests.

PART II

CHAPTER FIVE

North Caicos, Turks and Caicos Islands
British West Indies
January

The silver column of bubbles floated lazily toward the surface, leaving tiny globs of air to hang momentarily on the lips of the barrel sponge and plate coral above Jason's head. Despite the eighty-foot depth, the tropical sun was bright enough to make an artist's palette of color of the wall, a natural drop that fell into the hazy blue hundreds of feet below.

His artistic eye was oblivious to the spectacular quality of his surroundings. Instead, his attention was focused on something else as he hung motionless over the abyss, concentrating on a small hole in which he could see a spider crab. Though it was small in body, the crustacean's legs and claws were large enough to make a meal for two, a meal of the sweetest meat Jason had ever tasted. He wouldn't taste this one, though, unless he could get it out of its lair. The crab had retreated far enough back that it was out of reach, and Jason had left his spear in the boat. Nothing to do but remember the spot and come back.

That tangle of branchlike black coral would make a good marker, he thought as he flicked his fins and slowly moved on.

His dive watch told him he had still had a good twenty minutes before the pressure of depth presented any danger of the bends.

He watched a leopard ray glide by, its wings rippling in a graceful simulation of flight.

Then he heard it: an angry buzzing like the sound of an electric razor, growing louder. An outboard. Inside his mask, his eyebrows curved into a frown. On an island as sparsely populated as North Caicos, there were plenty of places for the natives to fish without dropping a line on the section of wall he was diving. Surely they could see the boat and would know he was down here. Maybe they'd go on by.

Somehow he doubted it.

As if to confirm his suspicions, he heard a splash and watched an anchor pull its line down to the sandy shelf forty feet above his head as the motor died. Jason waited, expecting to hear the thunk of a sinker on a hand line as it hit the water. He wanted to see where the treble hooks preferred by the locals were hanging rather than risk getting snagged. No fishing line, sinker, or hook was forthcoming.

Strange.

Unless the boat's occupant wasn't fishing. Unless somebody had come out here for him.

He bit the soft rubber of his regulator's mouthpiece in annoyance. There would be only one reason for somebody to come out here after him, and they were supposed to leave him alone for the next three months. Two jobs a year—that was it, the max. It had been only weeks since the affair on St. Bart's.

In fact, it would be fine if they overlooked him for a year or two. The work had paid well enough for him to retire as it was, enough to mandate that he reside someplace with no income taxation. His employer managed to satisfy the IRS by means Jason felt were best not inquired into, but sheltering his income where he lived was his responsibility. Hence his present residence. He had built the house as a vacation home, an excuse to claim residence in a tax haven. Now it was where he lived, had been home since his life had been turned upside down and shaken out as though the gods were emptying a paper bag. Ever since . . .

He pushed the thought out of his mind and glared up at the hull of the newly arrived boat. Well, if they were determined to intrude on his dive, they damn well could wait until he finished.

Maybe that crab was back on the edge of its hole.

A pair of passing jack rolled shiny button eyes at him in curiosity.

Twenty minutes later, Jason reached the surface and tossed the crab into his boat, followed by his flippers and weight belt. From the water he could see Pangloss, barking wildly, back into the stern, as far as the dog could get from the wildly thrashing crustacean. Pangloss hated crabs. His irrepressible curiosity had led to more than one painful experience involving the creatures' massive claws. Regardless, the dog insisted on joining Jason on dives, running into the water with baleful howls every time Jason tried to leave him ashore. Apparently barking at dolphins and seagulls was sufficient compensation for sitting in the boat for an hour while Jason probed the wall for lobster or crab.

Jason climbed into the twelve-foot Boston Whaler, his back intentionally toward the small craft rocking next to his in the gentle swell.

On the horizon he could see a sportfisherman. A charter from nearby Providenciales, Jason guessed, some rich dude paying a grand or so a day to troll for marlin even though the big-billed fish weren't expected in the area for months yet. The sun shot a brilliant reflection from something on board, perhaps the glass of a porthole, a woman checking her makeup in a mirror. There was something that didn't fit, something not quite right about that boat. What—

His thoughts were interrupted by a voice that had the musical lilt of the islands in it. "'Lo, Jason! You don' looks like you glad to see me."

Jason loosened the straps and slid out of the backpack tank harness before he turned toward the other boat. He was facing a black man whose age was indeterminate but whose disposition was always as bright as the smile he wore. It was annoyingly difficult to remain waspish around such cheerfulness, and Jason felt guilty for keeping the man waiting. He was, after all, only the messenger.

"I'm always glad to see you, Jeremiah. It's just you always bring bad news."

His mood undiminished, Jeremiah nodded. "Dat be right, I 'spose. But mon, you don' keeps no phone in yo' house; how else folks gonna get a'holt of you?"

Jason restrained a tart comment that the absence of a phone was fully intended to discourage contact. "I had a phone, Jeremiah, I'd never get to see you, now, would I?"

Jason was grinning in spite of himself. Jeremiah's smile was as contagious as the plague. As North Caicos' representative of the island's postal system, as well as UPS, FedEx, and DHL, he took his duties seriously. If a customer had paid for personal delivery, Jeremiah would see to it the service was performed as requested. Besides, occasional deliveries provided an excuse to visit with the constituency of his seat on the island's governing council.

Jason held out a hand and leaned over toward the deliveryman's boat. "Okay, give it to me and I'll sign for it."

Grateful he wasn't going to get any trouble from the reluctant recipient, Jeremiah handed over a cardboard envelope, using his other hand to rub Pangloss's nose. "I 'spect you be goin' like always when the package come."

Jason nodded absently, tearing the cardboard open. Inside was a Hallmark card, an invitation to a child's birthday party filled in for three days from now. Someone at the home office had a sick sense of humor.

It took Jason twenty minutes to navigate the convoluted, unmarked passage through the half-mile reef of fang-toothed coral that ringed the shallow lagoon in front of his house, tie off the Whaler to the buoy, and wade ashore with Pangloss splashing behind.

His house consisted of two structures elevated above potential flood tides by stilts. Between the buildings was a wooden walkway roofed with bougainvillea vines.

Pausing at the bottom of a flight of steps, Jason used a length of hose to wash sand from his feet while Pangloss lapped at the stream of cool, fresh water. Finished, both man and dog climbed stairs up to the building that served as kitchen/living room/studio. Years of island living had taught Jason the benefit of exposing as many surfaces as possible to potential breezes, as well as the wisdom of seg-regating light-requiring daytime activities from sleeping quarters that could be closed off against the tropical sun.

Inside, Jason ignored the panorama of golden beach and turquoise sea to glance again at the child's invitation in his hand. He had rarely been to the company's office. Most previous assignments, never more than one or two a year, had been hand-delivered. Idly, he wondered why the change. He tossed the card onto a table and looked out of the tinted glass that formed the building's front wall.

The houses's exposure to sea and sand had not been en-tirely for aesthetic purposes. The height of the walkway above the pancake-flat terrain gave him a 360-degree view of any possible approach. In front was the lagoon and its silent sentries of coral that would tear the bottom from any craft unfamiliar with the path through. Behind was a salt marsh, a saline, gelatinous muck soft enough to swal-low even the occasional iguana unfortunate enough to

wander there. To Jason's left, the beach ended in impene-
trable mangrove at the point of a tidal stream's juncture
with the ocean. To his right, sand the texture of powdered
sugar stretched in a three-mile crescent without intersect-
ing so much as a path connecting it to any of the three
small native settlements.

The latter approach was the only practical one, the
house's single vulnerability should someone choose to
trek miles across scrub bush and sharp rocks to reach the
shoreline. Discouraging as such a journey might be, Jason
had done his best to foresee the possibility.

Jason had not been surprised that Jeremiah had chosen
to deliver the packet by boat rather than the long walk
along the beach to a house that, to the untrained eye, was
only an attractive beach home somewhat difficult to
reach. In Jason's business, the more difficult, the better.

He walked into the kitchen area, pulled out a large pot,
and filled it with water from the cistern. Dumping the
still-thrashing spider crab into the water, he turned next
to rinsing out the dive equipment. Finished, he went to a
pine cabinet that housed the sound system. Seconds later,
notes of the first movement of a Mozart concerto grosso
filled the room.

Jason turned around and faced the glass that framed
the beachscape a few yards away. Between him and the
view, just inside the glass, was a canvas on an easel. Part
of a gecko, vibrant green, was staring back from a half-
completed cluster of bougainvillea. Tubes of acrylic paint
and brushes lay in the tray at the bottom of the easel. The
unfinished painting and art supplies were exactly as he
had had left them a lifetime ago. He and Laurin had gone
back to the States together without a suspicion that she
would never return.

Jason stared mutely at the canvas, as incomplete as his
own life. How many times had he picked up the brushes
to start again? More than he could count. Each time he
saw not lizard and flower but Laurin beside him, fasci-

nated as the canvas filled with paint. Each time he had replaced the brush in the tray, unable to concentrate. Twice he had vowed to toss the unfinished picture; twice he had been as unable to destroy the last thing she had watched him create. Not only was he incapable of finishing or destroying this specific canvas; it was as if his ability had drained away along with whatever passions and feelings he had formerly possessed. Brushes had become foreign objects, as strange and unfamiliar in his hands as an ancient war club.

There were times he feared he had lost the talent to paint forever. Other times he didn't care.

As though only partially aware of what he was doing, he went outside and followed the walkway to the building that housed his bedroom. Shuttered against the heat of the day, the room had a slightly musty smell that Jason knew would disperse as soon as he opened the windows to the evening's breezes. Overhead, a fan lazily churned the warm, humid air as he flipped on a light switch and entered a walk-in closet.

The space was more bare than occupied. On one side hung a few sundresses, the sort of beach casual wear appropriate for a place where shoes were optional at most. Repeatedly, Jason had vowed to remove them, to donate the lot to the local church for distribution. Each time he had removed one from its hanger to box it up, he remembered the last time she had worn it: the white with red polka dots she had on the night surprisingly rough seas had nearly swamped the Whaler on their return from a visit to a neighboring island; the green one with the exceptionally short skirt she wore to a friend's birthday party, provoking clucks and head shakes among some of the older native women; the blue stripe that she . . . Real or imagined, her clothes still had the scent of her, that musky, sweet odor he had come to associate with sex. Years later and the closet still smelled like she had just left it.

No use. He had given up, unable to part with the last

physical vestige of the woman he still loved. He not only couldn't remove her clothes; he couldn't go into the closet without tears blurring his vision.

Turning his back on the rack of dresses, he unzipped the clothes bag that contained what little remained of his business wardrobe. He slung a lightweight wool suit over one arm and, with some effort, extracted a cashmere overcoat. Jason scowled. In spite of his effort to stave off moths as ravenous as the sharks outside the reef, the insects had gotten to it. He'd better take it along, moth holes included, until he could replace it. It was likely to be cold where he was headed.

It took a few minutes longer to find his only two dress shirts and a tie. Now if he could only remember where he had put his suitcase . . .

CHAPTER SIX

That night

The number of things that had to be done before leaving the island always surprised Jason. Arrangements had to be made to refuel the house's generator every few days so that the contents of the freezer would keep; the bed linen needed to be stripped to prevent the mildew that bred in the humid air in any darkness; the cistern level must be checked to ensure a water supply upon his return. The alarm clock would have to be found so Jason could wake in time to take the Whaler over to Providenciales to catch the twice-weekly flight to Miami. Pangloss, along with appropriate rations, would have to be delivered in the morning to the native family who would keep him.

Pangloss.

The dog was scratching at the door, eager to enter where Jason was packing. Jason knew better than to let him in. The mutt recognized a suitcase and its purpose. With canine logic, the dog figured that if he unpacked the luggage, scattering its contents as wide and far as possible, Jason would not leave. It had taken Jason only one evening retrieving his underwear from the beach and his socks from the mangrove thicket to determine that Pangloss should be excluded from any area in which packing was taking place.

Closing the suitcase, Jason began to search for the tin of shoe polish he was certain he had bought only a few months ago. He found it under the sink in the bathroom. He sat on the floor to begin to try to remove the green mold that seemed to be devouring his only pair of toe caps.

In the background, Offenbach's overture to *Orpheus in Hades* cancanned through the sound system. Although he had never had any musical training, there was something about the symmetry of classical composers that Jason found restful. Contemporary pop, rock, or—worse—rap seemed to focus on the vocal, usually repetitive, and banal, with sharp elbows, rhythm without meaning. Or, in Jason's very private opinion, mere noise. He could endure the big band sound, the tunes of pre– and post–World War II, mostly long forgotten, but the classics of centuries past entertained him, setting a mood without the effort of trying to understand any particular lyrics.

He called it music to think by.

The heaviness of his eyelids told him it was well past his usual bedtime.

Pangloss had added a low growl to his persistent scratching. Putting down a shoe, Jason opened the door. Hackles raised, Pangloss had his lips pulled back, exposing long teeth. As if to make his point, the dog gave two sharp barks.

Then Jason heard it over the dancing violins: a low series of beeps coming from the system he had rigged in every room except the bath. The sound was what had so disturbed the dog, sound from wireless transmitters in the weight detectors he had buried at random intervals along the beach. Each device gave off a sound slightly louder than the previous one the closer someone got to the house.

Jason was not expecting visitors.

The sportfisherman he had seen that morning popped into his mind. What had made him notice it? There was no bone in its teeth, no white wake as it cut through the water. It hadn't been moving. The flash he'd seen had come from a telescope or binoculars. Instead of trolling for marlin yet to arrive, it had been observing him. Oversight like that could get a fellow killed.

But how . . . ?

The keys to the sailboat he had rented in St. Maarten's to sail to St. Bart's. The keys Paco had when he was captured. The float had the name of the rental company, and the rental company had . . . what?

Jason had used his employer's credit card, which matched his false passport, to rent the sailboat. Someone in Alazar's organization knew his face and recognized the fuzzy copy the rental company had made of his passport. The thought was less than comforting, but not as immediate as his present intruders.

In a single motion Jason removed something resembling a television remote and a pair of strangely configured binoculars from a dresser drawer and stooped to retrieve from under the bed a large wooden box clasped shut by a combination lock. Quickly touching a series of numbers, Jason opened the lid to reveal three fully assembled weapons with a loaded clip for each.

"Close," he said aloud, as though addressing Pangloss. "They're gonna get real close."

Letting the potential proximity of the intruders dictate his choice, he passed over a Chinese version of an AK-47 assault rifle and a stubby Heckler & Koch MP5A2 machine gun, a weapon designed to fill very small spaces with a maximum number of nine-millimeter Parabellum bullets, to select the bulkiest of the three, the military model Remington twelve-gauge fully automatic shotgun. The weapon had been designed for urban riot control, hence the name "Street Sweeper." At twenty-five yards or less it could fill an area fifty by fifty with painful but relatively harmless rubber projectiles or, using the loads in Jason's clip, deadly lead shot.

Outside, the moonless sky was black silk paved with diamond chips. Ducking below the railing of the deck to prevent presenting his silhouette against the stars, Jason scooted back to the other building, followed closely by Pangloss. Once inside, Jason went to the kitchen and out what served as the back door and down steps to a room originally designed as a garage. From there, man and dog went outside and circled the house to face the front.

Straining his ears, Jason could detect only the soft lapping of the tide at the beach and the wind's sigh through the few scrubby trees. He put one reassuring arm around Pangloss, using the other to hold the pair of night-vision binoculars to his eyes as he swept the beach. At the moment he could see only interlocking fields of dull green, the color the glasses used to concentrate all available light. Jason wished he had taken the time to buy the newer technology, vision aids that picked up heat to display images. Deep shadows might momentarily conceal something from the equipment he was using, but there was no hiding body heat from infrared.

He forgot his discontent as a green blob emerged from the darkness and took form. A man carrying . . . carrying . . . a long-nosed handgun. No, a handgun equipped with a silencer. Why go to the trouble of using a silencer when the nearest neighbor was miles away? Jason wondered. His curiosity was replaced by awe as four more figures followed the first silently up the stairs to the house's deck.

Five men for a single kill? In other circumstances, Jason would have been flattered his enemies took him that seriously. At the moment he had other things to think about.

Before moving, he swept the area a final time, to be rewarded with the green image of a sixth man standing guard a few yards between the beach and the house.

"Taking no chances, Pangloss," he muttered to the dog. "Damn! Too many!"

In any action movie worth a box of popcorn, Bruce Willis or Arnold would have successfully taken on all six assailants, defeating each in a spectacular display of strength, marksmanship, and agility, Jason thought ruefully. Unfortunately, neither of those two heroes was available tonight. Six men, each armed, presented impossible odds in the real world.

He could simply flee, disappear into the night. But where? Anyone who had tracked him this far was not going to be discouraged by not finding him at home, and the islands presented few hiding places. No, he was going to have to terminate this venture here and now, giving himself plenty of time to find another place to live. Subliminally, he had known this moment would come no matter how much he hated the idea of leaving these islands. He had hoped he would not need the preparations for defense even as he had made them.

Jason sighed. His fight had been from the first very, very personal. He had taken satisfaction from the expressions on the faces of men who knew they would be dead within the next second. Satisfaction and a small degree of revenge, a minute reprisal for his loss. Tonight there would be only impersonal killing, from which he would derive little vindication.

Well, with one exception.

Commandolike, Jason crept forward on his knees and elbows, the plastic device between his teeth and the shotgun held in both hands. When he was close enough to see the sentry against the sky, he stood.

"Welcome to North Caicos," Jason said softly.

He waited just the split second it took for the man to spin around and begin to raise his weapon, that nanosecond of hope he might survive.

The shotgun's muzzle flash burned into Jason's retinas

the image of the impact of six ounces of lead shot in the midriff, a blow that sent the man stumbling backward, hands flung outward if in one final, desperate supplication to his maker.

Before he could see clearly, Jason pushed one of the buttons on the remote. Instantly every light fixture or lamp in the building came on. Jason was standing just outside the rim of light that turned the surrounding sand a glossy silver.

Startled by the blast of the shotgun and the sudden brilliant illumination, two of the intruders ran out onto the deck, their weapons pointed in different directions. Even at this distance, Jason thought he could see shock and surprise on their faces. One had his mouth open, a black O in the bright lights.

"Come 'n' get it!" Jason shouted. "I've got a hell of a welcome waiting for you!"

Two more men joined the first pair in searching the darkness. Jason waited until one pointed at him before he dove headfirst into the sand at the instant he pressed another button.

Even with his face buried under his arms and eyes closed, the brilliance of the explosion lit the back of Jason's eyelids. He felt rather than heard the blast. By the time he raised his head, small pieces of debris and ash were floating down like a sprinkling of snow. Where the house had stood, timbers burned, sending sparks aloft in a Fourth of July fireworks show. There was no chance any living thing, including a recent infestation of mice, had survived.

Beside him, Pangloss whimpered.

He stood, running a hand up and down the dog's back. "Pangloss, looks to me like we're moving."

CHAPTER SEVEN

The next afternoon
Reagan National Airport
Washington, D.C.

Dirty rags of clouds squeezed oily moisture into rivulets that streaked the window of the 717. Jason gave his seat belt another hitch as the plane bucked in turbulence before thumping onto the runway. Winter-dried grass, shiny black pavement, and drab buildings emerged from the cloying fingers of fog.

Had he really begun the day with the glory of a Caribbean sunrise in his face, albeit diminished by the stench of the charred wood of his former home? Was it the same day he had dutifully reported to the island's sole constable, Stubbs, about checking a leak in the lines from his butane tank, the undoubted cause of the explosion? Had it been only this morning when he had counted out money under the gaze of the head teller at Barclays Bank, stuffed his sizable withdrawal into a money belt, and headed for the airport?

Pangloss, living up to his namesake, had eagerly sniffed the oversize dog carrier and even wagged his tail as he was locked into it. Now that they knew where he was, Jason couldn't risk leaving the dog until the unknowable time when his return could be made safely. The mutt would have to come along.

Jason felt he had traveled not only across space but also time. How often had he arrived back here? Hundreds? That was the difference, the disorienting factor. He was not returning home this time. The house in Georgetown and Laurin—neither was his anymore, no more than the life they had had.

He eased back in his seat and watched his fellow passengers stand and push into the aisle as the plane came to a stop. Idly, he watched as overhead compartments were opened and emptied. He hadn't brought much more than the clothes on his back, the rest having burned with the house. No problem. He could stop at one of the city's men's stores and outfit himself. With the money in the belt at his waist, he could dress himself however he wished.

The aircraft was almost empty when Jason finally stood. A blast of cold air from the open door made him thankful he had cleared customs in Miami. All he had to do was collect Pangloss and find a cab. There would, of course, be one stop, no matter what the weather, before he reached his hotel or a clothing store.

Reaching into the overhead compartment, he extracted his only luggage, a soft bag that contained toilet articles, extra socks and underwear, and a clean T-shirt, all purchased at West Indies Trading, North Caicos' only dry-goods store. He had declined to check the bag for two reasons. First, as an experienced traveler, he was all too aware of the chance of baggage taking an excursion of its own once entrusted to the airlines. The second was recent habit. A man waiting for his luggage to arrive on one of the crowded carousels was a man who could not move in a hurry if circumstances dictated. He saw no reason to break habits old or new.

CHAPTER EIGHT

Twenty minutes later

"Stop! Pull over for a minute!"

In the rearview mirror, the cabdriver's face was incredulous. "It's the Pentagon, mista. No stoppin' here."

Jason was already out of the cab, oblivious to angry horns as he dodged his way through traffic. He stood looking at what was arguably the world's ugliest office building as though experiencing rapture.

Along the west side, a single charred capstone was the only marker. In front of it were flowers, singly or in bunches, but Jason had no trouble recognizing the long green stems of white gladioli, her favorite. He had a dozen placed there every week.

The simple gold band he wore on a chain around his neck was the only trace of her found. There was no grave for him to visit, no other physical place to vent his grief. It was here, across a busy street around unattractive architecture, where she had spent the last seconds of her life, that he came to be as close to her as the living might get to the dead.

If you weren't looking for it, the repairs would go unnoticed. On that bright late-summer morning that had become America's darkest day, an airplane had slammed into the building.

It was like recalling an incident from childhood, so far away did 9/11 seem. First Lieutenant Peters, J., of the little-known and less discussed Delta Force, had been on temporary assignment here. His wife, Laurin, junior partner in one of the multitude of D.C. law firms specializing in lobbying activity, was in the building for an early morning meeting with the firm's largest client, the army.

The experience of going to work together was unique. Jason frequently was in places with classified names for indefinite periods of time. Laurin missed him, and the assignments were rarely to locales that could be described as garden spots. His paintings were acquiring a regular market, and her real estate investments, inherited from her mother, had become too large and profitable for her to manage and continue to work full-time.

They had decided to quit their present jobs in the next twelve months, spending the cold, wet Washington winters in the British West Indies and enduring the hot, equally wet summers in their Georgetown home. They built the house on North Caicos and spent an idyllic month there. They both loved it.

They were already counting the days.

Shortly before eight A.M. on September 11, 2001, he had shown her his temporary office in the Pentagon's second ring. She had a few minutes before her meeting.

"Can I bring you something from the canteen?" she'd asked.

It was much later he realized that most last words were probably equally banal.

"Sure. A large cup of coffee."

Nodding, she had set off, never to be seen again. Had she remained with him for the next five minutes, she would still be alive. The thought tortured him on nights he could only toss and turn with survivor's guilt.

It had taken a minute or two after the crash for Jason to learn what had happened and where. A number of fire-men suffered varying degrees of injury from a wild man trained to kill before MPs had succeeded in pulling Jason away from the inferno that had consumed his wife.

Once the adrenaline flow stopped, he had sobbed like a brokenhearted teenager. His rage was one of loss and im-potent fury. Delta Force kept a more or less current brief on the world's nasties. Even before the presidential an-nouncement, he had no doubt one or more of the terrorist groups had done this. He would, by God, get even.

But how?

His reverie in front of the Pentagon was interrupted by a hand on his shoulder. He spun around to look into the sympathetic face of a cop.

"Look, mister, I know you probably lost someone there, 'cause I see 'em all the time. But your cab's blockin' th' road. If you want, I'll hold up traffic an' let the taxi get to the parkin' lot. You can at least argue with them military assholes to let you stop there for a few minutes. Besides, you look like you're freezin'."

Jason, clad in only a T-shirt and a pair of light cotton trousers, had been oblivious to the mid-thirty-degree tem-perature. Even his moth-eaten overcoat would have pro-vided some warmth had it not been consumed in the fire.

Jason managed a weak smile. "Thanks, Officer, but I'll be going."

He could feel tears that were not caused by the cold on his cheeks as he climbed back into the cab.

CHAPTER NINE

Chevy Chase, Maryland
The next morning

Jason had found a hotel in Crystal City with a kennel for Pangloss. Both had spent a morose evening: the dog in unhappy confinement, Jason considering calling to get a table at Kincade's, one of the capital's better seafood places, before deciding the restaurant was too infested with memories. Instead, he elected to avoid his room's ever-remindful view of the Pentagon and eat in a dining room that justified every joke that had ever been made at the expense of hotel food.

A morning sky unmarred by clouds and a sun that turned a city of glass into gold improved Jason's spirits. Better weather did nothing for Pangloss, who barked most pitifully when Jason left the kennel after checking on him. Renting a car, he was at a nearby men's store when it opened. After purchasing two sweaters, slacks, and a Burberry raincoat with removable lining, Jason got on the Beltway and headed north.

When he exited the multilane road, he picked his way carefully, relying on memories two or three years old.

Where quaint towns had dotted the landscape, strip centers and outlet malls competed for space. Rolling farms had become subdivisions of McMansions on tiny lots. By equal parts navigational skill and blind luck, he finally saw the snaking brick wall that formed the boundary of the office park he sought.

Jason scanned the uniform plaques outside each building until he found the one he wanted: Narcom, Inc., one more acronymically named entity whose title did nothing to inform the observer of the company's function or distinguish it from its neighbors. Its one unique feature was a subterranean parking lot, a seemingly superfluous amenity in an office park where space was readily available. At the entrance to the down ramp, a wooden arm blocked passage until a ticket was taken.

Any semblance of normality ended with appearances.

Jason knew that while the car was waiting for the machine to spit out a ticket, scales set into the floor were weighing the vehicle. In less than a second, a computer compared the poundage to the manufacturer's specified weight, adjustments were made for a possible full tank of gas, and a formula applied for the number of occupants. Should the car exceed what the system deemed normal, a steel curtain would drop from the ceiling, preventing further access while probes extended from the walls to take air samples in much the same way bomb-sniffing dogs operated at airports.

The machine determined the rental car posed no risk, and Jason drove into a nearly empty basement. An elevator returned him to ground level, and he entered the three stories of smoked glass. Last night's rain was still a thousand diamonds on the carefully manicured lawn along the flagstone pathway to the entrance.

Almost all the buildings in the vicinity displayed signs announcing the services of one or more security companies. So did this one. Visibility was, after all, part of security. An intruder would, presumably, be less inclined to invade the premises of an establishment guarded by the usual electronic devices.

There were certain differences from nearby similar structures, had one looked in the right places, differences of which no ordinary burglar would have ever heard. But then, it was not the ordinary burglar Narcom wished to deter.

Jason knew his image was being transmitted inside by a series of well-concealed cameras. One step off the path would trigger sensors buried an inch or so deep under lush grass, green despite the season. The glass of the exterior was reinforced sufficiently to withstand any projectile smaller than an artillery shell. Well out of sight from below, the roof sprouted a forest of antennae. Window shades were rubber lined. When pulled, as they were anytime an important conversation was in progress, they made it impossible for listening devices outside to pick up vibrations in the glass caused by words spoken inside.

An electric eye opened the door as Jason reached it. The lobby, the twin of hundreds of others in the area, contained the usual potted plants and a reception desk manned by a woman who, by any measure, should have made an appearance on one of those reality shows where looks compensated for lack of plot. She had the pale, clear skin that went with naturally blond hair, and blue eyes without warmth.

As Jason approached, she watched with cold disinterest. From a few feet away he could read the tag pinned to the black camisole-type top, which, though not transparent, gave the impression of frilly lingerie underneath. He was not surprised to learn her name was Kim, nor would Lisa, Lori, or Ashley have been a shock.

He knew from previous observation that her fingers were never more than a few inches from a panel of screens that, when touched, could do everything from locking every door in the building to lowering a steel curtain between the entrance and the receptionist. Behind her, a mirrored wall was actually two-way glass, giving a complete view of the lobby to armed men who waited in perpetual readiness for whatever situation might arise. The place's security was second only to the White House's.

Kim imitated a smile, flashing teeth that would have inspired any orthodontist. "Help you, sir?"

"Good morning, Kim. I'm Jason Peters, and I'm expected."

She gave Jason a slow inspection, making no effort to conceal the fact that she was appraising him in the same way she might decide whether an insect was likely to sting or bite. Under other circumstances he might have taken a lingering look like that as interest, but her manner was of one who had no intent of inviting personal overtures. An expensive fur coat draped over the far corner of the counter explained a lot. He doubted Kim could have purchased it on her salary. She already had a "friend" with a bankroll.

Girls like Kim got minks the same way minks got minks.

"If you'll just step over here, sir."

Jason was familiar with the drill. Extending both arms, he placed the thumb of each hand on a screen that was part of the top of the desk.

She watched a monitor behind the desk. "Mr. Peters, I see you have a meeting in a few minutes. Know your way?"

"Indeed I do." He walked to the left of the desk, bowing slightly. "A delight to have made your acquaintance."

Kim had already returned to staring at the monitors in front of her.

A previously invisible door wheezed open, and Jason entered a small room, where he was patted down by one man while another, an M16A2 assault rifle in the crook of his arm, observed. A large dog of indeterminate breed sniffed for explosives.

The dog made Jason think of Pangloss, and he wished they both were back in the low-tech world of the Turks and Caicos. By now the day would be well under way there, the sun up hours ago. Reality intruded and he sighed, aware that it was unlikely he would ever claim North Caicos as a residence again, not if he wanted to stay alive. The place would be under observation.

"You'll have to empty your pockets."

Jason produced the rental car keys, a handful of change, and a small pocketknife.

The man not holding the rifle looked skeptically at the latter. "This some sort of weapon?"

"Not if you're attacking anything larger than a mouse. The blade is less than two inches long."

A moment of indecision. Jason could almost hear the line of thought: if box cutters could be used to take over airliners . . .

Jason handed it over. "Tell you what: you hold it till I come back through. If I have to kill someone, I'll do it with my bare hands."

"Thank you, sir." The man was clearly happy to be relieved of having to make a decision. "It'll be waiting for you."

As Jason stepped forward, there was a buzz, the snick of heavy bolts sliding, and the door on the other side of the room whirred open. A bank of two elevators faced him. Jason knew there were no buttons for selection of floors inside either. The cars moved at the direction of people elsewhere in the building.

Two floors up, another man greeted him with an expressionless face and voice to match. "This way, Mr. Peters."

Without waiting for a reply, he turned to precede Jason down a corridor flanked with steel doors.

The hall was deserted, filled with only the faint hum of electronic equipment and the sound of four shoes squeaking on linoleum. At the end a door swung open, throwing a beam of light into the otherwise dim hall. Framed in silhouette was a woman whose features appeared clearer as he drew close. Not old but not young, either. She wore listless brown hair in a bun behind her long, thin face.

She dismissed his escort and extended a slender hand to touch Jason's. The feel of her skin was as arid and cool as the first autumn breezes along the Potomac. She wore the fragrance he remembered, something that smelled of dried flowers.

"Bond, James Bond, to see M," he said in an overdone British accent.

She favored him with the threat of a smile. "Hello, Jason. Good to see you again. You're looking fit, all tan. The tropics must agree with you."

"Certainly more than Washington, Miss Tyson."

She clucked disapprovingly. "Now, now, Jason. We're happy to see you again."

He wondered if the pronoun included her boss. He had never known the boss to be happy about anything that didn't involve death, destruction, and mayhem of some sort.

"Nice to see you again, too."

Still holding his hand, she drew him across the threshold and the door silently swung shut.

Jason glanced around, noting the lack of change. The same bleak reception area, furnished with only a desk and secretarial chair that faced a worn leather couch. The walls were without windows or pictures. The room had the personality of a dial tone. He had often wondered how someone could spend time in such quarters, looking at nothing. Particularly if, as was the case with Miss Tyson, they never seemed to have anything to do. Perhaps she came in here only when her boss was expecting someone.

As though reading his thoughts, she pointed to the only wooden door he had seen in the building. "Go right in."

He knocked briskly, the comparatively mellow thump of wood somehow soothing after all the steel, and the door opened.

On the other side, the office was as lavish as Miss Tyson's space was spartan. Jason stepped onto the muted blues and reds of an antique Khurasan that cost more

than most houses. The rug's colors were softly repeated in
four original Renoirs whose gilt frames hung on fabric
wall covering. An Edwardian breakfront occupied most of
the far wall, behind its rippled glass a collection of eigh-
teenth- and nineteenth-century first editions. Floating on
the rug's center medallion like a ship adrift, a mahogany
partners' desk was topped with hand-tooled, gold-edged
leather.

Behind the desk sat an enormous black woman clad in a
flowing caftan with an African print. With a hand the size
of a catcher's mitt, she held the receiver of the telephone
that was the only item on the desk. With the other, she
motioned Jason into one of four Scalamandre silk wing
chairs arranged in a semicircle in front of her.

He was unable to understand the language she was
speaking, but, from the rare familiar word and hand gestures that accompanied each utterance, he guessed it was
some dialect of Arabic or Farsi. He sat and waited.

Jason had to smile as he watched her, the ultimate
minority-business-program beneficiary. An émigré from
Haiti, she was simultaneously black, female, and non-
Christian, embracing a belief in the African gods of
voodoo and Santería. She was the poster girl for politicians espousing egalitarianism above all. Unlike many
such recipients of government largesse, however, she had
qualifications beyond race, sex, and religion. As former
second in command of her native land's Tonton Macoute,
she was skilled at interrogation, torture, assassination,
and manipulation of the political process, a résumé the
awareness of which no elected official could admit. Had
anyone demurred at the government doing business with
a person previously associated with an organization
whose brutality made Hitler's Gestapo look like Boy
Scouts, he would have been denounced not only as a
racial and religious bigot, but sexist as well.

She served her only client well and was generously

compensated for taking on unsavory tasks to which no democratically elected government could admit, but which no government, democratic or otherwise, could do without. Any scruples she possessed related only to her "boys" and to the proper preparation of the fiery Creole cuisine of her homeland. Dealing with the nation's enemies of today required an unrelenting barbarity that made congressional stomachs churn. Narcom, Inc., provided the political antacid of deniability.

It was a marriage made perhaps not in heaven, but strong nonetheless.

In less than a minute she hung up and came around the desk. Jason stood to receive a hug that might have crushed the lungs of a man less fit.

"Jason! Good to see you again; always good to see one of Mama's boys!"

Mama's boys, the name she gave all her operatives, although Jason had met very few. By its nature, Narcom's business was strictly compartmentalized.

She relaxed her embrace, allowing Jason to draw a breath before he sat down. She returned to her chair behind the desk before speaking.

"How you doin' on that island of yours?"

"I'm not there anymore. I had some visitors."

As he related what had happened, she nodded. "Uh-huh. You stirred a stick in a bees' nest when you did Alazar down there in St. Bart's."

"You know that wasn't my fault. Whoever mixed the tranquilizing solution overdid it."

"I know, but somebody doesn't. Not that it matters. One less of those animals. I would have liked to ask him a few questions, though."

Alazar was fortunate, Jason thought, to be dead.

Mama continued. "Sounds like six bad guys won't be a problem anymore."

"At the cost of a damn nice house," Jason grumbled.

"With what you get paid, you can afford it," she said amicably. "But that's not why I invited you here."

She reached into a desk drawer and handed him a sheet of paper. On it was a series of lines in what Jason recognized as Russian. "This came off the computer you sent me, the one you took from Alazar."

Jason stared at the paper, unable to even guess what it was. "I speak a little Russian, but I don't read it."

Mama took the paper back. "Appears to be some sort of shopping list, an order for something that he supplied that was successfully used by the customer; refers to a type of new weapon. From the context, military intelligence thinks it's some sort of biochemical warfare, since it refers to 'containers.'" She wrinkled a brow. "Also talks about 'keeping it healthy,' like some sort of microbe."

The most oxymoronic of all government bureaucracy: military intelligence.

Right up there with legal ethics.

Jason leaned back in the chair, crossing his legs at the ankles. "And?"

The woman on the other side of the desk shook her head reproachfully, sending gold chandelier earrings flashing with reflected light. "I'll get there, Jason; just show me the courtesy of listening. Thing that got the attention over to Langley was the date this new whatever-it-is was used, last June."

Jason swallowed the urge to ask a number of questions, knowing Mama would answer most of them in her own way and in her own time.

"Last June, one of our coast guard boats in the Bering Sea found a Russian trawler, one of those supersize fishing boats. The whole crew had had their throats cut."

Jason hunched forward in his chair, impatient to get to the point. "So? We're not in the business of protecting foreign fishing boats, particularly those poaching in our waters like I'd bet that one was."

Mama nodded, multiple chins shaking. "Jason, you just

won't wait, will you? Whatever happened to manners? Anyway, this Russian trawler was just the beginning. Since then, there've been loggers in Georgia, a team of geologists looking for possible oil off Florida's west coast, an Indian chemical plant executive and his whole family, a Polish coal mine owner and . . ." She stopped and took a deep breath. "You get the idea. All found with their throats cut, no sign of any resistance."

Jason leaned back, letting the chair's softness envelop him. "Overfishing, timber cutting, petroleum exploration . . . All ecological hot buttons. We've seen people chain themselves to trees, lie down in front of earth movers, even blow up some labs where animal experimentation is going on. But murder?"

"Not the first time. There've been occasional acts of violence by the lunatic fringe. This time, though, it looks like a well-organized, concerted effort."

"And why does the client want to dump this in our lap?"

"I don't ask questions, Jason. I just take the money and perform the service. That's part of the company's success. If I had to guess, though, I'd say the present administration doesn't want to get involved with anything looks like opposition to environmental causes, even violent ones. This is, after all, right before an election year, and the president isn't the tree kissers' hero. On the other hand, the Feds can't just sit by while people get killed."

Jason thought that over. Made sense. "And none of them seemed to put up a fight? I mean, someone was trying to give me that close a shave, I'd at least try."

"That's part of the problem."

"Or a clue." Jason uncrossed his legs and sat up straight. "Any idea why they didn't put up a fight? Drugs, poison?"

Mama placed the report on her desk, sausagelike fingers squaring the edges. "Not a glimmer. Autopsies on the Russian crew and the loggers were no help. Only thing unusual was that each person had a slight amount of sulfates in the lungs and bloodstream, probably less than they would have inhaled from auto exhausts in any large city. And ethylene gas in the lung tissues."

"There aren't any cities in the Bering Sea. And what, exactly, is ethylene?"

"Dunno. Part of your job's gonna be to find out." She slipped the report across the desk. "Take this with you. It's classified, of course."

"Of course." Jason would not have been surprised if the people at Langley classified their grocery lists.

"That's jus' a summary. They got a complete one they'll deliver to you, a report on 'the Breath of the Earth.'"

"The Breath of . . . ?"

"Breath of the Earth. At least, that's how the note on Alazar's computer refers to whatever it is."

Jason recrossed his legs, this time at the knee. "Breath of the Earth, sulfur, ethylene . . . sounds more like halitosis to me. But then, halitosis is better than no breath at all."

Mama leaned forward, the desk groaning under her bulk. "Make all the jokes you like; our client takes this very, very seriously."

"So, you want me to do what?"

Mama shrugged. "First, we need to ascertain exactly what happened to those men on the fishing boat, the loggers, the others, see if there's any threat in this Breath of the Earth, whatever it might be. Then destroy it and whoever is using it."

"I don't suppose we have a name, an idea of who's behind this?"

Mama leaned farther forward, her elbows on the desk. "Matter of fact, we have an idea."

"Want to share it, or you'd rather I find out myself?"

She slowly shook her head in disapproval. "Sarcasm doesn't become you, Jason. There's an organization—if you can call it that—called Eco. Maybe you didn't know it, but the various conservationist groups around the world raise more money than the economy of a lot of third-world countries. Eco has gotten rich from unwitting but well-meaning green groups. Every concert in Japan to cease whaling operations, every T-shirt sold in Germany bearing the *Grün* logo, every contribution to a conservationist cause, even the sale of some ecology-friendly devices such as recycling bins and biodegradable trash bags, Eco gets a cut, either by contract or just plain, old-fashioned extortion. You know, 'We'll "guarantee" your rally for the three-toed tree frog will be peaceful' et cetera.

"Eco's agenda, so far as we can tell, certainly includes the industries where people have been killed, and they have the money. We don't have anything more concrete than that."

"So, why not infiltrate and see what they're up to?"

"Easier said. They don't have members in the conventional sense. The only reason they came to our client's attention was a large transfer of cash to Alazar's Swiss account from a number of banks around the world, all within twenty-four hours."

Although the Swiss still prided themselves on bank secrecy, they could do nothing to prevent a record of any wire transfer of funds by SWIFT, Society for Worldwide Interbank Financial Telecommunications, the Brussels-based clearing center for all electronic transfers. Most of the world, including international criminals, were ignorant of SWIFT's existence or its post-9/11 cooperation with the CIA, FBI, Interpol, and other agencies. Fortunately, so were American politicians, whose rush to expose the arrangement in televised displays of righteous indignation would have compounded the country's security problems.

"And the CIA traced those accounts."

Mama treated him to another gleaming grin. "Anytime that much money changes hands, they know about it."

And the American people still thought privacy existed.

"Anything else?"

"Running some cross-checks, our customer believes

Eco is run by a man name of Boris Eglov and some buddies from the Russian Mafia. They have the money to fi-
nance something like this but haven't been heard from
since the Russian police were hot on their trail a few years
back. Not likely they all became honest businessmen."

"They don't get involved in causes other than their own
pocketbooks. What's in it for them besides skimming and
extorting toad lovers?"

"Most of the ecology-friendly groups are honest and
nonviolent, but the word gets around when Eco strikes a
real blow—something other than chaining little old ladies
to bulldozers. You'd be surprised how many activists secretly cheer them on. After the murders on that fishing
boat, contributions jumped forty percent to worldwide
causes—and Eco gets a cut, remember. They want that
sort of cash. Also, when Eglov was running black-market
fencing and extortion schemes in Moscow, he was fanatic
on the subject of the ecology. May have something to do
with the fact that his parents and younger sister died from
radiation at Chernobyl when the nuclear plant blew. He's
suspected of personally strangling two of the surviving
plant managers with his own hands."

Jason was impressed. "You've done your homework."

She reached into the same drawer and slid two sheets of
paper across the desk. "I try. Here's what our friends in
the Moscow police tell us."

Jason studied the picture stapled to the top right-hand
corner of the first page. Though the image was grainy, he
saw a broad-shouldered man with a shaved head. The
eyes were hooded, slightly Oriental, while the rest of the
face had a Slavic flatness. Below was a list of attributed
crimes. Murder in one form or another was the most fre-
quent offense, with strong-arm extortion or robbery a
close second.

"I'm surprised they let a guy like this stay on the
streets," Jason observed, still reading.

"You'll notice he wasn't convicted of any of those charges."

"I also notice a high mortality rate of witnesses."

"Some people are just lucky."

"Not if the police want you to testify against this guy."

Jason finished the list. "Professional criminal, vegetarian, and passionate friend of the environment. Somehow it doesn't seem to add up."

Mama retrieved the papers and returned them to the drawer. "What? You saying a criminal can't be a nature lover? Seems to me the man has set up a worldwide scam of conservation organizations to fund his own agenda."

Jason groaned. "You're saying we're dealing with an idealist here, someone who kills in pursuit of his own utopian ideals. Or, not to put too fine a point on it, a nutcase."

"Perhaps, but a deadly one."

Jason stood, circling his chair. "The customer didn't hire us to do a job unless they need to be able to deny any involvement. What is it you're not telling me?"

The woman's eyes widened with mock surprise. "Are you suggesting I wouldn't tell you everything?"

"Not suggesting—clearly stating. Come clean; what's the hitch?"

Mama put her hands on the desk, fingers interlocked. "If we are talking about a chemical agent here, chances are Alazar's buddies didn't manufacture it—at least, not in his part of the world. Not much chance of setting up a laboratory when you're on the run."

"So, our clients figure whatever it was, it was concocted somewhere else, maybe some sovereign nation that might just resent foreigners conducting an operation on their soil."

Mama nodded. "You're smart, Jason. Looks like mebbe Langley finally figured out the sovereignty thing."

Both remembered the international outcry raised when an undetermined number of CIA operatives had snatched a terrorist suspect right off the streets of Milan. The Italian authorities had indicted six names on credit card receipts that indicated the kidnappers were American. Luck, rather than tradecraft, had stymied the prosecution when no real people could be matched with the credit cards. The only clue to surface so far was the fact that the cards involved were all Diners Club, a less than helpful discovery, even if the CitiCorp card did constitute less than three percent of the world's credit card charges.

Jason walked over to study one of the Renoirs, a woman lounging in the bow of a boat being rowed by a man in shirtsleeves and a straw hat. He was forever fascinated by the works of the earlier impressionists, pictures more likely created with palette knife than brush. At a few feet, the subject was clear. At close range, the whole thing dissolved into meaningless globs of paint. Only one of many things that didn't withstand minute inspection at Narcom.

He managed to forget late-nineteenth-century France and turned to face the desk behind him. "So, what now?"

Mama shrugged. "You're the one makes the big bucks. You know what facilities we have. They're all available."

Few third-world countries had the intelligence and military resources of Narcom, Inc.

He paced over and stood directly in front of the desk. "For a starting point, I'd like to see whatever reports were made, see if they took specimens, fluids, any of that really gross stuff. Run 'em by that spectroanalyst we use . . ."

Mama stood, handing him a plain white envelope. "Here's your contact."

Jason opened it, annoyed but not surprised to see what he took to be a single name and a phone number.

"Password is *fife*," Mama added.

"Fife, as in Barney?"

"As in fife and drum. *Drum*'s the countersign."

"Don't these guys know we're on their side? Or at least

they're paying us a hell of a lot of money to be." Jason held up the envelope. "Tell me this isn't going to burn a hole in my new suit when it self-destructs."

Mama grinned, one gold incisor sporting a diamond. "This isn't *Mission Impossible*, you know."

Jason nodded. "Yeah, I know. Question is, does the CIA? I wouldn't be surprised which bathroom is the men's and which is the women's is classified over there."

Mamma chuckled, her massive bosom quivering enough to shake the desk. "That might lead to interesting results." She swallowed, serious again. "You need anything, call."

Jason had been dismissed.

He was reaching for the door when she said, "Jason, I almost forgot."

He turned to see her holding out what looked like an ordinary BlackBerry, the combination cell phone and computer that had become the badge of anyone who wanted to be considered important.

"Thanks, but I have one."

She motioned him back with the hand holding the BlackBerry. "Not like this you don't. It's straight from the Third Directorate."

The CIA was divided into four compartmentalized divisions: Operations, or Ops, included the actual spycraft, cloak-and-dagger activities. Intelligence consisted of the satellite-picture-searching, communications-monitoring computer nerds. Supply, the Third Directorate, functioned somewhat like Q of James Bond fame. They had actually developed a gas-spraying fountain pen, a belt-buckle camera, and a poison-laden hyperdermic needle concealed in an umbrella. With the demise of the Soviet Union, the need for these "toys" had diminished to the point that Jason had had to search his memory to recall exactly what Supply did. The Fourth Directorate, Administration, included the bean counters, the cost analysts, procurers of equipment and the like.

Jason looked at the BlackBerry with renewed interest. "And it does what?"

"Functions just like an ordinary BlackBerry." Mama opened her other hand, revealing what appeared to be a newly minted quarter. "When you squeeze this, though, it goes bump in the night."

Jason took both, examining them closely. "How much 'bump'?"

"Enough that you don't want to be holding it."

Jason slid them both into a pocket. "I'll try to remember that."

"And keep the two in seperate pockets or you'll be singing soprano the rest of your life."

"I'll definitely remember that."

As he passed through the lobby, he waved to Kim. She ignored him.

In the garage he sat in the car a moment, planning his course of action.

He remembered his first job for Narcom, Inc.

After 9/11, after Laurin had . . . disappeared, the days and weeks had blended into a haze of equal grief and impotent fury. He was part of the most elite small-engagement organization in the world, Delta Force. He had dropped into inky darkness to places so deserted, so void of life that even the appearance of a scorpion had provided relief. He had slipped across borders into jungles that stank of decay, where boots rotted away in a week and both animals and plants were equally likely to be poisonous.

But no place had been as near to hell as the empty house on P Street in Georgetown, the home he and Laurin had shared. No encounter was as bad as being able to do nothing other than accept that she had been taken from him and there was nothing he could do about it. Getting even was out of the question; no life would equal hers. Still, he would gladly give years of his for just a chance at those responsible for her death.

Then Mama had called.

At first he had thought some prankster was playing a cruel joke. Then he remembered she was calling on a secure line, a phone that not only was unlisted but did not exist as far as any phone company knew.

It was as if she were intentionally playing Mephistopheles to his Faust.

The soft woman's voice named the members of his last squad and the code name of their mission, information so classified that less than a dozen people knew it. Would he be willing to take a high-paying job that desperately needed doing but carried far too much risk for politicians, a job ignoring national boundaries to stamp out international terrorist organizations, those who were perfectly willing to kill the innocent to impose their politics or religion on others?

Did a bear shit in the woods?

Did he have qualms about killing extremists, no matter their sex or nationality?

Did a shark ask questions before it fed?

A week later, Jason handed in his resignation from the army and Delta Force amid the sounds of debris removal at the Pentagon. That night he was on a plane for Munich, from where he would travel to a small town just across the Austrian border to a place the leaders of three European cells of Hamas were meeting.

Two days later he was on his way home, his rage at his loss partially slaked and his newly opened Swiss account over half a million dollars fatter.

It took the Austrian officials over a week to conclude that they would never find all the body parts.

Narcom had given Jason two things: wealth and revenge. There might be enough of the former in the world, but never the latter.

So much for Memory Lane. He had a new job to do.

CHAPTER TEN

Hilton Hotel K Street, Washington
That evening

Dressed in a new sweater and slacks as well as a warm and moth-free coat, Jason had cruised the Kalorama District, an area of restored mansions bordering Dupont Circle known locally as Embassy Row. Despite a number of sudden and unsignaled turns that brought the blasts of angry horns, he was still not sure he was not being followed. There was simply too much traffic to be certain.

Checking his watch for the third time in as many minutes, he was aware he was likely to be late for a rendezvous Jason considered useless at best. In typical CIA fashion, the phone number Mama had given him was answered only by the countersign, a time, and the bar of this Hilton as a meeting place. Simple courier delivery of the material Jason wanted would have served. The organization frequently reminded Jason of a group of kids playing at being spies, secrecy and stealth their own rewards. That love of the cloak-and-dagger mystique meant that if Jason were late, he'd miss his contact and have to go through the elaborate process of setting up another clandestine meeting.

He pulled to the curb in front of one the embassies, this one flying a flag he didn't recognize. As expected, a D.C. cop cruiser was behind him in less than a minute. In a world where alliances shifted like sands in a windstorm, the municipal government of the District made every effort to ensure that international antagonisms took only verbal form in its jurisdiction.

One cop stood just outside the driver's window of Jason's rental car. Another was checking the license plate.

The one beside the car made a motion to roll down the window. "You got a problem, mister?"

Jason shrugged. "Lost, I'm afraid. Can you direct me to the Hilton?"

The policeman shook his head in disgust. "Take a look to your left. And remember, visitor to the city or not, we enforce the no-stopping signs in front of these embassies."

During the brief encounter, Jason had seen no other vehicle stop to observe. It was the best he was going to do.

He was reluctant to hand over the rental car to the hotel's valet. Not having the keys in his possession eliminated one means of escape if something went wrong. That made him nervous.

Get a grip, he told himself. What could possibly go wrong with a simple delivery of papers, material Jason had requested?

But then, he knew Murphy had been an optimist.

His overcoat slung over his arm, he followed the sound of a piano mingled with voices. Just before the bank of elevators, he found a large, crowded room with an oak bar at one end. The sole entrance was clogged with customers coming and going. Tables surrounded by upholstered captain's chairs shared the rest of the space with a baby grand and banquettes against the wall opposite the piano. Jason skimmed the room with a glance. Drum, the voice on the phone, had given no clue as to how he might be identified.

Groups formed and re-formed like swarms of bees; no one seemed to be accompanied by anyone else. It was only after noting that there were roughly equal numbers of men and women that Jason realized it was Friday evening and he was witnessing that uniquely American mating rite, a singles bar. Had he given it any thought at all during the last several years, he would have guessed AIDS, herpes, and other unpleasant possibilities had culled the herd of unmarrieds seeking companionship, if not a relationship, in a saloon. Had he been asked, he would have assumed the ritual had joined the tea dance and church social on society's ash heap.

Jason grinned at snatches of conversation he could not help but overhear, words and phrases he had heard during his bachelorhood fifteen years ago: No woman ever came to such places except tonight, when she had simply agreed to accompany a friend. No man was driving anything less than a Porsche.

He smiled again, this time returning one from a shapely woman, her face surrounded by pageboy curls. It was too dark to distinguish all her features, but it would have been hard to miss the flat stomach that peered with a single eye over pants glued to her pelvic bone, or cleavage that threatened to spill out of a blouse utilizing less than half its buttons.

Undressed to kill.

Her interest looked a lot more personal than Kim's had been. She started in his direction, and for an instant Jason wished he were not here on business.

"Fife?" The voice came from behind him.

Jason reluctantly turned his head to see a man who, at least in the bar's dim light, looked no older than a college sophomore. More and more people seemed younger and younger, a sure sign Jason was experiencing what the advertisements euphemistically described as the maturing process.

Mature or not, he gave the low-riders another look. She was already talking to someone else.

"I have a room upstairs," the stranger announced.

Wordlessly, Jason followed him out of the bar and onto an elevator. The bright light confirmed Jason's impression that the guy was young. The heavy horn-rimmed glasses and dark suit did more to make him look out of place than older.

Still without speaking, the two men got off and trudged down a hall, stopping in front of one of a series of doors while the young man inserted his plastic key. Other than an overcoat draped across one of the beds and a briefcase on a table, there was no sign the room had been occupied.

"Wouldn't it have been easier to simply courier over the reports?" Jason bantered, throwing his coat beside the other and taking a seat in one of the two chairs. "You could have saved a pair of code names and the time you took to study my picture."

The other man sat in the remining chair across a small table, produced a key, and unlocked the briefcase. He handed Jason a form for his signature. "I assume you know the rules: classified documents are not entrusted to persons without appropriate clearances, and all copies have to be signed for."

The agency employment profile did not require a sense of humor.

Jason took a thin manila folder and quickly skimmed it. "This is the complete report of the incidents in the Bering Sea and Georgia?"

The young man was already relocking the empty briefcase. "It was what I was given."

"And if I have further questions about something?"

The agent's face betrayed confusion. "No one told me. My instructions were to deliver that file and have you sign for it."

Originality of thought was not a requisite, either.

Jason stood, stuffing the file under his belt at the small of his back and pulling his sweater down over it. "It's been a real pleasure to meet someone as charming and witty as you. I don't know what I would do without all your help. You want to leave first?"

Clandestine meetings broke up one at a time because single departures did not advertise the fact that there had, in fact, been a meeting.

The still-unnamed agent also stood, scooping a coat from the bed. "I'll leave first. Give me five minutes."

Then he was gone.

It was only when Jason picked up the remaining coat that he saw the young man had taken the wrong one. Instead of the tartan design of the Burberry's lining, there was dark faux fur. The remaining raincoat also lacked the belt that gave Jason's garment its distinctive shape.

The guy had been in too big a hurry to get away to notice. *Shit.*

Snatching up the coat, Jason rushed for the door.

Screw procedure. Jason wanted to retrieve his coat without having to drive all the way to Langley.

The hall was empty, and the elevator seemed to take forever.

As the doors sighed open, the vestibule containing the elevators was packed with a seething, shouting crowd, most of whom looked like they had come from the bar. A woman screamed; several men shouted.

Jason edged his way toward the hotel's exit, turning to a young woman. "What's happening?"

"Someone's been shot," the man next to her said. "Shot right here."

The pulsating wails of police sirens were becoming increasingly audible above the crowd as Jason worked his way through the lobby. Near the revolving door that led onto the arrival porte cochere, the crowd had formed a rough circle.

Jason felt as though he had stepped into a blast of arctic air as he peered over the heads of the people in front. He was looking at a man sprawled on the floor, a dark pool seeping into light carpet.

The man was wearing an overcoat.

Jason's overcoat.

CHAPTER ELEVEN

Hay-Adams Hotel
16th and H Streets, Washington
An hour later

Jason had made no effort to retrieve his rental car. Instead, he had again fought the crowds in the hotel lobby until he found his way to a side exit. Forcing himself to move at a normal, non-attention-getting pace, he took an irregular course for several blocks until he found an overhanging awning that afforded deep shadows.

For a full five minutes he waited, watching the way he had come, before crossing the street to a Metro station. He really didn't care where the train was headed. He simply wanted to put maximum distance between him and the overcoat-shrouded body in the hotel lobby.

The bullet that had killed the young man from the agency had been meant for him. They could simply have traced his credit card, one issued by Narcom in the same name as his alternative passport, the same one used to rent the boat, the same boat with the key in Paco's pocket. It would have led them straight to the hotel in Crystal

City. Then all they had to do was follow him embedded in the mass of Washington traffic, almost impossible to spot.

At some point, Jason exited the Metro and took a cab to the venerable old hotel across Lafayette Park from the White House. The woman at the desk was unable to conceal her surprise when he paid for the room in cash. It would draw unwanted attention, but the credit card would attract notice even less desirable.

One of the reasons Jason had selected this particular hotel was its dining room. The fare was good, but the location better. Seated at any one of several candlelit tables on the floor below the lobby, he had a clear view of anyone descending the well-lit stairs or exiting the elevators under overhead illumination. His first thought was to have a cup of coffee and tarry thirty minutes or so, observing. After only ten, the siren aroma of a passing dish reminded him he had not eaten in a long time. He asked for a menu.

His room was furnished with reproductions of late-eighteenth-century American pieces, a period reminiscent of the building's origins. The cabinet containing the TV and minibar was a highboy with brass pulls. The bed had both steps and canopy. Just to make sure, he checked the bathroom, satisfied the faux antiques did not include these facilities. Sitting in a Martha Washington chair at a Federalist desk, Jason began to read the report he had been given.

There were a number of items that had not been included in the briefer document Mama had given him, and one very interesting addition.

When he finished, he reread it, puzzled, before taking the BlackBerry-like device Mama had given him out of his pocket. The resemblance ended largely with the physical case. Although the gadget could receive and send voice and text messages, it could do so in nanosecond garbled bursts that both defied decoding without appropriate

equipment and sent false satellite coordinates that would
foil the most sophisticated GPS. In short, communications were secure both as to location and content.

He punched a button on the back that activated the special features and then a series of numbers, beginning with
the 202 D.C. area code, well aware that the actual phone
he was calling might be on the other side of the world.

Jason waited. There was no sound of ringing in the conventional sense. He was calling his agency contact whom
he used when he needed information on anything. *Anything* included pertinent weather updates in any part of the
world, scientific data, or impeding coups or assassinations.

The latter two, Jason mused, had been on a decline in
inverse proportion to increasing congressional inquiry.
Gone were the halcyon days when a people's revolution
conveniently removed a leftist-leaning dictator of some
banana republic, or a rival clansman used a single bullet
to end the anti-Western ravings of some sheikh or mullah.

The more moral American foreign policy, the more
chaotic the world became.

There was no salutation, no mention of a name, simply
a "Begin."

Jason was used to the abruptness. In fact, he had long
suspected he was speaking to a voice mechanically generated to make electronic identification impossible should
the conversation somehow be recorded. Machine or person, he had no idea with whom he was speaking, only that
the voice was always the same.

"Reference"—Jason held the written pages up to the
light—"document echo-tango-four-zero-two. Question:
The bodies found all had traces of silica and ethylene in the
lungs, though in quantities that should not have been fatal.
Couldn't that have come from natural surroundings?"

Pause.

"Unlikely with silica on the Bering Sea incident. Possible in Georgia, but the soil had low silica content. Unless

there were a sandstorm. There was no record of a sandstorm in the area."

Only a machine would exclude that possibility, given the locales. No, knowing the CIA . . .

Jason ran his eye down the page. "I note sulfates at almost uniform levels in all the victims' lungs, too. Isn't it unusual that persons with different-size lungs would have almost identical amounts?"

"Very."

Not exactly helpful. "Any explanation?"

"As stated, tissue studies show nitrogen also, as well as trace carbon. As in some sort of smoke inhalation."

"Smoke from what?"

"Unknown. Subsequent photographs of the ship and logging camp depict some sort of brush or scrub as the only flora nearby. One in a pot, the other beside the bunkhouse. None of it appears to have burned."

"Then what did the smoke come from?"

"Good question."

Jason thought for a moment. "Let's go back to the silica. That's a common element in rocks as well as sand, right?"

"Right."

"Any chance they breathed silica in the smoke?"

"Only if a rock was burning. Not likely."

"Okay," Jason went on, "any idea why they would be gassed at all? I mean, shooting would have been a lot more efficient."

"We don't know. That, Mr. Peters, is why we hired your company."

Jason thought for a moment. "Anything else that's surfaced since the report was written?"

Pause.

"There were traces of radiation. Very low rads, but ascertainable. Also some evidence of hydrocarbons in the blood, and ethylene."

Jason paused, trying to pry loose a distant memory.
"Ethylene is an anaesthetic, isn't it?"

"Was. Its use was discontinued in the sixties."

Jason stood, idly glancing around his hotel room.
"Don't suppose you have any explanation for the presence
of the hydrocarbons, either."

"You are correct."

Swell.

Jason was dealing with a form of anaesthesia mixed
with what amounted to sand, one or both radioactive, origins and purpose unknown. The agency needed a geo- or
biochemist, not a spy. "You've been a big help."

Pause.

"Always pleasure, Mr. Peters."

Was that a trace of mechanized sarcasm?

CHAPTER TWELVE

The National Mall, Washington, D.C.
The next morning

Shortly after sunrise, Jason had dropped by the Crystal City hotel to check on Pangloss. That had been a mistake. The big mixed-breed managed such a pitiful look from behind the bars of his kennel that Jason let him out and watched as the dog streaked for the backseat of the rental car Jason had just retrieved. *What the hell?* Jason rationalized. They both would be leaving Washington today, anyway.

The question was, for where?

At the moment, Jason was one of a number of people walking their dogs on the grassy mall in full view of the capital building. Restrained by an unaccustomed leash, Pangloss made a halfhearted lunge for a tourist-fattened squirrel, an effort Jason saw as more instinctive than motivated. Tail flicking indignantly, the intended prey unleashed a string of chattering rebuke while head-down on the trunk of a bare oak tree.

Jason gave the leash a tug, "Come on, Pangloss. You wouldn't know what to do with him if you caught him."

By now man and dog were in front of the original Smithsonian building, the redbrick Victorian pile that for years had housed the basis of the collection that now occupied most of the mall. Across the lawn was an unimposing structure, neither particularly modern nor classical. Its best architectural feature was that it was not of the type so common in Washington, a style Jason referred to as "Federal Massive."

Jason checked his watch and slowly walked over, watching the parade of joggers, dogwalkers, and bureaucrats scurrying to standard-issue desks in buildings that were visually indistinguishable from one another. Stopping as though to make certain where he was, Jason appeared to read the words above the entrance that informed him he was entering the National Museum of Natural History.

No one in sight paid him any attention.

He pushed his way through a revolving door and came face-to-face with a man in the uniform of the Smithsonian's security service. His name tag labeled him as W. Smith. Had Jason been asked, he would have guessed W. Smith had recently shaken Jim Beam's hand. Red-rimmed lids were puffy, almost closed over piglike eyes. He winced at any sound as though magnified, and hands were shoved into pockets, perhaps to conceal shaking.

"You can't bring the dog inside," the man said sternly.

The man's breath confirmed Jason's suspicions. He hoped W. Smith would stay away from open flames.

Jason glanced around furtively, a man not wanting to be noticed, although the foyer was devoid of tourists. "It's okay, Officer. This is a bomb-sniffing dog."

The man with the badge seemed little less assured. "Bomb?"

Jason shook his head, lowering his voice. "Nothing to worry about; just a practice run."

The guard glared at Pangloss. "Nobody said nothin' to me 'bout any dog, bomb-sniffin' or otherwise."

Jason managed a look of surprise. "Really?" He nodded toward a telephone hanging on the wall beside the door. "Why not give Dr. Kamito a call, tell him Jason Peters is here with the dog."

With one suspicious eye on the tail-wagging Pangloss, W. Smith punched in a three-digit number and grunted into the phone before turning to face Jason. "He says you know the way and for you and the dog to come on up."

It was clear W. Smith did not approve as man and dog walked across the entrance hall to a single elevator. *If ever Pangloss were to break house-training*, Jason thought, *Lord, let it be now*.

Prayers unanswered, Jason stepped into a long hall at the top of the building. He and the dog drew curious stares but no comments from people in white lab coats bent over microscopes, chipping at rocks, or working in a huge chemistry lab.

Unknown to most, the CIA was one of the largest contributors to the Smithsonian, particularly its natural history and aerospace subsidiaries. In return for its generosity, the agency had access to a number of the museum's scientifically oriented staff on a consulting basis.

For example, who better than a seismologist to predict, as far as predictions were possible, an upheaval of the earth's surface likely to disrupt or distract an uncooperative government for a few days? Even less known, for example, was the prediction within seventy-two hours of the Afghan-Pakistan-Indian earthquake of October 2005. The resulting destruction and chaos enabled a thorough search for terrorists camps in an area of Pakistan that the United States supposed ally had insisted the Pakistan Army had secured.

Jason had previously used the services of Dr. Ito Kamito, head of the museum's geology division and a specialist in geochemistry. Two years ago, Narcom had taken a rare job for someone other than the agency. The De Beers consortium of diamond fame was faced with rumors of gems allegedly mined in the Siberian permafrost. Knowledgeable sources told of gems indistinguishable from those of South Africa and half as expensive. The tension in the voice of the De Beers representative indicated that they took the threat very seriously.

The prospect of the loss of a few euros was one of two events that could provoke emotion from a Dutchman. Jason wasn't sure what the other was.

Posing as an international jewel dealer of shady repute and enormous resources, Jason had managed to smuggle one of the Russian stones from a mine inside the arctic circle and bring it to Dr. Kamito. Within a week he ascertained that the gems were not formed by carbon under intense geological pressure, the definition of diamonds, but were a form of Mesozoic era glacially ground glass with the same weight and spectrographic properties as the real thing.

The De Beers company expressed its gratitude by paying Nacom's bill promptly and without haggle, perhaps a first for the diamond consortium.

Near the far end of the hall, a small man stepped out of a door. Had Jason not recognized him, he would have mistaken him for a child in his parent's lab coat. Myopic eyes peered through bottle-bottom-thick glasses. An almost perfectly round face was split by a megawatt smile as he bowed slightly and extended a hand. There was only a trace of his native Japan in his speech.

"Jason! Good to see you again!"

Dr. Kamito might be Asian, but he was anything but inscrutable. Jason had never seen him in anything but a good mood.

The man clearly did not understand his world.

The two met with the doctor's usual enthusiastic handshake, a gesture that reminded Jason of pumping water from a very deep well. With his other hand, the scientist was scratching between Pangloss's ears, incurring a potentially enduring friendship.

"So, this is the dog you told me about? Can he truly smell explosives, as you told Mr. Smith?"

"Don't see why not; he sniffs everything. Whether he would know to alert us if he found any is another matter."

As he indicated that they should enter the open door, Dr. Kamito's slightly slanted eyes narrowed; he was unsure whether Jason was joking. "Bomb-sniffing or not, welcome."

The office was as Jason remembered it: imitation wood desk in front of a wall paved with diplomas, certificates, and other documents in multiple languages, including what Jason guessed was Japanese. Two prints, both depicting *Revenge of the Ronin*, added primary color. Between the desk and wall were a chair on casters and a small credenza, which left scant space for the sole visitor's chair. Nestled on the papers scattered across the desk was a plastic box, the sort that contained take-out food. Through the clear lid, Jason could see several slivers of what he gathered was raw fish.

Dr. Kamito followed his glance. "Some of the best-seeing—looking—tuna in a long time; makes a great breakfast."

Jason sat, certain his face didn't show the heave his stomach gave at the thought of raw fish first thing in the morning. "Better for you than a bagel, I guess."

The chemist smiled broadly, exposing more teeth than Jason had seen since Jimmy Carter. "You are familiar with sashimi?"

Jason managed a weak grin. "I grew up with it."

He managed not to add, *Except when I was a kid, we called it "bait."*

The doctor proffered the box. "I have some chopsticks here somewhere."

Jason put up a protesting hand. "Mighty generous of you, but I've already eaten."

Pangloss wasn't quite as eager to turn down the offer, but a gentle pull on the leash made him sit in front of the chair. Soon he was stretched out on the bare linoleum floor, snoring.

Kamito was digging around under the debris on his desk. "If I can just find chopsticks . . ." He produced an ivory pair from under a file folder, opened the box, and scissored a piece of fish into his mouth. "If you're sure . . ."

"I'm sure. Thanks."

Kamito smacked his lips in pleasure as he pursued another cut of tuna. "If you didn't come for the sashimi, you must have come for the company."

Jason reached into the pocket of his new jacket, producing both the report he had gotten from Mama and the one given him by Drum, or whatever the CIA man's name had been. He handed them across the desk, and Kamito read as he finished the tuna.

"That explains it," he said upon completing the reading of both papers.

Jason raised his eyebrows in an unspoken question.

"Your people, the agency . . ."

"Not my people, Doc. I'm just an independent contractor."

Kamito shook off the distinction as though all people in Jason's line of work were the same to him. "Ah, so. Yesterday some guy walked in here and handed me a package. Nothing unusual about that; we get samples of rocks and stuff all the time. This one, though, had no return address, no nothing other than a typed note asking that I do a chemical analysis with special attention given to trace ethylene. Just a test tube of what looked like clay, soil of some kind, with a few pebbles mixed in."

The chemist shook his head in puzzlement. "It would have been easy enough to at least let me know what to look for, who it was from, something. Sometimes I think you guys believe in secrecy for its own sake. Who else would send stuff like that anonymously? I'm surprised you people sign your Christmas cards."

"Not my people," Jason corrected again. "We just do jobs for them, same as you."

Kamito actually winked, two small boys sharing a secret from adults. "No worry. I can keep very tight mouth." He continued as he carefully placed the food container in the trash. "I went ahead and did tests. . . ."

Jason straightened up in his chair. "And?"

"I found silica, the usual thing you'd expect in any soil or clay, the ethylene, too. I also found traces of sulfides, slight radiation, the kind you'd assume around volcanic activity."

"But there aren't any volcanoes anywhere near where those samples came from."

Kamito shrugged. "You asked for an analysis; you got an analysis. And that's not even the real puzzler. I had to guess, I'd say the soil came from somewhere around the Mediterranean basin."

Fascinated, Jason leaned forward, waking up Pangloss. "Lemme get this straight: you do tests on soil and a few pebbles from Georgia and a trawler's rock garden and determine they came from halfway around the world? How did they get there?"

Kamito leaned back in his chair. "That's what your employer pays you to find out."

Jason sighed, despairing that the scientist would ever accept that he, Jason, was not employed by the CIA. Elbows on his knees, he said, "You're probably right. Let's start with how you came to the conclusion that this stuff is from the Mediterranean."

Kamito stared at the ceiling a moment, as though the answer might suddenly appear there. "Although most soils contain common elements, the proportion of those elements varies. For instance, I would expect the water-leached soil of, say, a rain forest to be very low in chemical nutrients like nitrogen. On the other hand, desert sand would be high in nitrogen but, without life-sustaining water, low on hydrocarbons."

Jason leaned back, aware that he had opened the jar and now the genie was going to take its time getting out.

"This particular sample is very rich in sulfides, which suggests past, present, or future volcanic activity."

"Yeah, but there are volcanoes . . ."

Kamito held up a silencing hand. "To my knowledge, only one of the tectonic plates of the world contains these exact proportions of sulfides, sulfur nitrates, and the like."

Jason searched his memory. "Tectonic plates? You mean those pieces of the earth's surface that more or less float on a sea of lava?"

A smile, almost condescending. "Not exactly, but very, very close. There are a number of plates that rub up against each other. One may override another or submerge under it, usually with cata . . . cata . . ."

"Catastrophic," Jason supplied.

"Ah, so. For instance, the plate that is the Indian subcontinent slid under the larger Asian plate a few years ago, causing a massive earthquake. The San Andreas Fault is the line between the plate to which North America belongs and that of the Pacific Ocean. One day—tomorrow, aeons from now—everything west of that line is likely to slip into the sea."

Submersion of the Hollywood glitterati was a pleasing thought. Likely to raise the average IQ of both the Pacific and United States.

"Along these fault lines, the magma below sometimes boils to the surface. Volcanoes are least common where there is no fault line activity."

"I don't recall any volcanoes in the western United States," Jason said.

Kamito grinned yet again, explaining as though to a small child. "Possibly the largest volcano in the world is in the western United States, We call it Yellowstone National Park."

It took Jason a moment be sure he had heard right. In the meantime, the chemist continued. "Not all volcanoes are above surface to begin with. If you consider the amount of thermal springs that regularly erupt under pressure—Old Faithful, for instance—there must be huge amounts of pressure in the area. It can go dormant or, in days or aeons, erupt, taking Montana and Wyoming with it."

Not as gratifying as California dropping into the ocean.

"Okay, I get the picture, but the Mediterranean basin is a little large. Could you be more specific?"

Kamito shook his head, the overhead lights shooting rainbow-colored streaks from his glasses. "Afraid not— not my area of expertise." He reached into a desk drawer, fumbled around, and produced a card, handing it across the desk. "Call Maria Bergenghetti; take her what's left of what you people sent me. She's one of the world's top volcanologists."

Kamito stood, extending a hand; the interview was over.

Jason studied the card, hardly surprised it was in Italian. Like those of most of her countrymen, her business card bore a bewildering list of phone numbers. "Exactly which one of these should I call?"

"The agency surely knows how to find people. Or you could try calling her office and asking where she is."

JOURNAL OF SEVERENUS TACTUS

Cave of the Sibyl
Cumae, Gulf of Naples
Campania, Italy
Nones Iunius (June 1)
Thirty-Seventh Year of the
Reign of Augustus Caesar (A.D. 10)

> My feet felt as though they were en-
> cased in lead, so full of dread was I, al-
> most as frightened of what I would hear
> as of my impending trip to the nether-
> world. My guide was silent, the only
> sound sandals on stone and the cooing
> of doves.[1]

I inhaled deeply, tasting the musty odor of earth mixed with rancid lamp oil. I saw the cave was largely man-made. Large, regularly spaced openings let in the light, making the dark shadows seem even blacker and obscuring my guide in the gloom. From somewhere in front of me a dim light grew brighter, and there was a moaning, keening sound like no human voice I had ever heard.

Then I saw her.

She sat on the stone floor of a tiny room, the oldest person I had ever seen, the woman who had asked for eternal life but not youth. A guttering lamp emphasized deep furrows the centuries had plowed in the sagging flesh of her face. Her uncovered head was bald, and she drooled from a toothless mouth.[2] Scattered around her were hundreds of tiny oak leaves. I watched her write on one, set it down, and begin another. According to Virgil, nearly a century past, she was composing prophesies. Should a breeze scatter her work, she would not rearrange the leaves.

She looked up with eyes as dull as unpolished stones, and I saw she was blinded by cataracts.

But how could she write if . . .

She either saw or sensed me, for she pointed a sticklike finger, its arthritic joints the size of chestnuts, before throwing herself onto her back and writhing with an animation that belied her age. She was mumbling something I could not comprehend. It was only outside that my guide repeated the words she had spoken, something in verse that sounded like [translation]:

> "To meet your father you will go,
> Even though he is not there below.
> No harm are you about to receive,
> If you are one who will believe."[3]

I waited for her to finish for a full minute before realizing she had begun to snore.

"But what am I . . . ?" I asked the priest when he had given me her prophecy.

My only answer was the production of a clay dish held by the attendant who had led me in. It was time to leave an offering for the gods in payment for the prophecy.

I reached into my *subucularm*[4] for my purse. "But . . . but I have no idea what she meant. I mean, she made no sense."

But then, sibyls didn't have to.

Although I had never been there, legend and literature were full of the riddles spoken by the Delphic oracle in Greece, as well as this Cumae Sibyl. If the priest's rendition was verbatim, she had delivered hers in almost perfect trochee.[5]

Sensing the growing impatience of the cloaked figure, I dropped a gold denarius onto the plate. Far more valuable than indecipherable prophecy, but it does not pay to be cheap when dealing with the gods.

Leaving the cave, I climbed the gentle hill to the temple of Jupiter. Actually, the temple of Zeus, I suppose, since the Greeks had originally built Cumae, as they had most of southern Italy. Had the Sibyl been here then? No matter—I left another gold coin at the foot of the god's statue that stared off across the sea as though it might be searching for Aeneas fleeing the ashes of Troy. Satisfied I had done all I could, I took the path down to the city gate, where the groom held my horse that would take me the few miles south to Baia.

And to Hades.

NOTES

1. Doves, pigeons, and even swallows abound in ancient descriptions, symbols, and pictures of oracles. Since no form of prophecy can continue long without being right occasionally, many scholars believe that carrier birds were used to bring immediate news of far-off events that could then be "prophesied" weeks or even months before the news arrived.

2. While the oracle at Delphi supposedly made her forecasts under the influence of narcotic gases from a cleft in the earth, the Cumae Sibyl is commonly believed to have made her predictions while in an epileptic seizure.

3. By "translating" the ravings of an epileptic, the priests could often utilize the information gained as noted in 1, above. They were certainly adept at ambiguity.

4. The *subucular* is commonly translated as a shirt. Actually, it served more as an undergarment. Severenus was carrying his money in such an unusual way as to suggest he had reason to fear of robbers.

5. The long-short meter of the seven types of Latin verse.

PART III

CHAPTER THIRTEEN

North Caicos, Turks and Caicos Islands
British West Indies
The next morning

Jason was the only white or male in the line outside the cinder-block building that Barclays Bank shared with Island Hair and Beauty. Although he had stood in this very spot more times than he could count, he already felt like a stranger here. He had spent last night in a resort hotel on Providenciales, the islands' tourist destination, where he knew no one. This morning, he had hired a stranger to bring him to North Caicos by boat.

After leaving Dr. Kamito yesterday, Jason had taken Pangloss to one of those high-end kennels found in cities where a large segment of the wealthy population were frequently unable to take their pets on their excursions abroad, a place where treatment of four-legged guests was designed to soothe the consciences of two-legged owners. Jason had stayed in hotel rooms—nice hotel rooms—that cost less per diem than Pangloss's temporary home. Of course, hotel rooms rarely came with soundproofing, regularly scheduled exercise, or personal attendants. The dog's quarters were even video monitored so separation-anxiety-racked owners could view their pets on closed-circuit TV accessible from the establishment's Web site.

Despite the glory of a tropical morning, Jason was in a black mood not entirely attributable to Pangloss's absence. Generally the homeless had a cardboard box, a street corner, a bridge, some familiar place that included that sense of belonging that tethered the human soul to reality. Jason was truly homeless. He was domiciled no place at all, had no location where he belonged. Annoyed at his own self-pity, he reached in a pocket to make sure he still had his real passport and bankbook. The homeless weren't standing in line to move a high six-figure account. He felt a little better.

He could have simply had Barclays wire-transfer the money, but anything done by computer was theoretically subject to hacking. If his new enemies, Eco or whoever they were, knew he had been living here, it would be logical for them to watch for the transfer of funds to learn his new location—of which, at the moment, even he was uncertain.

He'd had a couple of other details to clear up, too. Jeremiah would sell the Whaler for him and reap the political profit of donating the proceeds equally to the island's four or five churches. He had succumbed to a compulsion to sift through the charred remains of the house to make sure there was nothing of Laurin's that was salvageable.

There wasn't.

He planned to spend no more than half a day in the Turks and Caicos before beginning a convoluted series of international flights. Even if the islands were being watched, he should be able to get in and out before his enemies could muster an attack.

The door opened and a dozen or so native women queued up inside. He was the sole bank customer.

The solemn-faced teller dolefully counted out the

money, a large stack of hundred-dollar bills, as Jason had specified by a phone call to the bank's main branch in Grand Turk. The request was facilitated by the fact that the U.S. dollar was the currency of the islands, rather than pounds sterling. He was leaving when he spotted Felton, the island's constable and entire police force.

It was not unusual to see Felton in his uniform of starched white jacket and red-striped navy trousers. It was unusual for the policeman to have an old Welby revolver stuck in his shiny black belt. Since most crime on North Caicos involved drunkenness, fighting, or petty theft, there was little or no need for Felton to be armed. Sentences, imposed by Felton acting as prosecutor, judge, and jury, consisted of confinement for a day or two in the constable's guest room, which doubled as the jail. The prisoner served his time by playing endless rounds of dominoes with his jailer.

More unusual yet were the two young men walking beside Felton, two men whose uniforms identified then as police from Grand Turk.

Someone was in trouble, and Jason had an uncomfortable feeling he knew who.

Felton and his two companions stopped, blocking Jason's path.

" 'Lo, Jason," the constable said, his eyes refusing to lock onto Jason's.

"Morning, Felton," Jason replied. "There a problem?"

Felton, clearly unhappy to be the harbinger of ill tidings, nodded. " 'Fraid so. Police over to Grand Turk got a 'nonymous call day or two ago, say some folks were killed 'fore your house blew up."

The coffee and island fruit Jason had eaten for breakfast felt like a cannonball in his stomach. He didn't have to guess at the source of the call.

Felton continued, "Police from Grand Turk came over, looked 'round. Sure 'nough, there be human remains where yo' house was. Police figger you burned the house to hide the evidence."

"Why would I do that? If I had killed someone and wanted to hide a body, I'd dump it in the ocean or bury it, not burn down my house."

Felton nodded, acknowledging the logic of Jason's argument. "Mebbe so, but they wants to talk to you over to Grand Turk." He produced a pair of rusty handcuffs. "Sorry, Jason. I hates this, but you gonna haff to go wid' dese here fellas."

Jason thought about making a run for it and discarded the idea. Even if he succeeded, where on the island could he hide?

"If I'm being arrested, I get a telephone call, right?"

"You can call from Grand Turk," one of the policemen said.

Felton snapped the cuffs closed around Jason's wrists and handed the key to the man who had spoken, visibly relieved to no longer be in charge. "Like I say, Jason, I hates this."

As he was marched away, Jason turned his head and spoke over his shoulder. "Not your fault, Felton. I'll be back and kick your black ass at dominoes."

The constable's face lit up. "Dat'll be de day!"

Jason hoped Felton believed the match would take place more than he did.

CHAPTER FOURTEEN.

U.S.–Canadian border
Near Sumas, Washington
The same day

Rassavitch handed his Canadian driver's license and passport through the car window to the fat immigration and naturalization officer. Neither had his real name nor address. False identification was a cottage industry along the northern side of the U.S.–Canadian border.

The official retreated to the small customs building beside the road, presumably to run the fictional name into the computer for a useless comparison with known terrorists. Since Rassavitch had made the name up, he was less than worried.

Sure enough, the man returned, handing the documents back. "Canadian citizen?"

Rassavitch nodded. "Yes, sir."

No further identification required.

With millions of foreigners in Canada due to the most lax immigration standards in the western hemisphere, Rassavitch and his group caused no suspicion. No one was surprised when they availed themselves of equally lib-

eral welfare laws so they might devote full time to their
true purpose.

Even in December of 1999, when Ahmed Ressam had
been apprehended near here with a carload of explosives
with which to celebrate the new millennium, the Canadian authorities had done nothing to tighten security. It
was the Americans, not the Canadians, who had to worry.
Ahmed's target had been the Los Angeles airport, not
something in Canada. Besides, prosecuting or even extra-
diting accused terrorists was contrary to the country's
open-door policy to all people, a policy that endangered
their neighbor to the south, much to the glee of most
Canadians.

United States bashing had replaced apathy as the national pastime of Canada.

Don't offend, don't interfere, don't get involved. Canada's
national mantra. A national character that rivaled cottage
cheese for blandness. And why not? Any external threat
would be met not by the few largely ceremonial troops of
Canada's military, but by U.S. military might. Like most
recipients of charity, Canada was resentful, believing it
could avoid global conflict by political correctness and
siding against their protector on every issue.

Rassavitch smiled, showing yellowed teeth, as the officer waved him across the border. Didn't even ask for the
keys to inspect the trunk. That would be racial profiling,
hassling someone to whom English was not a native language. And America, the democracy, would not treat any
of its minorities differently from its majority.

Apparently dogs were immune from political correctness. The black Lab had sniffed its way around the car
and wagged its tail in a most friendly manner. Of course,
there was nothing in the car for the dog to smell. Only
Rassavitch, who intended to be much more effective than
a few hundred pounds of explosives.

He returned the officer's wish that he have a good day
and entered the United States. When he was out of sight

of the border station, he pulled to the side of the two-lane road and waited for a fully loaded logging truck to pass before he flicked a flame from a cigarette lighter and burned the driver's license and passport to unrecognizable ash.

The he turned east and began the long drive to the opposite coast.

CHAPTER FIFTEEN

Grand Turk
That afternoon

On the few occasions he had visited there, Jason had been impressed with just how unattractive a tropical setting could be made. Grand Turk was a center for off-shore banking, corporations and individuals who were willing to pay handsomely to remain below the radar of any number of tax-collecting authorities and the lawyers who served this very specialized clientele. One-story office buildings, mostly concrete block, crowded one another for space along one side of Front Street. Any number of colors, apparently based on the availability of paint at the time of construction rather than aesthetics, had been used. Across the street, a beach, framed by tired palm trees, had probably once been a spectacular crescent. Today, litter and garbage of every description covered the golden sand and floated in the turquoise surf as though a giant party had just ended.

The business of Grand Turk was business. Scenic vistas belonged elsewhere.

Jason sat in the backseat of an ancient Ford between

two burly officers who reeked of sweat and stale tobacco smoke. The prison occupied two blocks of the town's less desirable real estate, ten-foot-high stone walls topped with broken glass that sparkled in the sun with a cheerfulness that seemed out of place.

Upon arrival, he was taken to a small, airless room where the smell of lye soap was strong enough to make his eyes water but not sufficient to conceal the odor of old urine, feces, and despair. He was stripped and searched by two other officers and fingerprinted with a kit J. Edgar Hoover would have discarded as antiquated. His clothes, minus belt and shoelaces, were returned to him. The size of the eyes of the guard examining the contents of the money belt told Jason what was in the man's mind.

"Barclays has a receipt for issuing every dime of that," Jason said. "I'd hate to have to make a claim for any that was missing."

The glance exchanged between the two guards did little to reassure Jason.

"And I believe I'm entitled to a phone call."

The two looked at him as though he were speaking in tongues.

"A phone call," Jason repeated, holding a fist next to his ear to simulate the device.

One of the men grinned. "Mon, dis ain' some hotel on de beach."

The other nodded. "Yeah, we ain' got room service, neither."

The first twisted Jason's arms behind him with more force than was necessary and shoved him forward. "An' you don' gets a choice of view wid de room."

A short walk down a hallway brought them to an enclosed square, each side lined with six cells. The man behind Jason gave him another push that sent him stumbling into darkness and crashing into the far wall.

"You does git a private room, though!"

Both found this extremely funny. A barred door clanged

shut, and the two men were laughing as the sound of their footsteps faded.

Jason guessed the room was about six by six. A single bunk with a soiled cotton-tick mattress occupied one entire wall. Opposite from the entrance, a barred slit of a window was next to the ceiling. Below that, a seatless commode and a stained basin with a single handle added to the austerity of the room. A cursory inspection showed the walls to be island limestone, a porous material that was likely to seep water in a driving rain but hard enough to resist any efforts to escape.

A colony of mold was prospering on one wall.

Jason examined the barred door closely. Although the lock was of the old type that required a key, the lock plate was firm and, as far as he could tell, well maintained.

He stretched out on the bunk for lack of a better place. If they didn't know already, Eco's minions would soon be aware he was confined, locked up with no chance of escaping whatever they had in mind for him. The memory of Paco's headless body was enough to guarantee he would not accidentally doze off.

CHAPTER SIXTEEN

Providenciales International Airport
Providenciales, Turks and Caicos Islands
British West Indies
The next morning

There was something downright strange about Charlie
Calder's four passengers, the ones who had just gotten off
the international flight from Miami.

They didn't smile, unusual in a place where the sun was
almost always shining, the beaches and water almost always beautiful. People were mostly happy to get here and
smiled a lot. It was the eyes, Charlie thought, dark, almost
black eyes that seemed to scowl from faces that looked
very much like they had spent time in a boxing ring, faces
very much like those of the six men he had seen here at
the airport last week.

Those men, he understood, had chartered a fishing boat
run by his cousin Willie, but had done nothing but drift
outside the North Caicos reef and look at the beach
through binoculars before having Willie put them ashore
at North Caicos's only dock just at dark. As far as Willie
knew, they were still over there.

Now here were these men, just as dark, just as grim, and just as big and muscular, who wanted Charlie to fly them over to Grand Turk in the charter service's aging Piper Aztec just as soon as they had recovered their baggage from the airport's sole carousel.

Odd. Their only luggage appeared to be one briefcase apiece, leather attaché cases that could easily have been carried on board. Why check such little luggage? Hard question, unless maybe there was something in the cases they didn't want scanned by security before the boarding gates. What would somebody bring here like that?

Willie said his customers carried only briefcases, too, ones they never relinquished once they took them from the baggage claim. Strange, too, that they were willing to pay to charter the Aztec, because Turks and Caicos Air had a flight to Grand Turk that left in a little over an hour. The Twin Otter, a ten-passenger job, was a lot roomier than the Aztec, but Charlie guessed they were in a hurry, something no native ever was.

In these islands, people in a hurry usually got angry when things didn't move fast enough for them, and these men looked like they were angry about something the minute they got off the international flight and walked into the charter office. Charlie wasn't sure what, but they spoke back and forth between themselves in a language he had never heard before, one that seemed as angry as they did.

Another thing they had in common with those others, the ones Willie had taken to North Caicos: although they wore golf shirts and jeans like any visitor to the islands might, all the clothes were new. Wherever they had come from, apparently they didn't wear golf shirts and jeans.

Of course, wanting to go to Grand Turk explained a lot, Charlie guessed. Most people who went to Grand Turk weren't going for fun. That might explain why they carried only the briefcases.

Well, it wasn't any of Charlie's business. They paid him in cash, crisp new dollar bills. Providenciales and Grand Turk were only about seventy miles apart, a distance even the old Aztec could cover in a half an hour, including climb-out. In thirty minutes or so, he'd be on the ground, waiting to take his big, unhappy passengers back.

At the same time seventy miles away, Jason was rubbing eyes he had fought to keep open all night. If he was being held here for interrogation about the fire on North Caicos, no one seemed in a hurry to ask the first question. The only official he had seen had been the white-haired old man who had brought him supper and now stood outside his cell with breakfast. As though serving an animal, the old man stooped without a word and slid a steaming bowl under the bars of the door. If last night was the standard, he would return to collect the empty cheap plastic container and fork in a few minutes.

Jason was more interested in the ring of keys jingling on the jailer's belt than in the meal he had brought.

From the bones sticking out of the steaming dish, Jason guessed he was getting another serving of bonefish and grits, a strong-smelling yet bland native dish. It was a meal to be eaten carefully and slowly. Swallowed, one of the sharp bones would likely puncture something vital on the way down the throat.

The thought gave Jason an idea.

Cautiously probing the grits with the fork, Jason extracted a four- or five-inch section of bone with a wickedly sharp point at one end. He finished his meal and listened to the conversations shouted between cells. He was unable to understand most of the words, either because of dialect or because they were in the Spanish of the Dominican Republic, or in Creole, the combination of French and African peculiar to Haiti, both less than a hundred miles away.

* * *

At fifteen hundred feet, Grand Turk was visible from ten miles out. Charlie squinted into the morning's haze for the airport. Constructed as a part of the Atlantic Range recovery station during the early days of the United States' space program, the runway was unusually wide, built to accommodate cargo aircraft, a broad black asphalt belt across the island's southern tip.

"Got the field," Charlie said into his headset, noting that he was the only aircraft on the frequency this morning. "We're out at fifteen hundred."

With the prevailing if fitful southeast breezes, the landing clearance that came back almost immediately was no surprise. "Cleared to land runway niner, wind light and variable, one-two-oh to one-four-oh, altimeter two-niner-niner-eight."

He and his passengers would be on the ground in a few minutes. If he was lucky, Charlie would have time to go over to the TCA office and see how his application was coming along. Flying for the charter service beat fishing for a living, but the airline paid a lot better.

The seals in the windows and doors of the Aztec were worn, making Charlie raise his voice to a near yell to be heard over the engines and airstream as he asked the man next to him, "How long you reckon you'll be 'fore you wants to go back?"

His question provoked a chilly stare from eyes like brown ice. "You've been paid enough to wait."

CHAPTER SEVENTEEN

Grand Turk

The jailer reached an arm through the bars to accept the plastic bowl Jason was handing to him. The bowl clattered to the floor as Jason moved with the speed of a striking snake. In a single movement, the old man was snatched up against the bars and the daggerlike point of the fish bone pressed against his throat.

"Nice and easy," Jason said calmly. "You take those keys off your belt and unlock the door. Do like I say and you don't get hurt."

The men in the cell opposite Jason's saw what was happening and began to shout. Although he couldn't understand the words, Jason guessed they were clamoring for their freedom, too. It wouldn't take many minutes before someone came to investigate the disturbance. The jailer was fumbling with the ring of keys.

Jason pressed the bone harder against the man's throat. "I got nothing to loose, mon. Somebody come before you get this door open, you die."

Either the threat was effective or the old man had already found the right key. The door swung open with Jason still holding his captive through it. He let go of the arm long enough to snatch the key ring. He shoved his former jailer into the cell and slammed the door shut before turning the key. He was gratified to hear the lock's bolt click into place.

Jason tossed the key ring into an adjacent cell as he sprinted down the hall. He could hear other cell doors opening amid excited voices. The escapees wouldn't get far, not on a twenty-five-square-mile island, but they would provide the distraction Jason needed.

At the end of the cell block was a steel door. Jason shoved but it didn't move. It was locked from the other side.

Curious, Charlie watched his passengers carry the attaché cases into the sole taxi parked outside the one-room terminal. He was almost certain he had heard the one who spoke English ask to be taken to the jail.

Surely not.

He shrugged. None of his business. He looked at his watch. There was nowhere on the island that would be more than ten minutes away by cab. Figuring in, say, ten minutes for his passengers to go wherever they had business, another ten to do that business and another ten to return, he had at least a half an hour to spend at the TCA office, trying to get his application moved to the top of the pile.

For some reason, he was thinking about those briefcases as he crossed the street. Maybe they had business papers in the little cases and were planning on flying back to Miami that day. Except the Delta flight on which they had arrived was the only departure today, now long gone.

He shrugged. *Mon wants not to carry fresh clothes in this heat, that be his problem, not Charlie's.*

Jason turned from the locked door and dashed back down the cell block behind the last group of prisoners to escape their cells. He stopped long enough to snatch a thin mattress from a cot before joining the rush to the prison yard.

Outside, the dozen or so prisoners overpowered two guards. As a leaderless mob, they seemed unclear as to what to do next. With a few quick steps, Jason was at the base of the wall. Grabbing the mattress by one end, he swung it up and across the top of the glass-encrusted stone. Taking a few paces back, he got a running start and jumped, his fingers digging for purchase but finding none.

He slid back to the dusty yard and tried again just as truncheon-swinging reinforcements surged out of the jail and began clubbing the unfortunates within reach. As Jason made his second attempt, six or seven prisoners were beginning what looked like some sort of organized resistance.

This time Jason got high enough to hang one arm across the mattress and get a grip on the rough stone on the outside of the wall. With his feet scrabbling against the rocky surface, he managed to propel himself upward and over, dropping onto the ground below with an impact that buckled his knees.

He stood, turned, and looked straight into the shock-widened eyes of a woman carrying a huge bowl of mangoes on her head.

He nodded politely. "Mornin', ma'am." Then he bolted for the police station in front of the jail.

It was unlikely, he reasoned, that the police would anticipate his return after escaping. The emptiness of the building verified his assumption. It took him less than a minute to empty several open lockers in the room with a coffee machine and two worn Naugahyde couches. As he had hoped, neither of the two officers who had taken his money belt had trusted the other enough to allow its removal from where it was hidden under a pile of odoriferous laundry. A quick glance satisfied him that most, if not all, the bills were still there. More important, so was his passport.

Now he was good to go. The question was, where?

From the sounds coming from the prison yard, there wasn't a lot of time before the would-be escapees' resistance collapsed and the police on duty returned.

As calmly as he could manage in shoes with no laces, he sauntered outside, hands in his pockets to support beltless trousers, and merged with the foot traffic. He could easily walk to the airport; it was less than a mile away.

He had gone one, perhaps two blocks when the squeal of rubber against asphalt split the air. He turned just in time to see four men spilling out of an eighties-model Lincoln on which a faded TAXI was still legible. Jason's attention was not drawn to the passengers themselves as much as the briefcase each was opening. He didn't have to look twice to recognize the collapsible-stock Uzis. It was the same gun, carried the same way, as the Secret Service's presidential detail.

He had hoped to get the hell out of Dodge before Eco's disciples, Eglov or others, arrived for their revenge. A few more minutes and he would have made it.

Jason ducked into an alley along the back of Front Street, trusting the shade to make him difficult to see by the gunmen standing in brilliant tropical sunlight. He never knew if the theory worked. A string of shots showered him with concrete fragments as they dug into a wall above him.

He tried to pull his head into his chest like a turtle into its shell. In these narrow confines, the ricochets and cement chips could be deadly.

There was screaming from behind him, a terrified woman in shock, mixed with shouts in Russian that were getting closer.

The alley was only a couple of blocks long, ending in an open park just off the beach where Jason would have no cover at all.

Desperation made a decision for him.

He snatched at a door leading into one of the buildings, finding it locked. He had better luck with the second, pulling it open only wide enough to slip inside and locking it behind him.

He was in a well-lit, air-conditioned corridor lined with offices. In those with the doors open, Jason could see guayabera-clad solicitors and consultants advising clients or speaking softly on telephones as they conducted the financial affairs of those who did business where income and property taxes were only nightmares. From the voices he heard, both blacks and whites had spent time in England. There wasn't a native accent among them. A couple of heads came up with curious stares. Jason made himself walk slowly and calmly, as though looking for someone in particular.

"Can I help you, sir?" a well-dressed native woman asked in Oxfordian tones. "Is there someone you wish to see?"

Jason tried to push his pursuers from his mind long enough to remember the name of the Irish-born solicitor who had handled the purchase of the property on North Caicos. "O'Dooly, Seamus O'Dooly. Is he in?"

One eyebrow twitched in what might have been annoyance. "I believe Mr. O'Dooly has his offices next door."

Jason gave her the best imitation of embarrassment he could manage as he headed toward the front of the building. "Thanks."

He stood in the reception area for a moment, trying to see past the four or five people plastered to the plate-glass window that looked out onto Front Street and the beach.

"What's going on?"

"A shooting," someone said without turning around. "Some idiots just started firing guns in the middle of the street and looks like someone's hurt."

Edging closer, Jason saw ten or so people gathered in the middle of the street. Behind them, its doors still open, was the Lincoln. The gunmen were nowhere to be seen, no doubt checking each door off the alley behind him.

Soon enough they would come around front to check on those they couldn't enter. Jason didn't intend to wait.

With purposeful steps he strode into heat made all the more intense from his brief exposure to air-conditioning. He hardly noticed that his shirt was instantly sweat-plastered to his back. He kept his face away from the buildings and alley, fighting the urge to look around for men with guns. He gave only a cursory glance at the crowd gathered in the middle of the street. Shielded from view by the morbidly curious, a woman was wailing. From the few words Jason heard, her child had caught a stray bullet.

He should, he supposed, have felt some degree of guilt. Had he not been here, there would have been no blameless victim. The child lying on the pavement had been no more deserving of that bullet than Laurin had been of a hijacked airliner. His well of remorse was long dry.

Besides, he did not have the luxury of debating hypothetical fault. If he didn't make the right moves, any guilt he might bear would become academic.

The Lincoln was empty, its doors open and the engine running. Jason cast a thankful glance skyward. As usual, luck was going to play a stronger hand than skill. No one noticed as he shut all but the driver's door and climbed in behind the wheel. The interior stank of stale tobacco smoke, the headliner had long ago been replaced with some sort of ragged and gaily colored cloth, and the seat's loose spring was trying to castrate him.

Whatever amenities the car lacked were more than compensated for by the opportunity. At the moment, he would gladly have settled for a garbage truck.

As he slipped the balky gear into drive and eased away from the center of town, he could hear a siren. He crossed his fingers that the ambulance from the island's only medical facility got there in time.

He might be fresh out of guilt but he had a full tank of hope.

In minutes, the stubby control tower was visible above the low brush along the road. Jason pulled into one of the three parking places outside the small cement-block passenger terminal. The absence of other cars told him no arrivals were imminent. Getting out of the Lincoln, he walked past the terminal and onto the tarmac of the general aviation area, that part of the airport reserved for private aircraft.

Under the shade of the only tree nearby he recognized a familiar face and walked over to where a young native in a white shirt and dark, well-pressed pants was sipping the last swallow from a drink can.

Jason extended a hand. "Charlie, how you doin', mon?"

Charlie looked up with a smile showing perfect, brilliant white teeth. "Doin' fine, Jason." He shook the hand briefly. "Sorry t' hear 'bout that fire over to yo' place, though. Folks say you gonna leave."

In these latitudes, custom required polite conversation before coming to the point. Jason opted for brevity instead. "Charlie, some men are after me. There's already been some shooting in town."

Charlie's smile was replaced by confusion. "Mens? Mebbe four big guys, carryin' briefcases?"

"Those are the ones, yeah. I—"

"But dey can't," Charlie protested. "I mean, can' nobody bring guns into the Turks 'n' Caicos, not 'less you gots a permit."

Jason just stared, thinking of the collection of firearms that had gone up with his house, weapons that had sailed through local customs when accompanied by a liberal "gift" for the inspector. Charlie, like anyone else who lived here, knew full well that a few dollars placed in well-connected hands bought the right to do just about anything.

Capitalism was alive and well in the Turks and Caicos Islands.

Charlie turned his head to look down the road toward town. "That noise I heard . . ."

"Gunfire, shots aimed at me."

What Jason was about to ask suddenly dawned. "Listen, Jason, I got me a charter, gotta wait on 'em to come back. They kill me, I go off an' leaves 'em."

Jason pulled his shirt out of his pants and dug into the money belt. He slowly counted out ten one-hundred-dollar bills. "Tell you what, Charlie: you go back to the terminal, buy yourself another cold drink, take your time. You hear a departure, you just finish refreshing yourself there in that nice air-conditioned terminal. You come out, your plane's gone . . . well, you walk—don't run, walk—over to the police and report it."

Charlie's eyes flicked between the money and the Aztec parked fifty or so yards away. The door was open in the vain hope of a breeze to cool the interior. "Jason, I can't . . ."

"Can't what, Charlie? You know how many planes were stolen in the Caribbean last year, snatched just to make a single dope run, then abandoned? Hell, look how many old dope wrecks you see in the water 'tween here and Provo! Your plane gets stolen and it's unfortunate but not even unusual."

"But in the daylight, right here at Grand Turk?"

Jason began to slowly fold the bills up as though to return them to the money belt. "I'd thought theft was the reason the man who owns your charter service paid for insurance. But that's okay, Charlie. I understand you can't take a risk to save my life from those men with guns. I understand. . . ."

Charlie's hand grabbed Jason's. "You let go that money, Jason." He gave the area a quick, nervous survey, the look of a small child checking to see if parents were watching. "Jes' you sit here; let me get into the terminal. What you does then, that be yo' bidness."

"Remember: about thirty minutes before you report the plane stolen."

Charlie nodded. "You be in Haiti, the DR by then."

"Never mind where I'll be."

Charlie stood and walked away, then stopped and turned. "Jason?"

Jason looked up.

"Good luck!"

There wasn't time for a complete preflight inspection of the aircraft. Jason only unscrewed the caps to the plane's two gas tanks to visually verify they were full. He had never flown a Piper, let alone an Aztec before. He had, however, taken the hours of flight instruction mandatory for all Delta Force officers. He could only hope there was enough similarity between the Aztec and the light miliary trainer to keep him from killing himself.

His first glance at the panel was both encouraging and a little frightening. What gauges were present were familiar: altimeter, turn and bank, and their like. A number of empty holes told him he would have a single radio and navigation unit, no transponder or other electronics common to even small aircraft.

The switches were double what he had been used to, one for each engine. He flipped the first one on the right to ON and did the same with one marked PUMP. He heard the reassuring whine of a fuel pump. He gave a winged switch a twist and the left prop began a slow rotation. Keeping the knob turned, he used his other hand to work the fuel-flow lever in the middle of the panel back and forth. He was delighted when the small plane quivered and the prop caught, disappearing into a blur.

He was about to do the same thing with the right engine when something made him look up in time to see an old Buick almost collide with the parked Lincoln as it came to a stop. The four men piled out, this time not even taking the trouble to conceal their weapons. They had not noticed the Aztec yet as they looked around for Charlie before running into the terminal.

Now acquainted with the procedure, Jason had the second engine started and was rolling toward the runway in less than a minute. There was no time to seek taxi and takeoff clearances from the tower. Instead, he went to the western tip of the runway and prepared to do a run-up, the procedure by which magnetos, fuel-flow, and propeller pitch were given a final check.

Through the aircraft's windshield, he saw the four men racing across the general aviation area, guns held out. They might have missed him earlier, but even the poorest of shots was going to hit the Piper somewhere if they could get within the Uzi's limited range.

So much for the run-up.

Jason pushed the two center levers flat against the panel and the Aztec began to creep forward.

The four men certainly saw him now. They were gesturing in his direction.

The airspeed indicator was quivering around twenty-five knots. The white arc showed Vmc—liftoff—to be between sixty and sixty-five.

Nothing to do but press the fuel levers harder, hoping for any increase in power. The outside-air-temperature gauge read eighty-two, and standard humidity here was at least the same, adversely affecting power. Too bad he wasn't trying to escape from an arctic desert.

The four men stood in a line, Uzis raised. The guns were designed for massed fire at close range. The Aztec would be at the outer limit of the weapons' accuracy and reach. The plane was going to take some punishment, but not nearly as much as it would have from twenty-five yards closer. The fragile aluminum skin was too thin to protect vital parts or Jason from the bullets that did get that far.

The gauge's needle was crawling past forty knots. If only the damn plane would accelerate a little faster . . .

The needle hovered between forty-five and fifty.

Parts of his brief aviation instruction came back with the suddenness and impact of a thunderbolt. There was a way to get this thing off the ground quicker.

His looked at the bottom of the panel, where he saw an

oddly shaped switch. Pulling it down produced a whir of electronics, and the plane unweighted like a diver about to leave the board. He had hit the flap switch, lowered the flaps at the back of the wing. A procedure designed to slow the aircraft for landing, it also changed the airfoil of the wings, producing more lift, if less speed.

The small plane clawed its way into the air, with Jason pulling the control stick back far enough to keep the stall warning screeching. A stall would occur when the aircraft's angle of attack could no longer be sustained by available power and the plane simply quit flying. It was an acceptable landing maneuver, but to have all lift spill from the wings only a hundred feet or so in the air left neither time nor altitude for recovery.

But no more fatal than a hailstorm of automatic rifle fire.

There was a loud sound like the clap of hands, and the plane shuddered. At least one of the men had hit the mark. Jason could only hope no essential had been struck. The gauges told him nothing.

At five hundred feet he let the nose down to only a few degrees above the horizon. Turning his head, he could see Grand Turk shrinking in the distance. He lifted the flaps, anticipating the sinking of the aircraft with the loss of extra lift. At a thousand feet he leveled off, pulled the power back to his best guess of economy cruise, and put the Aztec into a slow right turn until both compass and gyroscope indicated a few degrees east of due south.

He sighed as he looked around the small cockpit. He gave the rudder pedals an experimental push, testing the force required to operate each. Maybe flying was like riding a bicycle in that you didn't forget how.

Quit kidding yourself, he thought. *You've got to land a plane you've never flown before and with possible characteristics of which you're ignorant.*

Oh well, his other self—the pilot self—replied, *you've already seen the speed at which this baby comes right up to a stall, and what is a landing but a stall into the ground?*

You'll be fine as long as you can find a nice long, deserted beach to put her down. Nothing to it.

A flicker of a needle caught his eye. The left fuel gauge was bumping against the empty peg. Gas gauges in airplanes were notoriously inaccurate; hence the visual check of the fuel level before takeoff. Still, the wing tank could have taken the hit he had heard. He quickly searched the floor between the two front seats and found a lever for each tank. He switched the left engine to feed from the right tank. He was unsure exactly what that would do to the balance of the aircraft, but better another unknown than the certainty of a fuel-starved engine.

Squinting, he peered into the blue haze. Clouds made dark patterns on the water easily mistaken for islands. Each form had to be examined closely. Where he was headed, he would quickly run out of altitude at a mere thousand feet. The mountains were some of the Caribbean's highest.

In a pocket in the door beside him was stuffed a tattered map, a color chart published periodically by the United States government's Coast and Geodetic Survey. Jason unfolded it carefully, fearful it might tear. To his pleasant surprise, the side that did not show part of the Turks and Caicos depicted the north coast of the island of Hispaniola. It was well out-of-date—he would not be able to rely on the printed radio frequencies—but he had no intent of making contact with facilities that could well have been alerted to the theft of the airplane. The depiction of the physical shape of the coastline, however, would be valuable.

He glanced up from the map in time to see shadows ahead coalescing into a definite form. A strip of foamy white surf along a golden beach confirmed his arrival. The question was, exactly where?

He turned to fly almost due east along the coast and passed over what was clearly a resort area. A golf course was laid out amid a jungle; the blue of a swimming pool twinkled in the sun. He was low enough to see people on the tennis courts. A few minutes headed the other way and he was over a finger of land running east and west. It took only a glance at the map to confirm he was over the Samana Peninsula of the Dominican Republic's north coast. Now to find a place to land.

There were several airstrips carved into the jungle, distinguishable from roads only by their straightness and the fact that one or two aircraft were visible on the ground. Tempting, but Jason decided not. Leaving a stolen aircraft where it likely would be found would start a trail he would prefer did not exist.

He descended slowly, his eyes on the beaches below him. Over a slight ridge, a muddy river formed a small delta along the coast. As far as Jason could see, there were no roads or other signs of habitation nearby, probably because the silt from the river's mouth spoiled the beach for swimming and sunbathing.

With one eye on the airspeed gauge and the other on the altimeter, he entered a lazy downward spiral. He made one final check, a low pass over the coast to spot rocks or other obstructions along the beach, before he lowered the gear and let the flaps back down. With the wheels hanging in the airstream, the Piper settled faster than Jason had anticipated. He was reluctant to add power, which would increase speed, which, in turn, would extend the length of beach required to stop. He eased back on the controls until the stall warning's bray began.

With a nose-up attitude, the Aztec slammed its wheels into sand that felt far less solid than it looked. There was the sound of tearing metal and the plane dipped to the left as it careened across the beach toward the river. One of the gear struts had collapsed. Now Jason was a mere passenger with no control over the aircraft. He could only flip off the power switches and hope.

The plane took a couple of spins before the left wing dug into the riverbank and came to a tooth-jarring stop.

Either the frame or the door had been bent, because Jason had to put his back against the exit and use his feet against the other side of the Piper to force it open. Panting with exertion, he dropped into wet, cool mud.

His shoes, still without laces, were underwater, invisible in the brown flow. Holding on to the crippled plane, he climbed onto the bank and surveyed his location. Palm trees screened anything more than a few yards behind the beach. Unless someone happened to be flying along the coast, he doubted the Piper would be seen for some time. Within a day or two, it was likely the force of the river might push it underwater, where it would never be found.

He sat, took off his socks, and wrung them out before putting his shoes back on and beginning what he knew would be a long trek to the resort he had seen. Before rounding a curve of the beach, he stopped and took one last look at the little twin engine.

Old pilots' lore: any landing you can walk away from was a good one.

CHAPTER EIGHTEEN

Santo Domingo, Dominican Republic
Two nights later

The warm night air brought whiffs of salsa music from the band on the beach sixteen stories below the balcony of Jason's hotel room. He could also hear party voices, although he could not tell if the words were in Spanish or English. He had had a spicy Spanish dinner, the name of which he could not remember but one he suspected he would continue to taste for hours, if not days. He had washed the meal down with several El Presidentes, the light Dominican lager. If he was going to make the early flight out in the morning, he needed to go to bed soon.

But he really didn't want to end the evening. He had never been in a city quite like this. He had been to tropical climates before, in the slums of dusty settlements on the Horn of Africa, where the rodent population outnumbered humans and the smell of rotting garbage and open sewers were strong enough to make the eyes water. If he had been lucky, he had arrived by aircraft, fixed-wing or rotor. More often, he and the members of his six-man Delta Force squad had reached their destination by parachute—HALO (high altitude and low operations)—at night into leech-ridden Asian jungles where the night brought fever-bearing mosquitoes that filled the moisture-laden air with buzzing, and where cotton uniforms were always damp.

The enemies he had been sent to bring out or leave for others to bury frequently did not live in the resort spas of the world.

Santo Domingo had the same humid air Jason associated with snakes, insects, and rot. But here, the night's fragrance hinted at tropical flowers. Here in the city, he had seen more high-rises than tin-roofed hovels. Cars filled streets lined with high-end shops. People smiled at one another and laughed a lot.

Sort of like an egalitarian St. Barts with a Latin beat.

The band below launched into a samba, and Jason took a sip from the Brugal rum and tonic he held.

The old life was behind him. Instead of risking his ass for a soldier's pay, he was rich. Instead of chasing petty warlords, he sought the major pooh-bahs of world-stage nasties. He could afford good hotels and flew first-class only, thank you.

He thought of the Aztec and the cashier's check he had instructed his Swiss bank to send its owner to cover any insurance deductible. Mostly first-class, anyway.

The bigger the game, the higher the stakes. No matter how high, he'd trade it all for a final five minutes with Laurin, a chance to say a proper good-bye rather than wait for a cup of coffee that never came.

The rum, he guessed, was making him maudlin. High stakes, big money. Had he been asked to, he would have hunted at his own expense the animals who killed the innocent. He had a major score to even. Moslem fundamentalists with a hijacked airplane, a shadowy group who killed those who earned a living in a manner they didn't like. Terrorists were terrorists whether using a bomb or a secret weapon. Jason would take pleasure in eradicating them like the vermin they were.

He patted the money belt, fattened this afternoon by the arrival by diplomatic courier of three passports, each with supporting driver's permits, credit cards, club memberships, and the like. One even had a Dominican Republic entry visa already stamped in it. Mama thought of everything.

Tomorrow he would take a number of flights that would eventually end on the other side of the Atlantic.

Rome, then to Sicily, where Dr. Bergenghetti was currently doing some sort of research, according to Mama. He frowned.

Rome.

It was a city he and Laurin had planned to visit in the spring of '02. She had already begun the planning, looking at hotel brochures, reading guidebooks.

The glass in Jason's hand shattered before he realized how hard he had been squeezing it. He went inside and wrapped a towel around his bleeding palm, so absorbed in his mental anguish he did not feel the throbbing of sliced flesh.

CHAPTER NINETEEN

Taormina, Sicily
Villa Ducale
Two days later

Taormina spilled down the side of a mountain, ending at the Strait of Messina. The slope upon which the town had its tenuous grasp was not what snagged the visitor's eye, however. The center of visual attention was Mount Aetna, a dark mass in the haze to the northeast. At eight in the morning, its white beard of heat-generated clouds was the only blemish in an otherwise blue sky.

Jason sat at one of only four tables on the hotel's piazza, sipping coffee with the consistency of molasses. He would not have been surprised had it sucked the spoon out of his hand. Probably enough caffeine to make Sleepy, one of Snow White's dwarves, into an insomniac.

He was just about to help himself to the breakfast buffet of fruit, cereal, cheese, and meats when the hotel's manager stepped outside. "Mr. Young?"

Jason's passport, the one with the Dominican entry and exit visas, proclaimed him to be Harold Young of Baltimore.

"Mr. Young, the package you asked about has arrived."

The parcel was heavy for its size. Besides his name, it had no other markings. If the manager found the private delivery of a package to a foreign guest unusual, he didn't show it.

Giving the man a few euros as a tip, Jason abandoned breakfast for the moment to return to his room, a white plaster-walled backdrop for paintings of the flowering cacti that covered Sicily. Once alone, he tore the brown paper from a box made of heavy cardboard. Inside was a holster with a belt clip, a SIG Sauer P228, the same type of weapon he had carried on St. Bart's, and two clips loaded with thirteen rounds each. A quick inspection revealed a third clip, also loaded, already in the weapon.

Jason slid the extra magazines into his pocket and fastened the gun onto his belt at the small of his back, where it would be concealed under the loose-fitting guayabera he had purchased for that purpose. For the first time since arriving, he felt completely dressed.

Maria Bergenghetti was waiting for him when he returned to the lobby.

He had anticipated a middle-aged academic, perhaps with the dark skin and short stature of most Sicilians. Instead, he was looking at a young woman of five-nine or -ten whose sun-streaked hair was tucked into a bun under a pith helmet, the sort of headgear one would expect to see on a British archeologist of the last century. She wore khaki shirt and shorts, loose fitting but not enough to conceal a figure that would be perfectly at home on a beach on St. Bart's.

Blue eyes peered at him quizzically. "Mr. Young?"

Jason managed to shake off his surprise. "Er, yes, you must be Dr. Bergenghetti."

"Well, I am hardly Dr. Livingstone. Do you stare like that at everyone you meet?"

He felt himself flush as he extended a hand. "Only the ones who look more like a swimsuit model than a volcanologist."

She shook. Her hand was cool, as though it had some-how managed to evade the growing Sicilian heat. "I am not sure what a volcanologist looks like." There was a sparkle in her eyes. She was obviously enjoying the repar-tee. "And that remark borders on sexism, something I un-derstood you Americans abhorred."

He couldn't place her accent, if indeed she had one. "Only unattractive women, Doctor. The pretty ones enjoy being admired, as they do in any country. Join me for breakfast?"

He led her out onto the piazza, gratified to see his table was still vacant. They sat, and Jason filled her coffee cup. "You speak excellent English."

She smiled, showing a gap between her front teeth that was somehow rather sexy. "I should. My father was with the Italian diplomatic corps in Washington. I spoke En-glish before I could even pronounce Italian." She took a sip of the coffee, wincing from the bitterness. "In fact, I did my undergrad work in the States."

"In volcanology? Seems an dangerous field, climbing up mountains, dodging hot lava, never knowing when things are going to blow up."

She treated him to another glimpse of gapped teeth. "Dangerous for a woman, you mean. Your sexism is showing again."

Jason held up his hands, palms outward. "I'm sorry; I didn't mean . . ."

"Of course you did," she said pleasantly. "And it is re-freshing. Did it ever occur to you that women get just as tired of political correctness as men? Anyway, I got inter-ested in geology, went to the Colorado School of Mines, came back to Italy with my parents, got bored, got mar-ried, got even more bored, and got divorced. I was look-ing around for something to do, something that would sufficiently shock my ex into finally accepting the fact that I was no longer his playmate. Studying volcanoes seemed perfect for all the reasons you mentioned, plus the fact that you get really grimy." She reached into her purse, producing a pack of Marlboros. "Don't suppose you speak any Italian?"

"Not much. Just a few situational phrases picked up in bad company."

"Such as?"

Jason watched her light her cigarette. *"Muova quel rottame, cretino!"*

She laughed, an almost musical sound. "You must have been driving in Rome. 'Move that junk pile, you cretin!' "

Jason grinned. "Then I learned, '*Ma perche e chiuso il museo oggi?*' "

"Why is the museum closed today?"

"Ma perche il museo e chiuso domani?"

"Why is the museum closed tomorrow?"

"And '*Quanto tempo starano in sciopero?*' "

She laughed again. " 'How long will they be on strike?' What do you do for a living, other than Italian phrases?"

Jason was unprepared for the question. "Well, I have a business back in Baltimore. . . ."

"One that involves the geographics of volcanic material?" She arched a skeptical eyebrow. "That is pretty lame, Mr. Young. Or whoever you really are."

He grinned. "Dr. Kamito said you were the best. He didn't say you were perceptive, too."

"Being married to an Italian man makes you perceptive. Suspicious and skeptical as well. Remember Casanova?"

"The greatest of lovers, at least according to him."

"Perfect description of my ex. But so much for my life and hard times. Exactly what is it you want me to do?"

Jason produced the vial of material Kamito had given him. "Tell me where this came from."

She accepted the glass tube, holding it up to the light. "Where did you get it?"

"From Kamito."

She sighed loudly. "I mean, what is its origin?"

"Apparently somewhere around the Mediterranean. Exactly where is what we want to know."

She took the sample and stood, her coffee cup still full. "I hope you are more generous in paying for my time than you are with information. I have a crew checking monitors up on the hill"—she nodded toward Aetna—"and I need to make sure they do it right. One mistake and a lot of people around here would be unhappy."

"Unhappy or buried?"

"Both, most likely." She turned for the door. "But I should have whatever answer there is by the end of the day."

Jason walked beside her, stopping to open the door that led to the postage stamp–size parking lot. "Figure out what I owe you. And if it isn't too much trouble . . ."

She regarded him with a mocking expression. "Let me guess: you would like me to show you the town and have dinner."

Jason chuckled. "Close. I was going to ask you for your recommendations as to restaurants, but I like your idea better. What time suits?"

She opened the door of a dusty Ford Explorer, one of only two cars that nearly filled the lot. "I will be here about seven or so." The door slammed shut and she cranked the engine, her head out of the window. "In the meantime, there is an old Norman fort at the top of the hill you might want to explore. At the bottom, there is a pretty well preserved Greek amphitheater. I would invite you to come up Aetna with me, but we would be in areas closed to the public."

"And as you said, it's both dangerous and grimy."

He watched as she backed out and drove downhill, shading his eyes until her car disappeared around the first of the series of hairpin turns that was Taormina's only road.

CHAPTER TWENTY

Piazza del Duomo, Taormina
That evening

They sat in a café facing the piazza that was the center of Taormina. Since no motorized vehicles were allowed in this part of the town, the only sound came from the square's baroque fountain, which, along with the fortresslike cathedral of San Nicola, was radiating with the Chianti red glow of sunset. A few blocks away, faint shouts came from a street soccer match between several boys, each of whom wore the jersey of a different team. Jason drained the last of a beer; he felt dehydrated from an hour's tour that had included everything from Palazzo Corvaja, the Norman building that had housed the first Sicilian parliament in the fifteenth century, to the ancient Greek amphitheater.

Tourism, he decided, was thirsty work, particularly when every third building sold adult refreshment.

Maria nursed a glass of Sicilian white wine, a product Jason had determined would have better use in removing paint. Her streaked hair was down, giving a softness to her face. Her simple black dress was adorned only by a brightly colored scarf around her neck, an embellishment Jason instantly recognized as Hermès.

The signature blue and red of the silk had given him a shock he was not sure he had been able to conceal. Hermès—one of Laurin's few extravagances. She had adored the colors and patterns unique to the French designer, keeping each in its signature orange box. At thirty-five and a half by thirty-five and a half inches, the square was large enough to serve as scarf, shawl, skirt, or even a top. Utilitarian as well as decorative, Laurin had described them.

Maria glanced down, checking the neckline of her dress. "I hope it is my scarf you're admiring."

"Uh, yeah," Jason managed. "Hermès, isn't it?"

She smiled. "Something men do not usually recognize unless they've bought several."

"At three hundred per, they're hard to forget."

Would he ever find a place where Laurin was absent, somewhere a phrase, a landscape, a scarf wouldn't remind him of her loss? He hoped not.

He forced his attention back to Maria. The dress she wore displayed her figure to more advantage than did her work clothes. Jason was deciding she was more than simply attractive. She was receiving admiring glances from almost every man who passed.

"Well," she said, "you have now pretty much seen everything except the Wunderbar."

Jason stopped watching men watch Maria and faced her. "Wunderbar?"

"Favorite haunt of your Liz Taylor and Richard Burton, movie stars."

"Thirty years ago, wasn't it?"

"People here still talk about it."

Jason drained his glass, noting the surrounding buildings, some of which dated back to the Hellenistic period. "I don't doubt it. Probably still talk about Ulysses passing thorough on his way home from Troy, too."

She looked up from making concentric circles on the tabletop with the bottom of her glass. "I thought Americans loved their celebrities."

"Want to try getting a waiter's attention when Tom Hanks is at the next table?"

She laughed. "Point taken. But I doubt Liz and Richard are at the Wunderbar tonight."

Jason signaled to the waiter. "Hungry? Where's a good place for authentic Sicilian cuisine?"

He paid the tab and she slipped an arm through his as they walked down the cobbled streets. Greek, Norman, Ottoman, all had left their imprint. They had gone only a few blocks when she veered into an alley, stopping in front of some tables in the street. From inside came recorded accordion music.

"Best *spada alla ghiotta* on the island," she announced.

Jason started to ask for an interpretation, thought better of it, and pulled a chair out for her. "I'll take your word for it."

Over more white Sicilian wine and beer, he asked, "The samples, could you determine where they came from?"

She spoke to the hovering waiter in the harsh Italian dialect of Sicily and then nodded, digging in her purse. "The percentage of sulfates, the presence of certain igneous similarities such as the radiation level . . . they differ with each volcano."

Jason shook his head. "Whoa! I appreciate your work, but I don't need a tutorial."

"No doubt about it, the Campania."

He waited a moment for the sole waiter to set down the *prima platte*, a steaming plate of *pasta con le Sarde*. "Campania? You mean around the Naples area?"

She was spooning half of the macaroni, sardines, and wild fennel onto her plate. "Yep."

He reached for what was left, noting it was considerably less than half. "What volcanoes are around Naples? I mean, Vesuvius hasn't erupted since, what, 1944?"

She took a tentative taste, sighed with satisfaction, and said, "The sample was from a volcanic area, not necessarily an active volcano. Besides, the whole Bay of Naples has seen volcanic activity. The ancient Greeks and Romans regarded the thermo-mineral water that bubbled up in the Phlegraean Fields to be curative of a number of—"

Jason's fork stopped halfway to his mouth. "The *what*?"

"Phlegraean Fields, in Baia." She saw his puzzled expression. "At the northern end of the Bay of Naples. Mount Nuovo erupted there in 1538. Then there's Lake Averno, a perfectly round lake that surely was a volcanic crater."

"The whole Bay of Naples area is pretty large."

He took a bite of the appetizer. Now he understood why the local wine had an astringent, puckering effect: the native food had a salty quality, sort of like anchovies out of a tin.

"Couldn't you be a little more specific?"

She had nearly cleaned her plate and was eyeing his. "Just why would a Baltimore businessman want to know, Mr. Harold Young?"

He finished the last of his appetizer before meeting her gaze. "Does it matter?"

She sat back in her chair, fished around in her purse again, and produced a pack of cigarettes. "Do you object?"

"They're your lungs."

A lighter appeared and she puffed greedily. Blue smoke disappeared into the surrounding darkness.

"Does it matter?" she mused. "I suppose not, not if we say good-bye tonight."

Jason was surprised to realize he very much did not want to say good-bye at all.

"On the other hand, as you Americans say, if we remain, er, friends, it matters very much. You see, Harold, or whoever you are, I was married to the ultimate liar. I think I mentioned him."

"Casanova."

"Yes, him. Just like some people have a violent reaction to, say, penicillin, I am allergic to liars. I know damn good and well some businessman from Baltimore didn't come all the way to Sicily to see me just because he had a personal curiosity as to the geographic origin of some soil and rocks. I also listen to my colleague Dr. Kamito at various professional gatherings. I cannot say I know, but I sure suspect that he does work for some people who are not in it for the pure science."

Jason started to interrupt but she went on. "No, let me finish. What Ito does and for whom is none of my affair. But I view with suspicion anyone he refers. I don't really care what your 'business' is." She made quote marks in the air with her fingers. "But I do insist on knowing who the hell you really are. Short of that, we will enjoy the meal, part on good terms, and I hope you enjoy your stay in Sicily."

Jason was silent while the dishes were removed and the swordfish served.

"Answer enough," she said, tearing off a piece of bread and dipping it in the small dish of olive oil. "I hope you like the entrée."

They ate in silence, the only sound music piped from inside. He would never know if he had eaten the best swordfish cooked in vegetables on the island, but he was certain that the meal would not be easily bested. He was even beginning to tolerate, if not enjoy, the local wine.

Leaning back on his chair's rear legs, he looked up and down the narrow alley, where unevenly spaced streetlights created archipelagos of illumination in a sea of darkness. An old woman, dressed in the traditional black, leaned from an upper window to shake a tablecloth free of the evening's crumbs. Another reached to tend to a window box of listless flowers. Men gathered around a pair of cardplayers inside gave grappa-induced laughs.

Jason broke the silence between them. "This is authentic, Liz and Richard notwithstanding. Seems like the real

Sicily. No TV, no iPods, no ringing cell phones. Totally un-Americanized."

Maria looked up from her plate with mischief in her eyes. "You sure about that?"

"About what, that this is one of the most non-American-like places I've seen in Europe?"

She put a hand behind her ear. "Really? Just listen."

The canned music that he had hardly noticed. It was the theme from *The Godfather*.

A few minutes later, they were walking back to Maria's car when Jason said, "I'm at a bit of a loss: I know the samples came from around Naples, but that's too large an area to be of any help."

Maria stopped, turning toward him. "I would like to help, but I don't even know your real name, let alone what you are looking for."

" 'Where ignorance is bliss, 'tis folly to be wise.' "

"Milton, *Paradise Lost*. Knowledge is its own reward."

"Ben Franklin?"

"Maria Bergenghetti."

Jason grinned. "Okay, you got me. . . ." He stopped midsentence, his attention drawn to the sound of an engine. "I thought you said cars weren't allowed. . . ."

Maria was looking over his shoulder, a question on her face. "They are not, only delivery vehicles and garbage pickup, both in the early morning."

Jason turned and saw it: one of those trucks peculiar to European cities with narrow streets. Not as large as a small pickup, but larger than a conventional sedan, the truck filled the alley. Its headlights were dark, it showed no intent of stopping, and there was no room on either side for Jason or Maria.

Jason didn't have time to think; he reacted.

Roughly shoving Maria into the first recessed doorway he saw, he began to run. There was no hope of outdistancing the truck, but the farther he got from Maria, the less likely the driver was to take the time to try to harm her also.

He thought of the SIG Sauer clipped to his belt and discarded the idea immediately. A bullet ricocheting from the sides of the buildings lining the narrow alley would be as likely to hit a resident as the truck driver. Besides, there was always the chance the driver had gone to sleep at the wheel, had a heart attack, or was motivated by something other than homicidal intent.

And there was the certainty that gunshots would bring the attention of the police, something that could end Jason's mission as certainly as that truck.

The sound of the small engine at high rpms told Jason how fast the truck was gaining on him. At one point, he hoped he could make it to an intersection with a wider street, giving him more room to dodge the oncoming vehicle.

His pursuer was now so close, he imagined he could feel the heat of the engine.

And there was no intersection to be seen.

But there were window boxes like the ones he had seen from the dinner table.

With hardly a break in stride, he gave a leap, adrenaline adding a Michael Jordan quality to his jump. His fingers touched the rim of a ceramic window box and managed to close before gravity reclaimed him. His prize was much heavier than he had anticipated, but at least he could move it using both hands.

Half running, half stumbling, he made it to the next recessed doorway. As anticipated, the truck swerved just enough to aim a fender at him.

At the last possible moment, Jason took advantage of the truck's effort, stepping into the narrow angle between where the front bumper angled toward the door and the wall of the building. The truck was committed, although brakes screeched in futility against cobblestones before the left front fender smashed into the edge of the doorway at precisely the place Jason had been. At the instant of impact, Jason swung the window box at the windshield.

He was rewarded with the sound of crunching safety glass and a yelp.

Without stopping his forward motion, he had a hand on the truck's door handle and wrenched. He didn't slow to bend over and look. Instead, he grabbed the first thing he touched and snatched.

There was another yell and Jason held a man by the shirt collar. The man struggling in his grip had the same bulky build, the same slant to the eyes and shaved head as the man whose picture he had seen, Eglov. But it wasn't the same man.

The man was reaching inside a pants pocket when Jason took a hand from the shirt's collar to grab his assailant's wrist. As Jason pulled it upward, light reflected from the long, thin blade of a stiletto.

Jason saw not only the knife but flames of that September morning. He heard screams, one of which could have been Laurin's. The agony of his loss, coupled with his anger at nearly being run down like a dog in the street, ignited a fury that erased any rational thought.

Grabbing the hand with the knife, Jason snatched the arm level, at the same time bringing the heel of his other hand crashing down on the wrist.

Jason thought he could hear the ulna snap a split second before there was a howl of pain and the clatter of steel falling onto stone.

His former assailant was moaning as Jason changed hands to take the shattered wrist in his left hand while stooping to scoop the knife from the street with his right. Blade in hand, he drew back for the underhand stroke that would drive the blade under the protection of the rib cage and up into the heart.

"Stop it!"

Startled, he whirled to see Maria standing only a couple of feet away.

"Stop it!" she commanded again. "You are not going to kill that man!"

Something in the tone of her voice made Jason hesitate just long enough to think rationally. Lights were flickering on up and down the street. No doubt the sound of the truck's crash had drawn more than one person to their window. Poor light or not, Jason was not going to bet someone wouldn't be able to identify him to the police.

Instead of the coup de grâce he had begun, Jason drew back his hand and threw the knife as far as he could before slamming the would-be assassin against the wall.

"A little something to remember me by," he said, delivering a kick to the man's groin.

There was a grunt, and the man melted into a groaning heap on the cobblestones.

Maria had Jason by the arm. "We must go. Someone's surely called the police by now."

As though to verify her observation, the pulsating wail of a siren could be heard.

Jason let himself be led down the alley and into another.

Damn, he thought. Someone must have found the plane on the Dominican shore. That discovery, coupled with a liberal application of cash to Dominican officials for a search of names on exit visas as compared with recorded entries, as opposed to mere stamps on a passport, would have revealed that a Mr. Harold Young was the only person within days to depart the Dominican Republic without having first entered it. Having apparently dropped out of the sky, Young then departed Santo Domingo for Paris via Air France. It would have taken simple hacking into reservation computers to determine that Mr. Young had taken Alitalia from Orly to Rome, thence onward to Messina.

They had arrived at Maria's Explorer. She was fumbling

with the keys. "Whatever your real business is, somebody is displeased by it."

He took the keys from her shaking hand. "Apparently."

The lock popped open and he held out the keys.

She was staring as though seeing him for the first time. "You really were going to kill that guy."

Jason was walking around to climb into the passenger seat. "Think of it as returning the favor. He very nearly ran over both of us."

Now Maria was having trouble getting the key into the ignition. Jason got out and opened her door. "You're in no shape to drive. Let me."

Wordlessly, she climbed over the gearshift and brake and sat.

Jason started the engine. "Where to?"

For a moment he wasn't sure she heard him. Then: "You really were going to stab him."

She was looking straight ahead.

Jason bit back a retort and said, "Maria, we don't know that he was alone. I'd suggest we not hang around to find out. Where to?"

She shook as though the words had shocked her back into reality. "To? Your hotel, I guess."

Jason was turning the car around, stopping only to allow a blue-and-white police car, siren wailing, to pass, headed in the direction from which they had come.

"Not a good idea. If that guy knew where to find us, he—or one of his pals—must have followed us. They know my hotel. Next time they might get lucky. Where are you staying?"

She turned to look at him, the hint of a nervous smile tugging at her mouth. "I thought I had heard every come-on there was, but this is the first for 'I need to stay with you tonight because someone is trying to kill me.'"

"Delighted to have exhausted another possibility of human experience," Jason said. "I might remind you that truck driver was perfectly willing to kill you, too. Which way?"

Her eyes grew large. "Me? He had no reason to want to run me over!"

"You want to bet your life on that? Which way?"

She pointed. "Right, up the hill past your hotel."

They were quiet for a few minutes until she said, "I think it is only fair to warn you: I do not do sleepovers with men whose real names I do not know."

He nodded, keeping his eyes on the serpentine road but taking his right hand off the wheel to extend it. "Jason. My pleasure."

She shook it. "Certainly not mine. Nearly getting killed is hardly my choice of a date. This sort of thing happen to you often?"

He was steering around a hairpin turn to the left. "Often enough. Comes with the job."

"Which is?"

"Now a job description's a prerequisite to staying at your place, too?"

"Okay, so I can guess." She looked out over one of the turns. The town below was a handful of jewels. "You really were going to kill him, were you not?"

Jason nodded. "Someone very like him and his pals killed someone very dear to me, along with about three thousand other innocent people, all in the same morning. They're terrorists, Maria, just the same mind-set as any other bunch willing to kill to achieve their political or religious aims. Civilization as we know it can't coexist with people like that."

"'Civilization as we know it'? Don't you think you are being a little extreme?"

He took his eyes off the road just long enough to give her a questioning glance. "Extreme? I don't think so. There's only one way I see of solving the problem: exterminate them like any other vermin."

"I take it your business involves just that."

"You could say that."

"Surely there are good people with extreme ideas."

"Ideas are free. It's when someone is willing to kill any-one who doesn't share them that the trouble starts. Not to put too fine a point on it, but General Sheridan could have been speaking of fanatics, religious or political, when he defined a good Indian: a dead one."

"Turn right here." She pointed to a barely discernible path leading away from the road. "You don't really believe that."

He was squinting, trying to make sure he stayed on the dim track. "Let's say I believe most beliefs have their good and bad people. Culling one from another is the problem." A small building took shape in the headlights. "That it?"

She nodded. "The government rents it for staff when we are working at Aetna. There is a spare bedroom."

He turned off the lights and ignition. "Lucky me."

She looked over her shoulder as she reached for the door. "Lucky you, indeed. Believe me, it always was the spare room or the foldout."

Jason got out and shut the door. "And here I thought my charm, wit, and good looks would prevail."

She produced a set of house keys from her purse. "I am almost as allergic to violence as I am liars. I would say we have a real personality conflict."

She opened the door and flipped on the light. From be-hind her, Jason saw her body stiffen as she emitted a frightened squeak. In a step he was beside her, the SIG Sauer in his hand.

The single living room/kitchen/dining room was a wreck. Drawers had been pulled out, emptied, and left on the floor amid their contents. Drapes lay in heaps or thrown over chairs or a sofa from which the cushions had been re-moved.

Weapon in hand, Jason searched the two adjacent rooms.

" 'Fraid they've been tossed, too," he said, putting the gun away.

Tears were running down Maria's face, whether from

anger, fright, or both, Jason couldn't tell. "Who . . . What did they want; what were they looking for?"

Jason righted a chair and picked up what looked like the matching cushion. "If I had to guess, I'd say they were looking for the samples I gave you."

She was still gazing around the room, dazed. "I left them at the portable lab, not here. But why would they . . . ?"

Jason slowly raised his hands, nodding toward the still-open door. "I'm afraid we're about to find out."

On the threshold stood a tall, bald man, the one Jason had seen in the photograph, Eglov. He held what Jason recognized as a Colt M733, a true submachine gun not much larger than a pistol. Delta Force had used them in the jungles of Asia.

Jason's eyes cut toward a window.

"Don't bother, Mr. Peters," the intruder said in almost accentless English. "I'm not alone."

"Jason," Maria asked in an unsteady voice, "who are—"

"You can bet they're not among the 'good' idealists we were talking about."

The man with the weapon made a motion, and Jason heard a rear door crash open, making Maria give another frightened squeak. Rough hands grabbed Jason from behind, and he felt the weight of the SIG Sauer being lifted from his belt while a hand groped into his pockets.

A voice behind him spoke in Russian that Jason couldn't follow.

"Who are you? What do you want?" Maria had regained enough composure to start getting angry.

In a step, the man with the Colt was beside her. He slapped her with the back of his hand hard enough to send her staggering backward.

"Silence! You'll find out soon enough!"

Instinctively, Jason started to move toward her until he felt the jab of a gun's muzzle in his back. Maria slid down a wall, sitting splay-legged on the floor.

The man who had hit her motioned to whoever was behind Jason. The gun muzzle moved, and another man, this one with a mustache, carrying an AK-47 with a full clip, walked over to a table and deposited the contents of Jason's pockets along with the SIG Sauer.

"Okay," Jason said. "Now that you've made yourselves at home, exactly what is it you want?"

Eglov smiled, showing one shiny steel front tooth. "Allow me an introduction. My name is Eglov. Aziz Saud Alazar was a friend and business associate. You have caused considerable inconvenience, Mr. Peters. But I what I want is information. We will start with why you have consulted Dr. Bergenghetti."

"Consult?" He shrugged. "She's an attractive woman. I like attractive women."

A nod from Eglov sent Mustache over to where Maria was still sitting on the floor. She screamed as he yanked her to her feet by her hair. Transferring his rifle to his other hand, he ripped away the top of her dress and roughly grabbed her bra. Maria whimpered in pain and fright.

"Perhaps you will be amused watching my friend enjoy the woman," Eglov said. "I can assure you she will not find it pleasant. Or perhaps you will slice to the chase, eliminate the cow excrement." There was no warmth in his smile. "You see, I have mastered your American idiom." The smile vanished. "The information I seek, Mr. Peters. Or the woman suffers."

Jason sighed his resignation. "Let her go and I'll tell you what you want."

"Do you take me for a fool, Mr. Peters? I let the woman loose and the place swarms with police like angry bees defending a hive."

"You don't let her go and she dies here after you've learned what you want."

Eglov shrugged. "She lives; she dies. It is a matter of your choice."

"Yours, not mine."

"You are not in a place to argue, Mr. Peters. The degree of her suffering is in your hands. Now, why are you here?"

Jason had no illusions that either he or Maria was going to walk out of this house.

Unless . . .

"Look, leave her alone. The information you want—it's all on the BlackBerry." Jason was pointing.

Eglov stepped over to the table, picked the device up, and handed it to Jason. "Summon the data you say is here."

Jason punched a series of keys and scrolled up the beginning of a paragraph before handing it back.

Eglov scowled. "It is encrypted! Do not play games with me, Mr. Peters. You will have ample time to regret it."

Jason pointed again. "Those coins that came out of my pocket. One of them has the decoding key."

Alternating quick glances at Jason, the Russian used the hand not holding the Colt to sort through a dozen coins. "The American quarter?"

"That's it." Jason held out his hand. "Let me have it."

Once he held the twenty-five-cent piece, Jason turned it heads up, offered the closest thing to a prayer he had said in years, and pressed Washington's head. Pretending to concentrate, he said, "Look closely at the screen now."

Eglov brought the BlackBerry nearer to his eyes. "I see nothing but—"

What happened next was a phenomenon Jason knew well from combat: the brain's slowing things down to better comprehend what was happening. It was like watching a film in slow motion, where every movement was as deliberate and sluggish as though performed underwater, and there were one hundred twenty seconds to the minute.

With more of a whoosh than an explosion, a sound like a stove's gas ring catching, the BlackBerry erupted. A single yellow flame blew the front of the device into Eglov's face.

Between the detonation and the Russian's howl of pain, Jason had the SIG Sauer in his hand.

Mustache never had a chance.

Before the man could let go of Maria's bra and raise the rifle, Jason fired off two shots close enough to sound like one. The AK-47 flew across the room as though levitating on its own as Mustache slammed into the wall. He stood openmouthed before his head bent down as if he were contemplating the two bright red splotches that were blooming on his shirt.

He muttered something and fell face-forward to the accompaniment of Maria's terrified screams.

The other man had a chance but not enough of one. A third shot from the SIG Sauer doubled him over. No longer interested in combat, he staggered outside.

Less than a second had passed since the BlackBerry had blown up. Jason whirled to take care of Eglov. The machine gun, along with a puddle of blood on the floor, was all that remained. Other than Jason and Maria, the room was empty of life.

Jason dove through the open door into the darkness outside rather than present an illuminated target. Even before his eyes became completely adjusted to the dark, he heard hurried feet moving unevenly on the pebbles of the driveway and saw a form moving at a staggering run away from him.

He took two quick steps in pursuit and stopped. There was no way to know how many others might be out there, nor whether there would be another attempt made on Maria and him that night. He wanted little more than a chance to finish Eglov then and there, but prudence told him getting out of the area was the wiser move.

But where?

CHAPTER TWENTY-ONE

Autostrada A18
Between Taormina and Messina
Thirty minutes later

Maria had said nothing since Jason had draped a blouse from the closet around her bare midriff and bundled her into the Explorer. Tears she made no effort to wipe away coursed freely down her face, leaving trails that glistened in the light from the dashboard. Jason had been primarily occupied with the rearview mirror, making sure they were not followed, but the only traffic at this hour of night was trucks availing themselves of the deserted four-lane to make good time to their next destination.

He had left the house occupied by Mustache's body and whatever other evidence the police might find. Sanitizing the scene would have taken more time than he was willing to risk in case Eglov had others nearby. Leaving additional firepower behind was contrary to any training Jason had, but he elected to leave the AK-47 where it had fallen. Should he be stopped, he wanted no part of explaining to authorities, who would take a dim view indeed of an unregistered, fully automatic weapon in the hands of an American traveling under a false name.

For the first time, he noticed that Maria was shivering in the warm Sicilian night. A chill or the onset of shock? Reaching an arm around her shoulder, he gently pulled her against him, sharing body heat. She made no effort to resist, nor gave any acknowledgment of the gesture.

"You okay?" he asked.

She gave the bare minimum of a nod and snuggled closer.

He was slowing down for one of the numerous automated tollbooths when she finally spoke. "Where are we going?"

"For the moment, as far from Taormina as I can get. The ferry from Messina to Calabria runs twenty-four hours a day."

"And then?"

"I'll surprise you."

"In other words, you do not know."

"Let's say only that I'm not yet sure."

She pulled away to sit up straight. "I think I want to go back to my office and volcanoes."

Jason pulled out to pass a lumbering truck. "I wouldn't recommend it. You saw what those guys were willing to do to you."

She turned in the seat to face him. "You are saying I need to stay where you can protect me? I am not helpless, you know."

Jason simply gave her a wordless look.

"Okay, okay, so we stay together for a while. I will call in to take leave."

She put her head back on his shoulder. In minutes she was snoring gently.

JOURNAL OF SEVERENUS TACTUS

Gulf of Naples
Campania, Italy

The sun was beginning to set behind the mountains to the west when I reined

my horse in at the top of a hill. The Bay
of Baia shimmered gold in the setting
sun. Even though the town at the bottom of the hill was only a mixture of
white marble and lengthening shadows, the thought of my coming visit to
the underworld somehow gave it a sinister pall.

As I started downward, I could see
the villa of Agrippa,[1] a place I had once
visited long ago with my father. The
general had been old then and must now
be ancient, but I knew he still had the
ear of the emperor for whom he had
won so many battles.[2] He and my father
had had a long relationship that ended
for reasons I knew not when I was
barely twelve. Should I survive my or-
deal, I decided to pay him a visit.

Spurring the horse forward, I made
for the inn where I had taken a single
room. There, sometime in the night, I
would be taken away to a place unknown, to a bath, where I would be purified by steam and by magic potions for
two days before entering Hades.

In the inn's courtyard, I let the thirsty
horse plunge its nose into the *implu-
vium*.[3] Once the beast was sated, I
handed the reins to a waiting groom and
swung a leg over the animal's back.

"Be quick to dismount, Severenus,"
came a voice from behind me.

Turning, I saw a figure in a black
cape, his face concealed both by its folds
and the final darkness of the night.

"Who tells me when to dismount?" I

snapped, unused to taking orders since my father's death.

Undaunted, the stranger replied, "The dead tell you. In your room you will find suitable *vestmenta*. Once you have put them on, come outside and follow the slave with the torch."

"It is dark. Any slave on the street will be carrying a torch for his master."

"Then you must select the correct one."

The stranger stepped back into the deeper of the shadows. By the time I reached the spot where he had been, the man was gone.

On the way to my room I was accosted by a young girl, perhaps ten or eleven, her face gaudily painted. Prostitutes were not allowed to solicit business at respectable inns, since several men occupied the same bed. The farther one got from Rome, the less enthusiasm the local authorities had for enforcing the rule.

I shooed her away. As she slunk down the stairs with a sultry look far beyond her years, I wondered what such a meeting might portend.[4]

I retired to my *cubiculum*[5] to change. On top of the rough-woven covers was a cloak similar to the one I had seen in the courtyard below. Stripping off my horse-sweat-soaked clothes, I exchanged them for a clean tunic, over which I tossed the new cloak and went back downstairs. Outside the gate to the inn, a lone slave waited with a torch.

I followed down dark and deserted alleys, fearful of robbers or worse, until we came to a marble-lined doorway dug into the side of a hill. The hair on the back of my neck felt as though it were rising when the door swung open without sign or sound from my guide. Inside, a long hallway was lit by lamps.

My guide wordlessly stood aside and pointed to an open door through which I entered a small room. Its dimensions were such that I could neither lie down nor stand erect. As the door shut, the light of lamps revealed the most terrifying paintings on the walls: people with various deforming and hideous diseases, old age, hunger, death, insanity, and all matter of evil were vividly displayed.[6] Had I known I would be left alone to confront such fearful images, visited only on occasion, as food and drink were brought by silent figures who left after refreshing the lamps, I might have wavered in my resolve to come here.[7]

Whether day or a night—I could not tell—a single bowl was placed before me filled with vegetables cooked in strange spices. After each meal, a different god or spirit would appear, though none would converse with me.[8] At other intervals, my keepers would bathe me with strange-smelling waters and massage my body with oils.[9]

I know not how long I remained there, but at least twice priests in black robes with high, pointed headgear[10] sacrificed one of the bullocks I had provided, examined its liver, and, finding the lobes flawed, postponed my journey. With each delay, the spirits who visited me became increasingly angry, and I began to wonder if I would go mad.

NOTES

1. Not to be confused with his father, Marcus Vipsanius Agrippa, senator and statesman.

2. Notably Actium, a sea battle in which the forces of Antony and Cleopatra were defeated 31 B.C.

3. A small pond that was the opening to the cistern common to villas and inns where the viaducts did not run or did not supply sufficient water.

4. Few things in Roman life were without possible significance in foretelling the future: the formation of a flight of birds, the frequency of croaking frogs, persons accidentally met on the street. Like most ancient cultures, the Romans used a number of methods to ascertain their fortunes: *extispicy*, or augury by inspection of animal entrails, particularly the liver, oracles, and omens. Interestingly, astrology did not become a popular method of divination in Rome until about the time of Christ, although other cultures—Babylonian, Egyptian, Greek—had seen the future in the stars for millennia.

5. A closet-sized, windowless room usually large enough to hold only the bed. Any activity other than sleeping was conducted elsewhere. A stone slab was covered with a stuffed cloth mattress.

6. Virgil's *Aeneid* gives a similar description of such a room.

7. Alone, confronted by his fears, perpetual light, cramped and uncomfortable quarters, sleep deprivation, visited only by those bringing suste-

nance, at the mercy of unknown keepers—
Tactus's captivity bears a remarkable resemblance to so-called brainwashing techniques or
modern interrogation methods designed to break
down the subject's resistance and perception of
reality.

8. Pliny the Elder tells of a number of hallucinogenic plants with oracular connections, such
as thorn apple, whose roots were made into a sort
of tea; and henbane and nightshade (belladonna), both deadly poisons if used carelessly.
Indeed, Greco-Roman oracular history is full of
pilgrims to the underworld who never returned,
their "spirits having been retained by other
shades." Other accounts tell of travelers to Hades
whose dispositions were forever changed or who
died within months of their return. Coincidence
or misuse of drugs?

9. The skin, the body's largest organ, is absorbent, as anyone who has ever used anything
as common as suntan lotion knows. What is frequently overlooked is the skin's ability to absorb
drugs applied as salves or ointments.

10. The conical hats of religious penitents, medieval witches, and the Ku Klux Klan.

PART IV

Chapter Twenty-two

Over the Tyrrhenian Sea
The next day

Maria slept most of the brief flight. In fact, she had slept most of the previous day once they had checked into a small hotel. Jason supposed it was a means of avoiding thinking about what had happened and what had nearly happened.

Jason had used the time the day before to make a call from a pay phone to an unsecured number in Sardinia. Without his BlackBerry, getting a secure message to D.C. presented a problem, since all calls worldwide were subjected to monitoring, not just the few that raised the political ire of the civil libertarians in the United States. The redeeming feature, of course, was that no entity or country possessed the assets to actually translate and evaluate any but communications between persons of interest. The truly unnerving fact was the question of the security of the system. Who might be monitoring the monitors? Despite the howls of politicians who knew the truth anyway, privacy had become no more than unexamined information, or, in the current euphemism, data at rest.

Even so, if someone was sophisticated enough to hack into ECHELON, they certainly could set key words to flag any specific communication. He longed for the days when a pay phone guaranteed anonymity.

Jason finally decided on an innocuous telegram he could only hope would be correctly interpreted.

> *MAMA STOP BAD BOYS BROKE BLACKBERRY AND LOST TRAVEL SUPPLIES FOR SELF AND WIFE STOP WILL WAIT REPLACEMENT TELEGRAPH/POSTAL OFFICE CALABRIA STOP JASON*

Fairly transparent, but it was unlikely the other side would ever guess something as primitive as a transoceanic telegraph would be used. Additionally, since the nearly ancient Atlantic cable carried the few messages that still were exchanged in this manner, no one had bothered to develop the technology to monitor such messages. Satellites could not intercept messages on landlines.

Like most European countries, Italy's telephone and telegraph functions were operated by the postal service. Jason left the post office, checked on Maria (still asleep), had lunch, and took in the few sights Calabria had to offer, then spent the one-o'clock-to-four-o'clock siesta sipping espresso and reading a two-day-old *International Herald Tribune* at an outdoor table at a small trattoria.

His patience was rewarded in the late afternoon when he returned to the post office. A courier from the American attaché in Naples had delivered a plain brown paper package.

Back at the hotel, Jason hurriedly unwrapped the parcel, removing a United States passport jacket for Ms. Sarah Rugger of Tampa, Florida, presumably the wife of William Rugger, the name and residence on Jason's second set of identification. Also there was an appropriate Florida driver's permit blank, Visa and American Express cards, a small digital camera, a gadget similar to one used to impress notary or corporate seals on documents, and another BlackBerry.

Why Florida? he wondered. Nice place to visit, but you wouldn't want to vote there.

A note from Mama cautioned more care in the future.

Slowly waking to Jason's persuasion, Maria needed no encouragement to apply makeup and brush her hair once she saw the camera. Jason took two pictures of her, being certain the background was different in each.

Down the street, he found a UPS business center, where he had the pictures printed. Back in the room, he glued the pictures onto the passport and used the press to apply a reasonable facsimile of the U.S. seal. There was little he could do with the driver's license other than make sure the application of the photo was smooth and hope that the holograms would pass muster. It was the passport that got the closest scrutiny anyway, he told himself.

Finished, he had gone back outside and deposited camera and seal in different trash bins before finding an Alitalia office and booking two tickets to Rome the next day.

If Eco hacked into the reservation system, they would find of interest any American couple and would have someone watching the airport to make a positive sighting.

This morning they had indeed driven to the small airport and parked the Explorer in a conspicuous place in the lot. Jason had then signaled a cab for the short ride to other side of the field, where the five- or six-plane general aviation fleet was based.

After some discussion with the field's only charter service, they boarded a DeHaviland Twin Otter, a high-wing, fixed-gear twin designed for takeoff and landing on short, rugged terrain. Jason had patiently explained that he was interested in being transported to a specific location that was unlikely to have an airstrip.

Language was only a minor barrier, since English was the international language of aviation. A Russian Aeroflot pilot approaching Hong Kong International Airport would speak English with the Chinese air traffic controller. The only exception was France and spheres of French influence, where the sanctity of the French language was deemed a greater priority than air safety.

For that matter, the French deemed it a greater priority than anything Jason could think of, with the possible exceptions of wine and sex.

Luckily, he was not dealing with the French, a fact for which he was always grateful.

Maria was asleep before the tires left the ground.

The jaw-jarring return to earth gave truth to the hoary pilots' axiom that a landing was only a controlled crash. Had he not tightened Maria's seat belt, she would have been thrown to the floor.

From the window, Jason could see nothing but dust swirling from the field in which they had landed. The right engine shut down, the plane pivoted, and one of the two crew members came back from the cockpit to open the door.

"These es eet," he said in accented English. "Th' coordinates you wanted."

The jolt of the landing had Maria wide awake. "This is no airport," she observed, sitting up straight and peering out the window. "This is some sort of a farm."

The dust had almost settled when they reached the bottom of the aircraft's three steps. They had no sooner put both feet on the ground than the door retracted while the pilot restarted the right engine, taxied downwind, and took off almost straight up. Both Jason and Maria closed their eyes against a cloud of flying grit of Saharan proportions.

When they finally dared open dirt-encrusted eyes, they were facing a man standing in front of a battered Volvo. He was perhaps six feet tall with a huge white walrus mustache. Silver hair was visible underneath a tweed cap he wore despite the season. The headgear was the same color as his jacket. A dress shirt, complete with tie, was stuffed into corduroy pants, which, in turn, were bloused over the tops of knee boots, the rubber sort the English called wellies.

As the last of the dust settled, he used both hands to brush himself off and approach. When he got within handshaking distance, his blue eyes twinkled as though with a wry story he was impatient to tell.

Instead of shaking, he embraced Jason with a squeeze any grizzly bear might envy. "Jason, lad!," he exclaimed. "It's been too long! Welcome to Silanus."

The accent was guttural, yet musical, the sound of his hereditary Gaelic, a language common in Europe half a millennium before Rome existed, now clinging tenuously to the continent's westernmost fringes. The tongue was fading but, for the time being, secure in his native Scottish Highlands.

Jason managed to extricate himself and turned to Maria. "Adrian, this is Maria Bergenghetti. Or should I say *Dr.* Maria Bergenghetti?"

Maria involuntarily flinched as the Scot approached, fearful she, too, would receive a suffocating hug.

Instead he bowed from the waist, extending a hand. "A pleasure, lassie. Welcome to you also. The lout ye're with's too uncivilized for a proper introduction. I'm Adrian Graham, major, Her Majesty's First Grenadiers, retired." He winked at Jason. "I'd be pleased if you'd just call me Adrian."

Maria seemed uncertain whether her hand would be shaken or kissed. She held it out nonetheless, showing relief at the conventional shake.

"Adrian's an old, er, business associate," Jason added. "Retired here to Sardinia."

Actually, Adrian's affiliation with the grenadiers, Her Majesty's or otherwise, had been extraordinarily brief. He had hardly finished basic training when his fierce competitiveness and total lack of fear of any man (or rank) had brought him to the attention of Special Air Services, SAS, a semiclandestine, small-unit combat force generally considered to be made up of the best commandos in the world. The service had a lot more to do with *special* than *air*, the name dating back to World War II, when its men were usually parachuted behind enemy lines to perform the service's raison d'être: murder, arson, and general mayhem.

In large part the American Special Forces, the parent of Delta Force, had been patterned after SAS.

Jason and Adrian had met during the chaos of the Bosnian Conflict, when both English and American "peacekeepers" were taking fire from both sides, Muslim and Christian, each intent on exterminating the other.

That day both men had been separated from their individual units and from their communication equipment.

By pure circumstance, each was being pursued by Bosnian rebels intent on driving foreign powers from the area to be able to ethnically cleanse Muslims at their leisure. By even more extraordinary circumstance, each man had chosen the same wooded crest of a small hill as a likely place to make a stand.

Each was delighted to discover the other and that their defense had just increased by one hundred percent.

"Jason Peters, Delta Force," were the first words Jason had spoken.

"Adrian Graham, SAS."

They glanced at each other with the admiration elite forces share for one another.

"Say, mon, how many of yon blokes're after your scalp?" Adrian had asked, looking over Jason's shoulder.

"No more than ten or so," Jason had said calmly. "And you?"

" 'Bout the same," Adrian had said. "We'd best not let them see we've joined up until they're in range."

Jason peered down the slope, waiting for the first of his pursuers to show himself. "And why's that?"

"If they know there're two of us, the sodding bastards'll run."

The timely arrival of a low-strafing, rocket-bearing F-16

fighter actually scattered the attackers, but neither Jason nor Adrian would ever admit that the plane's arrival was more than an intrusion by air forces with not enough else to do.

After the conflict they had kept in touch, spending boozy, ill-remembered evenings in places most people had never heard of, until Adrian's retirement a few years ago.

Like most Highland Scots, Adrian was intensely proud of his heritage and equally eager to leave its desolate landscape and dreary weather.

In the seventeenth century, Cromwell had had one of Adrian's ancestors hanged by the neck—but not until dead—then castrated and drawn and quartered. Although presumably no longer of interest to the victim, his component parts had then been buried at various unmarked crossroads. Years later, such remains as could be found had been entombed in a grand sepulchre in St. Giles in Edinburgh. It was a fact of which Adrian was extremely vain, but no more so than that his bloodline had three centuries earlier stood with Robert the Bruce at Bannockburn, with somewhat happier results. Even family pride, though, could not overcome the misery of the nine-month Scottish winter.

Like so many British, he and his wife had sought warmer climates. Unlike most English expats, he had not chosen the southwest of France, Tuscany, or Spain. His hobby of archeology had drawn him to the stone structures of the early Bronze Age that dotted the hills of the island of Sardinia. Through either beneficence or indifference, amateur exploration was not discouraged, and the cost of living was some of the lowest in western Europe, and life expectancy the highest.

Adrian and his wife had purchased a small farm in the rocky mountains that formed the spine of the island near the tiny village of Silanus.

Adrian held the door of the Volvo open. "You've no luggage?"

"We didn't have time to pack," Jason said. "Figured we could pick up what we needed when we got here."

Adrian helped Maria into the front passenger seat, motioning Jason into the back. "Aye, well, there's no Fortnum and Mason or Harrods in Silanus. Clare, m' wife, will have a spare frock or two. An' you, Jason—I think I can put something on yer back till you find suitable clothing."

"I don't look good in kilts," Jason said.

Adrian was turning the key, the Volvo's starter grinding. "An' I'm not insultin' th' Graham clan tartan by givin' ye th' loan of any."

The starter motor had quit whirring and simply clicked its solenoid.

"Damn piece of Swedish junk! Doesn't like the Guinea climate." Adrian got out and withdrew a cudgel from under the seat. "Just raise the bonnet and give 'er a tap."

Jason could feel the blow to car's engine.

Satisfied, Adrian climbed back in, tossing the club into the backseat next to Jason. "Like any woman, she needs to be shown who's boss once 'n a while."

Jason was thankful Clare wasn't present to hear that.

Adrian turned the key. This time the engine purred. Adrian engaged a groaning clutch, shifted reluctant gears, and they were in motion.

He was grinning. "An' Antonio, th' closest thing we have to a real mechanic in these parts, wanted more'n a hundred euros to repair what a good thrashin' could accomplish."

They drove along a barely discernible trail among the foothills of the Gennargentu Mountains. Parched and sloping pastureland feuded unenthusiastically with jagged rock outcroppings. Gray rock was everywhere—in the path they were driving, intruding bluntly into scatterings of meadow, and rising into mountains. Rare patches of green stubbornly forced leaves up between stones. Scattered herds of sheep and goats added cotton fabric to the otherwise threadbare landscape. The vista was largely unforgiving and barren. Other than the terrain's stinginess with green, it was,

Jason thought, remarkably similar to Adrian's native High-lands.

At the end of a dusty, rocky path only generosity would call a driveway, the Volvo pulled into a dirt yard. At the far end sat a one-story cottage made from thě gray native stone. Two stunted trees, perpetual combatants in the battle with the mountains' winds, flanked the single front door.

Adrian gave a cheery toot on the horn, and a smiling, white-haired woman popped out of the door as though she had been waiting for the signal. Her round face was reddish and split by a smile as she trotted toward the car, wiping her hands on an apron.

Jason barely got out of the car in time to accept her embrace.

"Jason! It's been so long. . . ."

Tears glistened in her eyes. Despite differences in background and age, Laurin and Clare had become fast friends during the one time Jason and his wife had visited the couple in Scotland. The two women had exchanged e-mails on a regular basis, and Clare and her husband had appeared as grief-stricken as any blood relative at Laurin's memorial service. Jason would always appreciate the time and expense involved in their attendance.

Clare dabbed a sleeve to her eyes and turned to Maria.

Dropping her arms from Jason's shoulders, she gave a gesture that, in earlier times, might have been called a curtsy. " 'Lo! I'm Clare."

"Th' present Mrs. Graham," Adrian added.

"Auld fool!" Clare nodded toward her husband of over thirty years.

Maria extended a hand as she climbed out of the Volvo. "Maria Bergenghetti."

"*Dr.* Bergenghetti," Adrian added.

"Maria will do fine," Maria said, darting a glance at Jason.

Clare looked from Jason to Adrian and back again. "Have they no luggage?"

Adrian was herding Jason and Maria toward the house as he tossed over his shoulder, "None at all. I'm sure you have a gown or two you can share with the lass."

Clare hurried after them. "Of course. Not that anything I have here is high fashion."

The inside of the cottage was somewhat more inviting than the outside.

Entry was into a large living room with a vaulted, beamed ceiling. A number of comfortable-looking leather chairs and a couch faced a fireplace large enough to hold man-size logs. Surmounting the rough wooden mantel was a huge double-edged sword, its burnished metal attesting to regular care.

Adrian followed Maria's gaze. "A Graham swung that claymore beside Bonny Prince Charlie at Culloden Moor. 'Twas what you might call the Stuarts' last stand. Y'see—"

"I think they'd be more impressed with something to eat," Clare interrupted before her husband could reach full speed. "Not much, just a typical local lunch."

Behind her, a long wooden table was spread with a white cloth. Four tumblers guarded a bottle of red wine and a plate of *carta da musica,* the native flatbread so thin it did, in fact, resemble a sheet of music. A large slice of whitish-yellow cheese—Jason guessed pecorino—was next to a bowl of some sort of vegetable stew, probably eggplant, tomatoes, and fava beans. Not exactly the meal one would expect from a Highlander.

Adrian was the typical paradoxical Scot: thrifty to the point of parsimony, yet a generous and congenial host.

Perhaps apocryphal, certainly believable, was the story repeated to Jason by more than one of Adrian's former subalterns as lore in the regiment. Nightfall on base brought young Lieutenant Graham prowling the enlisted men's quarters, ostensibly to verify that no one had taken unofficial leave. His actual purpose was revealed in the morning, when a dearth of toilet paper in the latrine was noticeable. Young Graham, it seemed, had an aversion to spending his meager officer's pay to purchase necessities so readily available.

A few of his peers called him Leftenant Bum Wad until the day he retired.

But Adrian had no compunctions about sharing the "last wee dram" of single-malt scotch or a Cuban cigar. On his sole visit, Jason had wanted for nothing. Jason supposed the generally hostile climate of his friend's native Highlands disposed him to waste nothing but offer bounteous hospitality to those who sought it.

Adrian ushered them into cane-bottom chairs, poured the red wine, and raised his glass. *"A cent'anni!"* He took a sip and grinned. "Sardinian greeting and toast; means 'live a hundred years.'"

Adrian dipped a generous serving of the stew onto Maria's plate before serving Jason. "I'll not be inspectin' th' teeth of any gift horses, but I'll admit to a certain curiosity as to why you called, wantin' to visit Clare 'n' me all o' a sudden."

Jason gave Maria a slight shake of the head. He would explain.

"Maria was doing some work for my employer. We encountered some, er, unhappy customers and decided it would be best to let things cool off."

Adrian gave Jason a long look, a smile tickling his lips, before he nodded his understanding and changed the subject as adroitly as a running back shifting field.

"You'll be interested to see th' farm Clare 'n' I got."

"I thought you came here because of the archeology."

"That, too." Adrian took a mouthful of stew, chewed, swallowed, and continued. "I spend as much time in yon old stone dwellings as I can. But it's not like we have a butcher and greengrocer convenient. We raise most of our vegetables, slaughter most of our meat. Even raise a few grapes." He held up his glass. "Not a fine claret, but sufficient."

And far better than Sicilian.

"I can't think of anything that would go better with what we're having," Maria said tactfully.

Adrian rolled his eyes at her. "Clearly ye've not had good wine, lassie, but thanks."

After the meal, Adrian leaned over his wife's chair, planting a prim kiss on her cheek. "Mind, now, Mother, there's more'n enough of yer bonny stew for lunch on th' morrow if it's put up proper in th' fridge."

Clare rolled her eyes, a woman who had kept house for a lifetime only to have her retired husband begin to tell her how to do it.

Adrian took Jason by the elbow. "Let me show you my projects," he said pointedly.

Outside, behind the house, Jason saw perhaps an acre or so of vines, the young green shoots limning the stumps of last year's harvest. From nowhere a dog appeared, a large, shaggy animal with a tail wagging with pleasure.

Adrian stooped to pet the broad head. "Name's Jock."

"What kind is he?"

The Scot shrugged. "Never asked, but he's good at roundin' up the wee lambs that get lost, stays out of the henhouse, and generally makes good use o' himself."

Jock barked as if to confirm the résumé.

It was something Pangloss might do. Jason reminded himself to check on his dog's well-being the next time he communicated with Mama.

They walked past a half acre or so of sprouting vegetables. Jason was surprised to see tomatoes already blushing with ripeness so early in the season. Yellow zucchini buds were visible through thick leaves, and there were the herbs mandatory for any Italian garden, basil and oregano.

Brown-spotted chickens scratched rocky dirt in front of a fenced shingle coop. A few feet farther they came to a run delineated by stout logs. Two of the biggest pigs Jason had ever seen stopped their rooting to watch through red, feral eyes.

Jason put his hand on the top rail and leaned over, the better to see. "Damn, Adrian, I've never—"

Adrian snatched him backward just as one of the animals charged the place where he had placed his hand. The animal moved faster than anything that size Jason had ever seen. Its head struck the wood with a force hard enough to shake the thick timber rails. Its teeth were grinding into the wood.

"Laddie, you've never seen swine like these, obviously. Both hog 'n' sow are specially bred for size—have shoats that measure up to some full-grown pigs."

Jason looked at the space between rails where one had stuck its snout through, exposing large, yellow tusks. "Not exactly friendly."

"That's why I keep 'em fenced rather than let 'em root wild. If I hadn't pulled you back, ol' Goliath there'd be chewin' on yer arm."

Jason looked from the pig to Adrian. "I didn't know pigs were carnivores."

"Omnivorous," Adrian corrected. "Most pigs'll eat anythin' they can chew or swallow. The mate to Jock, the dog there, somehow got into that pen. Wasn't much left of her, time I got here. Ever' time I herd the sheep, I go way 'round, make sure none of 'em wander into that pen there."

As they turned to go back to the house, Adrian produced a pipe from one pocket, a tobacco pouch from the other. In minutes he was puffing something that smelled like a combination of silage and wet dog hair, so bad that Jason checked the soles of his shoes before ascertaining that the pipe was the source of the odor.

Adrian sucked noisily on the pipe's stem. "Clare won' let me smoke in the house anymore . . ."

Small wonder.

". . . and I can't get the good tobacco I used to enjoy."

Surprise!

"You used to smoke cigars, I recall."

But nothing that stank like that pipe.

"Still do when I can get Havanas."

Adrian stopped, blowing a perfect smoke ring that shimmered in the daylight, then warped and disappeared. "If I'm pryin', say so, but should I be on the watch for any, er, unexpected company?"

Jason shook his head. "Don't think so, but you never know."

"Perhaps you'd enlighten me. I'd be interested in hearing as much as you can tell me without breachin' whatever security you're operatin' under."

Jason shrugged. "You're letting me hide out here; you're entitled."

While Adrian was staring into the bowl of his dead pipe, Jason took a quick breath of fresh air.

Striking a match with one hand, Adrian coaxed smoke from the briar. With the other, he indicated a woodshed and took a seat on an upright log. "We can talk here."

Jason stared into the sky, wondering exactly where to begin. "Back last winter, I had a mission to snatch one of the bad guys, an arms dealer. He didn't survive the process. One of his customers is afraid somebody knows too much or will find it out. . . ."

"An' who might that be?"

"We think they're an organization that calls itself Eco, run by former Russian Mafia turned eco nut."

"There's always a chance they might figure you know nothing. Bad blood makes trouble."

Jason remembered a two-hundred-year feud between Scottish clans, Graham as the House of Montrose on one side, the Campbells on the other, but he decided to say nothing.

Instead, he continued. "Whatever this thing, this weapon—they call it Breath of the Earth—is, it's something that renders an enemy helpless while the bad guys cut his throat. Some minerals were included, minerals that came from somewhere around the Bay of Naples."

Adrian was poking around the bowl of the again-dead

pipe with a matchstick. "And your kit is to find out what that weapon is, destroy it, and manage not to get your own throat cut in the bargain."

"As we used to say in the army, 'kee-rect.'"

Graham struck a fresh match and applied it to the pipe. "I'm curious: why render someone defenseless and then kill 'em? Why not just apply lethal force to begin with?"

Jason edged away from the stream of smoke that insisted in drifting into his face. "Don't know, but a good guess would be that having some natural substance make an enemy helpless has a certain appeal to radicals, those who believe they alone can save the earth. Sort of like Mother Nature's revenge."

"How involved is your . . . friend, Dr. Bergenghetti?"

"With me? She's not. I mean, she's a leading volcanologist. I asked her to do some tests and those bastards are threatening her to get at me. Seemed expedient not to leave her."

"Expedient because she's a bonny lass or because she's really in harm's way?"

Jason told him about what had happened in Sicily.

Adrian smiled around the stem of his pipe. "The one who got away—Eglov—he'll not be on your trail?"

"I booked a flight to Rome, swapped IDs, and took a charter over here. I'd guess it will take Eglov a few days before he discovers we aren't in Rome. By that time, I'll no longer be imposing on your hospitality."

Adrian was tapping pipe on the heel of a boot, knocking the contents onto the ground. "Aye, let's hope."

Jason grinned. "Hope what? That they won't find us, or we'll be gone in a few days?"

Before Adrian could answer, Maria came out of the house, lighting a cigarette. Clare's ban on smoking applied uniformly.

CHAPTER TWENTY-THREE

Office of Aero Tyrrhenian
Aeroporto Calabria
At the same time

The two men were not from Sicily. Their Italian was unlike any Enrico had ever heard. Or, rather, the Italian of
the one who spoke. Guttural and harsh, with little distinction between the soft and hard Cs, as though he had
learned the language from a book without speaking it.

There was something about them that made Enrico uncomfortable. Perhaps the bandage that covered the whole
right side of the face, including the eye, of the man doing
the talking, the mispronouncing. He must have been in
some sort of accident recently, because bloody splotches
were showing through the gauze.

Enrico was also uncomfortable about what the man
wanted: information concerning a woman and an American man who might have chartered one of Aero Tyrrhenian's planes.

Had they?
Where?
When?

Although no actual threat was made, Enrico got the feeling that the consequences of withholding information might be unpleasant. Very unpleasant.

Enrico had struggled for six years to establish his flying business, his one true love (besides Anna, his wife at home, and Calla, his secretary and mistress, of course). He had built the company up from one four-seat Cessna to a fleet of four aircraft, including the turbo-prop, twelve-seat Islander. Someday he would be able to afford a used jet.

He ran a business, not an information agency. To give out the information these men sought seemed like a betrayal of a customer. If a man had no integrity, he had nothing.

Enrico's resolve was solidifying when the man with the bandaged face put a stack of hundred-euro notes on the counter.

The resolve became a little mushy around the edges.

"*Mille*," the man said.

There was no problem understanding the number. A thousand euros.

The old Beech 18E, the radial-engine twin he used to haul cargo, was going to need the number two overhauled after a few more hours of flight time, and Enrico was fairly certain it would require one or more new pistons, very expensive pistons. A thousand euros wouldn't cover the cost, but it would sure make it less painful.

Still, there was the matter of integrity.

The man with the bandage doubled the number of bills on the counter.

"*Due.*"

Enrico could feel Calla's eyes burning into his back from her desk behind him. Two thousand euros would not only cure the Beech's problem; it would pay for the dress Calla had seen in the window of the shop just off the Quattro Canti in Palermo last week.

The bills disappeared into Enrico's pocket.

CHAPTER TWENTY-FOUR

Silanus, Sardinia
1840 Hours (6:40 P.M.)
The same day

Adrian shared Jason's taste in both music and drink. The two men sat in front of the empty fireplace, glasses of single-malt whiskey in hand. Violins were singing the first movement of Handel's Second Symphony. The only thing preventing Jason's serenity was the odor coming from the kitchen. Whatever Clare and Maria were preparing for dinner smelled suspicious enough to make him verify that Jock, the dog, was still alive and well.

"Haggis," Adrian commented, obviously aware of his friend's apprehension. "For you, we've killed the fatted calf. Or, in this case, the fatted sheep."

"You really shouldn't have."

Jason could not have been more sincere.

The thought of a sheep's heart, liver, and lungs minced with suet, onions, and oatmeal and boiled in the animal's stomach was less than appetizing.

Adrian licked his lips in anticipation. " 'Tis the dish of the Highlands, of all Scotland, for that matter."

And Jason had always thought it was Scotland's abysmal weather that had caused centuries of Scottish incursion southward.

Maria came in from the kitchen and sat beside Jason. "Clare does not need any more help."

The expression on her face betrayed feelings similar to Jason's regarding the impending meal.

" 'Tis a complicated dish," Adrian said, fishing his pipe from his pocket. "Sometimes it's easier to do it yoursel' rather than teach another."

Like mixing a Borgia poison.

"I am sure I was more hindrance than help," Maria offered, her tone unable to conceal gratitude at being released from the experience.

Forbidden to light up, Adrian was making sucking noises on the pipe. "So, tell me exactly what it is you seek, Jason. You mentioned that the poor sods on that fishing boat appeared to have traces of sulfur and various hydrocarbons, including ethylene, in their blood, and that Maria here says the mineral samples are linked to the area of the Bay of Naples."

"I'm to find out exactly what this 'Breath of the Earth' business is all about, see what these extreme nuts have come up with, where they got it."

Adrian took another sucking draw from the pipe, removed it from his mouth, and regarded the empty bowl sadly. "Damn nuisance, having to go outside to light a pipe I've been smoking thirty years. Things we do to please the womenfolk."

Jason was tempted to remind his friend of his comment about demonstrating who was boss, but said, "So far, only thing I've learned is that this guy Eglov takes keeping a secret very seriously."

"Bad sport, that lad." Adrian tapped the pipe's stem against his teeth. "You think the sailors were gassed?"

"Only way I can think of to get those chemicals into the body short of an injection."

"And if th' bleedin' Ecos were that close, they bloody well didn't need all those chemicals."

"Exactly."

Pipe temporarily forgotten, Adrian stared into space for a moment. "Y' know archeology is my passion."

Puzzled as to the connection, Jason leaned forward in his chair. "Yes, but—"

"Subscribe to the magazines, popular and some academic." Adrian stood and went to kitchen. "Clare, where've you been puttin' me archeological journals 'n' stuff?"

"Try lookin' in th' shed," came the disembodied answer.

Adrian turned away, grumbling. "Shed, indeed! All my valuable research material in a leaky auld building . . ."

"If it's leaky," came Clare's voice, "it's not because I haven't asked you a score of times to see to th' roof!"

Adrian was still griping as he walked out of the door.

Moments later he returned with a stack of magazines.

Dumping them in front of the chair he had occupied, he sat and began to page through each. "Year or two ago, I saw an article on Greek Baia. Two or three millennia after the Bronze Age dwellings here in Sardinia, so I didn't give much mind to it."

"Baia?" Jason asked. "What's Greek Baia?"

"Oldest Greek settlement in Italy." Maria spoke for the first time. "It is in the Naples area."

Adrian was still turning pages. "Had something to do with gases, I think." He held up a gray-backed journal. "Ah, here it is. Written by a Professor Calligini, translated by one of your American chaps."

"Eno Calligini, of the University of Turin?" Maria asked.

Adrian moved the magazine a little closer to his face. "Aye, a professor at Turin. Y' know th' man?"

Maria smiled. "Our fields, volcanology and archeology, are not unrelated, at least not here in Italy. He and I participated on a symposium on the Vesuvius eruption of A.D. 79, the one that buried Pompeii."

The look on her face told Jason it was likely she and the

professor were, or had been, more than professional colleagues. He felt a twinge of jealousy. Irrational, but nonetheless real.

Adrian glanced from Jason to Maria. "Y' may want to read what th' professor has to say, Jason. I recall it, he speaks of hallucination-producing vapors."

Clare appeared in the kitchen door, holding a serving tray. "Supper's ready. I—"

The first bar of "Scotland the Brave" chirped from Adrian's pants pocket and he pulled out a cell phone.

"Sorry. Only have the bloody thing so th' kids can keep in touch." He snapped it open. "Graham here."

His face went blank as he listened before a single, "*Grazie.*"

From Clare's expression, Jason guessed they didn't get a lot of phone calls from their kids or anyone else.

The phone disappeared back into Adrian's pocket. "Peppi." He turned to Jason in explanation. "Runs the local trattoria, closest thing about to a pub. A man was asking directions here."

Jason squinted through the windows at the collecting darkness. "Any description?"

Adrian nodded. "Big, shaved head, didn't speak Italian like a local. Or an Italian, for that matter. Had half his face bandaged."

"How many others?"

"Peppi didn't see anyone else. I gather this chap is an acquaintance of yours?"

"I'd guess he's the same one I told you about. You can bet he's not by himself. How long would you guess it'll take him to get here?"

Adrian gave a grim smile. "Depends on how long it takes him to figure out that Peppi's directions are leading him astray."

"Your friend gave him misleading directions? Why?"

Adrian shrugged. "Could be because Peppi knows we don't have many visitors. Could be because he dinna like

the cut o' the man. Probably was a combination of the locals' distrust o' strangers an' the perverse Sardinian sense
o' humor."

"He sent the guy out to the boonies as a joke?"

Adrian nodded as he crossed the room toward Clare,
taking the tray and setting it on the table. "Aye, havin' a
stranger lost in these hills would be very funny to th' natives, particularly a stranger Peppi'd taken a dislike to."
He looked over his shoulder at Clare. "Mother, if you'd
gather some bottled water from the shed, along with a few
tins we can open for supper later . . ."

Clare left the room.

Adrian went to a low chest, removing several blankets.
Underneath them was a long object wrapped in an oil-
spotted cloth. Jason inhaled the familar smell of Hoppe's
gun oil. It took only a moment before Jason was looking at
SAS's favorite weapon, a Sten Mark IIS. From the silhouette, Jason noted that his friend had the model with a
lengthy silencer built onto the barrel. The machine gun
was clearly recognizable from the thick canvas sleeve
around the rear of the silencer, the only protection a
shooter had from a heated barrel. With the Sten, automatic fire was unadvisable except under the direst circumstances. Still, the British commandos had had an
affection for the gun and its predecessors since before
World War II, when it had been manufactured by British
Small Arms along with the oil-spitting, brake-failing BSA
motorcycle.

The British saw romance in ineffective machinery;
hence the long life of the Jaguar automobile.

Adrian slammed one of two thirty-two shot clips into
the gun. "Looks like we're about to have company."

Jason took the SIG Sauer from its holster in the small of
his back, checked the magazine, and put it back. "I don't
know how they found us unless they went to the charter
service."

Adrian was stuffing the Sten's extra clip into his belt.

" 'Th' best laid plans of mice and men gang af't a'wry.' Or so th' bonny bard Bobby Burns tells us. Reason enough to keep me old weapon handy and ready."

Jason was in no mood to discuss either alliterations or Scotland's most beloved poet. "I doubt we have the firepower to fend them off."

Adrian tossed one of the blankets to Maria and pulled out a Savage Model X20 nightscope, something any hunter in America could purchase at his local gun shop. "Wasn't plannin' on a fight, not with women around . . ."

"Don't let me keep you boys from your fun," Maria snapped.

Adrian cocked an eyebrow. "An', as I was about to say, only th' Sten an' a pistol between us."

Unspoken was the fact that, unlike in Bosnia, retreat was not an viable option.

Clare reappeared, carrying a military knapsack. "I've got enough water and food to last us a day or two."

Motioning Jason and Maria to follow, Adrian headed for the door. "We'll not be going far, but we need to hide the car, make it look like we're gone, perhaps off on holiday."

"What about that?" Clare was pointing to the tray with the still-steaming haggis.

"Canna leave hot supper around, now, can we?" Adrian thought for a moment. "Much as I hate it, we'll have to let the swine have it."

Jason had never imagined he would be indebted to ecological terrorists.

"Ah, wait!" Adrian exclaimed. "I'll take a wee second to turn off the ginny motor."

"Ginny motor?" Maria asked.

"Aye, lass, the generator that provides the 'lectricity for the house. We dinna have a local power company out here."

The house went dark, and Adrian returned seconds later holding a flashlight. "It's on our way we are then."

The Volvo cranked on the first try. They drove less

than a hundred yards into a deep ravine carved into the hillside that would make the automobile impossible to see unless someone knew where to look or was very lucky. From the car, Adrian led them uphill to a scattering of large stones Jason had seen earlier and dismissed as just one more of the island's rock formations. Only when Adrian played a flashlight across the surface did Jason see a horizontal opening leading under an overhanging boulder.

"One of the early Bronze Age dwellings," Adrian said, ducking to get into the space beneath. "Phoenicians and Romans invaded the Nuragic settlements along the coast, forced the indigenous population to retreat here into the ridges. They built homes that were difficult to find, easy to defend."

Jason followed Adrian's light. They stepped down into a cave—no, a room perhaps thirty by thirty. The walls still showed marks of the ancient chisels that had pried away the stone. At the back, the cool night air entered through a hole in the roof, a primitive fireplace, recognizable by smudges of soot still visible on the wall. The closer he looked, the more Jason realized the habitation was not as primitive as he had thought. The streaked wall behind the fire pit would have been heated by the flames, radiating warmth throughout the small room.

Adrian switched off his flashlight. "Make y'sel' comfortable, but cut off the torches. Don' wan' th' light givin' us away."

As his world went dark, Jason heard, rather than saw, Adrian stretch out on his stomach at the slit that was the cave's entrance. He could see the outline of the Scot studying his house with the nightscope. "Dinna take 'em long."

Jason felt the glass pushed into his hand. At first he saw little other than the disconcerting hues of green and black produced by concentration of ambient light. As he watched, the colors assumed the recognizable shapes of the house, trees, and rocks. He saw nothing that did not belong.

"Over by the far corner of the house," Adrian whispered.

There was a blur of monochromatic green as Jason shifted to his right. At first he observed nothing that wasn't part of the landscape.

Then something moved, a ghostly flicker edging toward the front of the house. Then another. Jason made a minute adjustment to the scope, and several images jumped out of the background with starling clarity.

"Six of them, by my count," he whispered to Adrian, although the distance would have prevented the intruders from hearing anything less than a shout. "The usual AK-47s. Looks like they're deploying to cover all windows and doors. How'd they get here, anyway? I didn't hear a car."

"You wouldn't. These hills can block sound sometimes, amplify it at others."

Adrian was reaching for the return of the scope.

Jason took one last look. "One of 'em has the right part of his face bandaged, all right. Can't be sure, but I think he's the one we ran into in Sicily."

"Th' one w' th' bandage, he's the leader," Adrian observed. "Tellin' 'em to search th' house."

It took the new arrivals only a few minutes to ascertain that no one was home.

A few minutes later, Jason caught a snatch of a voice, although he couldn't make out the words. "What's happening now?"

"They dinna find us in th' house, an' now the man with th' bandage, he's pointin' in different directions, tellin' 'em to search for us, I'll wager."

From behind him, Jason heard an intake of breath, a gasp. He could not tell if it was Maria or Clare. It was more for their benefit than Adrian's that he said, "They'll have a tough time finding us here."

"Aye, laddie, a tough time indeed, long's we keep quiet and our heads down."

"And even if they do, this is as perfect a shelter as we could want. It'll take a high-explosive device to get to us here."

"Don' be too sure o' that. A few shots through the slit here in front an' the ricochet'd be like grenade fragments off these stone walls. Best we lie low like a fox in his den till th' hounds have tired."

Jason checked the luminescent face of his watch, surprised to note that only fifteen minutes had passed since they'd fled the house. He watched that fifteen stretch into twenty, then thirty. Waiting for action was one of the most difficult things in Jason's line of work. There was nothing to do but think, and thinking frequently complicated the problem.

Jason slid his sleeve over the watch's face and stared into darkness.

Minutes, an hour later, he heard footsteps crunching on the rocky soil outside. One, no, two men were following a course that would lead them straight to the cave.

Jason thumbed the SIG Sauer's safety.

Adrian backed farther inside, making sure that no errant source of light gave them away by reflecting from the nightscope.

Jason felt someone beside him, Maria. He gave her hand a reassuring squeeze and she would not let go, her grip tense and damp. Even so, Jason took pleasure from her touch.

Looking up toward the entrance, he could see them now, or at least, he thought he could make out two sets of legs from the waist down. Two ill-defined masses of darkness against a slightly less dark night. One moved slightly, the activity quite clear against the pinpricks of stars in the dome of the ink black sky. One said something, low, guttural words Jason could not hear clearly, and the two sets of legs moved off to his left, the sounds of grinding rocks and gravel growing gradually dimmer.

A hand, not Maria's, tugged at his sleeve.

"May as well get some sleep, laddie," Adrian whispered into his ear. "I'd bet a month's pay they'll not be leavin' us till they're sure we're gone. I'll stand a three-hour watch, then wake you."

Like any seasoned combat soldier, Jason took an opportunity to sleep whenever it presented itself. Head on his hands, he was breathing deeply in less than a minute. His sleep was light, the sort that gave rest but was not so deep he could not come instantly awake. He pretended not to be awakened when Maria lifted his head and placed it in her lap.

CHAPTER TWENTY-FIVE

Silanus, Sardinia
Dawn, the next day

The morning did not begin with a slow grayness. Instead, the red of a cardinal's robe streaked the eastern sky momentarily before buttery light began to chase the night from the far ridge. In an instant of déjà vu, Jason was with Laurin, watching the sun climb to the lip of the bowl that was Aspen, Colorado. He had been so absorbed in the colors, he had forgone the ski slopes that morning for an opportunity to capture the scene on canvas.

Laurin. The places they had shared.

As always, the emptiness was filled with a sense of rage, a fury illogicaly directed at the men from whom he was hiding.

In minutes the cave would be in full daylight. Slipping out of the entrance, Jason used the last of the shadows to tend to bodily functions before returning to a refuge without comfort facilities.

Maria had much the same needs, and he met her as he entered. He pointed to the valley below that was quickly filling with daylight. "Hurry."

She started to reply, a sharp remark, he guessed, thought better of it, and disappeared behind a nearby boulder.

Not far below, somewhere near Adrian's chicken coop, a rooster belatedly proclaimed what was already fact.

Carefully holding his weapon behind him rather than risk an errant reflection of the early sun, Jason stretched. Muscles, including some he had temporarily forgotten, ached from sleeping on the rocky floor. He winced as he rotated his neck in a vain hope of working out the soreness. He gave up on the stiffness going away anytime soon and he surveyed the farm below.

Two men in military fatigues were poorly concealed beside the house's door. Two more were covering the approach up the driveway. Assuming he and Adrian had seen them all last night, that left two unaccounted for. Jason guessed they would be concealed somewhere along the turnoff from the road to the house. Or on the ridge behind the cave. Or both.

Or neither.

"No tellin' where th' sods might be." Adrian had come up behind him, one military mind reading another. "Could be that we dinna know exactly how many of them there are."

"I thought of that," Jason said, not taking his eyes from the view in front. "Question is, how long do they plan to stay?"

Adrian shook his head. "Long as they want, I'd think, waitin' for us to come back home. Folks 'round here pretty much mind their own affairs rather than constantly botherin' their neighbors. Could be a month or so 'fore anyone comes 'round."

"You've got your cell phone, right? You could call the cops," Jason suggested.

"Not in here. These rocks shield us from satellite contact. We might try calling the nearest carabiniere, about a hundred kilometers away, if we can get outside tonight and risk being overheard."

Jason had a better idea. "I'd as soon not have to answer the questions they'd ask, and I'm not sure how much scrutiny my papers will take. Tell you what—if they're still down there by dark, I have another way to handle it."

If Adrian had doubts about that, he didn't show them.

The rest of the morning was spent alternating watches from the cave's mouth.

Shortly after noon, Maria observed, "They are still searching for us, looking behind every rock, checking out every building. Except one."

Jason snorted derisively. "And that one is the pigsty."

Maria didn't take her eyes from the men below. "And that would be because . . . ?"

Jason shrugged. "They may well know those pigs would go for them. Plus, how eager would you be to wade through pig slop up to your knees?"

Surprisingly, Maria smiled, the first time since leaving Sicily. "I thought these people were nature lovers. Pig shit is part of nature, is it not?"

GET UP TO 4 FREE BOOKS!

You can have the best fiction delivered to your door for less than what you'd pay in a bookstore or online—only $4.25 a book! Sign up for our book clubs today, and we'll send you **FREE* BOOKS** just for trying it out...**with no obligation to buy, ever!**

LEISURE HORROR BOOK CLUB

With more award-winning horror authors than any other publisher, it's easy to see why CNN.com says "Leisure Books has been leading the way in paperback horror novels." Your shipments will include authors such as RICHARD LAYMON, DOUGLAS CLEGG, JACK KETCHUM, MARY ANN MITCHELL, and many more.

LEISURE THRILLER BOOK CLUB

If you love fast-paced page-turners, you won't want to miss any of the books in Leisure's thriller line. Filled with gripping tension and edge-of-your-seat excitement, these titles feature everything from psychological suspense to legal thrillers to police procedurals and more!

As a book club member you also receive the following special benefits:

- **30% OFF all orders through our website & telecenter!**
- **Exclusive access to special discounts!**
- **Convenient home delivery and 10 days to return any books you don't want to keep.**

There is no minimum number of books to buy, and you may cancel membership at any time. See back to sign up!

*Please include $2.00 for shipping and handling.

YES! ☐

Sign me up for the Leisure Horror Book Club and send my TWO FREE BOOKS! If I choose to stay in the club, I will pay only $8.50* each month, a savings of $5.48!

YES! ☐

Sign me up for the Leisure Thriller Book Club and send my TWO FREE BOOKS! If I choose to stay in the club, I will pay only $8.50* each month, a savings of $5.48!

NAME: _____

ADDRESS: _____

_____

TELEPHONE: _____

E-MAIL: _____

☐ **I WANT TO PAY BY CREDIT CARD.**

☐ VISA ☐ MasterCard ☐ DISCOVER

ACCOUNT #: _____

EXPIRATION DATE: _____

SIGNATURE: _____

Send this card along with $2.00 shipping & handling for each club you wish to join, to:

Horror/Thriller Book Clubs
1 Mechanic Street
Norwalk, CT 06850-3431

Or fax (must include credit card information!) to: 610.995.9274. You can also sign up online at www.dorchesterpub.com.

*Plus $2.00 for shipping. Offer open to residents of the U.S. and Canada only. Canadian residents please call 1.800.481.9191 for pricing information.

If under 18, a parent or guardian must sign. Terms, prices and conditions subject to change. Subscription subject to acceptance. Dorchester Publishing reserves the right to reject any order or cancel any subscription.

CHAPTER TWENTY-SIX

Silanus, Sardinia
That night

The day seemed interminable, as long as those days Jason had lain in hiding before a night operation. Only this time he had little equipment to check and recheck to pass the endless hours. Jason and Adrian had decided that only one person at a time should keep watch, the other three remaining invisible in the cavern's recesses. Whether caused by darkness or apprehension, anxiety in the cave had reduced conversation to monosyllabic whispers and grunts. Even so, Jason feared they might be overheard by an unseen prowler.

When evening's shadows finally flowed across the small valley, they brought relief to the tension like flotsam on an incoming tide.

Twenty minutes after the first star winked on, Adrian surveyed the area with the nightscope. "Sodding rotters still surrounding the house, far as I can see. Now's as good a time as any for whatever you plan to lay on."

Jason retreated to the far reach of the cave, a flashlight in one hand, his BlackBerry in the other.

"You canna get satellite reception back there," Adrian reminded him.

"Don't have to. I'm inputing a text message. Once I'm done, I'll step outside and send it."

Adrian cocked his head. "An' jus' to whom would you be sendin' such a message, the U.S. Marines?"

Jason's grin was visible in the flashlight reflecting from the stone. "Close guess."

"An' those blokes down there." Adrian jerked his head toward the cave's entrance. "You're betting they have no way of intercepting or tracing . . . ?"

"Omnidirectional. If they had such equipment, it would tell them the message came from all three hundred sixty degrees. Second, transmission time to the satellite is in the nanoseconds, less time than it takes a lightbulb to go dark when you turn off the switch. Someone staring at a direction finder wouldn't even have time to see the indicator move. Finally, it's encrypted. Anyone listening in would hear only a single beep."

Adrian's eyebrows arched. "All this in a simple Black-Berry?"

"It only looks like one."

Finished, Jason moved to the front of the cave.

"Be careful," Maria whispered as he crept by.

"I'm not even going all the way out," Jason said, extending an arm through the opening. "There, done."

"That quick?" she asked.

CHAPTER TWENTY-SEVEN

Aboard the USS Carney *(DDG 67)*
Eastern Mediterranean
Ninety minutes later

PO 2d Class Shawana Davis had a tough choice to make: her enlistment would be up in three months, and the navy would provide a substantial sum for tuition to any of the three colleges to which she had been accepted. Conversely, she had come to like her life in the military. It was something very different from the endless flat fields of dusty clay where soybean field met soybean field, where being able to buy something you wanted depended on the harvests and excitement was defined by whatever movie was on HBO. The job offered a genuine chance of advancement, too, not some bogus showcase job where the occupant's chief value was to demonstrate the company's commitment to equal opportunity for women and minorities. Any promotion she got in the navy would be one she earned.

She liked that, relying on ability rather than her sex or race, to get ahead.

She also liked the prospect of being not only the first

person in her family to graduate from high school, but the first from college, too.

Tough choice.

What if she—

There was a loud buzz that startled her before she realized the ship was receiving a message. Unusual for this time of day—must be important. As the sole person on duty in the communications room, she watched an incomprehensible series of letters and numbers march across the screen. In the old days—at least, according to the old war movies she loved—the message would have clattered through the printer louder than two skeletons making it on a tin roof. Now, only the buzzer alerted her to incoming traffic.

She waited for the characters to stop and then picked up a phone on the bulkhead next to her station just below the bridge. She waited a second or two before Lieutenant (J.G.) Wade, tonight's duty officer, picked up.

He must have been daydreaming, too. Woolgathering, her daddy would have called it. Easy enough to do when the only sounds were the rhythmic throbbing of the engines and swish of the hull parting a flat sea.

His voice sounded as though she had woken him up. "Wade."

He didn't have to identify himself. His drawl was right out of North Carolina's tobacco fields.

"Sir," Shawana said, "incoming message received."

"From battle group, fleet?"

Shawana frowned and held her head back from the screen as if that might answer the question. "Don't think so, no, sir. Copy to fleet and battle group, but the communication appears be code ten."

There was an audible intake of breath. "The navy department? Direct to the *Carney*?"

"Looks like it, sir."

Thank you, Davis. I'll be right down."

The immediate clang of hard leather on metal stairs

made good on the promise. Less than fifteen seconds later, Lt. (J.G.) Robert Lee Wade was looking over her shoulder. From his breath, Shawana guessed the spaghetti sauce in the officers' mess had been heavy on the garlic.

"That's something I've never heard of," he said. "Why would Washington communicate directly with a guided missile destroyer instead of going through channels?"

"Maybe somebody's in a hurry," Shawana suggested. "Maybe you ought to get this to the captain on the double . . . sir."

"You may be right, Davis. I've never seen that particular cipher before."

Neither had she, but she said nothing as he ripped the page from the printer and bolted for the companionway.

It took Cmdr. Edward Simms a full ten minutes of playing with his encryption computer to decode the message, and another ten to confirm he had done it correctly the first time.

"Balls!" he said to no one in particular. "This makes no sense at all."

The other four men in the room, Wade and the three men who had been playing bridge with the ship's captain, looked at one another before one said, "It's from Washington. It doesn't have to make sense."

Old joke. More truth than humor.

Simms held the offending paper up to the light as though there might be a secret message in light-sensitive ink. "We're to program the specified target location into one of those experimental aircraft, launch, and recover it."

"But sir," one of the men protested, "We have no armament for the Thing, only dummy bombs to test its stability and accuracy."

"The Thing" was the nickname the *Carney*'s crew had given the CRW (canard rotor/wing) X50A UAB (unmanned aircraft, bomber). The X designated the machine experimental. As one wag had noted, it looked like a helicopter and a Piper Cub had had sex with a resulting miscarriage. It had wings and propeller at the rear, but also rotor blades above. The aircraft had vertical takeoff and landing capacity, making it able to act as either an attack or observation vehicle. Its composite skin made it a poor radar target even if it should climb higher than the terrain-hugging altitude suggested by the bulbous radome at the front end. The only thing in general agreement was that it was the ugliest object in the military since, along with the front parts, the rear end of mules had been retired.

"I don't get it," someone else piped up. "Launch an experimental drone to drop phony bombs?"

"You don't have to get it," Simms said, studying the map posted on the bulkhead. "It's an order. Not ours to question who or why, et cetera. It is ours to confirm with fleet, however."

Simms knew too many horror stories where careers had been sunk by following unusual orders outside the chain of command, only to have some REMF (rear echelon motherfucker) deny issuing such orders when the excrement was being distributed by the ventilating device. Confirmed orders were undeniable orders. Undeniable orders covered one's ass nicely. He wasn't about to risk having his nineteen years end in front of a court-martial.

"Say," the captain continued, "look at these coordinates. We're conducting a phony strike on Italian territory, Sardinia, to be exact."

"Perhaps that's why Washington wants to use the Thing. Suppose it involves some sort of spook operation. The plane doesn't officially exist, being as how it's experimental. They could deny responsibility under adverse circumstances."

Simms glared at his junior officer. "Wade, you sound like a politician."

It was not a compliment.

CHAPTER TWENTY-EIGHT

Silanus, Sardinia
Three hours later

Jason had insisted everyone gather up whatever few possessions they had brought to the cave and be ready for a speedy departure.

"Y' tellin' us the cavalry's gonna come chargin' o'er yon hill?" Adrian had asked, only half joking.

"Something like that," Jason had replied enigmatically.

"Exactly what will happen?" Maria wanted to know.

"I'm not sure," Jason confessed. "I just know we're gonna have to move in a—"

He was interrupted by a flash of light. Half a second later, a sound like a thunder reached the cave. All four peered out of the entrance to see smoke rising from a patch of ground near the house. Fifty feet away, a second burst was followed by the same roar and dense smoke.

Adrian was chuckling. "Practice bombs! Little noise, lots of smoke to show where the thing hit. 'Less a man knew, he'd think he was being assaulted by ground forces."

Against the billowing smoke, additional flickers silhouetted men running in every direction, firing at imagined attackers. One or two bullets whined off the rock at the entrance to the cave.

"We'll never have a better shot at it," Jason said, rolling out onto the rocky ground. "Let's go!"

With his hand on Maria's elbow, Jason dashed up the hill, followed by Adrian and Clare.

It must have been the loose pebbles and scree that cascaded from each hurried step that drew the attention of the ecoterrorists below. First one shot, then two, then a fusillade split the air above their heads.

Maria moaned in fear.

"Bloody sods dinna know where we are, just shooting at th' sound," Adrian puffed.

Maria ducked her head as though she might be able to dodge a stray bullet. "They do not have to know if they hit us."

As they crested the edge of the gully where the car was hidden, Adrian took the lead. He seemed to know their position from memory rather than whatever he could see with the nightscope. The steep hills blocked all but the stars directly overhead. It seemed to Jason they had been on this trek for hours, although his watch told him they had left the safety of the cave only minutes before.

Behind them, the sound of both rifle fire and practice bombs had stopped. Apparently, Eglov and company had realized they were not under any serious attack.

A glimmer of light on metal told Jason they had arrived at the place they had left the Volvo.

Adrian opened the driver's door and swiftly disabled the interior light. "Briskly, now."

The whine of a nearby rifle shot suggested they had not been quick enough.

"Somebody saw the courtesy light," Jason surmised, piling into the backseat just as the rear windshield became a spiderweb of cracked glass.

"Never mind," Adrian said, pulling his wife in beside him. "We'll be outta here . . ."

The sentence died with the empty clicking of the car's solenoid and the thump of two more rounds hitting sheet metal.

"Jesus wept!" Adrian was back out of the car, handing the Sten to Jason through an open window. "Spiteful ol' bitch! She picks a hell of a time to demand attention!"

Jason was considerably more interested in getting the Volvo going than attributing malevolent intent to it. He was using the butt of the machine gun to clear the remaining glass from the back window so he could see to shoot if necessary. "If you can't get her started, now's the time to run for it. They don't see us yet, but that interior light gave somebody the general location."

As if to verify the observation, a bullet kicked up pebbles as Adrian slammed the hood down. "Give 'er a try, Mother!"

Clare leaned across the seat and tried the key. The feminine touch was no more successful.

Jason opened his door. "Hey, you saved over a hundred euros, remember?"

"An' where's Antonio when you need him?" grunted Adrian.

"Not exactly the time to play mechanic, Adrian. We need to make a run for it."

"I dinna think so. In th' dark you'd na' be able to follow me. You'd be lost in five minutes, left to the tender mercies of our friends back there once the sun came up."

"So, what the hell do you suggest?"

Adrian leaned against the post of the open driver's door. "I suggest you bloody push on t' other side. There's a steep swale a few yards away an' we might be able to jump 'er off."

There was no time for argument. Jason put his shoulder against the car door, his feet scrabbling in the loose, rocky soil. The car didn't budge, and he saw one, two muzzle flashes as their opponents drew closer. Fortunately, the shots were still wild.

They wouldn't be much longer.

"Give 'er a shove, now." Adrian gasped. "On th' count o' three. One, two . . ."

The Volvo seemed to move forward a few inches before rolling back, but at least a ton or so of inertia had been overcome.

Jason ducked as a bullet sang by, too close for his liking. Ignoring a second, he heaved again.

This time the car began moving ahead, tires grinding at glacial speed against loose dirt and rocks.

"Should we get out?" Clare wanted to know.

"Nah. We get this thin' goin', there'll be na' time to stop for you," Adrian puffed.

If *we get it going.*

The Volvo was picking up speed, reaching the pace of a steady walk. A bullet buzzed past Jason's ear like an angry bee.

"Any chance that lot has access to night-vision equipment?" Adrian panted.

Jason was thinking the same thing. "Who knows?"

The automobile was now moving at the velocity of an octogenarian's brisk walk as four more shots sprayed Jason with biting, stinging dirt. "But I'd say it's a definite possibility. We're not in accurate range of the AK-47s they carry."

"When will we be?" Maria's voice asked from the floor of the backseat.

"No time soon, I hope, lassie. Jason, jump in."

This was going to be it. Either the balky Volvo cranked when Adrian popped the clutch or they had lost valuable time trying to escape. At least they had the chance, Jason thought. Had the Volvo an automatic transmission, there would have been no possibility of using the car's own motion to replace the starter motor.

The Volvo shuddered and jerked, its tires skidding on the dirt, then stopped.

Nothing.

"Not fast enough yet. We'll give 'er a go again," Adrian said with unwarranted optimism. "Jason, kin ye fend those lads off a bit?"

The Sten wasn't known for its accuracy at any sort of range, and Jason would have cheerfully exchanged the silencer for a flash suppressor. A shot would be hard to trace by sound in these hills, but the fire from the muzzle would pinpoint their location.

Jason rested the machine gun on the roof of the automobile and flicked the selector to single fire. "Soon's there's a chance of hittin' anything. How 'bout you get this buggy going?"

His answer was another shuddering jerk as Adrian popped the clutch again. This time the effort was rewarded with the sound of the engine. The Volvo fishtailed with the sudden application of power, steadied, then lurched forward. Jason fired two or three rounds behind them before jumping into the rear seat. Unlikely he would hit anyone, but it served notice to their pursuers to keep their distance.

"There's a paved road coupla kilometers on," Adrian announced. "We get there—"

The Volvo hit a bank, lifting the right wheels.

"If you dinna turn on the headlights, we'll na' make it to the paved road," Clare observed. "Easy to run right inta the edge o' the' combe w'out seein' it."

"She's right," Jason observed. "We're at the edge of their range, anyway. More chance of us crashing into something or running over a cliff than getting hit."

The road in front of them was suddenly visible in the car's lights. Jason marveled that they had not smashed the radiator against one of the boulders lining the rocky trail like irregularly spaced sentries. Or hit the unforgiving rock that, in several spots, towered above the path. This

would have been difficult four-wheel-drive territory. That
the Volvo had not left its oil pan or transmission housing
along the way had to be the sheerest of luck.

"'Ere we be." Adrian was turning onto what at first
looked like a continuation of the uneven path they had followed. Closer observation revealed dirt-colored pavement,
cement or asphalt, Jason couldn't be sure. Whatever the
material, it served to join a series of tooth-loosening pot-
holes.

At least here there was small chance of unexpectedly
hitting a stone larger than the car. As it was, the road was
carved from the hills that formed the spine of the island, a
serpentine, narrow two-lane that looked barely wide
enough for two medium-size vehicles to pass.

Over Adrian's shoulder, Jason could see the speedome-
ter wavering around eighty-five kilometers, less than fifty
miles an hour. Even so, he nearly hit the headliner with
each bounce.

He tightened his seat belt to the limit, noticing Maria
doing the same.

Through teeth clenched for fear of biting his tongue, Jason asked, "Where're we going?"

"Cagliari," Adrian answered, not taking his eyes off
the road.

"Where?"

"Cagliari," Maria said. "Provençal capital. Italian naval
base."

"Only town of any real size on the island," Adrian
added. "Figgered you could head to wherever you were
goin' and I could drop Mother off, send her home to visit
with the wee grandchildren back in Scotland until all this
blows over."

"You need to figger again," Clare said. "I'll not be
shipped off like some mail-order parcel, not after th' years
I spent waitin' for you while you were in the service,
waitin' to see if you came home upright or in a box."

"But y' kenna come along," Adrian argued. "There's people back there mean us all harm."

"I'm no more in danger than th' lass," she said, referring to Maria.

Swell.

Barely escaped from Eglov's killers and Jason was listening to a domestic argument that sounded like which child would get to use the sole ticket to the county fair.

He was about to speak up, thank Adrian for his implicit offer to help, and decline, when the interior of the Volvo was filled with light from behind.

"Jesus wept!" Adrian grunted. "You'd think this was the bleedin' M4. Somebody's drivin' way too fast."

It didn't take a clairvoyant to guess who.

Jason guessed Eglov and his men had reconnoitered the area well enough to know the paved road was the likely, if not only, escape route. They had also obtained a car with a lot more power than the aging Volvo. It was gaining quickly, already well within range of the AK-47s.

"Anywhere we could turn off, maybe lose them?" Jason asked.

"Na' but winding road for the next ten kilometers," came the reply.

A burst of gunfire, this time close enough to hear, came from the right front of the pursuing car and went wide right.

Jason involuntarily ducked.

The swaying, bucking motion of fast travel made any sort of accurate shooting unlikely. Whether the silver-bullet-firing six-guns from Silver's back by the Lone Ranger or a Walther PPK from a speeding Aston Martin driven by James Bond, a hit was the result of far more luck than skill. The sudden shifts in wind, direction, and elevation all made a moving gunfight more spectacular than deadly.

Nonetheless, Jason felt compelled to fire a few shots in return, with equal lack of result.

"They'll be right up beside us in minutes," Jason observed. "Got any ideas?"

Adrian nodded. "Aye. In a moment we'll reach a wee straight. Remember the bootleg?"

Jason did.

He sat back down in the seat to cinch his seat belt tighter. "Ladies, I'd make sure your seat harness is supersecure."

"Jesus!"

The sudden expletive made Jason forget his seat belt.

The edge of the headlights was reflecting from a truck pulled across both lanes of the narrow road.

The Eco men must have had a backup crew farther down the road, one that could commandeer the truck now effectively hemming the Volvo in. They also could not have picked a better spot: to the right was sheer wall, to the left the abyss.

Adrian slowed as though to surrender. Jason knew what was coming and hoped Clare and Maria had followed his suggestions to make themselves secure.

"We have enough room?" Jason asked, instantly wishing he had kept his concern to himself.

"Na' matter," Adrian said, keeping an eye on the rearview mirror as the car behind closed the gap. "Goin' over th' edge's better 'n what those sods have in mind for us."

At a point no more than fifty feet from the truck, Adrian hit the gas, momentarily gaining on the surprised driver of the pursuing car. Just as the gap started to close again, Adrian stood violently on the brake, at the same time snatching the wheel toward the emptiness of the road's outer edge.

The snap of the steering mechanism broke any adhesion between rubber tire and paved road. At the same time, centrifugal force threw the automobile's rear end outward, causing a spin.

"Chicago! Al Capone!" Adrian chortled. "Elliot Ness!"

The maneuver had its origins in Prohibition bootleggers' moonshine-filled cars dodging pursuing revenue agents, one of a number of driving tactics taught in commando training worldwide, perhaps the only one with truly American roots. Although Jason suspected the trick was more at home on the winding dirt roads of Appalachia than the streets of Al Capone's Chicago, he had to admit Adrian executed it perfectly.

At the exact moment the car was facing the opposite direction, Adrian hit the accelerator, regaining traction, and the Volvo leaped like a springing cat in the direction from which it just come. Jason had only an instant to see astonished faces as they whizzed past the chasing vehicle.

Unable to stop or turn so unexpectedly, the car that had been behind—it looked like an older Mercedes as it flashed past—skidded into a sideways drift. For an instant the two left wheels pawed empty air, and Jason thought it might roll over.

But there was no time for a roll. Instead, Mercedes met truck with a crash of splintering glass and tearing sheet metal.

"Hold it; stop!" Jason yelled.

Before the Volvo was entirely still, Jason bolted from the rear, dashing toward the mass of metal that was hissing and steaming like the death throes of some mythical dragon.

Jason sprayed the carnage with nine-millimeter bullets until the Sten's firing pin clicked on an empty chamber and the barrel burned his hand through the canvas cover.

Slamming another clip into the weapon, he took two steps forward before he was restrained by Adrian's hand on his shoulder.

"No time to put a bullet in each of 'em, laddie. We canna ken if there's more about. Best we make our way while we can."

Jason reluctantly agreed with the wisdom of the observation, if not the sentiment. He would prefer not to chance facing any survivors later, survivors who would be less than appreciative of his bounty in letting them live.

CHAPTER TWENTY-NINE

Il Giardino de Mare Risorte
Sardinia
The next afternoon

After the highway was effectively blocked by the collision, Adrian had been forced to reverse course, taking an all-night alternate route to put a protesting Clare on a flight to Edinburgh via Rome and London. Like it or not, she would visit with her grandchildren for a few weeks.

Jason was as happy to have the Scot join him as Adrian was to see action once again. The pastoral life, though simpler and potentially longer, lacked excitement, the addictive narcotic from which Adrian had not entirely withdrawn since his retirement from SAS. Neither man knew what to do with Maria, a question largely mooted by her stubborn refusal to join Clare out of harm's way, and the fact that she would provide the introduction to Dr. Calligini as well as translate the questions Jason had.

The one thing the remaining three had agreed upon was that a couple drew far less attention than two men and a woman. Adrian had set out for Turin while Jason and Maria would follow in a day or so.

Jason and Maria spent a day on the Costa Smeralda, on Sardinia's northeastern coast. It was, Maria informed him, the ritziest part of the island. The scalloped coastline consisted of hundreds of small stretches of narrow beaches, each containing one or more resort hotels. Many were so close together that "ocean view" consisted of craning one's neck left or right even to glimpse the water between buildings. The beach, the water, and the decor of the Holiday Inn–knockoff hotel were interchangeable with south Florida, if slightly less tacky. The major difference was that even the Sunshine State's major hotels would have blanched at prices rivaling the French Riviera.

In a bikini from one of the hotel's several overpriced shops, Maria drew less than covert glances from male vacationers whose chubby wives and loud children were also reminiscent of Florida. Jason watched her tan on the beach while he stretched out on a lounge, where he could watch the single path from the hotel.

He was the only sunbather wearing a shirt. He was also probably the only one with a pistol tucked into the waist of his swimming trunks.

In the late afternoon, Maria produced another of her Hermès scarfs, this one in brown and gold depicting horses' heads, riding whips, bridles, and other stable gear Jason didn't recognize. He had no idea how it had survived the last few days, and even less where it had been.

Tying two corners around her neck, she turned for him to knot the remaining ends behind her back. "See, a backless blouse."

Just as he had done for Laurin a hundred times.

"How very clever," he said.

She turned before he had finished, startling him. "You don't sound surprised. Maybe you tied some other woman's scarf for her."

"Maybe."

She started to say something, thought better of it, and

nestled against him like a puppy seeking warmth from its
mother. "I'm getting chilly. Let's go in."

He would have preferred the touch of her body against
his to any comfort inside. Strands of her hair tickled his
nose pleasantly. Instead of the smell of salt water, her skin
had a musky, pleasant odor that was not the residue of her
tanning lotion.

He started to put an arm around her shoulder and
stopped in midair. He wasn't here for romance and neither
was she. Maria, after all, had voiced the request that had
made the eyebrows of the hotel's otherwise circumspect
desk clerk give a slight quiver of surprise: Mrs. William
Rugger of Tampa, Florida, insisted on *una camera con
due letti*, a double room, an accommodation usually requested by European families traveling on a budget.

Jason had pointed out that any variation on the norm
was potentially dangerous. Maria had countered that the
danger of sharing a bed was more than potential.

Jason was well aware of the futility of arguing with a
woman: an apparent victory simply meant the fight wasn't
over.

Besides, they would be staying only a single night, two
at the most.

Jason struggled up from the lounge with a mixture of
disappointment that a possible romantic moment had
slipped away and relief at its escape. He led the way to the
pink stucco building and down a hallway with wallpaper
exhibiting blue and pink seashells. Uncharacteristically,
Maria chatted aimlessly: the quality of the beach, the
warmth of the water.

He stopped when he reached the door of their room.
Squatting, he surveyed the doorknob.

"Looking for fingerprints?"

He shook his head as he stood. "Nope. When we left I
used spit to stick a hair between the frame and door. It's
still there."

It took her a moment before she nodded her head. "If anyone had gotten into our room . . ."

"We'd know about it," he finished, pushing the door open.

She stood in the hall. "You think . . . ?"

"I think it pays to be careful."

She stepped across the threshold behind him, shoving the door shut. "Playing spies is fun for just so long. Yesterday when those people started shooting at us, I thought . . ."

Her lips quivered and a single tear tracked down her cheek, the trickle before the dam broke. She covered her face with her hands, and her shoulders heaved. Between sobs, she blurted, "I hate acting like . . . like such a weak person." She hiccupped. "But I cannot take it, the killing, the brutality of . . ."

Impulsively, Jason wrapped his arms around her. He tried to think of something comforting to say but couldn't come up with anything, only a very hollow, "It'll be okay, really. Everything will be fine. . . ."

She pushed off against his chest, regarding him with red-rimmed eyes. "It will *not* be okay! You and those, those . . . people!" She spit the word as though it were a curse. "You and they will keep it up until you are all dead, and God help anyone who gets between you! And for what? Some macho, male bullshit!"

He was tempted to point out that opposing the use of deadly force to impose environmental views was hardly a personal vendetta. He doubted the observation would do much good.

Her eyes were locked onto his. "Violence only makes for more violence. Do you not understand? Killing one another is not the way to resolve differences!"

Tell that to Laurin, he thought. But he said, "Think, Maria. Both the, er, incidents began by them attacking us."

She used a forearm to wipe her eyes, smearing mascara and leaving dark areas under her eyes like a raccoon. "Jason, one side has to stop, to try to reason with the other. Can you not understand?"

He understood perfectly. One didn't reason with rabid dogs, a life-form he held in a great deal more esteem than fanatics. A dog didn't choose to go mad.

She sniffed and gave voice to the perennial pacifist platitude: "War is not the answer."

Depends on the question.

"Oh, Jason," she said with an imploring look, "I am frightened. I've never been shot at before, never had people want to kill me. It is not a good feeling."

No shit.

It might have been her look of desolation, of utter helplessness, or it might been something more biological; Jason never knew nor cared. He took her back into his arms, squeezing her close. His lips brushed hers. For an instant she drew back and then pressed her mouth against his.

In seconds clothes were flying and the two were writhing on a bed amid moans, grunts, and sounds defying description.

Later, Jason lay on his back, watching the room's Venetian blinds paint zebra stripes on Maria's bare back as she snuggled into the hollow of his armpit. This was not the first time since Laurin's death he had found sexual release, but it was the first time he had felt no guilt, no sense of betrayal.

Suddenly, he realized he had no independent recollection of his wife's face. He could recall thousands of shared incidents, but every time she appeared in his memory, he saw a face from one of many photographs. Maybe he was finally letting go; maybe Laurin was finding peace.

Maybe . . .

A sharp rap on the door sprang him out of bed, his hand reaching for the SIG Sauer in its holster.

Weapon in hand and back against the wall next to the door, he nodded to Maria. "Ask who it is."

Maria rattled off a question in Italian. A woman's voice, muffled by the door, replied.

"The maid. She wants to know if we want the beds turned down."

Jason let out a deep breath he had not known he had taken. "Later."

As he returned to the rumpled bed, Maria began to weep again, silent tears leaving shiny trails on each cheek.

Jason sat beside her, reaching out.

She pushed him away. "No."

"But . . . ?"

"Jason, I care for you—care for you a lot more than I ever wanted to."

"And I you," he admitted. "That's a reason to cry?"

She nodded wearily. "No matter how I feel about you, Jason, we are finished after I've helped you with Dr. Calligini as I said I would."

"But—"

She put a finger across his lips. "It will not be easy getting over you, Jason. I do not . . . what did we used to say in America? I do not fall for guys that often. I might even learn to accept what you do, even if it makes me sick. Even sicker because you enjoy it. Some Old Testament sense of vengeance, I suppose. I gave up on one man because he was a cheat, a liar. I might learn to accept what you do, but I cannot bear to be there for you when you do not outdraw the other fellow at the OK Corral, the time when you do not see it coming."

"Maria—"

She silenced him with a kiss as her hands reached for his groin.

The next day they rented a car and drove to Palau, a small port town a few kilometers north. Seated in front of a trattoria across the tree-lined street from the crescent-shaped harbor, they lunched on stewed baby octopus washed down by an astringent white wine that originated in the nearby hills. They watched ships come and go.

A table away, four young men in navy whites made no

effort to disguise their admiration of the pretty woman
seated with the American. Several made remarks, the tone
of which Jason understood, if not the words. Just as Jason
was wondering whether chivalry required him to flatten
each of them, Maria turned. Radiating charm, she spoke
in machine-gun Italian. The sailors' faces went from surprise to embarrassment. They quickly finished their beers
and left.

"What the hell did you say?" Jason wanted to know.

Maria tossed her head, treating him to that Wife of Bath
smile. "I told them their mothers would be ashamed of
them for saying things about a woman closer to her age
than theirs. Italian men always worry what Mama might
think. Even long after she is dead."

"Even if they don't live with her anymore?"

As an Italian, Maria was fully aware that many Italian
men never left, simply bringing a wife to their childhood
home.

"They are from that ship." She pointed toward the harbor where a white, military-looking ship rode at anchor.
"The new Italian navy."

Jason nodded. "No doubt equipped with a glass bottom
so they can see the old Italian navy."

He ducked the half loaf of bread she threw at him.

After lunch, they took the ferry across the Golfo dell'
Asinara to empty, wooded hills. A single road led to the
crest that held the tomb of the unifier of Italy, Giuseppe
Garibaldi. People stood in line at souvenir and refresh-
ment stands to enter the small building. Instead, Maria led
Jason up a slight rise and into a rare copse of dense foliage.

"Wha . . . ?"

He never finished the question; her lips were pressed
too tightly against his. Oblivious to the crowd screened by
folage only fifty feet or so away, they made love even more
passionately than the night before.

Afterward, as they returned to the parking lot, Jason

was certain some of the people were staring at them. If so, Maria didn't notice.

They made the ferry from Cagliari to Naples with only minutes to spare. During the drive, she pointedly changed the subject whenever he mentioned any future beyond the next few days.

JOURNAL OF SEVERENUS TACTUS

I know not how many days I remained in the tiny painted room, my only companions my fears and such spirits as might visit. On two occasions, cowled priests entered my cell to inquire as to my father, the more easily to summon his shade.[1]

From the darkness, I knew it was early morning when two young boys brought me forth from the painted room to sacrifice a ewe. By the light of a torch, a priest examined the liver of the animal and pronounced the signs to be favorable. I was removed to another room, this one much larger, where I was bathed in herb-scented water[2] and given peculiar-tasting drinks I did not recognize.

Once so purified, I was clad in a white toga and my hair bound with white ribbon. I was girded with a belt with a bronze sword and given a golden branch of mistletoe to carry in my hand.[3] To my surprise, the ancient crone, the Sibyl herself, appeared, robed in scarlet, to guide me on my journey.

Behind us came the priests, dressed in black with pointed headdresses and only slits through which to see. They drove the livestock I had purchased to be sacrificed at various stages.

We had gone but a short way along a dark and descending pathway when we reached the Dividing of the Ways. To the left went a return to the world, should I choose it. To the right, the final descent into Hades. I had come this far to consult the spirit of my father, and chose to continue into dark and the increasing heat and stench of sulfur.[4]

We took a turn, and, to my amazement, the sheep and cattle that had been following us were now awaiting our arrival! We paused for another sacrifice and another study of the liver before proceeding down a sharp incline. As we progressed, the odor of sulfur grew stronger, along with other noxious smells. At least twice we passed a sparse type of bush that immediately burst into flame but did not burn.[5]

The deeper we went, the hazier my vision became and the more uncertain my step. At last we reached a point where the black-hooded priests stood aside, framing the place where the River Styx impeded further progress. Between them I could see Charon standing in his small coracle.[6] Though I could not see the dog, I could hear the howling of Cerberus.

The boatman wore only a ragged cape that looked as though it had never been cleansed, a supposition consistent with his filthy, matted white beard. Without a word being spoken, the Sibyl climbed into the fragile craft and I followed, leaving the priest on the shore.

Thus was I truly committed.

NOTES

1. More likely to produce a credible likeness. By skillfully interrogating the pilgrim, the priests would learn something not only of the deceased's appearance, but his personality.

2. See note 8, previous chapter.

3. Mistletoe had spiritual connotations throughout the ancient world. Since it bore berries in winter, when other plants were awaiting spring, it symbolized life amid death.

(4) The origins of the Christian concept of hell as fire and brimstone?

(5) *Dictamuus albus*, also known as *dictamus fraxinella*, native to Asia Minor and parts of southern Europe. The plant exudes a flammable vapor that is subject to spontaneous combustion of the gas without its own leaves being consumed. Likely this is the burning bush from which God spoke to Moses. Other flashing or sparking plants include henbane, white hellebore, and belladonna, all of which had their uses in oracular mysticism. It is odd that no one seems to have undertaken a study of self-combustible plants in modern times.

(6) A craft used in nontidal waters made of skins stretched around a basketlike frame.

PART V

Chapter Thirty

Via Della Dataria
Rome

Inspectore Santi Guiellmo, *capo, le Informazioni e la Sicurezza Democratica*, chief of Italy's security force, removed his glasses and glanced down from his third-story corner office at the Piazza del Quirinale and its obelisk and fountain flanked by equestrian statues of the twins Castor and Pollux. Crossing to the other side, he noted the dress-uniformed carabinieri standing at attention outside the Palazzo del Quiriale, the old papal palace that now housed Italy's president, the man whose security, along with the rest of the country, Guilellmo was sworn to protect.

The Chief, as he liked to be called, returned his attention to the hand-tooled, gilt-edged leather top of the boulle desk that rumor attributed to Victor Emmanuel I, the first king of a united Italy. Royalist sentiment had become unfashionable after the last Victor Emmanuel's abrupt departure from Rome in 1944 in the face of determined German defenders and the equally resolute Allied advance. The desk had been relegated to oblivion until the

Chief had restored it, if not to its former glory, then at least enhanced status above that of the petty bureaucrat in whose office he had found it.

Guiellmo replaced his rimless glasses and scowled at the papers that blemished the usually immaculate desktop. He picked up the top of the stack as he plopped into a leather swivel chair.

As chief of national security, he had the job of keeping the country . . . well, secure. Secure from invasion, subversion, or infiltration, though it was hard to imagine by whom. After all, Italy had had sixty-plus governments in the last sixty years. Fascists, Communists, socialists, and everything in between, including a female porn star elected to parliament.

In this country, everyone's allotted fifteen minutes of fame was their term as president.

Now this.

A week or so ago, the police in Taormina had found a man, apparently not Italian, shot to death in a rental house. Scorched paint hinted at some sort of explosion. A Chinese version of the Russian AK-47 automatic rifle had been nearby. Not the usual baggage for a tourist, a visitor to Sicily with no driver's permit, no passport, no identification whatsoever. Nearby bloodstains suggested at least one other person had been wounded.

At the time, Guiellmo had paid scant attention. This was, after all, Sicily, home of the Mafia, which tended to settle quarrels on a permanent basis.

But the dead man in Taormina wasn't Mafia. At least, not in the traditional sense. The cut of the clothes, the facial structure made it almost certain the man was from Eastern Europe. The poor quality of dental work—iron fillings, one steel false tooth—made Russia likely. The ideology of Marx and Lenin had produced dentists more qualified to repair Oz's Tin Man than teeth.

Okay, so there was the possibility the Cosa Nostra boys had had a falling-out with one or more of the organization's heroin suppliers from the poppy fields of Turkey,

Afghanistan, or Pakistan, trade the Russians crime cartels largely controlled. It was a guess, but a reasonable one.

One less narco trafficker, a slightly better world.

Then, two nights ago, the local *polizia* in the wilds of Sardinia had come upon a multifatality wreck. Nothing unusual about that in itself, either. After all, every Italian male fancied himself a Formula One driver.

But in Sardinia, all fatalities, all four, had been foreigners. Again, no identification but bullet holes and empty shell casings in abundance, as well as the AK-47s common to third-world militia, terrorists, and anyone else seeking the most inexpensive and easily obtained automatic the international arms market had to offer.

Again, dentistry that few who could find better would choose, dentistry peculiar to the USSR before its collapse.

Coincidence that there would be a double instance of Russians armed with automatic weapons? Mere chance that they had been shot?

Unlikely.

Then there were the reports of some sort of explosions earlier that same evening. Investigation had been cut short the next day when the American Embassy announced apologetically that somehow one or two of its special aircraft drones carrying little more than training fireworks had broken their electronic tethers and crashed in Sardinia somewhere in the neighborhood of the auto accident. Brief as it had been, the probe of the scene had revealed harmless amounts of pyrotechnics but no trace of aircraft, drone or otherwise.

A fluke?

Why was it every time the Americans apologized for some sort of incursion across Italian boundaries, Guiellmo's imagination could see Uncle Sam, his index finger just below his eye, tugging the lower lid down ever so slightly, the Italian equivalent of a knowing wink?

One was an isolated incident; the second part of a pattern.

A pattern of what?

The Chief hated mysteries and puzzles, be they involving words, like the English crosswords; numbers, like the current rage for Sudoku; or multiple homicides, like the reports in front of him. Mysteries and puzzles represented a form of disorder. Unlike his countrymen, he found confusion and turmoil to be anathema. He hated the snarled traffic, comic corruption of government at all levels, social disarray. He suspected somewhere in his ancestry lurked a non-Italian.

Perhaps a German.

He straightened the papers back into a perfect stack. He hated disarray. That was why he had never married. Sharing a dwelling with another human being, let alone one with lace underwear, hose, cosmetics, and other unimaginable accessories, was to invite bedlam into his well-ordered life.

As was letting these killings go unsolved.

The answer, of course, was to look at the problem logically.

First, although Italy had sent a small contingent to fight with the coalition in Iraq, there was no national enemy as far as the inspector knew. The killings, then, had to be either based on something else or committed by a non-Italian. For that matter, the shell casings and slugs in Sicily and Sardinia were definitely not all from Czech, Chinese, or Russian versions of the AK-47.

So far, he was unsure what that meant.

He had few leads as to who the warring factions might be.

Little clue, but not no clue.

He looked at the e-mail that had come in from Interpol at his request that morning.

A week or so ago, five, perhaps six men had perished in a fire someplace in the Caribbean. He thumbed the corner of a page. The Turks and Caicos Islands, a British crown

colony. In itself, that was insignificant. The interesting fact
was the only parts readily identifiable were dental work.

Russian dental work.

The house's owner, one Jason Peters, holder of an
American passport, had been suspected of setting the fire
to conceal the deaths. A search of the ashes also turned up
a number of firearms, both AK-47s and a couple of other,
somewhat more exotic specimens. Even more intriguing
was Mr. Peters's escape from the local jail by stealing a
plane under a barrage of gunfire from unknown gunmen
who had made their own disappearance before the Royal
Police, or whatever they called themselves in that part of
the world, could arrest them.

Whatever was going on, there definitely was bad blood
between this Peters and an as-yet-unknown group of Russians, a feud the island authorities had done little to
squelch.

Guiellmo indulged himself in a snort of contempt. Ineffective police work was offensive to him no matter
where.

The plane Peters had stolen turned up in . . . He turned
another page. The Dominican Republic and Interpol concluded he had fled from there to parts unknown, presumably under some other name.

Jason Peters, American.

Guiellmo leaned back in his chair and stared out of the
window without actually seeing the Roman skyline framed
in fire by a setting sun. The Cold War was over. Why
would Americans want to strew the landscape with dead
Russians? Yet, it appeared that, in at least one instance,
this Jason Peters had done just that.

A guess, admittedly. But then, few things were certain
in the Chief's line of work. The time line fit. He had found
someone with an apparent if unknown reason to do violence to Russians. Now all he had to do was find Mr. Peters. And if the Chief were a betting man—which he most

certainly was not—he would have bet a lot that Peters would be found in Italy, where the Russian fatality rate had taken a large jump.

Exactly where he might be was unknown, but, happily, there were leads.

The house in Sicily was owned by the Italian government, some obscure bureau that dealt with the study of volcanoes. The chief moved a couple of sheets of paper. The Bureau of Geological Studies, that was it. At the time of the incident, one of its employees, a Dr. Maria Bergenghetti, had been in residence, studying Aetna. The morning the local authorities found the shooting scene, she had called in to announce she was taking a few of the sixty or so vacation days enjoyed by government employees.

An explanation for the glacial speed at which the government accomplished anything.

Dr. Bergenghetti, though, had taken no leave for two years. This must be special.

He thumbed sheets of paper until he came to a photograph. Black-and-white, slightly fuzzy from being faxed. Still, the doctor was an extremely attractive woman—attractive enough, he hoped, to be remembered by the countless law enforcement officials to whom it had been distributed, along with the notation to notify him immediately if she were seen. Report, not detain.

Nor had there been an explanation as to the source of the Chief's interest. He had learned the painful lesson that sharing information about an investigation was the same as calling a press conference. The story wound up in the papers either way.

Inspectore Guiellmo was curious as to the company she might be keeping.

CHAPTER THIRTY-ONE

Piazza San Carlo
Turin, Italy
Late afternoon

The cobblestoned square had become world-famous from television coverage of the 2006 Winter Olympics. The only differences were that the red tile roofs were not snow covered and the crowds were nonexistent. As Jason and Maria sipped espresso in front of a trattoria, he studied the white limestone baroque churches of San Carlo and Santa Christina at the southern end of the piazza, his fingers drumming a nervous tattoo on the table. Somewhere nearby was the small café where, supposedly, vermouth had been invented, a mecca for martini drinkers worldwide. In the distance, purple shadows were blurring the jagged edges of the Alps.

This time there had been no unusual requests for rooms at the small hotel just off the arcaded Via Roma, the main street of the historic district. They had left a message for Adrian before Maria had called Eno Calligini, whose arrival they now awaited.

Maria glanced around the piazza as she took a Marlboro from her purse without exposing the pack. She ignored Jason's grimace of disapproval as she lit up and exhaled a jet of blue smoke. "Did you watch the Olympics here?"

Jason shook his head. He had not owned a television since he left Washington. "Missed it." He swiveled his head, scanning their surroundings. "This professor friend of yours usually on time?"

Punctuality was not an Italian virtue.

She leaned back in her chair, squinting through the smoke drifting into her face. "My, are not you the chatterbox?"

His attempt at a smile was a failure at best. "Don't like sitting out here where we can be seen by people we can't see. Makes me nervous."

Maria took a long drag as she looked around the square. "You are paranoid."

"I'm still alive."

They sat in the silence of an uneasy truce until Jason leaned forward to pull the magazine containing the summary of Dr. Calligini's book from his pocket. He had read all but the last two chapters on the train they had taken after the boat back to the mainland. Flying would have been quicker but would have involved security likely to turn up his weapon. The SIG Sauer would have been hard to explain.

"I appreciate Adrian giving this to us." He held it out. "Want to read it?"

She stubbed her cigarette out in a small glass ashtray. "Read the book when it first appeared. I do not know if . . ."

She stood, leaving the sentence unfinished. Jason followed her gaze across the piazza to where a tall man was striding toward them. Hatless, with a full mane of shoulder-length silver hair that reached a shabby cardigan. Faded jeans were stuffed into rubber-soled boots. As the man approached, Jason saw tanned features, the skin wrinkled from exposure to wind and sun.

It was not until he stood at tableside, his long face split by a dazzling smile, that Jason realized the man was more than old enough to be Maria's father. That did little to diminish a twinge of jealousy as the two embraced.

Jason stood as Maria turned to him. "Jason, I want you to meet Dr. Calligini. . . ."

The doctor extended a hand with a firm grip. "Eno, please." He immediately returned his attention to Maria with a stream of Italian before stopping and turning back to Jason. "*Mi dispiace.* I'm sorry. I have not seen little Maria long time."

Jason arched an eyebrow, looking at Maria. "'Little' Maria?"

Eno nodded. "*Si.* Beeg Maria, she my seester, marry to Maria's poppa."

For reasons quite understandable, Jason felt relieved. "A pleasure, Dr., er, Eno. You speak good English."

Jason was treated to a smile that could have served as an ad for toothpaste as the doctor held thumb and index finger an inch or so apart. "Only a leetle."

The three sat, and Eno barked Italian at the waiter, who scurried away, returning almost immediately with a tiny cup of espresso.

The professor's eyes fell on the magazine on the table, and he smiled even wider. "You read?"

"Interesting," Jason said without commitment. "I'm not sure Greco-Roman mythology is going to be helpful in finding what I want."

Eno turned to Maria, obviously seeking a translation.

They exchanged sentences Jason didn't understand before she said, "It is no myth. He believes that the Roman's journal is an accurate representation of what happened."

Jason lowered the coffee cup he had almost put to his lips. "It's real; he thinks it's real? That there really is a hell?"

Eno apparently understood the gravamen of that. He shook his head. "No 'hell.' Hades."

"There's a difference?"

"*Si.* Difference."

The professor ignored his coffee to speak rapidly to Maria. His gesticulations confirmed Jason's belief that an Italian unfortunate enough to lose both arms would be struck dumb also.

When he had finished, or at least subsided, Maria said, "There really is—was—a Hades, complete with River Styx and all. It was the place of departed spirits, a place of darkness, of heat and volcanic activity, hence the fire and brimstone the Christians associate with hell."

Jason leaned back in his chair, unconvinced. "If it was real, where was it?"

"Baia, or in the old Roman Latin, Baiae."

"The place in the article."

She nodded.

"But how—"

Eno interrupted with another stream of italian.

When he finished, Maria said, "General Agrippa blocked it in, perhaps on the orders of Augustus Caesar, his friend and patron. That would have been sometime A.D. 12 or before."

Coffee completely forgotten, Jason rested his chin on open palms, elbows on the table. "You mean they sealed it off?"

She shook her head. "No, they tried to completely fill it in. Like Nero's Golden House in Rome."

He shook his head.

"When Nero died, years after Augustus, Vespasian filled the palace with dirt. It's been excavated for only a few years. Hades at Baia was the same, filled in."

"Then how . . ."

She held up a hand, rushing on. "A chemical engineer, an Englishman by the name of Robert Paget, retired to Baia and became interested in the local antiquities. In

1962 he and a native crew excavated part of it. They could work only in fifteen-minute shifts because of the heat and the gases, but he cleared the passageway to an underground river, the Styx. Along the way were sacrificial altars—"

"Gases?" Jason's interest quickened.

"They did no analysis, but there was some kind of gas that made them sleepy as well as prone to hallucinations."

"Ethylene?" Jason was twisting his cup around on the tabletop.

Maria shrugged. "Possibly. They were amateur archeologists, not geologists."

Eno was following the exchange closely. "The *Inglese*, Paget, he want to find Greek Hades, no geologist."

Jason straightened up, palms flat on the table. "Okay, so it looks like I'll have to go to . . . where?"

"Baia," Maria and Eno said in unison.

"Not so easy," Eno added. "After Paget explore there, Italian government . . ." He made a motion of touching his hands together in silent applause. "How you . . . ?"

"The Italian government shut up the entrances, said it was too dangerous," Maria said.

"Nobody's been in there since 1962?" Jason was incredulous.

Eno explained something to Maria, who turned to Jason. "Another archaeologist, Robert Temple, convinced the authorities to let him explore further in 2001. He reported the gas levels had subsided, as had the intense heat reported by Paget. He took some pictures and wrote a book about it, *Netherworld*. Then the government sealed it off again."

Jason drained the remains of what was by now very cold espresso. "Why? I'd think the archeological value of the real Hades would be worth keeping it open."

Eno motioned to the waiter for refills and joined in. "Government say too dangerous. My guess, Church wanted closed."

"Despite what the politicians say, the Catholic Church has tremendous influence on Italian politics," Maria explained. "Having a secular or pagan model of hell open for inspection would not be something the Holy Father would have supported."

Jason thought about that for a moment. "According to Eno's book, or at least the English summary of it, this place at Baia was filled with hallucinogenic gases, which a sect of scheming priests used to basically fleece people who believed they could meet the dead. The gases were there naturally, so the priests created Hades centuries before Christ. But why not in Greece?"

"Cumae oldest Greek city in Italy," Eno said.

"Besides," Maria added, "they had little choice. Just the right gas combination was at Baia, so they had to create the Netherworld there. It was probably the only place in the Greek world with just the right characteristics: a cavern, gases, an underground river, and easy accessibility."

Jason nodded. "Disney World for wealthy ancients."

Maria lifted her head to nod thanks to the waiter as he set another cup in front of her and whisked away the old one. "Natural gases that were the product of a system of underground volcanic activity."

"Part of the 'fire and brimstone' of the Christian hell, as Eno noted in his book," Jason said, exchanging his cup for the fresh one. "The physical evidence indicates that whatever minerals were involved in the Bering Sea incident and the Georgia National Forest came from around Naples, so I'd have to guess the ethylene blend did, too."

Maria dunked the sugar-encrusted stick that came with her coffee. "Which raises a truly interesting question."

No doubt the same question that had been nagging at Jason's subconscious, an unexpressed idea that had first lurked in the back of his mind like a wild animal at the edge of a campfire until his conversation with Adrian.

Maria voiced the issue Jason had thought about since Adrian had made his suggestion. "Why would the terrorists go to the trouble to find the source of a hallucinogenic gas? Why not simply kill their victims rather than gassing them first?"

"These people want to make a statement. Having something from the earth incapacitate the victims, in their minds, is a sort of revenge by nature."

"But whatever it is does not *kill* anyone," Maria protested. "These men, these eco . . . ?"

"Ecological terrorists," Jason supplied.

"These men do the actual murder of helpless people."

Jason leaned back in his chair. "There's no understanding the thought process of lunatics, fanatics, but making a natural product of the earth they believe their victims are destroying makes the ecology—nature—a partner in revenging what they see as an evil done to the earth."

Both Maria and Eno were giving him skeptical looks.

"Okay, Okay, so I'm just guessing. We may get the real answer at Baia."

"Or Cumae," Eno added.

"Cumae?" Both Jason and Maria were staring at the professor.

"Cumae," he repeated. "The gases, they could have come from there. The Sibyl, she maybe . . . how you say? High? Yes, she maybe high on some sort of gas when she give future statements."

"Your book suggested epilepsy, not gas," Jason noted.

Eno shrugged. "A guess. Who for sure know why make statements?"

"Prophecies," Maria corrected.

"Prophecies," Eno continued, grinning. "She only one high in Vatican."

Jason looked at Maria, puzzled.

"The Sistine Chapel," she explained, "Michelangelo included the Cumae Sibyl in the group of prophets around the edge of the ceiling. According to readers of Virgil, she foretold the coming of Christ; at least, the emperor Constantine thought so. She's the only pagan figure on the ceiling."

Jason absorbed this information before saying, "Another question: how did Alazar, the Moslem who sold whatever this is to Eco, find out about gases in an ancient Greek religious site, one that wasn't even in Greece?"

Eno shrugged. "Arabs long know Greek culture," the professor began before lapsing into Italian.

Jason waited impatiently for Maria to translate.

"When Rome fell to various hordes of barbarians," she began, watching Eno, "much of the Greco-Roman knowledge was in danger of being lost, in addition to what the Greeks and Romans had learned from the Egyptians, Babylonians, Sumerians, and whoever else. A lot of wisdom was lost forever. The Moorish traders in the Mediterranean, the Arabs along the ancient Silk Road, the Byzantine, then Ottoman emperors saved what they could use. Had it not been for them, Greek and Roman sciences—and the ancient knowledge before that—in medicine, astronomy, mathematics, would have been lost. We would not know the geometry of Euclid, Ptolemy's geography or astronomy, or Pliny's history. During the so-called Dark Ages, much was forgotten that had originated in Europe and been learned by the Muslim merchants. It was only during the crusades that some of this knowledge began to filter back west. Even then, most forms of science were bitterly opposed by the Church, hindering even further the restoration of ancient learning in the Christian world. Eno says he wouldn't be surprised if the Arabs haven't known of Baia and Cumae longer than current Western civilization. After all, the stories of Virgil and Homer, the plays of Euripides, were known and enjoyed in the Mideast while most of Europe was divided into tiny, warring principalities run by kings who could not even read their own languages. An Arab arms dealer was only passing along something adopted by his culture a long time ago."

Jason was quiet for a few seconds. He turned to Eno. "Any chance of the government giving us grief about going down into whatever it is in Baia?"

Eno shrugged, a man asked a question to which there was no apparent answer. "They have it closed, but I do not know if they guard it. Entry is prohibited."

If the country observed that law to the same degree as traffic laws, there would be no problem.

"Obviously somebody's been there. That's where the ethylene seems to have come from," Maria observed.

"Perhaps," Eno said. "Many such places are closed but not guarded. This one may not be watched by the authorities, but these people you seek will be watching, I theenk."

Jason said, "I'll keep that in mind when Adrian and I get there."

"Adrian, you, and *I*," she added.

"Thought you were through as soon as you'd helped me with Eno here."

"And miss a chance to observe an underground volcanic system that, with two exceptions, has been closed off from study for two thousand years?"

CHAPTER THIRTY-TWO

Albergo del San Giovanni
Via Roma, Turin
The next morning

Jason's head was buried alternately in the *International Herald Tribune*, the *New York Times*, and the *Washington Post*'s English-language newspaper distributed throughout Europe. He was sitting in the hotel's small dining room, where a buffet breakfast of breads, sausages, fruit, jams, cereals, and juices was lined up on white tablecloths. Across the table, Maria was finishing her third coffee.

Jason lowered his paper long enough to glance at the one inches away. Like an old married couple, he thought, each too engrossed in the morning's papers to engage in conversation. Just as well. Other than ecological extremists trying to kill them, exploring hell, or last night's sexual acrobatics, what did they have to talk about?

An article on the front page drew him back to the news. He read, then re-read it, then sat in silent thought for a moment. He folded the *Herald Tribune*'s front page and shoved it over the top of Maria's paper like an invading army breaching a castle wall.

She lowered the barrier long enough to give him a peevish look. "I thought you read that paper only for the comics."

"It's the only one that still carries 'Calvin and Hobbes.'"

"Oh, that makes a difference."

He used the hand not holding the paper to point. "Look at this."

Washington—The president announced a new environmental initiative yesterday. A previously undisclosed conference is scheduled for next week.

The president and members of his cabinet will meet with leaders of various ecological and conservationists groups, such as the Sierra Club and the American Green Party, largely organizations that have been critical of the president's handling of such issues as global warming, oil exploration in Alaska, and relaxing of clean air and water standards.

A White House spokesperson said any organized group with an interest in the environment will be welcomed on a space-available basis.

As an act the same spokesperson described as "showing good faith," the president intends to pardon those accused of crimes in the name of conservation, such as those who are presently charged with trespassing on national forest lands by chaining themselves to trees to be cut, or blocking access to oil fields. Asked if this pardon would include violent crimes, the White House appears to be undecided.

Senator Sott (D-Mass.) described the announcement as "A shockingly trans-

parent and cynical effort by the environment's sworn enemy to drum up votes
from those he has ignored too long."

The exact site of the conference in
Washington has yet to be announced.

Frowning like a primary school teacher accommodat-
ing one of her less bright pupils, Maria scanned the article. "So?"

"The man's nuts," he said. "He'll never make peace
with those people any more than you could placate a rat-
tlesnake."

She finally laid her paper down, regarding him with a
mixture of annoyance and amusement. "Your president is
'nuts'? And to think how many Americans got angry
when we Europeans first made the observation. Do you
think he is any different from any other politician? A
politician would be willing to forgive and forget the
biggest mass murder in your history if he thinks it will get
him reelected."

"Like Jimmy Carter trying to negotiate with Iran to free
American hostages? It lost him the next election."

She smiled. "Perhaps now it is your role to give political
advice?"

She stood, went to the buffet and selected a pear, and
returned to her chair. She took a noisy, moist bite before
sitting down. "And so?"

He put the paper down, subject exhausted. "If Adrian
and I go . . ."

She held the pear out to him for him to sample. "If you,
Adrian, and *I* go."

The fruit seemed to turn to a mellow syrup in his
mouth. Like most Italian fruit, it was fresh, flavorful, and
just ripe enough—So good that Jason suspected there was
an official Italian fruit manufacturing agency that produced synthetic goods. He'd never sampled anything that
good from Mother Nature.

He swallowed before saying, "Your choice. Eno was right: if Cumae or Baia is a supply of the gas, somebody will be watching."

"Is that a fact?"

Neither Jason nor Maria had seen Adrian emerge from his hiding place behind another paper in the far corner of the room.

"Truly alert you are, laddie," he gloated to Jason. "Coulda killed you a dozen times. Ye're na' payin' attention t'er surroundin's." He pointed to the half-eaten pear. "Or too busy wid the forbidden fruit in this garden."

The SAS man was right: Jason had given scant notice to the other diners, any one of whom could have been Eglov himself hiding behind a copy of *la República*. He had felt so good, so happy as a result of last night's lovemaking, he had momentarily forgotten a darker world where inattention was frequently a capital offense.

As Adrian planted an avuncular kiss on Maria's cheek, Jason dared envision, just for a second, a life where it wasn't necessary to get neck cramps looking over your shoulder. A life . . . well, a life pretty much like what he and Laurin had planned before she was taken from him.

The reflections shattered like crystal dropped on bricks when Jason realized Adrian was asking questions.

"Was Professor Calligini helpful? Be we off, then? Where to? Baia? Will we be needin' special kit?"

It was the latter question that had brought Jason back to reality. "According to the last explorer, the gas wasn't a problem. Still, I asked Maria to request air tanks so we won't be taking the risk. They should be waiting when we get there."

"And where would 'there' be?" Adrian wanted to know.

"Naples. We can be there in a few hours."

As they left the room, Jason looked back to where the *Herald Tribune* lay in the chair he had occupied. There was something about that meeting in Washington that he knew without being aware of his knowledge, something . . . Past experience told him the thought was not yet ripe enough to fall into his full conscious. It would become clear in its own good time.

He only hoped that would be soon enough for . . . what?

CHAPTER THIRTY-THREE

114 Taylor Street
Queens, New York
The same day

Rassavitch had no trouble blending into the enclave of
Russian emigrants. Every evening and twice on Sunday he
attended the concrete-block building that had begun life
as a grocery store and now served as an Orthodox church.
It still had a faint odor of spoiled fruit. He was a religious
man, a man convinced he had survived the communists to
serve God by restoring the Master's will on earth.

He did God's will, and he had been called here by like-
thinkers to make certain others did, too. At the moment,
God was displeased with the use being made of the Earth,
the despoliation of His greatest gift to man. It was far past
time someone, some group, wreaked vengeance on those
who defiled the Earth.

Rassavitch had finally found just such an organization.
That was God's will, too.

If there was one thing distinctly Russian, it was a peasant's love for the land, a commodity for centuries owned
exclusively by the State, by the Czars, then the Party. Now,

at least in theory, any Russian could own a few hectares. The catch—and in Russia there was always a catch—was that only the wealthy could afford to buy, the very people who raped the earth with poisonous fertilizers, who polluted the rivers with chemicals and defiled even the air all had to breathe.

The injustice of it made Rassavitch grind his teeth.

But the Russians here didn't seem to care. Oh, a few of the old babushka tended thumbnail-sized patches of sickly vegetables, but most of the populace had no interest in the land that had been the sustenance of the Russian people since before the czars. Instead, the young people would rather work at jobs in the city and spend their leisure time wearing American blue jeans, the dye from which Rassavitch was sure polluted some stream, and listening to the noise they called music.

At first, he worried his fellow Russians who had shed the old ways might notice him, perhaps report him to the authorities. Then it dawned upon him that nobody cared. In America, everyone was far too busy making a dollar and watching television to be interested in what someone else did.

Including defiling the earth, the water, the air.

Soon, very soon, Americans would realize the earth could and would strike back.

CHAPTER THIRTY-FOUR

Via Della Dataria
Rome
That afternoon

Unlike most Romans, *Inspectore* Santi Guiellmo did not leave work between one and four o'clock, the hours when offices, museums, shops, and even churches were closed for employees to enjoy a long lunch and, perhaps, a restorative nap. A crisp salad brought to his desk to eat while he scanned the day's headlines was all the break he required from routine. The lengthy recess in the city gave him time to think. It silenced the disruptive telephone and halted the parade of subordinates seeking answers to questions they were too lazy to find for themselves.

Even had the Chief been in the habit of taking the allowed time off, he would not have done so today.

This morning, Dr. Maria Bergenghetti had surfaced. Well, perhaps not surfaced, exactly. She had telephoned a coworker at the Bureau of Geological Studies, requesting certain equipment: six air tanks with three regulators and backpacks, as well as spelunking gear such as miners' helmets, harness, and rope. She also wanted some scientific apparatus, the function of which was unclear, something the names indicated had to do with detecting, analyzing, or measuring gases.

Guiellmo stared at the inventory as though ordering it to give up its secret. The volcanologist was going to explore the crater of a volcano or a deep cave. Unfortunately, Italy was riddled with both. Since no fire retardant clothing had been requisitioned, it was a safe bet the woman and her companions were not headed for the caldera of an active volcano. Yet why else would she want a source of breathable air?

If she was, in fact, in the company of this American, Peters, what interest did he have in caves, volcanoes, or gases? It was not likely he would find more Russians to kill in such places.

Not that Guiellmo was particularly sympathetic to Russians. Their national image since the fall of communism was one of lawlessness, of crime, corruption, and violence that made the old American West look tame. Although many people decried stereotypes as based on prejudice, Guiellmo saw them as based on observation. And observation of crime in Russia was not encouraging for law enforcement.

But Italy was not going to tolerate its soil being used to stage an open season on Russians or anybody else, lawless or not.

He stood and went to look down on the Piazza del Quirinale, now empty other than the presidential guards, still as statues, and the resident pigeons, busily searching for the last crumb of pizza crust dropped by the morning's horde of tourists.

Breathable air in a cave? Unlikely it would be needed. That left extinct volcanoes. The most obvious was Vesuvius, killer of Pompeii and Herculaneum, inactive since 1944. Was it considered extinct?

He returned to his desk and sat heavily. No matter. Bergenghetti had requested the equipment be assembled at the old Vesuvius Observatory, the nineteenth-century structure that served as a base for recording data, the research facilities having moved to Naples. A good choice. The building was known by few, and there would be only one or two technicians present.

As usual, Guiellmo preferred the involvement of as few people as possible in an investigation.

CHAPTER THIRTY-FIVE

Vesuvius Observatory
Mount Vesuvius
Late the next afternoon

The drive from Turin had been exclusively on the Autostrada, Italy's equivalent of the interstate system, until the last thirteen kilometers south of Naples. They parked in front of a red-and-white neoclassic building that resembled a wealthy family's villa more than a structure dedicated to scientific endeavors. Other than the Volvo, the spacious square in front held only one car, a motor scooter, and a tour bus chugging diesel fumes. Maria, Adrian, and Jason climbed out of the Volvo, stretching and yawning from hours on the road.

Jason worried that the car, lacking its rear windshield and sporting suspiciously round holes in the coachwork, might draw attention.

"In Rome, mebbe," Adrian assured him. "In Naples, many o' th' cars are rolling junk heaps."

Perhaps. But did they look like the former owners might have been Bonnie and Clyde?

Jason paused to admire the view of vineyards and small settlements nestled in the folds of the volcano's verdant slopes. "Doesn't look like anyone's worried about another eruption anytime soon."

"The soil's rich in alkali and phosphorus," Maria said, turning to share the view. "Perfect for grapes. The Lacryma Christi wine comes from here."

"It'd suit the growin' of malt f' good whiskey, too," Adrian observed. "But it's na' for the bonny scenery we're here."

Inside, the building housed an impressive polyglot library and a huge collection of minerals, presumably the vomitus of the mountain itself. Maria led them around a group of thirty or so white-haired tourists, listening intently as a blond tour director lectured in German as she pointed with an umbrella to indicate a large boulder.

Maria paused in front of a small elevator until its door slowly parted, revealing an open platform designed to carry freight more than passengers. Inside the shaft, a simple switch gave a choice of only two floors, the main one and one above. They exited the elevator after a wait that made Jason wonder if the contraption really was moving. A short, dimly lit corridor ended at an open door.

A twelve-by-twelve-foot office managed to contain two metal desks back-to-back, computers, and an array of machines that seemed to be drawing graphs, recording temperatures, and completing functions at which Jason could only guess. A man and a woman interrupted a conversation as the three entered, looking up in surprise.

Or was it guilt?

Maria's smile faded as she asked a question, *"Dove Guiedo?"*

Where's Guiedo?

The two technicians exchanged glances before the man replied.

Maria nodded her head, asked another question, and

received a slightly longer response. "Our gear is on the loading dock around back. One of the people who usually works here packed it for us."

The woman gave Jason and Adrian a stare that was far more steady than curious before she asked another question, to which Maria responded by introducing Jason and Adrian with an explanation that Jason's very limited Italian couldn't follow.

This time the man inquired, to which Maria shrugged before answering.

The number of queries were making Jason uncomfortable. He sensed Adrian shared his feelings when the Scot said, "Best we're off, lassie. Bid your friends farewell."

As they were loading the gear into the back of the Volvo, Jason asked, "What was all the question-and-answer about?"

Maria opened a canvas bag, removing and returning three regulators. "The man was curious about where we will be using the equipment. I told him there are a series of caves around Lake Averno that we were investigating."

"Lake Averno?"

"I mentioned it that night in Sicily. With what happened, I can understand your not remembering. One of the Phlegraean lakes near where we are actually going. Lots of underground volcanic activity. In fact, there are places where the ground itself is hot. The Greeks thought the entrance to Hades was nearby, as we learned from Eno that it is. 'Averno' comes from the Greek *a-ornom*, without birds. Apparently in ancient times, the vapors were suffocating, deadly to anything flying over it."

Adrian hefted an air tank in each hand. "That's why we would need to get kitted out. Good thinking."

Maria started to lift a third and nodded gratefully as Jason took it. "I certainly was not going to tell them we were going someplace forbidden by the government, even if Guiedo had been there."

"You knew those two?" Jason asked.

"Never saw them before. There are not that many people who work for the bureau. I thought I knew them all by sight."

Adrian put down the tank he was lifting as Jason asked, "And Guiedo, the one you made inquiry about, he was someone you know?"

"Known him for years. The woman said he'd gone to Rome to see to his sick mother."

An hour later, Jason was driving the Via Nuova Marina, a wide, six-lane boulevard skirting Naples's harbor. The water was to his right. On his left, the city's hills swept upward abruptly, festooned with apartments displaying the day's wash on a thousand clotheslines.

He had expected the traffic of Rome, the mostly absent stoplights, kamikaze dashes through busy intersections, and the use of horns rather than brakes. Naples presented different but equally traumatic hazards: Without warning, cars would pull over to park two or three deep along the curb, doors opening into traffic. Or a vehicle would simply choose to park in the middle of the street, occupants stepping fearlessly into lanes of moving cars, trucks, and scooters. Jason not only feared hitting someone nonchalantly getting out of an automobile, but that the casual merging of pedestrians and cars would conceal an ambush until the last second.

By the time the Nuova Marina became Via Cristforo Columbo (having already been Via Amerigo Vespucci), Jason was certain of two things: they had exhausted the list of Italian navigators, and Neapolitans all had death wishes.

He felt relief as the Volvo began to climb the ridges that seperated the city from the inland. At the top, Maria promised they would find another Autostrada, this one heading west to Cumae.

As the number of vehicles began to thin out above the city, Jason noticed a lone motorcycle keeping a consistent distance behind them, always at least two cars back. Jason lifted his foot and a Fiat passed with an angry horn blast.

But the bike simply slowed and fell in behind an egg-shaped Smart.

"We've got company," Jason said, putting out a hand to prevent Maria from turning around.

Adrian knew better than to telegraph the fact that their tail had been spotted. "How many?"

"A single motorcycle."

In the rearview mirror Jason could see Adrian nod. "We're only being observed, then."

"Looks that way."

"Y' ken how long?"

Jason shook his head. "Dunno."

"Since the observatory," Maria said.

Jason risked cutting his eyes from the road to her and back again. "The observatory? How do you know that?"

"Guiedo."

"Your friend who was visiting his mother in Rome?"

Maria nodded slowly. "Yes, but I just remembered, Guiedo's mother lives in small town just outside Bologna."

"How well do you know him?"

She shifted uncomfortably in the seat. "Not too well. He was young, just out of university. I think he . . . what did we say? Yes, I think he thinks I'm hot."

Guiedo at least had his priorities in order.

Jason flicked a glance to the rearview mirror. The bike was still two cars back. "Any chance she could have moved since you last talked to him, maybe to a nursing home or something?"

She was staring straight ahead. "Italians, most of them, would be humiliated to pack a parent off to let someone else care for them. It is possible the woman moved, though, I suppose."

"Not bloody likely," Adrian piped up from the backseat. "Having not one but two sods that Maria didn't know back there, we can bet we're being followed."

"By who?" Maria wanted to know.

So did Jason.

"I dinna think we want to be findin' out," Adrian observed, unfolding a road map. "Try exitin' yer nex' chance."

Jason wasn't surprised when the motorcycle followed. "Still there."

"Bastard's not 'xactly subtle," Adrian growled. "Doesn't give a damn if we know he's there."

"Or he thinks we won't notice."

"I'll . . ." Jason stopped midsentence. "He's gone!"

"Gone?" both Adrian and Maria chorused.

"We turned right; he turned left."

"Guess we became excited over nothing," Maria ventured.

"Maybe," Jason said. "But I wouldn't bet on it."

"We were meant to see the laddie on the cycle," Adrian explained. "Long as we concentrated on him, we wouldna ken there was another when the first turned away."

Jason stopped, backed up, and returned to the Autostrada. There were several suspicious cars, but each eventually passed the Volvo.

"Unless they've got multiple tails, I can't identify any," Jason admitted.

"So, let's flush 'em out,' Adrian suggested.

Once again, Jason left the multilane highway system with cars both in front and behind. Minutes later the Volvo was laboring up a steep hill behind a truck. Several automobiles were strung out along the winding road for half a mile or so. Without giving a signal, Jason pulled onto one of the periodic overlooks that gave the casual traveler a panorama of Naples across an azure bay.

The rumble of passing traffic faded from Jason's mind as he imagined the pigments he would use to transfer the scene to canvas.

If he ever painted again.

No one seemed interested in the Volvo. Jason elected to continue along the scenic if narrow two-lane that skirted

the northwestern corner of the Bay of Naples. He was
growing less certain they had been followed at all.

Then an idea evaporated what little complacency he
had enjoyed.

"Maria, you've traveled this road before?"

She glanced at him, curious. "One or two times, yes."

"It goes where?"

"Miseno, both the lake and the town. The town sits just
south of the ruins at Baia and farther south of the ruins at
Cumae."

"Are there any turnoffs, roads that go somewhere
else?"

She pointed to the slopes above and the steep dropoff
into the water below. "Where would one build any such
towns? Other than a few private villas, I think there are
no crossroads till we get to Miseno."

From the backseat, Adrian voiced what Jason was
thinking.

"There's no need to follow us. Have someone wait
ahead, another to make sure we dinna double back, and
we're like beetles in a bottle."

The analogy was less than comforting.

CHAPTER THIRTY-SIX

Miseno
An hour later

Miseno looked like a resort. Roads branched off in seemingly random fashion like spaghetti, leading to cottage-lined small lakes. The almost perfect circles of the shorelines gave a clue as to origins as volcanic craters. Large restaurants were flanked by even larger parking lots. The area anticipated a successful tourist season.

For now, traffic was light.

Jason pulled onto a grassy embankment that fell steeply off into a lake the color of midnight despite the sunny blue sky above. The few vehicles that passed paid them no attention.

Adrian and Jason exchanged puzzled looks before the latter said, "Guess we weren't followed after all."

The Scot shook his head slowly. "Aye, but dinna be dropping your guard yet."

Maria stretched her arms and yawned. "Where first?"

"Cumae, I think," Jason answered. "I know Eno's book attributed epilepsy to the Sibyl, but I'd like to check to make sure her cave isn't a source of that ethylene, too. How far?"

"Maybe four or five kilometers. Let me drive."

The reason for her request became quickly obvious. Climbing and descending, she took what seemed a haphazard course. From one hill, Jason could see the lakes, from another the sea in the opposite direction.

At last she pulled into a small unpaved parking lot with no indication as to its purpose, turned off the ignition, and got out.

Jason followed, staring up at the surrounding low hills. "This is it?"

Maria nodded, walking around to the trunk. "It is."

"But there's no . . ." He was looking at a deserted ticket booth and an iron gate hanging open on the last of its hinges.

"No tourists?" She filled in the blank. "Cumae is not one of the popular destinations. Few people other than archaeologists come here."

Cumae must be remote indeed if no one was selling tickets, picture brochures, or cheap souvenirs. Jason suspected that, in Italy, tickets would be printed for a dogfight if it could be anticipated in time.

Maria was digging through the trunk. "I doubt we will encounter the gas you seek here, but we will test the air." She held up a device with a meter attached to a hand pump. "This will tell us if ethylene is present." She handed a miner's helmet to both Jason and Adrian. "And you will need these."

She led Jason and Adrian along a dirt path that skirted the base of the hill to their left. After the trail made a ninety-degree turn, she stopped. The trio were looking at a passageway cut along the side of the hill. The exposed rock was yellow in color, the tufa Maria had explained was native to the region. Rather than round, the opening was square for its first three or four feet, then towered upward about eight feet in a lopsided A shape. Like floor-to-

ceiling windows, open spaces alternated with stone. Even
from outside, Jason could see the effect of equal areas of
light and dark as the end of the tunnel vanished into
shadow.

"You're right," Jason said. "Too open. No gas could be
held there."

Maria entered. "The Sibyl's cave is not so open."

The passageway was not quite wide enough for two
abreast. Gauge in hand, Maria led the way, followed by Jason and Adrian. Without looking behind him, Jason rested
his hand on the SIG Sauer in its holster, and he sensed
Adrian also was prepared for whatever might happen. Although only a few feet away, Maria appeared and disappeared in much the same way described by Severenus
Tactus two millennia ago.

Jason wondered what other parts of the Roman's account would prove accurate.

The alternating spaces that admitted light came to an
abrupt end. Jason and Adrian put on the helmets, turning
on the light on each. The artificial illumination gave the
yellow walls a reddish tint as though washed in blood.
Every few feet a niche was carved into the stone, stands
for ancient lamps, judging by the halo of soot above each.

A few more steps brought them to the end of the passage. To their left was a cavern, a low-ceilinged, square
room carved into the rock. Lamp niches were on three of
the four walls.

"The Sibyl's cave," Maria said, as she worked a small
hand pump. "No sign of anything but normal air here,
oxygen, nitrogen . . ."

Adrian held up a hand, a signal for silence.

Jason heard only the echo of his own breathing,
then . . . a scrape, the sound of a shoe on stone or something hard against rock.

Maria and Adrian needed no signal to turn off the
lanterns on their helmets as Jason did the same. "Any
other way in?" he whispered.

He could only see Maria's dull silhouette shake its head, no. "Not that has been discovered."

Taking each by the arm, Jason eased Maria and Adrian back the way they had come. Even if they had no other means of escape, they had one advantage: the location of the Sibyl's cave would force whoever had entered the passage to enter successive squares of light, while Jason, Adrian, and Maria remained in concealing darkness.

Pressing the two others against the wall, Jason drew his weapon. The slight rustle of clothing told him Adrian had unslung his Sten. Jason thumbed off the safety and heard the echoing snick of the Sten's bolt being cocked.

Though he knew better, an eternity seemed to pass before Jason saw indistinct shapes flitting between the light and dark sectors of the long passage. Had he not reined it in, his imagination could easily have seen long-robed priests leading a young Roman to hear his fate foretold.

Instead, he made out four distinct figures, each moving with hands clasped in front as though carrying a weapon at the ready, each progressing in synchronized movements designed for a minimum of exposure to the sunlight and a maximum of coverage by his comrades.

Jason pushed Maria toward the first opening, speaking with his lips to her ear. "When they move next, you go through outside."

He felt, rather than saw her nod.

When the four figures simultaneously slipped from one patch of dark to the next, Jason shoved Maria, knocking her forward and out of the corridor. He lunged after her, half expecting shots.

There were none.

Outside, Adrian stood, dusting himself off while holding the Sten, its stock still folded. He had it trained on the passage they had just exited. "Get a look at 'em?"

Jason shook his head. "No. But they move like they've been trained, not some pickup gang of thugs."

He wasn't sure if that was better or worse.

Adrian helped Maria to her feet. "Any way out of the area without passing by the entrance?"

Instead of speaking, she motioned. Jason followed, keeping the gun's muzzle pointed at the slots in the cave's side. Where were they, the people who had entered? Was it possible they were only tourists visiting an obscure place?

Not moving in concert, as he had seen. More like military. Then why . . . ?

Possibly they had been blinded by emerging into light; possibly they hadn't seen Jason, Adrian, and Maria's exit.

Possible, but unlikely.

They were walking up a stone-paved path that wound its way around the hill into which the Sibyl's cave had been carved. Idly, Jason wondered if the rocks had ben worn smooth by the feet of ancient Romans. The trail ended at steep stairs carved into naked rock and long ago polished by use and the elements.

"Temple of Jupiter, highest point in the site," Maria announced. "We should be able to see them when they come out of the cave."

Jason started to reply and decided to save his breath for the ascent.

Minutes later they stood among broken and tumbled columns. From the stubs still in place, Jason guessed there had originally been six to a side, with two across the front and back. Rubble of columns and pediment were strewn around a large stone platform atop crumbling stairs that had led into the floor of the temple. To his right, Jason could see a number of figures slowly working in a field beyond two large arches.

"Archeological dig," Maria explained, following his line of sight.

Adrian was looking the other way. "And that would be?" He was pointing to a similar collection of ruins slightly below and across a dirt path.

"Temple of Apollo."

Adrian took a step back as four men emerged from below, turning their heads in deferent directions. The dark suits they wore were out of place, both as to location and climate.

"Th' lot look like coppers," Adrian observed.

"Whoever they are, we can bet they're not here to help," Jason said, squinting against the reflection of the afternoon's sun on the ocean to his left. "Is there another way to get back to the car?"

Maria nodded. "We can go down to the excavation site"—she pointed—"and then around the bottom of the hill."

"No good," Jason observed. "They've split up. We'd run into at least two of them."

"So much the better," Adrian said. "We ken where they are. They dinna have but an idea as to us. I say we divide up, too, an' take 'em on."

Maria looked nervously from Jason to Adrian and back again. "Surely you are not going to shoot these men when you do not even know . . ."

Adrian grinned. "Na need to be shootin', lass, if we right surprise 'em." He pointed. "Jason, you 'n' Maria go back th' way we came. I'll go 'round."

Jason wasn't wild about the idea, but it made more sense than waiting to be surrounded. He nodded, and he and Maria set off down the hill, his hand on the weapon at his back as they descended the stairs.

They had just reached the last step when two men rounded a bend in the path below. Both were red-faced from the exertion. The older of the two, overweight and white-haired, was puffing loudly and was watching carefully where he placed each footfall.

His companion was the first to see Jason and Maria. His right hand went inside his suit jacket. Jason glimpsed a flash of blue steel.

The advantage of carrying a weapon in the small of the back rather than a shoulder holster was that the shooter could assume a firing position without waiting for his gun to come to bear. Jason was in a two-handed stance, the SIG Sauer covering both men, before the other man had cleared his Beretta.

Both of the suited men slowly raised their hands.

Jason turned his head in Maria's direction, unwilling to take his sight off the men for an instant. "Tell them to use their left hands to take their guns out and drop them on the ground."

They complied, the older man speaking angrily as Jason kicked the two automatics well out of reach down the slope.

"He says they are National Security Service and that you will never see the outside of prison if you do not put your gun down immediately and surrender."

Italians knew the second-person form of the verb?

"Ask him to show identification. Slowly."

Before Maria could translate, both men were holding wallets with badges attached. Jason looked carefully, aware that he wouldn't recognize the bogus from the real. Again the older man spoke irately.

"He says you are Jason Peters and you are wanted for questioning by the British and Italian authorities. He also wants to know about an incident that occurred on the highway in Sardinia day before yesterday."

Sardinia? How could he . . . ? The Volvo's tag—the car was registered in Sardinia. Jason leaned closer to read the name on the official ID. From the men's quick response to the request for identification, he suspected one or both understood a fair amount of English. "Please tell Signore Belli he's not exactly in a position to make demands, and ask him what makes him think I'm the person he's looking for."

This time, Maria translated in full before there was a response. Belli jutted out a defiant jaw in a manner reminiscent of pictures Jason had seen of Mussolini. In fact, take away the white hair and he might have been looking at *Il Duce* himself.

Maria translated. "It is no consequence how he knows who you are. You are arrested."

Jason's gaze followed the line from his gun muzzle to the security man's head. "Maybe. But I'm the one holding the gun." He jabbed it forward in a threatening manner. "And I'm not afraid to use it. Tell him he's got about ten seconds to answer my question."

Jason was now certain the older man understood English. He puffed out his chest in the pose that had become associated with the Italian dictator, as he spoke to Maria.

"He doesn't, er, submit to threats from criminals. To do so would dishonor his country, his service, and himself."

With studied indifference, Jason squeezed off a shot that missed Belli's ear by no more than an inch, close enough that the man could feel its hot breath as it whined by and chipped a piece of rock from the incline behind him. Both Italians were flat on the ground before the first echoes bounced from hill to hill like a volleyed tennis ball.

Maria's eyes were larger than Jason would have imagined nature allowed.

"Tell him the next two will take his ears off one at a time."

Dishonor, it seemed, was preferable to disfigurement.

Belli spoke quickly, shifting an uneasy glance from his prone position from Jason to Maria as he talked.

"The chief of their agency was notified of the body of what appeared to be a Russian in the house in Taormina. Since the bureau I work for is the owner and I had suddenly taken holiday time, they wanted to question me. Then that wreck in Sardinia with all those bullet shells and more dead lying about—he made a connection. You were the only person Interpol suspected of killing Russians, at least outside of Russia, and . . ."

Jason held up a hand. He had heard enough.

Maria was looking at him warily. "Jason, what are you going to do . . . ?"

"Do?" A voice came from behind them. Adrian was

marching the other two suits in front of a pointed pistol Jason recognized as a government-issue Beretta. The Sten was again slung over his shoulder. One of men looked somewhat worse for the wear. "We'll leave 'em in their bleedin' car an' toss the keys."

"Good idea," Jason concurred.

Moments later the four Italians were stripped of their cell phones and handcuffed inside a black Lancia from which the radio had been removed.

Adrian stuck his head in the open window, making sure all were secure. "Nice 'n' comfy, 'r ye?"

"*Vaffancula!*" the oldest one muttered.

Adrian grinned. "He's suggestin' I commit an anatomical impossibility."

The tone had suggested as much to Jason. "C'mon; let's get outta here before more show up."

"But they have our license plate number," Maria protested. "Will we not be stopped by the first policeman we see?"

Jason was already climbing into the driver's seat. "It's not the tag that helped them find us, believe me. Besides, isn't Baia just over those hills? We'll be there before dark."

Minutes later, Jason pulled off the pavement beside one of several roadside restaurants, partially shielded from view by a row of plane trees. He waited until two cars, a Smart and a Fiat 1500, parked and disgorged what looked like local workmen.

"On th' way home from work, I'd guess," Adrian said, stuffing his pipe. "Stoppin' by f' their pint."

"Grappa's more like it," Jason observed, hoping the pipe wasn't going to get lit until he could get upwind.

He was disappointed. He smelled the sulfur of a match, followed by a sour stench that reminded him of the time Pangloss had gotten too close to a charcoal grill. On second thought, he was maligning the aroma of scorched dog hair.

It was as if Adrian had read his mind. Or seen the wrinkled noses of both the other passengers. "Na' t' worry."

He got out of the car and lay down to look under it.

"There she is!"

He stood, the pipe clinched in his teeth, puffing in exul-
tation. He exhibited a small square of metal about the size
of the bar of soap Jason would expect in a hotel bathroom.
He trotted off across the parking lot, smoke trailing behind him like a locomotive. He stopped and knelt beside
the Fiat.

"What is he doing?" Maria wanted to know.

"Replanting the bug."

Her expression said he might as well have been speaking in Aramaic, Swahili, or jet-propelled Sanskrit.

"The bug, that little black thing he took from under this
car. The reason the police didn't have to follow us is because they had a homing device stuck somewhere underneath. Some satellite did their surveillance for them.
Good thing about that kind of satellites, though, is that
they only 'see' the impulses from the tracking equipment.
They don't see whose car it may be attached to."

"But where . . . ?"

"My guess is at the observatory."

"Why not arrest us there?"

"Then they wouldn't know where we were going or if
others might be involved in whatever they think we're doing, would they?"

"I guess not. But that car over there, the one Adrian is
attaching—"

"Somebody's going to have a real surprise on the way
home."

CHAPTER THIRTY-SEVEN

Via Della Dataria
Rome
That night

Inspectore Santi Guiellmo paced the floor of his office, oblivious to the late hour. *Zuccone!* Belli was a fool! Had it not been for a couple of teenagers on bicycles looking for a deserted place to fornicate, Belli and his men would have spent a miserable night handcuffed to their own police car. Guiellmo almost wished they had. They certainly deserved it!

Belli had followed that farce with an even greater one.

He had commandeered one of the lovers' cell phones, checked in with his headquarters, and called every available *polizia* and carabiniere within a hundred kilometers in the name of the *forze dell'ordine*, a security force that was now the joke of every cop south of the Alps. It had required nearly thirty armed officers to apprehend two elderly, unarmed, and grappa-besotted stonemasons on their way home from work in a Fiat.

Guiellmo had little sense of humor, none where his agency was involved. Under Italy's civil service, firing someone was even more impossible than it was in the private sector, but Belli would reach retirement in Italy's remote northeastern Adriatic coast, the Marche, chasing Gypsy sheep thieves.

No doubt they, too, would outsmart him.

At least the imbecile had been able to give descriptions. The woman was certainly Dr. Bergenghetti, something already known. What remained a question was her involvement with the two men, and in what were they involved? Judging by the Volvo's registration, one of the men was a Scot named Adrian Graham, who had retired from the British army and resided in Sardinia. Belli had heard the woman call the second man Jason, confirming his identity.

What was going on? Peters was likely responsible for the death in Sicily and four more in Sardinia. But why? Surely the man was not on some campaign of his own, simply out to reduce the Slavic population. Such a goal might be commendable, albeit illegal, but certainly profitless. Peters was after something else.

But what?

Guiellmo spread a map of the Bay of Naples across the top of his desk, his forehead wrinkled in thought. What was Peters doing at Cumae, seeking aid from a Sibyl who had not been in residence for two thousand years? What else was there at Cumae other than ancient Greek ruins that could be of interest? He ran a finger along the crescent of the coast. If archaeological sites were of some sort of significance, the closest to Cumae would be Baia.

There was something about Baia. . . . He couldn't remember.

Stepping across his office, he opened the drawer of a small table, taking out a number of tourist guidebooks. He had always intended to take a summer vacation, exchange the sauna that was Rome in August for the sea breezes of the Amalfi coast. These books were the closest he had come to fulfilling what he now realized was little more than fantasy.

He flipped pages of bright photographs until he came to Baia. What he read sounded more like myth than fact. Fact or fiction, whatever had brought Peters to Cumae was likely to take him to Baia or Pozzuoli next. Both were sites of significant Greek ruins. Only one, though, was likely to require self-contained breathing apparatus.

He went back to his desk and picked up the telephone. This time he would lead the operation himself, confide in no one, and have only himself to blame for failure.

CHAPTER THIRTY-EIGHT

Port of Savannah
Savannah, Georgia
0942 EST of the same day

The rusty freighter left a creamy wake in the mocha-colored waters as its Liberian flag hung limply in the morning's increasing humidity. There was nothing to distinguish the ship from any of the others plowing along within yards of the cobbled streets of the city's historic waterfront area, certainly no clue that the ship was owned and operated by Pacific Oriental Shipping, a partnership of entities that included the Sheikh of Dubai and Hutchinson-Whampoa. HW had controlled ports at both ends of the Panama Canal since one of America's lesser lights had used his presidential office to give that waterway to Panama. The idea could have come to him only as dementia from a peanut field's heat and been mistaken for divine inspiration. After all, God frequently gave him personal direction.

What had not been revealed from on high was that Hutchinson-Wampao was owned by the Chinese army, hardly a force friendlier to the United States than its partner from the United Arab Emirates.

The containers stacked on deck, equally ordinary, would draw no attention, either. Specially ordered form plastic and auto parts from Japan, exotic wood from Malaya, and reproduction antiques from Taiwan (the Chinese saw no reason to let a political quarrel with the latter interfere with Western-style profit).

The ship's log included a stop at Naples, where a single container had been taken on board, marked simply, LANDSCAPING GOODS. The question of why any shipper would detour across the globe for such a small and mundane cargo might have caught the attention of port authorities had their union not repeatedly told them that questioning logs and cargo manifests was Uncle Sam's job, not theirs, and performing such a task gratuitously could only jeopardize the next contract negotiations.

Once quayside, the landscaping goods were lifted off the deck by a crane like any other bit of cargo and stacked on the dock five or six containers high. There was approximately a one in one hundred chance its contents might actually be inspected. The funding of the Transportation Security Administration was far too stretched to permit both the high-profile confiscation of passengers' cigarette lighters at the nation's airports as well as the far lesser known investigation of the millions of tons of shipping entering ports annually.

Few voters passed through marine ports of entry.

A large German shepherd, trained in detection of explosive material, did lead his handler down the corridor of stacked containers. Whether he discerned something or felt only the urge to leave a pee mail message for the next canine to pass this way, he cocked his leg as he panted in the increasing heat.

That was as close an inspection as the crate would receive in Savannah.

JOURNAL OF SEVERENUS TACTUS

My journey is to me a dream, as I see it now. The tiny craft, weighted by two men and the spare form of the Sibyl, wallowed precariously across a river that so reeked of rot,[1] I put a cloth over my nose.

Charon had hardly touched the far bank with his oar to hold the little boat in place when the Sibyl jumped to shore with a nimbleness I would have expected in a much younger woman. As I have said, all the underground was enveloped in a dark haze, but I saw this other side of the river as though through a veil as well as eyes that did not want to remain open.[2]

We were in a domed cavern of some sort, the size of which I was unable to measure. The landscape was one of the most scant of features I had ever encountered, scattered sparse bushes and huge rocks. Surrounding us were faceless forms, spirits of the departed clad in hoods that shadowed faces. All were unknown to me but moaned in a manner most pitiful. As the Sibyl led me past them, many held out supplicating arms as though they suffered some torment I might relieve.

We had not gone far when the Sibyl held up a hand to restrain my further progress. In front of me stood a figure silhouetted in the fuzzy light. He was as tall as my father, but his face, like the others, was concealed by a hood. Yet I could see light reflecting from his eyes and make out the line of the wound he received when as a boy he fell from a horse.[3]

He said nothing but gazed at me with a steady look.

"Father," I said, "it is I, your son, Severenus, come here to the place of the dead to speak with you."

If he heard, he gave no sign.

I tried again. "Father, my mother—your wife, Celia—sends you greetings, as do your other children."

Again there was no response and I was beginning to wonder if the dead had no ears.[4]

"Father" I said, raising my voice to be certain it might be heard above the moans of the other shades. "At your death, the granary was near empty; there were few goods in the storehouse and less in the treasury. Surely you removed these things elsewhere. Pray share with your family that location."

I feared, once again, that I would receive only silence as an answer.

Instead the form spoke in a whisper that could have been my father's voice or that of the wind in the spring leaves. "What you truly seek has been removed beyond your reach[5] to be placed in the care of the servant of the god."

This made little sense. My father, although careful to offend no deity, was not a religious man, worshiping only Augustus, the man-god emperor.

He turned and began to walk away.

This was no answer but a riddle. I had

not journeyed this distance nor spent funds that my family needed for other purposes to leave with only an enigma. I started after him, but the Sibyl stood in my way. I stepped aside to get around her.

Just then there were flashes of fire and I could see the flaming bushes were burning. As before, they consumed not themselves, but there were rocks placed next to each plant that began to glow from the flames. I thought I saw a mist emanate from stone, as though a spirit therein were being liberated.

My memory is a blank slate from that point until the time I awoke from what must have been a deep sleep, tormented by Morpheus.[6] I was in a plain room with no idea how long I had so been. Almost immediately robed priests appeared, carrying some sort of stew, which I consumed in its entirety. They would answer neither my questions as to how long I had remained in these quarters nor what had happened in the place of departed spirits after the bushes began to burn.

Instead, they interrogated me closely as to my experience. Had I seen my father? Was I certain it was he? Had I received the answer I sought? These questions were not asked in the manner of a friend making inquiry, but rather with the intensity of one determined to receive information.[7]

At last I was free to go. I was shocked to discover that a full four days had passed since I entered the Netherworld.

But I could not go home, not without

the information for which I and my family had paid so dearly. Then, like a vision from Jupiter, I recalled the view of Agrippa's home. Surely an old family friend, particularly one so powerful, would render such assistance as he could, perhaps intercede with the priests or even force them to restore part of the fortune I had spent.

The villa was as glorious as I remembered, high on a cliff overlooking the sea. Its walls enclosed three full acres,[8] with a path winding to the beach below, where strange and exotic fish swam in ponds.[9]

I entered the enclosure and gave my name to an inquiring slave. I had hardly dismounted to sit in the shade of a towering fruit tree[10] when I was led into the coolness of the house.

Agrippa himself, older and more enfeebled than I remembered, greeted me dressed in a shining white toga trimmed in purple.[11] He took my elbow in his bony grasp, taking me to a room that opened onto an inner courtyard, where we were furnished cool wine and sampled figs and dates. After solemnly noting his sorrow at my father's death, he asked what he might do for me.

I told him as much of my experience in the underworld as I could remember, including my father's shade's strange remark that his fortune had been placed in the "hands of the servant of the god."

The problem, of course, was which servant of which god, a puzzle the old

man promised to consider. I could see
the riddle disturbed him but I knew not
why, perhaps because of the great price I
had paid for a mere puzzle to solve. He
suggested I remain his guest until he ascertained the best course of action, an
invitation I was hardly in a position to
decline.

NOTES

1. Severenus uses the word *putrescere*, the
Latin verb for "to rot or putrefy." Knowing what
we do today of the area, it would be safe to assume the air was heavy with sulfuric fumes.

2. Consider the smoke from lamps or torches,
the fumes previously alluded to, and the drugs he
had been fed over the last few days.

3. A well-known scar easily reproduced by
cosmetics?

4. Hearing.

5. *Extra manum*, literally, "out of hand."

6. Greek god of dreams.

7. It could be speculated that the visitors to
Hades who did not return were those who were
skeptical of what they had seen and heard.

8. A rough equivalency. The actual words were
"fifty by fifty *heredia*." One hundred *heredia*
equals approximately ten thousand square meters.

9. Ponds of fish, both fresh- and salt-water,
were a competitive display of wealth among Romans with seaside villas. The occupants of these
ponds were frequently edible, and the more uncommon the species, the better. At least one full-
time servant would be required to monitor the
water level and temperature, feed, etc.

10. Since few fruit trees "tower," it is likely

Severenus refers to a date palm, which would have been imported from Africa, another Roman version of conspicuous consumption.

11. A color allowed only to senators and other nobles.

PART VI

CHAPTER THIRTY-NINE

Baia
Early the next morning

Jason had finished all but one chapter of the article in Adrian's archaeological magazine in the waning hour of daylight as the Scot drove the short distance from Cumae. They had parked the Volvo in a lot near Pozzuoli's ancient forty-thousand-seat Greek amphitheater in hopes it would remain unnoticed. Jason and Maria had taken a cab to Baia, leaving Adrian to find a van large enough to carry both him and the gear from the observatory.

They had found a single room in a small pensione. Jason had handed over the false passports and made sure the elderly proprietor had returned to his quarters before admitting Adrian, who had spent the night in a less than comfortable chair. Jason had hoped that the police would be looking for a trio, not a man and wife.

Early the next morning, Jason attempted to retrieve the passports after letting Adrian out through a window. The proprietor was not to be found, and Jason made a mental note to regain the documents later in the day. Now they waited among the crumbled walls of a Roman temple of

Venus on a terrace above the present town. Below were
the domes of the baths of Mercury and Venus, therapeutic
springs used well into the Middle Ages.

The rising sun painted the bay the color of pink roses until it cleared the horizon, leaving the sky a cloudless blue
tinged with purple, an expanse marked only by the twin-
kling eye of a single morning star until it, too, winked out.

Jason stood and stretched. "Do we know how to find
wherever it is we're going?"

Maria pointed up a slight slope. "There."

Jason squinted. In the early light what he had mistaken
for the rock face of a nearby hill bracketed by stumps of
columns was in fact a single slab of cement. Closer inspection revealed a razor-wire fence partly concealed by
scrub bush. He could not make out the words on a couple of faded signs. He was fairly certain they didn't offer
welcome.

"The Great Antrum to the underworld," Maria announced.

"Not exactly hospitable," Jason observed. "Someone
sure doesn't want us in there."

"The Italian government," Maria said. "They claim that
it may collapse and it may be filled with poisonous gases.
It has been sealed since 2001, remember?"

Jason helped her sling her air tank and regulator over a
shoulder before picking up his own. "Since Robert Temple's exploration."

She was walking up the gentle slope. "Yes."

They stopped at the strands of wire. A few minutes with
a wire cutter from Adrian's pack made a narrow but pass-
able entrance. Now they stood at the base of a slope of
some twenty feet, a solid face of concrete.

"This may na' be so deft," Adrian observed. "We canna
spend th' day chippin' through cement."

Jason, his hand touching the wall, was moving slowly to
his left. He felt what he thought was a crack. He was looking at a rectangular cut around an area about five and a

half by three, just large enough to admit a man. Someone had made an effort to conceal the seams with vegetation pulled from nearby.

Adrian took a few steps back, arms akimbo. "Y' may have found a way in, but I'm doubtin' th' three of us kin lift such a slab."

"Someone obviously can," Jason replied. "Otherwise cutting it in here wouldn't have made sense."

Maria reached out a hand to run it across the surface. "This is not cement."

"Not cement?" Jason echoed.

There was a flat thumping sound as Maria rapped her knuckles against the surface. "Not at all. Plastic."

Adrian reached out and confirmed what she had said. "Someone must've cut a hole here and replaced it with lighter material."

"Only reason they'd do that," Jason said, "is so they can come in and out whenever they wish."

There was no doubt as to who "they" were.

It took little effort to remove what was no more than a cleverly customized plastic form, one that a single person could easily lift and replace from inside. The three checked their regulators before struggling into the backpacks with heavy their air tanks and tested the lamps in their helmets. Adrian and Jason both made sure their weapons were readily accessible.

On his knees, Adrian leaned into the entrance. The hungry darkness swallowed the light of his helmet lamp. "Ye're right, laddie, aboot someone comin' in 'n' out. There's a ladder here."

Sure enough, the entrance dropped straight down to a floor about six feet below before the passage disappeared under the hill. Jason helped Maria down.

Jason stood at the gates of Hades. He tried to remember how many people had prophesied his arrival.

Gas detector extended, Maria led the way single file down a corridor wide enough only for single file. Even so,

Jason's shoulders brushed against the walls constantly, and he bowed his head. The corridor wasn't built for the size of a twenty-first-century man. Anyone who didn't believe in evolution should try strolling through a passage carved two thousand years ago.

Rubble, either from Agrippa's attempt to close the passages or moved there by one of the two explorations, littered the stone floor, sometimes piled so high that the trio had to crawl between it and the roof.

The lights on their helmets revealed chiseled marks on the low ceiling as the passage began a gradual descent. At regular intervals, the rock was streaked with black above small ledges that had once held lamps. There was the smell of long-dead earth and a silence that rang in the ears, a quiet that seemed to resent the interruption of footsteps upon stone. At the periphery of his light, Jason could see moving things, large insects, he guessed, indignant at the intrusion. They silently swarmed, divided, and reunited in hazy clouds before disappearing back into the sea of gloom.

He shined his light on a handheld compass for a few steps, surprised to see the excavation had been placed in a precise east–west orientation. How could that have been done underground before compasses were invented?

A few minutes later they entered a vaulted chamber, the roof invisible above. In the center, a slab of the native tufa rock had been carved with figures of gods and animals, still quite clear.

"A sacrificial altar," Adrian whispered as though in a church. "Where animals were slaughtered, I'd guess."

Past the chamber, the passageway took a sharp turn. Maria was so intent on the gas detector she bumped into the far wall before she saw it.

"*Stronzo!*" she exclaimed, backing into Adrian.

Jason was fairly certain the exclamation had not invoked the name of a saint. "You okay?"

He could see Maria rubbing her nose. "I will be fine," she grumbled in a tone that said she didn't believe it.

Jason took a step backward, the light on his helmet probing shadows he had not previously noticed. He looked closer. A slit carved into the rock led into an even narrower passageway that seemed to go in a direction that intercepted the angle made by the turn like the hypotenuse of a triangle. On one side, crumbling iron hinges were still visible.

Adrian had somehow managed to turn around despite the bulk of his backpack. "A concealed path, I'd say."

Jason nodded. "One that would put the priests and animals in front of the visitor when they had been behind, just as Severenus described. That must have seemed like magic."

"Na' chance we could squeeze through wearin' this kit?"

Jason shook his head. "We'd have to leave the air tanks here."

"That would be unwise." Maria's head was poking around Adrian's body. "If what Jason says is correct, we will see where this path comes out anyway."

With Maria still holding the gauge in front of her like a crucifix leading a choir's procession, they continued until they reached another chamber with its sacrificial altar. To the altar's left was another ancient doorway, probably the end of the passage they had discovered a few minutes earlier. On the other side of the room, the slope decreased and flattened out.

Shortly past where the passage began again, they came to a dry riverbed. Their lights shone into only a void, the far shore being too far away to see. The water had been hardly three feet deep, but the sharp edges of the banks indicated the current had been swift. The streambed was mostly polished slabs of stone, making their crossing fairly easy.

The River Styx had been about a hundred feet wide, although the dark and the time it would have taken to pole against or across the flow could have made the distance seem longer.

The far bank was an immense cavern, sloping gently upward from the riverbed. Its walls soared like the nave of a cathedral until vanishing into darkness beyond the beams of their lights. A sole bat, disturbed by the illumination, flew erratic circles before disappearing into the dusk from which it had come.

"See here." Adrian was kneeling over what at first looked like a slight depression in the rock floor. "It's a hole with what looks like a tunnel at th' bottom."

"That would allow the 'shades' of the dead to appear and disappear," Maria observed, pointing to several more.

Very interesting, Jason thought—but not what they had come to find. Walking slowly to avoid falling into one of the openings, he played his lantern across the nearest wall.

"Maria," he called, "what do you make of this?"

She was beside him in a moment, both looking at a series of round gray boulders. Between each a scraggly, seemingly dead bush had been inserted into a hole cut into the rock floor. How could anything grow in such darkness? It couldn't, Jason concluded. Someone had placed them here. But why?

Maria knelt on the hard-packed earth, running a hand over one of the rocks.

"Pumice."

The word took Jason back to the house in Georgetown, to Saturday mornings when Laurin, clad in rubber gloves, goggles, and coveralls bearing the logo of some oil company, would begin work on an obvious piece of junk rescued from one of the local shops. Before the day was out, her abrasive—sandpaper and pumice—usually produced a treasure that had been hidden below years if not centuries of chipped paint and blackened varnish.

Even here in Hades, she followed him. She had always threatened she would. He pushed the thought away to concentrate on the problem. Laurin went reluctantly but with understanding.

"You mean like what people use to sand furniture?"

Adrian had joined them as Maria said, "It can be used as a fine sandpaper, yes. It is a volcanic glass, very poor, er . . . full of holes."

"Porous?" Jason suggested.

"Very porous. And I will guess that it will match exactly the specimen you brought me." She passed her meter over the stone, "Yes, just like the one you brought, I am receiving indications of ethylene gases. I have never seen such a property of volcanic rock before."

"But why," Jason asked, "would someone take rock from here halfway around the world, unless—"

There was a flash almost in front of Maria's face. One of the bushes had begun to burn. More correctly, flame danced just above it, leaving the plant unconsumed. Almost immediately nearby stones began to give off a thin trail of smoke.

"The rock is giving up its gases as it heats," she snapped. "Put your regulators in your mouths, and don't breathe through your nose."

As a scuba diver, Jason had no trouble doing just that. He was relieved to see that the other two seemed equally at home with the arrangement. He stood back as yet another of the scruffy plants seemed to burst into flame soundlessly. He could imagine the reaction of the drugged, susceptible young Roman, Severenus.

Or was it another sound that overrode the whisper of the flames? He listened intently. Had the solitary bat returned? No, what he heard was not the beating of tiny wings. It sounded more like . . .

Like footsteps from the darkness in front of them.

Chapter Forty

Amtrak
Somewhere between Washington, D.C., and Atlanta
1430 EST the previous day

Rassavitch had wanted to fly from New York to Savannah, but being subject to scrutiny both when he boarded for Atlanta and when he changed planes for Savannah was putting too much credibility in the Americans' insistence on nonethnic profiling. That a post-9/11 United States would decline to detain someone spekaing heavily accented English to check his background and purpose for being on the aircraft more closely rather than offend someone was simply beyond belief. The Americans were polluters and despoilers but not idiots. Their much-proclaimed willingness to search and inquire of an equal number of blond Scandinavian and abaya-wearing, dark-skinned women who might well conceal anything under their loose-fitting robes was not egalitarian; it was suicidal.

Rassavitch didn't believe a word of it.

With Rassavitch's poor language skills, flat, Slavic face, and ghostly white skin, the authorities would surely study the New York driver's permit he had effortlessly obtained.

They would question him for hours. Somehow they would know he was here to destroy them.

So, he took the train, where there were no security precautions.

The cars were clean, quiet, and mostly empty. At first he wondered why more Americans did not use this mode of transportation. His answer came at every place the tracks paralleled a highway: automobiles sped by far faster than the train. So did the buses he saw.

He would have an opportunity to ride one of those buses from Atlanta, where the train would go on to New Orleans. From the bus to Savannah, he was to go to an address he had been given by a man who had sought him out yesterday and handed him a copy of Chekhov's plays with the correct passages underlined. In the book had been ten one-hundred-dollar bills and an address in Savannah.

There was no indication as to what Rassavitch should do when he reached the Georgia port city, nor instructions as to how the money should be used, although it was obvious some of it would be spent reaching his destination. Once he got there, he would figure out what to do next.

CHAPTER FORTY-ONE

Baia

In front of Jason, Adrian stiffened, his head cocked to listen.

"Wha . . . ?" Maria took the regulator from her mouth, then froze.

Jason inhaled and removed his regulator, whispering, "I'd say we've got company."

"But who . . . ?"

"You can bet it ain't the Sibyl."

He pointed to the light on his helmet as he turned it off. Maria and Adrian did the same, leaving them in a darkness punctuated with the flare of the bushes that did not burn. The gaseous flames cast flickering shadows that danced menacingly across the walls to make forms of fanciful creatures of all descriptions.

In fact, Jason thought at first that it was these imaginary creatures he saw emerging from the hazy darkness at the farthest point of the cavern. The thing looked insectlike, round eyes occupying a full three-quarters of a face with a tube for a mouth. Approaching with a low shuffling motion, it was something out of a bad sci-fi movie, although there was noting fictional about the automatic weapon it carried.

Jason's hand went to his own face, searching for a leak in his breathing equipment that could have allowed him to inhale the hallucinatory fumes of the steaming rocks. As far as he could tell, the ethylene gas had nothing to do with what his eyes kept insisting he was perceiving and his brain kept trying to dismiss as impossible.

Another of the creatures emerged into the shimmering light, and Jason realized what he was actually seeing, ashamed of the relief he felt. The fire dancing above several bushes was reflecting off the glass eye ports of old-fashioned gas masks, their air hoses a trunklike connection to the air purification system on each man's back.

Jason counted six of them. Mere men or not, they were now probing the reluctant shadows of the cavern with flashlights, both sweeping the floor with each step to prevent falling into one of the numerous shafts to the tunnel below, and searching every crevice. It required no effort to guess for whom.

Jason could see Adrian, a solid form of darkness to his left. Keeping a low profile, he pulled Maria behind as he duckwalked over, took a breath, and removed his mouthpiece. "We need to back out of here, same way we came."

"That a fact?"

On all fours, hands outstretched, searching for unseen openings that could result in a fatal fall, Jason, Adrian, and Maria shuffled across the rubble-strewn floor.

Any doubt as to the intentions of the men in gas masks dissolved when a beam of light exposed Jason. He rolled violently to his left, shoving Maria away as a stream of gunfire chipped an explosion of tiny, shrapnel-like fragments from the stones where he had been. The sound was still booming off the walls and unseen ceiling as Adrian rolled onto his back and fired two single rounds from the captured Beretta in the direction of the muzzle flash. He was rewarded by a yelp of pain.

"The river," Jason said, trying to keep his attention on the floor they were crossing. "If we can make it to the riverbed we should be able to see them better than they can see us."

"Aye." Adrian grunted. "But then, there're a lot more of them than us."

Adrian, always the optimist.

By the time the three slid down the steep bank of the riverbed, the flaming bushes were little more than a glow in the distant darkness, not enough light to frame their pursuers.

"We can put the breathing equipment away," Maria whispered.

"You can read the gas gauge in the dark?" Adrian wanted to know.

She held it up, showing a tiny green light.

Thankful for the smallest of favors, Jason wriggled out of the heavy backpack, helped Maria off with hers, and led the group to the far side of the dry river. Without the equipment, they should easily outdistance those behind them. Halfway up the embankment they stopped, each looking over a shoulder.

"Sodding bastards're comin' right on," Adrian whispered, seeing the beams of light sweeping the gully. "Wee long for a shot."

"A bit long for their flashlights, too," Jason said, starting back up the incline. "I wouldn't be revealing our position by taking a shot at them."

Jason reached the top first and reached back to take Maria's hand.

"I can manage," she said tartly.

Was it the tension or had he made some unknown misstep?

Once all three were atop the bank, they began to feel their way along the narrow passage through which they had entered. Here, at least, there were no holes concealed in the dark.

There was, however, endless rubble.

As Adrian tripped for the third time, he swore softly. "I'll be bloody killin' meself; I canna see."

"If we turn on our lights, somebody else will do it for you."

"Look!" Maria spoke aloud.

At the instant she spoke, Jason saw a glimmer of light ahead, a mere flicker that could just as well have been his imagination.

Adrian had seen it, too. "Bloody hell! Now they're in front as well!"

"Feel your way along the wall," Jason advised. "Somewhere along here is the sacrificial chamber where that other passageway comes in."

"An' what is making you think we're the only ones knowin' aboot it?" Adrian asked. "They could jus' as well be comin' through there, too."

Adrian had the optimism of a man mounting the gallows.

CHAPTER FORTY-TWO

I-95, between Savannah and Charleston
22:21 EST the previous day

Eighteen-wheelers owned the interstate late at night. They rushed by with a blaze of headlights and a whoosh of air that made the old flatbed truck shiver, sometimes so hard that Rassavitch feared the single container on the back might come loose from its restraints.

The container.

When he had arrived at the Savannah bus station, a man had brushed by him, shoving a slip of paper into his hand. The paper bore what Rassavitch thought was a street address, a guess confirmed by the cabbie who had driven him away from the Greyhound terminal. In minutes, the taxi had been cruising through a seedy neighborhood where the few functioning streetlights showed houses thirsting for paint and weedy yards hosting rusted hulks of automobiles. The occasional resident strode quickly along cracked sidewalks as though in a hurry to get off the street, casting only a glare of resentment at the wealth implied by a taxi ride.

The cab slowed and the driver was scanning the few street numbers. He stopped in front of a house showing no lights but with a flatbed truck in the dirt driveway. "This looks like it." He turned his head, looking up and down the deserted street as if expecting an assault any minute. "You want, I kin wait here till you inside."

Rassavitch shook his head, peeling the fare off the wad of bills that was ever diminishing.

As the cab's taillights hastily retreated to an area where passengers were more likely, Rassavitch circled the truck. Through the slats of the sides he could see a single large box on the flatbed. He looked around. Surely someone had been watching the vehicle. In this neighborhood, it would not have still been here otherwise.

The door to the cab was unlocked. As he heaved himself into the driver's seat, he noted that the key was in the ignition and a road map of the eastern United States was taped to the dash. He cranked the engine, surprised at an even purr inconsistent with the shabby body. He made one last effort to peer into the shadows around the house before putting the gear into reverse.

So far, the ride had been uneventful, the silver-on-green mile markers slipping by rhythmically. Between eighteen-wheelers, the symphony of a late-spring night in the South flooded the cab through an open window: the constant argument of the katydids, the chirp of crickets, and an occasional shriek of some night raptor. The sounds were almost hypnotic, totally unlike the moan of the night wind across the Siberian steppes of his youth.

Another behemoth of the road roared by, drowning out the music of living things and snapping Rassavitch's attention back to the highway in his lights.

I-95 had been marked in red on the map with a small town in Virginia just south of Washington circled. On the margin, in Russian, had been the words for *tomorrow night*. He had torn them off and shredded the small slip of paper. He had no idea why he must deliver the truck and its cargo overnight, nor would he ask.

He would simply do it.

Chapter Forty-three

Baia

Jason no longer touched the carved stone wall; only empty space. With his hand holding Maria's left, he probed the darkness.

"We must be in the chamber," he whispered. "The secret passage is here somewhere on the left."

The flicker of lights from behind them as becoming a constant glow.

"Aye," Adrian replied sotto voce, "but can we find it in time?"

"Only if we all try. Let's spread out as far as we can and still hold one hand; use the other to search the wall."

Jason was moving when he heard voices echoing in the tunnel in front of them. Lights were getting close enough that he could distinguish gray forms that were Adrian and Maria. He estimated that the two groups would meet in minutes.

With the three of them between.

"Here!" Maria said triumphantly. "I found it."

She pulled Jason toward her to verify that there was a void in the stone. As soon as his hand could define the

opening, he pushed her inside, using his other hand to tug
Adrian along. The passage was too narrow. Not only did
Jason's shoulders touch both sides, but he had to stoop to
avoid smacking his head on the ceiling. Turning his body
would have been difficult.

He managed to look over his shoulder in time to see six
or seven men pick their way single file along the main corridor behind them, each carrying a flashlight in one hand
and a pistol in the other. They wore no gas masks. Their
bulky Kevlar body armor attested to the fact they expected trouble of a more ordinary sort. Jason felt Maria
tense, and he became aware he was holding his breath
rather than risk the sound being heard.

When the dark finally swallowed the reflection of flashlight beams, Jason gave Maria a gentle push. "If we're
lucky, we can make it back to the main passage and out of
here. . . ."

He was interrupted by a shout, words distorted as they
echoed down the long tunnel. The staccato burst of an automatic weapon was followed by the popping sounds of
pistols.

"Who in hell . . . ?" Adrian asked.

"In hell, indeed," Jason said. "Whatever's happening,
let's get out of here before they stop shooting at one another and start looking for us."

With shots and voices reverberating behind them,
Maria risked turning on the lamp on her miner's helmet.
Although it illuminated the narrow way, it did little to de-
fine the rubble over which the trio hurriedly stumbled.
The broad sweep of the light showed the intersection with
the main corridor just as Maria stopped suddenly.

Jason ran into her back as Adrian ran into his. "What?"

"Don't you feel it?"

"Feel what?"

Before she could reply, he had his answer. With each series of gunfire there was a faint quiver beneath his feet, as
though he were feeling the sound. A string of automatic

fire sent an almost imperceptible tremor through the wall Jason was touching.

Adrian spoke Jason's mind. "Best we be on our way, 'fore this bleedin' fox's burrow falls in on our heads."

As if in reply, a stream of dust poured from overhead, followed by a rock the size of Jason's fist.

"It's the vibrations," Maria explained needlessly. "There's nothing shoring the rock up."

Her observation was punctuated by a grinding sound overhead, another eruption of dust, and a crash as the top of the side tunnel they had just passed through collapsed.

This time Jason was less than gentle as he shoved her forward. "Move!"

Quick movement was difficult. The beams from their lights reflected from dust particles to form a choking, shimmering fog that obscured visibility more than a few inches in any direction. A short distance away, Jason heard the crash of larger stones striking the floor. His sight was wavering as the dust stung his eyes. Every breath felt as if he were inhaling sand. He coughed and tried to spit out the grit grinding between his teeth. His mouth was desert dry.

Were they behind or in front?

Adrian gave voice to the fear Jason was trying to stifle. "How th' bloody hell're we supposed to know which way is out?"

"A fifty-fifty chance," Jason said without the slightest intent of being facetious.

"Aye, laddie, but a certain chance of bein' crushed if we dinna move quick."

THE WASHINGTON POST
CEREAL HEIRESS'S HOME TO BE
SITE OF CONFERENCE
　　WASHINGTON—
　　The location of the president's envi-
ronmental conference was announced

today as Hillwood, the last home of cereal heiress and legendary Washington
hostess Marjorie Merriwether Post,
who resided there from 1957 until her
death in 1973.

Ms. Post's former husband, Joseph
Davies, served as ambassador to Russia
from 1937 to 1938, during which time a
cash-pressed Soviet Union was selling
art treasures confiscated from both the
Catholic Church and the deposed Romanov family. Ms. Post and her husband
became connoisseurs of Russian art,
and Hillwood contains the largest collection of such art outside Russia, including at least fifty imperial Fabergé eggs.

Located between Connecticut Avenue
and Rock Creek Park in the Woodley
Park residential area, the estate was left
to the Smithsonian Institute upon Ms.
Post's death.

The size of the property, its multiple
gardens, and towering trees will provide
privacy for the meeting, while its limited accessibility will aid security measures that White House sources have
described as "tight."

Further details, such as the names of
those attending and which conservation
organizations will be represented, have
not been made public. The president, in
a highly controversial move, has announced possible amnesty for those accused of crimes in the name of the
environment, such as the American
Greens, three members of which are accused of burning a corn-cloning labora-

tory in Kansas last year, which accidentally resulted in the death of a chemist.

"Someone has to start somewhere,"
Tony Blackman, White House press secretary, said. "If all sides can agree on the
future of our planet, what does it matter
who made the first move?"

CHAPTER FORTY-FOUR

Hillwood
4155 Linnean Avenue, Washington, D.C.

Shirlee Atkins was no more than a cleaning lady. Oh, she had a free uniform furnished by the foundation that supported this big ol' house, an' she had the benefit of a union contract, an' she was called a "custodian," whatever that was, but other than that, this job wasn't no different from the ones she'd had in homes of senators and representatives and them lobby people, houses some bigger than this one over to Georgetown an' Kalorama an' even Arlington. 'Cept Arlington wasn't really in Washington, was it? She wasn't sure.

Anyway, this job paid enough for a small apartment away from the projects where the kids could go to school without dodgin' between crack addicts, dope pushers, and hos, where the sirens didn't wail all night. Place like hers, the kids had a chance to grow up an' be somethin' more 'n a housecleaner.

But she'd never worked in a house furnished quite like this one. Ever' day she come to work, walk right up to the columned brick front an' into that room at the front door.

Foyer, yep, that was it, the foyer. Big, two-story entrance, whatever it be called. She never seen no chandelier like that before. Mr. Jimson, he say it be Louie somebody, some French king. Rock crystal, he tell her. An' those people lookin' down from their golden frames, most of 'em draped with more fur than your average black bear. Course, they be Russians, and Shirlee understood it got pretty cold in Russia. Still, it suit Shirlee jus' fine that most of them Russian pictures were out in the little house in the yard, the dacha, Mr. Jimson called it, a place Ms. Post built for her Russian art. Weren't no nesting dolls there, though. Jus' paintings and jeweled things.

Cabinets on either side of the foyer full of porcelain, too. Why anybody want to eat off somethin' painted with flowers 'n' stuff, she didn't know. Couldn't hardly tell if it be clean even when you wash it.

Mr. Jimson laughed when she said that. But then, he laughed at a lot of what she said. Not that shitty you-dumb-nigga laugh some folks had when she said somethin', but a warm chuckle, like she 'n' Mr. Jimson enjoyin' the same joke. He an' Shirlee, they had a lot of laughs together. Like the time he said Ms. Post done bought his place when she run out of husbands an' chose it over successive . . . monog, monag . . . mahogany. Shirlee hadn't unnerstood 'xactly what he meant, but she laughed anyways. It made Mr. Jimson happy for her to laugh. He unnerstood when one of her kids needed to go to the doctor or had a problem at school, too. Ain't easy raisin' three kids with no daddy. Mr. Jimson understood that, too.

She sighed deeply and wiped away a single tear rolling down one fat cheek.

Mr. Jimson.

Done got hisse'f keeled by a car, steppin' off the curb two days ago. Driver never found. D.C. cops be lucky they could find the fly on their pants when they needed to piss.

This new man, the one called hisse'f some Russian-soundin' name, look like somethin' outta one o' her kids comics: big guy, head shaved, and from some country other than this one. He hardly spoke to nobody, all nervous and such. Yesterday, he 'bout jump outta his skin when Shirlee come up 'hind him to ax if she could leave a few minutes early. Him standin' there, lookin' outta the dinin' room window into the rose garden.

Shirlee guessed he was thinkin' 'bout that meetin' gonna take place in that room. Must be some kinda meetin', needin' thirty chairs around the marble inlaid table.

She needed to vacuum that rug, polish the table again 'fore any meetin' started. She wasn't too sure 'xactly what sort of meetin' gonna take place, but she heard tell the president hisse'f gonna be there. She wasn't 'bout to have no president come in 'n' think Shirlee Atkins was no sloppy housekeeper, no, sirree, Bob.

Thing was, those men diggin' in the rose garden right outside the French doors. They prolly Russian, too, judging by the way they talk English jus' like the new man. Make sense, the house full of Russian art an' all. She'd have to keep watch on 'em, see they didn' track no dirt into her house. Funny thing was that most of the diggin' in the rose garden should be in winter, when the plants were dormant. She'd heard tell that some of the mens come to this meetin' wanted some plants of their own. Why? Them roses pretty 'nough for anybody.

CHAPTER FORTY-FIVE

Baia

Maria tugged at Jason's shirt. "This way."

He could barely hear her over the increasing clatter of falling stones. "You sure?"

"You are the one who said we had a fifty-fifty chance. I'd prefer to take mine in the direction from which the air is moving."

For the first time Jason noticed the swirls and eddies in the mistlike cloud of grit. They definitely had a consistent flow, a river of air that could come only from an opening to the outside.

But which opening? There could be unclimbable vertical shafts.

In which case he would be no worse off than he was.

Those odds he could live with.

With Maria leading the way and Jason holding Adrian's hand, the three made their way along the tunnel, pausing only as larger and more numerous rocks fell around them. No one spoke. The rumble of a shattering rock formation would have had made conversation difficult, and to open one's lips was to invite a mouthful of grainy dust. Jason even managed not to swear when he barked his shin on a jagged boulder.

The echoes below the earth had made it impossible to tell with certainty the direction of the gunfire. Wherever it had come from, it had ceased. Jason supposed the combatants had exhausted their supply of ammo or people to shoot.

Or were trying to get out before the shaft collapsed.

He listened for the sound of feet on the rock floor behind them, but he doubted he could have heard a team of galloping horses over the sounds of the tunnel falling in.

The billowing dust seemed to grow lighter and lighter until its shine actually hurt. He was squinting, eyes as close to shut as possible, when the air he took in was suddenly free of rock particles and he felt a gentle, warm breeze on his face. Instead of a dark tunnel, he was looking at a bay, the gold dust of sunlight sparkling across its blue surface.

Using a shirtsleeve to wipe away what felt like layers of grime several inches thick on his face, he gulped in the clean, salty air. Maria slid down the rock face as though her spine and legs had turned to wet noodles. Adrian was alternately tilting his water bottle to his lips and washing out his mouth.

"Hey," Jason said, "c'mon. We can't stay here. No matter who comes out of that entrance, they aren't going to be friendly."

Maria struggled to her feet. "I understand the first group, the ones with gas masks, were the same people who tried to kill us in Sicily and Sardinia, some sort of ecoterrorists. But the second?"

Adrian pointed to a pair of plain but shiny black Lancias. "I'd fancy them to be police of some sort."

"Makes sense," Jason agreed. "Somehow they guessed we'd be here. Good thing they came when they did."

"Good for us," Maria said, watching dust belch out of the mouth of the cave. "Perhaps not so good for them."

As though her words were prophetic, the hillside trembled for an instant, then was obscured in a tornado of dust and rocks. None of the three said a word for perhaps five full minutes.

"Those policemen," Maria finally said. "They are trapped inside."

"So are Eglov and his thugs," Jason added.

"Ye really think so?" Adrian asked.

"Who else would have been down there other than someone who was planning to use the gases emitted by the pumice? They were all equipped to deal with it."

"But of what use to them would be nonlethal ethylene gas?" Maria wanted to know. "It is effective only in enclosures."

"I don't know," Jason admitted. "A hallucinogenic, nonfatal gas, usable only in enclosed space. But at least we now know what the 'Breath of the Earth' business was about. I'll send the info to Washington and let them sort it out."

"Do that on the way," Adrian suggested. "We've na' business hovering aboot here like drunken sods after last call. You can be sure the local constabulary'll be on its way when those poor devils in the cave don't return. Let's get what little kit we left at that wee hotel las' night an' be gone."

Jason turned to walk down the slope, sidestepping pebbles and rocks still tumbling downhill. "Better yet, let's not go back to the pensione. If the cops knew we were here, they're gonna look around. They'll find that an American and a woman fitting Maria's description checked in and never checked out. They'll assume we're in that cave, too."

"Fine for you, laddie," Adrian observed, fishing a plastic bag out of his back pocket. "But sooner or later the lass has to go back to her work, an' I'd like to go home m'self."

"Easy enough for me," Maria suggested. "I was duped by the handsome American spy who made me think he,

too, was a volcanologist. By the time I found out otherwise, I was his captive."

Adrian had removed his pipe from the bag and blew
through it with a wet whistling sound. "An' was madly in
love, too blind to see the possible pitfalls."

Jason looked at him skeptically.

"I'm na' 'round th' bend, lad. 'Tis the stuff of Italian fiction. They love it."

"It might work at that," Maria agreed.

"So, you just go back to work like nothing happened?"
Jason asked.

The question did not come from idle curiosity. He remembered her vow to return to her job as soon as any
volcanic exploration was over. He had managed to avoid
thinking about it. Since Laurin's death, women had entered his life for an evening, occasionally a weekend, and
exited just as casually. In most cases he had watched their
departure with a relief he suspected they shared. They had
made his life less empty by supplying a diversion or even
an imitation of love, a masquerade that shriveled and died
in the morning's light

Not Maria.

He admitted he did not want her to leave. For the first
time since his wife's death, he could actually imagine a
more permanent relationship. There was something about
that gap-toothed smile, the tenderness they shared after
sex, even the ludicrously expensive Hermès scarfs. Mostly,
there was that unexplainable something, that feeling that
defining it would reduce it to the banal.

But had she changed her mind since that night on the
Costa Smeralda?

" 'Twould be best if she put a day or so between here an'
returnin' to her normal life," Adrian observed. "Wee bit
too coincidental, she manages to escape at joos' the time
her captor is buried under a hundred tons or so of rock. I
propose we leave the Volvo here, go back to Silanus for a

day or so. Nothing happens there without people knowing aboot it. I'll have m' neighbors sniff out what they can before you return to whatever volcano you're workin' on, lass. Give me time to see how much muck I've gotten m'self into, too."

Jason tried not to show his anxiety as Maria considered what Adrian had said.

He also tried not to show his relief when she replied, "You make sense. A few days, then. But how do we get back to Sardinia without being seen?"

Jason leaped in. "They won't be looking for us if they think we're under all that rock, particularly if we go separately."

"Separately?" She looked apprehensive. "But what if some of those . . . people are still looking for us?"

"Eglov's people?" Jason asked. "I'd guess they're permanently entombed in Hades. Talk about just deserts! If not, another reason to lie low at Adrian's place for a few days. He can use his neighbors there to let us know if someone's looking for us." He reached into a pocket and produced the BlackBerry-like device. "Right now I gotta phone home."

Adrian put out a hand, tugging Jason's sleeve. "Not now, laddie. Give us long enough to get as far from here as possible before someone comes to check on the coppers we left in there."

Jason was staring at his communication. "Something must have hit it. It's not working."

"Anything that canna wait?"

Jason shook his head. "Can't think of anything."

CHAPTER FORTY-SIX

I-95, between Richmond and Washington
At the same time

Rassavitch's eyes felt as though they were full of sand, and his back was telegraphing pain all the way down his leg, but he was thankful for the safe trip.

He forced his eyelids open a little wider to read the address the man had given him at the convenience store a few miles back, the last place on his primary instructions: I-95 to the Beltway, to Rock Creek Parkway to . . .

He rubbed the back of a hand across his face and bit his lip in hopes the pain would keep him awake.

He *would* complete this mission.

PART VII

CHAPTER FORTY-SEVEN

Naples, Cagliari Ferry
Later the same day

The ferry provided overnight accommodations, but, unlike a hotel, no passport was required; nor was there a metal detector to screech at the weapon Jason was carrying. Jason stood at the boxy stern, watching the sun sink into the Tyrrhenian Sea. Maria would be following tomorrow morning with Adrian on the afternnon ferry. After a day or so Jason would be leaving, even though he was unsure as to where. Washington, certainly, for a debriefing. He supposed he had rid the world of Eglov, entombing him with a number of his radical environmentalists.

But what else? He had discovered a very strange plant and a rock that gave off a nonlethal anesthetic, the hallucinogenic gas ethylene. Hardly a threat like a nuclear or biological weapon.

In fact, some might even enjoy the high.

More questions remained than were answered. Why would Eglov and his fellow eco-nuts commit the time and effort to exploit something of such limited use, Breath of the Earth notwithstanding? As a practical, rather than ideological matter, it made no sense.

He shrugged, a man with no explanation. His job was over. Time to find a place to get on with his life, as the talk-show shrinks said, as though living were some kind of task to be fulfilled.

Returning to the Turks and Caicos was out. Even if he were able to satisfy the colonial government as to his innocence in the house fire, that hiding place had been exposed. Pity. In the short time he had lived on North Caicos, he had grown to love the remoteness, the fact that the feel, the very essence of the island had not been sacrificed to the tourist dollar.

Yet.

He would probably choose another island, the smaller the better. A place with only occasional air service, or, better yet, none at all, small enough that the arrival of a stranger was noticed. One place he could not live was the United States, not with the sizable bank balances he had accumulated since going to work for Narcom, accounts in capital-friendly countries that saw the wisdom of holding foreigners' money, not confiscating it with punitive taxes. The very existence of the income produced by such accounts as could be found would attract the attention of the IRS, which would ask questions best left unanswered.

Besides, Jason had no desire to participate in the ever-growing and thinly disguised intent of American politicians to redistribute the wealth.

His wealth.

He turned and walked to the stairs leading up to the passenger lounge. Even though the sea breeze was blowing its salty air in his face, he imagined he could smell baking crusts from the cramped pizzeria that was the boat's sole dining facility. He climbed the steel steps and went inside.

Jason could not decide between the artichoke-mushroom and the multiple cheese selections. He ordered a square of each and made his way to one of the ten or so small tables, only half of which were occupied. He had taken only a bite out of the cheese pizza when he noticed a copy of the *London Times* crumpled on the adjacent table. Glancing around the room to be certain the paper was abandoned, he opened it up.

He scanned the day-old headlines. The lead story concerned a conference on the environment, a meeting in Washington whose main purpose, Jason guessed, was politics rather than statesmanship. The only agreement on allocation of the world's resources would come when they either no longer existed or could be produced artificially. Those who profited by exploiting the earth were not likely to voluntarily relinquish them.

He took a bite of artichoke and mushroom.

He was about to turn the front page when he happened to notice a reprint from the *Washington Post*. The word *Hillwood* sprang out at him. He had escorted Laurin to some sort of function there, one of the several charity balls to which she had dragged him annually.

He hated the things.

Disease balls. Benefit for multiple sclerosis, funding for breast cancer research, cure for whatever. Mostly social aspirants, those unable to attain membership in the better clubs—women more on the outside than the inside of Washington society, could put on a five-thousand-dollar gown and chance meeting the current social glitterati in the name of charity. God forbid they be subjected to disgusting and dreary work at a homeless shelter or soup kitchen, where they would never be photographed for the society section of the paper.

Or at even in the small magazines that sold subscriptions to the very people they covered.

Jason had pointed out that a two-hundred-dollar ticket to such galas meant the charity in question would be lucky to get fifty. Why not, he reasoned, simply give the institution half the cost of the unbought gown and go out to a good restaurant while others were busy climbing the social ladder?

After all, as a partner in one of the city's premier law firms, Laurin had multiple club memberships paid for by her partners. There was no need to spend an evening of bad food and worse company among social wannabes.

Laurin would have none of it.

She spent at least one weekend a month doing the true grunt work of charity—helping in a hospice, giving free legal advice at a halfway house—efforts that would never be rewarded by public recognition. So why not do the glitzy part, too?

He didn't remember the specific event or the malaise it celebrated.

Prevention of terminal flatulence, maybe?

He did recall the former home of the Post heiress. Far from the street, out of the way. Small for the wealth it represented but on a large estate, one that would be difficult to totally close off from the rest of the world.

He supposed the conference would be held in the dining room, where he had experienced a lavish buffet of overcooked roast beef, rubber chicken, listless salad, et cetera, by the yard. The usual poor quality of the food had been overshadowed by the appearance of a man whose name Jason had forgotten within minutes of hearing it, a doctor who attached himself to Jason like a human leech. He was typical of the tedious types that peopled such functions, unable to discuss anything but his golf score and his brilliance in the stock market.

Jason had introduced him to Laurin and disappeared, leaving the man trying to be discreet in looking down the décolletage of her ball gown while she frantically searched for a way to disengage herself.

It seemed ample revenge for her dragging Jason there.

He had escaped through the French doors that led into a garden, where rosebushes were just beginning to bloom.

Jason had guessed those doors could be left open, letting diners enjoy the fragrance of the flowers.

Or some other fragrance.

Like in a trawler in the Bering Sea.

Or at Baia.

The thought that had prowled the back of his mind now leaped from the tangle of his subconscious, a concept so powerful it would have struck him dumb had he had anyone to talk to.

He checked his watch. Hours before the ferry docked.

A ship-to-shore telephone on board?

He would certainly arouse suspicion by demanding to use it.

But he couldn't simply sit here and allow events to spin on their present course by his inaction. He had to do something, get the word to Mama no matter what.

But how?

CHAPTER FORTY-EIGHT

Hillwood
4155 Linnean Avenue
Washington, D.C.
1530 EDT

Shirlee Atkins had been right.

Them mens hadn't given a shit whether they tracked dirt into the house or not. Chattering in some language she had never heard before, they went about their work in the rose garden and they would walk right cross the Chinese Oriental rug to go to the bathroom without so much as wiping their dirty boots. Mr. Jimson, he wouldn'ta let 'em do that, but this new fella, the one whose head look like an Easter egg, he didn't much seem to care.

Prolly wouldn'ta much cared 'bout what Shirlee done found in one of the silver drawers in the sideboard, either. The drawer stuck and she'd had to give it a real tug. Thing fell out on the floor, spillin' knives 'n' forks everwhere. But underneath them knives 'n' forks was some kinda false bottom, a place Shirlee reckoned Ms. Post used to hide real valuables. Like the curve-bladed knife with a golden handle. She 'spected there be no reason tell the new man she near done broke that drawer, jes' put it back like it was.

Ever since that man what call himself Rassavitch showed up this mornin' in that big ol' beat-up truck, the mens with the shovels, they workin' harder'n Shirlee had seen all week. They was sho' gonna finish this afternoon, git the place ready fo' that big meetin' tomorrow.

Stuff on that truck strange.

Some kinda spindly little plant. Downright ugly, and hadn't no flowers on it. Then they unloaded a bunch o' rocks. Big, round white-colored stone, look like they coulda weighed tons. But they didn't. One o' them scrawny little guys could pick one o' them rocks right up an' carry it to where they were planting those scraggly little bushes between them rocks in a line right outside the floor-to-ceiling doors of the dinin' room.

Not near as pretty as rosebushes.

But then, what did Shirlee know?

She wasn't nothin' but a cleanin' lady.

CHAPTER FORTY-NINE

Naples–Cagliari ferry
At the same time

Jason looked up from the table, most of his two squares of pizza uneaten. His attention was focused on the man standing in the doorway talking on a cell phone and smoking a cigarette at the same time. Both hands occupied. Jason picked up his *London Times*, pretending to read while he kept his eyes on the man by the door.

The minute the conversation ended, the man turned, jamming the phone into a jacket pocket. Jason moved as quickly as he could while appearing to be just one more bored passenger with nothing to do but try to find an alternative to the ferry's tiny staterooms.

Outside, the bright lights of the car deck outlined everything along the edges of the passenger deck above. The man Jason was interested in was leaning against the rail as the breeze snatched sparks from his cigarette into the air like a child's sparkler.

Jason muttered something unintelligible and staggered against the side of the cabin, bouncing off the railing. He couldn't see the man's face, but he was pretty certain it was turned toward him. Jason stopped a few feet away, swaying with the ocean's swells like the drunk at sea he was imitating.

He waited until the next large wave, then lurched forward, colliding with the smoker.

"*Mi dispiace*," Jason mumbled. *I'm sorry.*

His victim never felt the hand slip into the jacket pocket.

The smoker gave Jason a gentle push as he stepped back. "*Prego.*"

The Italian word that translated as anything from *you're welcome* to *quickly* to a simple acknowledgment of an apology.

Jason staggered down the steel catwalk, trying not to seem in a hurry until he was certain he was out of sight of his victim.

Once in protective shadows, he held up the cell phone. Its keyboard lit up when he flipped it open. He turned his back in the direction of its owner. He hoped he couldn't be seen using the stolen device. He punched series of buttons, the number of the American consulate in Naples, one of several he had memorized before leaving Washington.

The voice that answered was definitely American and just as certainly bored. The person Jason wanted to speak with was gone for the evening, sorry.

"It's important," Jason said.

Not to the person on the other end of the line. "He's still not here."

"Your name?"

"What does it matter?"

"It matters," Jason growled, "because when I hang up, I'm calling the ambassador in Rome. I'm telling him he has some lazy little dweeb down here in Naples who doesn't care enough to get off his ass even where national security is involved."

"Oh, yeah? And who is this, the secretary of state?"

"No, but if you've got any sense at all, you'll put me on

hold while you contact extension two-oh-one in the Rome
embassy and tell them you're talking to one of Narcom's
people."

Two-oh-one was the extension number for the agency
office in the embassy, those supposed trade, cultural, and
military attachés whose actual work had nothing to do
with their titles.

Apparently the jerk in Naples at least recognized that
anyone who knew the extension number might be important. "Hold on."

Jason heard a loud, angry voice from above. No doubt
someone had found their pocket picked and their cell
phone gone. Jason moved farther back into the shadows.

The voice that came back on the phone was noticeably
chastised. "Yes, sir, what can we do for you?"

"I need a patch through to a Washington number."

"A secure patch might take a little while. Where can I
call you back?"

Jason had no way to know the number of the cell phone
in his hand.

"You can't."

"But I—"

"I'll hold."

He could hear steps clamoring on the steal deck overhead. More than one person.

"Listen," he hissed into the phone, "things are a little
busy at my end right now. Get the patch ready." He gave
the number Mama had monitored twenty-four/seven. "I'll
call you back in five minutes. Tell the recipient of the call
it's from Italy."

He hung up before the voice could protest. Hopefully
Mama wasn't running any other operations in Italy at the
moment.

Squaring his shoulders, he tried to stand as tall as possible as he strode purposefully toward the ferry's forecas-
tle, the location of his small stateroom. The two men, one
in the uniform of the ferry company, pushed by him, the

victim of the theft pointing toward the bow. Obviously they were looking for a drunk whose face had been obscured in the darkness.

Jason flipped on the single overhead light as he entered his quarters. He sat on the stingy bunk and redialed the Naples number.

Nothing.

He tried again with the same result.

He glared at the steel bulkheads that imprisoned the cell phone's signal as securely as any jail held an inmate. He wasn't going to be able to connect with the satellite from here.

Cracking the door, he checked the narrow hallway outside and climbed the companionway to the top deck. Other than a few passengers leaning on the rail, staring into the night, it was deserted. He descended to the automobile deck and selected a white van.

It was locked.

His next choice was a small Mercedes truck. The door opened at his touch and he slipped inside, settling into the darkest corner. He flipped the phone open and punched in numbers.

This time the voice from the consulate was polite, almost solicitous. "We have your connection, sir. Understand you're calling from an unsecured source. Anything said in this conversation is subject to interception."

Like any other call made by phone users the world over. Unless the ecoterrorists had somehow found the number he was calling and managed to alert a computer to scan all its calls, this conversation would be hidden among millions of others the same way a pickpocket relied on the numbers of a crowd to conceal him.

"Yes?" The voice was unmistakably Mama's.

Besides the volume of phone traffic, Jason knew brevity would help, though there was no guarantee of anonymity.

"Conference in Washington tomorrow. Hillwood." He paused, wondering if the words would trigger the search program of some monitoring device. There wasn't time for circumlocution. "Breath of the Earth. It's ignited from rocks by plants that spontaneously combust."

The silence that followed was only seconds, but it seemed long enough for Jason to wonder if the connection had been broken.

"Plants? Rocks?"

"Like the trawler. If the conference is held near open windows, like the dining room at Hillwood."

Another pause.

"I'm not sure I understand."

"The gas, ethylene, will make everyone—delegates to the meeting, security, everyone—both drowsy and delusional, but it won't kill them. That's the beauty of it. While everyone's on a high, someone will slip into the room from outside, slit a few throats, and disappear while the Secret Service guys are on the nod. No one to yell, cause a ruckus till it's too late. Or, maybe one or more of the Eco people'll have a breathing device concealed on him. When the gas dissipates, no one knows what happened. People have been murdered literally in front of their security and no one knows anything. The Earth will have claimed some sort of revenge with its natural products, the plant and the gas."

"My God, the president is planning to attend!"

"I suggest he make other plans."

"You can document this?"

"Not by tomorrow morning."

Another pause before Mama's rich Creole voice said, "This conference is important. He thinks he can become the person history will record as dedicating his life to reconciling industrialists and conservationists."

"He will. Just not the way he'd planned."

"We'll look like idiots if you're wrong."

"How will you look if I'm not?"

"I see what you mean. Tell you what: I'm passin' this

along to the CIA. They're our client and can do what they want."

In Washington, the buck never really stopped; it was in perpetual motion.

CHAPTER FIFTY

Near Silanus, Sardinia
An hour later

There were three men in the rented Mercedes that had pulled off the ferry two hours ago. The face of one of the men in the rear seat was partially covered by a large eye patch. One cheek displayed scars that were angry red, as though recently inflicted. All four wore the loose blouse and baggy pants of the local farmers for whom they easily could have mistaken.

Sardinian farmers, however, would have been unlikely to drive such a car. It was equally doubtful locals would drive through the night to a simple farmhouse, one where a thorough search demonstrated that the normal occupants were still not in residence and had not been for several days.

The refrigerator had a sour smell about it, containing only an open canister of milk long gone rancid. The source of the house's electricity, wherever it was, had been turned off, and flashlight beams revealed that a light patina of dust had begun to collect on flat surfaces. There was nothing remarkable in the house. A few inexpensive oils hung on the walls and a huge sword over the fireplace—a sword, though effective in its time, that would be no match for the weapons these men carried.

One of the men turned to the one with the eye patch, speaking in Russian. "You are certain the Scotsman and the American will return?"

The man with one eye nodded. "And with the woman. We will wait."

CHAPTER FIFTY-ONE

Cagliari, Sardinia
The next morning

Jason was careful he was not observed as he dropped the stolen cell phone overboard before being one of the first to disembark from the ferry. A quick survey of the harbor revealed fishing craft, private sailboats, a few motor launches, and no place to rent a car. Adrian had omitted that factoid, he thought sourly.

Taxis, though, were plentiful. He took one to the airport.

The ride through town began as one of no particular interest. Apartment houses of undistinguished architecture and recent vintage shouldered one another for room, screening the view of the ocean. The churches gave some small clue as to the island's multicultural history. Graceful Moorish facades were only blocks from chunky Romanesque fronts left by conquering Normans and Spanish. The ebullience of Italian Gothic, unlike any other of the period, was equally represented. It looked like every second street corner hosted an outdoor market.

The airport was featureless modern. Jason paid the driver and went inside the terminal, where boutiques, tour guide offices, and duty-free shops outnumbered the two ticket counters. Turning to his left to follow the signs, he crossed a neatly groomed patch of ground to another building housing rental car offices. There were no lines in front of any of them.

The Rugger passport had been left at the pensione in hopes of convincing the authorities that Jason had perished at Baia. He pulled a leather pouch from a jacket pocket and examined the other two IDs Mama had sent him before he left the Dominican Republic. The pictures on both driver's licenses and passports were the same. He selected the documents and cards in the name of Andrew Forest Stroud of New York City. He looked at the address. East Seventy-second Street.

Jason hoped he looked like someone from the tony Upper East Side. But then, New York's wealthy made a practice of shabby dress.

Eurocar had a selection varying from the largest Mercedes to the tiniest Smart Car, also by DaimlerChrysler, though the manufacturer was understandably ashamed to adorn it with the three-pointed star. Jason chose a four-door Peugeot, something that would attract as little attention as possible.

The drive back to town was unremarkable, other than the normal frustration of finding a parking space. Jason felt truly blessed when he pulled in behind a departing Opel only six blocks from the harbor.

From his table outside a waterside trattoria, Jason watched the ferry dock. As the cars drove off, the few pedestrian passengers disembarked. The bright colors of Maria's gold-and-blue scarf were visible all the way across the quay. Jason could only marvel how the woman always managed to come up with a different one. He had little doubt she could find a Hermès shop in the middle of the Sahara Desert.

Women possessed some sort of internal navigational system for such things. Laurin could detect the proximity

of a shoe store in cities she had never visited. Once in
Paris . . .

He pushed the thought aside, surprised at how easy it
was becoming to dismiss his former wife. He watched
Maria seat herself at a table identical to his but on the
other side of the small harbor. The plan called for her to
have a cup of coffee and remain where she was until Jason
verified that she was not being followed or observed.

Unlike their American counterparts, Italian and most
European trattorias, bistros, or whatever considered the
price of a single beverage to be a ticket to occupy a table
as long as the customer wished. In fact, the national pastime in many large cities was to order a sole glass of wine
and spend the afternoon watching the passing crowds
from the same table.

After forty minutes, the only interest in Maria that Jason
noted was the openly admiring glances for which Italian
men were notorious. He was amused by the persistence of
one who had tried to share her table and finally admitted
defeat after ten minutes of being intensely ignored.

He stood, reluctant to leave the pleasant morning sun,
and walked casually along the edge of the port, feigning
interest in first one sailboat, then another. He barely gave
Maria a glance as he passed within ten feet of her and
sauntered on. Without looking back, he turned away from
the water's edge and strolled up one of the two streets that
dead-ended into the harbor. He paused in front of a *gela-
terie*, seeming to marvel at the variety of flavors of ice
cream the small shop displayed. In the glass of the adjacent store's display window, he saw Maria turn the corner
and enter the same street.

She stopped, distracted by the size of the prawns on ice
under a sign proclaiming FRUTTI DI MARE. Although the
sidewalks bore some pedestrian traffic, no one showed
any lingering interest in her.

Jason took the time for admiration. She had a figure
Hollywood would envy, honed, no doubt, by scurrying in

and out of volcanic craters. The olive skin framed by crow-wing black hair she had let loose around her shoulders. He shook his head. The object of the exercise was to get her safely to Adrian's for a few days before she returned to her life.

He was in no hurry for that.

Periodic checks of reflections in shop windows confirmed that she was following him to the car at a casual pace. He had to fight the temptation to hurry, to rush to the moment he could take her in his arms.

He turned a final corner, waiting to see her follow.

CHAPTER FIFTY-TWO

Hillwood
4155 Linnean Avenue
Washington, D.C.
0746 EDT, the next morning

Shirlee hadn't minded comin' to work half an hour early, not at all. Wasn't ever'body, 'ticularly ever'body in her 'hood, was gonna see the president up close 'n' personal.

For the tenth time in as many minutes, she looked out the windows beside the front door, searching the driveway for that procession of long black cars she'd always seen on TV. For the tenth time in as many minutes, she smoothed her uniform, making sure no wrinkles marred its appearance. Shouldn't be none. She done took it home and washed and ironed it herse'f. For the tenth time in as many minutes, she walked back into the kitchen, making sure the big coffee urn was turned on and the doughnuts and other breakfast pastries were in neat rows on the trays that Mr. Jimson used for special events. This time, though, granola bars, high-fiber cereal, and fresh fruit occupied equal space on those things Mr. Jimson used to call salvers.

Why he'd call a silver tray *spit* was beyond Shirlee.

Mr. Jimson . . . Wouldn't he proud, he be 'live? Havin' the president hisse'f come to Hillwood?

The thought was interrupted by two men in dark suits entering the kitchen. Both in their mid-thirties, both with athletic builds. Both with small tubes in their ears and murmuring into the little mikes pinned to their lapels. 'Bout the fifth time one of 'em had come through here, lookin' into the oven and microwave like they thought mebbe Shirlee done put a bomb in there.

Them mens were 'bout the politest Shirlee ever seen. Always a smile that look like it be stuck on with glue, always, "Yes, Ms. Atkins, No, Ms. Atkins," when she axed questions. But they be so serious, they scary. But nowhere near as scary as them other fellas, the Russians, the ones that wore what looked like pajamas belted at the waist stuffed into knee boots. They *really* scary, lookin' around with angry expressions like they done eat a mess o' collards somebody done put too much pepper sauce on. They didn' much care 'bout the house like the mens in suits. 'Stead, they kept lookin' at them whitish-colored rocks and scrawny little bushes right outside the French doors in the dinin' room, doors Shirlee been tolt to open so the room wouldn't get all stuffy during the meetin'. What them Russians think, like mebbe them stones an' plants gonna disappear somehow? An' they didn' care much for women, either, least not Shirlee and Cornicha, the other custodian work there. Ever' time either Shirlee or Cornicha speak to 'em, even a "good mornin'" or somethin', them mens just glare like they angry.

The sound of sirens made her forget the two types of men. She rushed to the front door. Must be the president come a little early.

CHAPTER FIFTY-THREE

Between Cagliari and Silanus, Sardinia
1340, the same day

As the only one who knew the way, Adrian drove. At a place that qualified as a town only because it had a small piazza, he parked just outside the square.

"Victuals," he explained before either Jason or Maria asked. "Before we left the house, I tossed whatever was perishable." There was no mistaking his remorse for the waste. "The haggis we didn't eat, everything. Y' recall the last thing I did was switch off the ginny motor. No sense wastin' fuel, but no ginny, no electricity an' no refrigeration." He got out of the car. "Also, this is the only place I know of around here that sells dry ice."

"Dry ice?" Jason asked.

"Dry ice. Y' know, carbon dioxide in frozen, solid form. It'll take a bit for the fridge to cool down once it's restarted. Th' dry ice'll preserve what needs to be refrigerated."

Minutes later, all three emerged from the store laden with eggplant that seemed too purple to be real, tomatoes the size of softballs, peppers almost as large as the tomatoes, bread, cheese, and sliced sausage meats. Jason carried a carton of bottled water. When it was all loaded, they set out for Adrian's home, a journey of only a half an hour.

Adrian pulled up in front of the house. Taking the empty pipe out of his mouth, he got out of the car and whistled.

No response.

"Jock! Jock!" he called.

The hills gave him back a faint echo, but there was no sign of the dog.

"You think it was okay to leave him?" Maria asked.

Adrian filled the pipe as his eyes looked around. "Aye. He's not your city-dwelling lapdog. Plenty smart enough to seek sustenance from the neighbors. They'd feed 'm, f' sure."

"Maybe they fed him too well," Jason suggested, lifting the carton of water from the trunk. "He's decided to take up with them."

"'Tis possible," Adrian admitted, the levity of the words not matching the serious scan he was giving the surrounding countryside, "but a dog's not like a person. Y' canna buy his loyalty."

Jason was certain Jock was not what was on Adrian's mind at the moment. He was about to ask what the Scot sensed when he heard grunts from behind the house.

"Jock may be taking time off, but your pigs sound hungry."

"Always are. That's why they're pigs. May have to turn 'em loose to forage f' themselves if we canna find slop for 'em."

Adrian's eyes were fixed on the house.

"You're not thinking about the dog or the pigs," Jason said.

"There's somethin' not quite cricket here. I'm tryin' to figger out what."

In small, highly mobile strike groups like Delta Force or SAS, instincts were sharpened to the level of a sixth sense: a sudden quiet in the clamor of a jungle night, a pebble re-

cently knocked loose from a mountain footpath, an old
and battered automobile in a wealthy residential neighborhood. More than once, Jason had saved his own life as
well as those of his men by noticing some almost imperceptible incongruity.

He put the carton of water down, freeing a hand to go
to the weapon in the small of his back.

"What is the matter?" Maria asked.

Adrian shook his head. "Naught, lassie, jus' an old
man's years of paranoia."

Perhaps, but Jason noted that the Sten gun under the seat
was the first thing his friend removed from the Peugeot.

Each of the three loaded what they could carry. Adrian
used a foot to open the door.

"Unlocked?" Jason asked.

"Aye. Someone come by to be a-borrowin' somethin'
an' find th' door locked, I'd be regarded as an inhospitable
sod, or, worse, one who dinna trust his neighbors. 'Sides,
I dinna recall th' las' time I even saw th' bloody key."

Jason headed for the kitchen. "Where do you want me
to put the dry ice?"

"Th' fridge, along with the sausage, cheese, and vegetables. Also the bottled water. It's better cool."

Perhaps the first time Jason had ever heard a native of
the British Isles express a preference for chilling any beverage, including beer or drinks the rest of the civilized
world served over ice.

Maria came in, her arms full. She leaned over to stock
the small refrigerator. When she straightened up, her gaze
went to the single window, a view of the rear yard.

"What is that?"

Both men joined her. Just beyond the shadow of the
house, a small mound of fresh earth had been piled up.

" 'Twasn't there before," Adrian mused.

Jason was reaching for the back door.

"Please stay where you are, Mr. Peters."

The voice came from the kitchen's entrance to the rest

of the house. The doorway was filled by three men, all with shaved heads, two pointing AK-47s. The one in the middle had a patch over one eye and recent scars on his face. Even so, Jason recognized him instantly.

Eglov.

"Please do not make any move I do not request. I would be greatly disappointed if I had to shoot you right here and now." He leered at Maria. "I have much more, er, interesting plans. An eye for an eye, I believe your Bible says."

"The dog," Adrian growled. "You—"

"The filthy mongrel bit one of my men. We could hardly leave him to warn you we were here upon your arrival. For that matter, we would have slaughtered the pigs also, but their absence would have alerted you. Besides, no true lover of the Earth would want to needlessly kill something so nearly feral as those swine. Now, if each of you will assume the position against the wall . . ."

Adrian leaned against the wall, legs and arms spread-eagled. "It was th' windows, laddie. Th' bloody windows. Since na' person was here, they shoulda been dirty from th' dust that blows aboot, not clean enough to see through."

Having the answer was small consolation.

CHAPTER FIFTY-FOUR

Hillwood
4155 Linnean Avenue
Washington, D.C.
0801 EDT

Them cars was no presidential caravan; Shirlee could see that. Two District police cars 'n, a black SUV with blue lights behind the grille. 'Bout the time Shirlee made that determination, the mens in the suits was listenin' to their earpieces. She couldn't hear them, of course, but their hands went up to the little devices like touchin' the things would make them louder.

"Say again?" one of the mens said, his forehead wrinkled like he was hearing some sorta foreign language.

At the same time, the cars sqealed to a stop and men both in uniforms and suits came pourin' out like they was on fire. Shirlee was pretty sure she had enough doughnuts an' pastries, but these mans weren' interested in breakfast. Instead, two or three of 'em were carryin' guns an' the rest of 'em shovels.

Shovels?

Like they gonna garden?

Now?

Sho' 'nuff, while the mens with th' guns were lookin' 'round like they 'spected some kinda trouble, the others were digging at them ugly little plants jus' outside the dinin' room.

Then things got crazy.

One of them men who'd watched the plantings all week come screamin' outta the house, waiving this long, curved knife. He not be too smart, tryin' to cut the man with the gun, who shot him right there.

'Bout that time two more Russians—or whoever they was, ones been in and out the kitchen all mornin'—they pulled guns outta the drawers of the sideboard where Shirlee guessed they done hid 'em sometime in the las' few days. The two mens with the things in they ears, they got no guns, 'cause nobody 'sposed to have weapons on 'em for this conference. Still, they rush the mens with guns. There be two, three shots, so loud in the room Shirlee's ears ringin' and she stone-deaf. An' one o' the mens in suits, lyin' on the floor bleedin' bad.

The other Russian, he swing his gun around at Shirlee and shot. First she just feel a burn in her shoulder. Mutha-fucker done put a hole in her clean, starched uniform, one she done spent half the night ironin'!

Then it hurt. Oh, shit, did it hurt!

That same dude, he turn toward the other man in the suit, gonna shoot him, too.

Even months later, Shirlee was unclear exactly what happened next. She thought she remembered reaching with her good arm for the big coffee urn, the one she couldn't hardly lift with both hands. She definitely re-membered the clunking sound of that big pot hitting the Russian's head. She remembered thinking that she was in the shit now, coffee an' blood all over the rug along with one very unconscious Russian.

Then it all went black.

Next thing Shirlee knew, she was still in the dining

room but she was strapped to a stretcher. A woman in a pale blue uniform with EMS stitched on the pocket was standing over her, holding some kind of bottle attached to Shirlee's arm. Two men in their light blue uniforms were lifting the stretcher.

Shirlee tried to sit up but couldn't, either 'cause of the straps or because she jus' didn' have the strength.

"Lemme outta here," she croaked, surprised she could manage no more than a whisper. "Who gonna take care my kids tonight, I ain't home?"

"I will," said someone behind her. She thought she recognized the man's voice from somewhere but couldn't quite place where.

"Who that?" she asked.

A man in a suit stepped into view. The light from outside was in her eyes, so she saw no more than a silhouette. "Your children will be my personal guests until you're up and around."

He moved and Shirlee thought she was seein' things, sure. She was lookin' into the smilin' face of the president hisse'f.

"You're a very brave woman, Ms. Atkins. Without you, there'd be some children without their fathers tonight."

It was then that Shirlee realized it hadn't been the sun blindin' her; it was lights around a man holdin' a camera. *Shit!* Her one time on TV an' she gotta look like hell.

The president leaned over, taking one of her hands in both of his. "Your children will be well cared for. It's been since when, Jimmy Carter, that there was a small child in the White House? When you get out of the hospital, You'll come for dinner?"

At first Shirlee thought he wanted her to *serve* dinner. Then she realized he meant as a guest.

She'd be goin' to eat with th' Man hisse'f! Weren't that sumthin'? He wasn't foolin' her none. She knew he'd have his pitcher taken with her, meybbe get a few more black votes, but she didn' much care. Her babies were gonna have somethin' they'd talk 'bout rest of they lives.

And Shirlee?

Well, the folks down to the projects where she used to live would see she really had gone a long way, wouldn't they?

CHAPTER FIFTY-FIVE

Silanus, Sardinia
1521 hours

Stripped of their weapons, Jason and Adrian had been shoved into chairs, where they were watched by two of the men standing just out of reach. Maria was allowed slightly more freedom, although confined to the room. Jason had the impression they were waiting for something. His only guess was nightfall, when Eglov would kill them and leave in the dark, unseen by any passing neighbors.

"I am hungry," Maria announced. "Anyone besides me want something to eat?"

If food wasn't the last thing on Jason's mind, it was close to it.

Eglov nodded for one of the rifle-carrying men to accompany her to the kitchen. "Enjoy your meal; eat well." He smiled cruelly. "It will be your last opportunity."

"Tell me," Jason asked, "how did you get out of the tunnel at Baia?"

"Do you think there was but one entrance, Mr. Peters?" Eglov pointed to the still-unfinished condensed version of Eno's book, faceup on the couch where Jason had tossed it minutes ago. "Even your magazine there recounts a final exit out of the Netherworld before the descent into Hades."

More to start a conversation than out of curiosity, Jason asked, "Why go to the trouble of taking that ethylene rock all the way to the United States to be set off by the self-igniting bushes? Wouldn't it have been easier just to carry a bomb into the conference?"

The Russian frowned. "This was special. Think of the reaction of your countrymen when your president and his fellow despoilers of the Earth have their throats cut while the true friends of the Earth live. The knives for the job will be dropped into the special hiding places my men have created in the last few weeks, the same places in which they will rest until needed. No one other than a designated pair will even know what happened. No weapons, no one enters or leaves the room. Only the Breath of the Earth. It will be seen to the true lovers of our world as a miracle, the poor Earth striking back on its own."

It would be a display of insanity, Jason thought, but he said, "Why kill the president, anyway? He was willing to grant you and your radical environmentalist pals some sort of a pardon for the crimes they committed."

Eglov spit. "Forgiveness is not his to give; it is the Earth's alone! Pardon by the great rapist of the resources that belong to all?" He spit again. "As long as your country and the other greedy industrialist democracies exist, there will be no peace, no peace until their sins are paid for and the planet allowed to rest without being ravaged."

A second Dark Ages. Comforting thought.

It was difficult to carry on a conversation with someone who spoke in slogans. Still, it was important to conduct a discourse, anything to take the fanatic's mind off killing them, if even for a moment. Jason wondered what would happen if Eglov found out the details of the gas plot had already been given to Washington.

"Exactly how will you prevent your own people at the conference from falling asleep?"

Eglov smiled, proud of his ingenuity. "Two will have medicinal oxygen tanks for lung disease. They will do the Earth's work while the others are unconscious."

Jason was about to say something else when he heard water running in the kitchen.

"I thought the generator was off," he said.

"Doesn't run the water," Adrian explained. "There's an artesian well up on the hill, feeds water down a pipe by gravity."

Maria came in from the kitchen, carrying a platter of sliced bread, sausage, and cheese. She placed it on the table and returned for a pitcher of water.

"Would you like some?" she asked Eglov.

He scowled. "Eat sausage that contains meat, steal nourishment from the death of defenseless animals?" He looked slightly ill at the thought. "No."

Jason got up slowly and went to the table as Maria continued in the same tone she might have used had their captors been invited houseguests. "You will have some cheese, then? I expect when the police arrive, you will not get a chance to eat again for quite a while."

What the hell was she doing, trying to get them killed ahead of time? Jason's eyes met Adrian's and then looked away.

"Police?" Eglov scoffed. "Do not make yourself look foolish!"

She shrugged. "Your disbelief does not change the facts. We were to meet them here."

In one step the Russian was beside her. He gave her face a slap that could be heard across the room. She staggered backward and almost fell. Jason lunged forward, only to be prodded in the chest by one of the other men's AK-47.

"Stupid cow!" Eglov snarled. "You think I would believe such a childish trick? The police will arrive only to find your bodies."

She wiped a hand across her mouth. "Stupid or not, they *are* coming."

She was staring at Jason.

He had no idea what she was talking about, but he had to assume she had done something in the kitchen.

Then it hit him. As a volcanologist, she would be familiar with gases other than the ethylene. He had an idea what was coming.

He nodded imperceptibly at Adrian. "She's right, Eglov. The place will be swarming with cops anytime now."

Adrian's expression turned from bewildered to knowing. He gingerly got out of his chair and, back to the empty fireplace, inspected the food selection. Without looking at Jason, he shrugged, then put a finger to his temple. The two gestures meant something akin to, *I'm not sure what you mean but I understand*, the silent signs that acknowledged that action of some unknown type was at hand.

There was an explosion in the kitchen, followed by what could have been gunshots.

"In here!" Maria yelled. "We are here!"

The two armed men reacted by swiveling around to point their weapons at the anticipated incursion of gun-wielding police. The distraction lasted only a second at most.

But it was enough.

Leaning backward, Adrian reached behind his head and brought both hands down with the claymore, the huge two-handed sword that hung over the mantel. So swift was the blow, the light gleaming from the hand-forged steel appeared as a single arc. A fraction of a second too late, the closest man swung his AK-47 to bear, only to have the blade sever his shoulder from his body. Arm and weapon clattered to the floor in a geyser of blood.

Jason ducked under the barrel of another rifle whipping

back toward him, his shoulder throwing the muzzle upward as a burst of shots plowed into the ceiling. There was a downpour of plaster dust. Jason grabbed for the armed man's gun as the other hand stretched for the gunman's throat.

Intentionally or by chance, Jason's intended victim stumbled or stepped backward out of reach, leaving Jason staring at the leveled mouth of the AK-47 and the gleeful eyes of his victorious opponent.

Jason fully expected to die.

Instead, the man seemed to shift his shoulders slightly as his eyeballs rolled upward as though trying to see into the back of his own head. His knees buckled slowly as he sank to the floor and fell facedown. The knife used to slice the sausage protruded from between his shoulder blades. Behind him stood Maria, her blood-soaked hands clasped over her mouth.

She could not tear her eyes from the man sprawled before her. "Oh, my God, oh, my God," she whispered.

Then she spun, took a step, and vomited.

She shook off Jason's consoling arms. "Oh, my God," she repeated, "I've killed a man. . . ."

She bolted for the bedroom. Jason could hear her retching.

"An' what aboot him?" Adrian asked, his sword pushed against Eglov's stomach. "It'd be a pleasure to slice him up like so much pickled herring."

"Do what you will," Eglov sneered. "It cannot be worse than suffering at the hands of Russian police."

"Letting him go doesn't make a lot of sense," Jason said.

Eglov was looking at him without fear. "There is a deal to be had here. My organization could use men such as yourselves."

Jason snorted. "Swell. I'd be afraid to sleep, afraid I'd wake up with a knife between my shoulders. No, thanks. It isn't my thing."

Eglov's eyes narrowed, making them appear even more

slanted. "You are a fool if you think you can kill me and not pay for it. I command a virtual army of loyal followers."

Eglov's megalomania was becoming tiresome.

"I say we put th' man's disciples to th' test," Adrian said, gesturing to the gore-drenched floor. "Bit of a bother explainin' all this t' th' local constabulary if we turn 'im over to 'em."

"My cause will survive to see the capitalist-industrial complex crumble."

Jason literally saw red as a wave of rage surged through his consciousness.

For Laurin.

For Paco.

For three thousand Americans killed on a warm, clear September morning.

For the victims of all zealots who advanced their causes by killing innocents.

He nodded slowly. "For once, Eglov, you are not calling the shots." He ripped off the Russian's shirt. "We'll see how long the viper survives without a head."

Eglov watched with growing consternation as Jason began tearing the shirt into strips. "So, you will kill me."

Jason nodded. "Your lieutenants will have an opportunity to struggle on without you."

Eglov abandoned any pretext of unconcern. "What are you doing?"

Jason gave him a malicious smile. "Things are a little different when you are the one about to die, aren't they, Eglov? This time you're not slitting the throat of some unarmed fisherman or lumberjack. Makes you a little uncomfortable, doesn't it?"

"You are a fool to pass up the money you could make working for me, even more of a fool to bring the wrath of my followers down upon you."

Jason ignored him. Using the strips to bind the Russian hand and foot, Jason slung him over his shoulder. "Open the door for me, will you?"

Adrian did as he was asked. "But what . . . ?"

"We'll send our pal Eglov to meet his much-loved natural world in fitting style."

Jason headed for the back of the house.

Adrian and Eglov guessed what Jason had in mind at about the same time.

"Surely you're not . . . ?" Eglov said.

What false confidence Eglov had left vanished as he began to howl for mercy in English and Russian.

"Surely you would not kill a fellow human this way!"

"You'd rather I cut your throat?" Jason said, shifting the burden of the man's weight. "You're getting about as much of a chance as you gave your victims. Besides, letting nature's own creatures take care of you seems . . . well, appropriate."

The pigs grunted in anticipation.

As Jason returned to the house, the squeals of delight were becoming louder than the anguished screams.

Maria, pale and haggard, was leaning against the bedroom doorway. "I saw what you did."

"Fitting end, I thought," Jason commented. "By the way, brilliant move, mixing water with the dry ice."

"Huh?" Adrian asked.

Jason explained. "Carbon dioxide, when mixed in confinement with water, forms a gas. When the gas has no more room into which to expand, it explodes its confinement—in this case, the water bottles. Like gunshots."

"Bonny good!" Adrian applauded. "That little prank saved our lives."

Maria shook her head slowly. "Had I known what would happen, I don't know if I could have done it." She examined her hands. "I killed someone."

"If you hadn't, we all would have been dead soon," Jason said.

"And you . . ." She was pointing an accusing finger. "I saw what you did. That was . . . was . . . inhumane!"

"Inhumane? Like gassing unarmed workers so they

could peacefully be murdered? Like planning to assassi-
nate the president? And what do you think they would
have done to you when they tired of raping you?" Jason
asked. "If you hadn't stabbed that man . . ."

She was wringing one hand with the other as though
washing them. "Whatever they might have done . . . I cannot live with killing someone." She glanced at the door. "I
want to leave. Now."

"Maria," Jason reasoned, "give it a few days. We can—"

"No!" she almost shouted. "There is no more 'we.' Because of you, I killed another human being. I watched you
literally feed a man to pigs to be eaten alive. No, Jason, I
cannot be around someone whose business is violence."

"But—"

She was unconscious of the washing motions, Lady
Macbeth. "I love you, Jason, but I cannot live with what
you do. The sooner I start trying to forget you, the sooner
I will."

It was then that Jason realized that, quite possibly, he,
too, was in love. The thought surprised him. After Laurin,
he hadn't thought he was capable of it.

"Look, Maria, I don't have to keep doing this. I can . . ."

She shook her head. "No, Jason. I can never forget the
things you have done, even though I suppose you had to
do them. I will find some quiet college-professor type, get
married, and have a dozen or so children. I could not live
with a man who killed for a living."

"A college professor like Eno Calligini?" Jason asked
bitterly.

"Perhaps similar to him. They seem all similar. It is
none of your concern." She turned to Adrian. "Would
you take me to the nearest place I can get a bus to the
airport?"

Adrian looked at Jason.

"Go ahead," Jason said dully. "I can't make her stay."

Maria followed Adrian out the door, then reappeared.
Crossing the room with quick steps, she threw her arms

around Jason and kissed him. "Do you understand, Jason? I cannot live with what you do or what your duty requires. Even if you quit, you would resent me as the cause."

Then she was gone.

EPILOGUE

Ischia Ponte, Islade Ischia
A year later

Jason stood on the second-floor loggia of his villa as the triumphant clamor of Wagner's "Ride of the Valkyries" boomed from carefully placed speakers. He was concentrating on a group of buildings sloping up a hill a half a mile away. Brush in hand, he squinted as he tried again to catch in acrylic the exact hue the sun tinted the gray-white stone Cathedral of the Assnta, a golden sheen that seemed to radiate from within the stone of its craggy heights itself. The electric blue of the sea beyond looked more painted than real. Transferring these colors to canvas was a Sisyphean task; they changed by the minute. The challenge, though, was one too beautiful for any artist to decline, and his previous efforts had sold well in the artists' market in town.

His new house was an Italianate walled compound situated on a small hill. White with a red tile roof, it possessed little other than size to distinguish it from other island homes nestled among the rugged terrain. He loved the way the sun recolored its stucco every hour with a glow he had no hope of reproducing with mere earthly equipment.

He put down his brush and inspected the canvas in front of him.

Beyond the piazza enclosed by his own walls, he could see the sole approach to the tiny village of Ischia Ponte, a causeway dating back to 1438, joining it to the volcanic island of Ischia. The Argonese Spanish also built a castle, a monastery, and the cathedral, all protected by a shoreline too steep to harbor ships or land a hostile army. Subsequently, the island became a favorite of Bourbon royalty and, today, of landscape painters and tourists avoiding the more popular attractions of Europe by seeking the main island's black sand beaches or tumultuous terrain.

Jason had all but convinced himself his choice of residences was based on the single means of ingress and egress rather than the island's proximity to Naples, where he knew a certain volcanologist spent a great deal of her time.

He had moved there immediately after a week of debriefing by Mama and the various American intelligence agencies, all of whom owed him a debt they could never admit. Failure to timely access the Breath of the Earth project could have resulted not only in assassination of the president, but political recriminations that would have sent any number of department heads into early and obscure retirement.

In addition to the fee paid him by Narcom, he had asked only that the State Department do what was necessary to ensure that he was no longer wanted by the British Colonial or Italian authorities.

In the first instance, the British Colonial office was all too happy to forget the matter. After all, their Caribbean possessions were one of the world's vacation spots. Even the rumor of violence would frighten the tourists who were the islands' main source of income.

The Italians, understandably thorny when it came to activity by a foreign power on their soil, simply did not acknowledge that any such exercise had taken place at all. No one was certain exactly what had inspired *Inspectore*

Santi Guiellmo, *capo, le Informazioni e la Sicurezza Democratica*, to lead men into a shaft closed since antiquity. As was his custom, he had confided in no one. The old archeological site was far too unstable to risk any effort at retrieving the bodies. A simple Mass for the dead was said at the mouth of the hole and the matter officially forgotten.

Although the depth of the sea surrounding Ischia precluded scuba diving, the fishing from Jason's small skiff was successful enough. Dorado and other fish were plentiful, and what he didn't catch was available in the open-air market in Ischia Porto, the island's main town and ferry port. Pangloss seemed relieved that there were no crabs lying on the trays of ice, but the claws of the large prawns gave him pause.

Even with a dog, painful memories lingered.

Otherwise, Pangloss loved the people, color, and, above all, the smells of the market. Jason got the impression the dog would have preferred a car to having to keep his balance between the front wheel and Jason's feet on the floorboard of the Vespa, though.

Daily help was inexpensive and provided a form of company, once the old woman realized the dog was far more friendly than fierce. Her extended family basically adopted Jason, including him in an endless procession of weddings, saints' days, birthdays, and one funeral, all occasions for appropriate gifts to grandchildren, nieces, nephews, cousins, and others of whose relationship he was uncertain. The affiliation also provided him with numerous eyes and ears. Should someone come looking for him, he would know before they found him.

He took Italian lessons twice weekly.

At night he cooked, read, drank wine, or watched bad Italian soaps or, worse, American sitcoms on the rabbit-eared set the previous owners had correctly appraised as not worth taking with them.

Almost by accident one evening, he found the dog-eared magazine Adrian had given him, the one containing the condensed version of Eno Calligini's book. Only then did Jason remember he had not finished the misadventures of Severenus Tactus, the one facet of the Breath of the Earth operation still incomplete.

A glass of wine at his elbow, he had begun to read.

JOURNAL OF SEVERENUS TACTUS

Two days I remained in Agrippa's household. I began to despair that he would ever have restored to me what I had lost, for he rarely left the house, instead conferring for hours with men, many of whom I recognized as among the most powerful in Rome.

Late in the afternoon of the second day, I heard his guest depart and set out to speak with my host. I found him at the counting table[1] of his treasure house.[2]

He looked up as I entered and smiled with a greeting.

I was about to inquire as to what had been done when I saw a small gold stature of Dionysus[3] on a chest. The same figure had adorned the little temple at which my mother, unlike my father, had worshiped all and many deities. Like most of the household treasures, it had disappeared shortly before my father's death. Without thought, I reached out to examine it.

Agrippa moved with greater celerity than his age would suggest, clasping my wrist in an iron grip.

"That statue belongs to my family," I protested.

He shook his head. "There are legions like it. You are mistaken."

I lunged and knocked the little figure upon the floor. On its bottom was my family's mark.[4]

He did not release my wrist but said, "Your father owed much before he died."

As though delivered by the gods, the words of my father's shade from Hades only two days past came back to me: *In the hand of the servant of the god.* Not servants, not gods.

A single servant.

A single god.

Augustus, the emperor, was a god.

Agrippa was his most devoted servant.

In the two years before he died, my father had hoped to do business with the imperial household, to have intercourse with government. It was an ambition never voiced before, nor hoped for.

But, I surmised, it had been one for which he paid dearly.

"You," I said. "You took my father's money on a promise to return commerce from the emperor and state. You used your high office to induce him to believe you could do such things."

Agrippa finally released my wrist. "As Augustus's confidant I could. Your father was foolish enough to believe I would. Who told you?"

"My father's spirit," I answered. "And to him you will answer."

Agrippa laughed. "I answer to no one but Caesar. But I shall have a response

to the priests who revealed my business
to you."

NOTES
1. Abacus.
2. The villas of many wealthy noble Romans
included a treasury, or *thesaurus* (from the Greek
thesauros) within its walls. Usually small and
windowless, it would also be where business was
transacted.
3. Roman god of wine, equivalent to the Greek
Bacchus.
4. This would have been a simple picture, design, or mark not disimilar to cattle brands in the
United States.

Author's Note

The diary stops abruptly here. What may have happened to Severenus Tactus for confronting the second-most-powerful man in early first-century Rome is only a guess. We do know, however, that Agrippa had the Oracle of the Dead (Hades) filled in. Not buried—filled from the inside out, a task that occupied at least two years. We can only suppose that such thorough destruction was not the result of mere efficiency but to ensure that no more of the old general's schemes came to light, or as an example to others who might tend to reveal them.

Of course, we can never know, but this is one answer to the mystery of why Agrippa took such action.

Ischia, Bay of Naples

Jason had put the magazine down.

He had found a place to live and begun to enjoy life.

He was home free.

Almost.

He thought about Maria every day. Sometimes he brooded on the cosmic unfairness of falling in love twice and losing both times.

The affair with Maria, though, had had some positive results. He found himself painting again, as though his anguish at the loss of Laurin had been unlocked like some emotional jail. He also realized that, at least in principle, he might find romance again.

But not here, and he had no real desire to leave. At least, not until the artistic possibilities had been exhausted.

Pangloss's joyful barking almost drowned out Wagner, no trivial feat.

Someone was at the gate to the piazza.

Jason shaded his eyes and recognized Petro, one of his housekeeper's countless grandchildren, a young man who always had some small treat for the dog. Jason never was sure whether it was affection or tribute.

"It's unlocked," Jason called down.

Pangloss met the visitor before he could climb the steps to the second floor.

"Signore . . ."

The boy was nearly breathless. He must have run all the way from Ischia Ponte, a half mile uphill. Jason waited for him to finish gasping.

The lad blurted out his brief story. Cousin Anna, who worked in a dress shop in Ischia Porto, had called Stephano, her husband's brother, to tell him to notify Antonio, Petro's father, that someone had gotten off the SNAV hydrofoil from Naples and begun asking questions about Jason. Where did he live? Where could he be found?

No, no one had mentioned what the stranger looked like, only the questions.

Jason pressed a twenty-euro note into the boy's grateful hand, thanked him, and shooed him off the premises.

Someone had found him.

Painting forgotten, Jason went into the bedroom and knelt beside the bed. He pressed on the series of tiles forming a colorful abstract mosaic and a section of the floor sprang open. Inside was a small arsenal. A reliable weapon with both automatic and single-shot options, accuracy not requiring the surgical precision of a scope, and enough range to effectively cover any part of the villa was required. Jason selected a standard U.S. Army M-14 rifle with flash suppressor and banana clip. If one person had risked attention by asking about him, it was a safe assumption that a number of others had already arrived.

Jason inserted the clip as he lay on his belly, sighting the weapon on the gate as the most likely place of attack.

Damn, but this was getting old. He could, he supposed, summon the local police. But what could he tell them? That some unknown person had been asking questions about him? Hardly a crime. By the time the peace had been breached, it would be far too late to seek help.

Pangloss's ears perked up just as Jason heard it: the sound of a straining auto engine.

A second later a battered Ford Fiesta poked its rusted grille around a turn a hundred yards downhill, the last turn before Jason's gate.

The car sputtered to a stop just before the bars of the gate, hiding its occupants behind the wall. A figure in khaki came into view, head turning, searching for . . .

Looking for the bell, a loud, jangling device so unpleasant Jason swore it made his teeth itch. Had he visitors on a regular—or any—basis, he would have replaced it.

There appeared to be only one stranger. Others quite likely were surrounding the villa. As the bell clamored again with an angry insistence, he moved closer to the edge of the loggia in hopes of widening his view.

The only thing he could see was the brownish form below, brightened by a flash of brilliant green and fire engine red.

Red and green?

Like a . . .

Like a Hermès scarf!

He stood, dropping eight and a half pounds of M-14 plus clip on his bare foot.

"Shit!"

From below: "Jason, is that you?"

He was trying to pick up the weapon, hold his damaged foot, and not sound surprised, none of which he was achieving. "Yeah, yeah. I'll be right down."

"You sound cross."

Try a broken foot to improve your disposition.

Pangloss was already dashing for the gate in anticipation of another potential friend bringing treats.

Jason got almost to the stairs before he remembered the M-14. Leaving a weapon in view wasn't a smart move, not when he would be trying to explain how peaceful his life had become.

"Hold on," he shouted. "I'm coming!"

"So is Christmas!"

His weapons cache again concealed, Jason stumbled down the stairs and across the piazza and opened the gate.

"I thought I was being turned away," she said.

"No chance," he said.

Pangloss ran in circles, barking during what he clearly considered an unreasonably long embrace.

The Fiesta drove off.

Jason picked up a single suitcase. "I'll take it upstairs."

"What makes you think I am staying?"

"You've got a hell of a walk if you don't."

"You will not take me back to town?"

"Not a chance."

"Good."

The piazza, stairs, and bedroom floor displayed a trail of increasingly intimate apparel. By the time they rolled onto the bed, she wore only the scarf.

Later, they both lay breathless, letting the overhead fan lazily stir the humid air.

"How'd you find me?" he asked.

"You kept in touch with Adrian. So did I."

Jason sat up, slipping a thin gold chain over his head, the chain with a simple gold wedding ring dangling from it.

"You do not need to do that," Maria said.

Jason folded the chain carefully, almost reverently, and put it in a drawer of the bedside table. "Yes, I do."

Jason was running a hand along her ribs and hips. "He convinced you to come?"

"He gave up on that months ago. I decided myself."

His hand had stopped in a particular place. She was beginning to breathe harder. "Either way, I am glad."

"Nice of you to say. I was beginning to wonder."

"As long as you are here."

She was moving in rhythm with his stroking hand. "I am not quitting my job."

"Good thing. You'll be supporting an artist."

"No more violence?"

"There're those who say I do it to my subjects with my brushes."

"I can live with that."

"For how long?"

She rolled away from him to stare at the ceiling. "Until tomorrow. Then I shall rethink it."

Jason was confident there would be a lot of tomorrows.

THE JULIAN SECRET

GREGG LOOMIS

Don Huff was Lang Reilly's friend, and now he's been brutally murdered. Could someone be willing to commit murder to prevent the book he was writing from ever seeing the light of day? What secrets are worth killing for? Lang is determined to find the truth, but the organization that killed his friend is just as eager to kill him if he gets too close.

The trail of secrets leads Lang on a deadly chase across Europe, deeper and deeper into a mystery that has been concealed since the days of the founding of the Catholic Church. Danger follows Lang with every startling revelation. But at the end of the hunt lies a final secret that will shock even Lang—if he survives long enough to find it!
